HIS WICKED KISS

"Why don't I remember you?" she asked. With his great height and very handsome head he was hardly invisible. "This is all quite astonishing."

His thumb caressed her soft lips. "You couldn't see me, You were guarded well."

"I see you now," she whispered, her gaze drawn to his mouth.

"Now you are mine." He bent his head and brushed his mouth across hers. She stopped breathing altogether. His lips felt soft and warm, and when she didn't recoil, they lingered, slow, tender, coaxing. She melted inside. Her eyelids sank. She felt his arms stealing inside her cloak, around her waist, pressing her to his torso. His heat, his scent—a musky blend of cognac, fire, and something else, more intoxicating than the sunny air or the salty breeze—tantalized her. He kissed her as one enjoyed a scoop of cream—thoroughly, unhurriedly. The tip of his tongue dampened her lips, seducing them to part for him. Though hesitant at first, she complied. Her tongue touched his, and a heady wave of pleasure swamped her.

Low sounds rose in his throat as her response gathered confidence and their kiss deepened. His mouth was no longer tame but hot and needful . . .

GREAT BOOKS, GREAT SAVINGS!

When You Visit Our Website:
www.kensingtonbooks.com

You Can Save Money Off The Retail Price
Of Any Book You Purchase!

- **All Your Favorite Kensington Authors**
- **New Releases & Timeless Classics**
- **Overnight Shipping Available**
- **eBooks Available For Many Titles**
- **All Major Credit Cards Accepted**

Visit Us Today To Start Saving!
www.kensingtonbooks.com

MY
WICKED
PIRATE

RONA SHARON

ZEBRA BOOKS
Kensington Publishing Corp.
www.kensingtonbooks.com

ZEBRA BOOKS are published by

Kensington Publishing Corp.
850 Third Avenue
New York, NY 10022

All Kensington titles, imprints, and distributed lines are available
at special quantity discounts for bulk purchases for sales promo-
tion, premiums, fund-raising, educational, or institutional use.

Special book excerpts or customized printings can also be created to fit specific needs. For details, write or phone the office
of the Kensington Special Sales Manager: Attn. Special Sales
Department. Kensington Publishing Corp., 850 Third Avenue,
New York, NY 10022. Phone: 1-800-221-2647.

First Printing: November 2006
10 9 8 7 6 5 4 3 2 1

Printed in the United States of America

For Iris—
my mother, my heroine, my heart, my brightest star.
I love you.

Special thanks go to:

Zeev Sharon,
Dana Sharon,
Dror Peled,
Eli & Shula Gorenstein,
Tali Dowek,
Tali Yekutiel,
Niza Abarbanell,
Yael Ron,
Shay Gamliel,
Yael Yekutiel,
Dania Broukman,
Chilik Hochberg,
and to Evan Marshall and John Scognamiglio—
for making my dream come true.
Thanks!

CHAPTER 1

> *Tingoccio replied, "Lost? If a thing is lost, it can't be found; so what on earth would I be doing here if I were lost?"*
>
> *"That's not what I mean," said Meuccio. "What I want to know is whether you're among the souls of the damned, in the scourging fires of Hell."*
>
> —Boccaccio: *Il Decamerone*

West Indies, September 1705

Alanis opened her eyes in response to the loud banging on her cabin door. She sat up, intoxicated by the smell of salt and sea blowing in through the ports and by the sweet fragments of her dream. She was running barefoot on a white, sandy beach dotted with palm trees. She remembered an azure ocean and roaring waves breaking into white foam. *She was free.*

"My lady, may I come in? It's urgent!" John Hopkins, the chief mate of the *Pink Beryl,* insisted beyond the door, his voice strained with concern.

Alanis heaved a sigh, letting her dream fade away. "Yes, Mr. Hopkins. Do come in."

The door opened. Hopkins's lamp pierced the darkness. His face looked grim. "I apologize for disturbing you at such an ungodly hour, my lady, but—" His voice caught at the sight of her.

Blinking lazy cat eyes, she pulled the sheet up to her chin and swept back tangled locks, which appeared more silvery than golden in the moonlight. "Yes, Hopkins, what it is?"

"Pirates! We are under attack—"

Cannons roared on the horizon, discharging an ear-splitting broadside, and a terrible blast hit their ship. Walls shattered. The ship tilted sharply. Mayhem ensued outside her door. Thrown against her pillows, Alanis heard officers bellowing, sailors scurrying on deck, guns firing.

"Bloody hell!" Hopkins dropped to his knees beside her bed. "My lady, are you all right?"

"Yes, yes, I'm fine." Alanis gasped, shaken but still in one piece. "And you?"

"Fine." Hopkins stood up, yanking his navy jacket back in place. "We must get you off this ship, my lady. Pardon my cheek, but you ought to dress and make haste about it, for they will be upon us in minutes. We can only hold head to a warship for so long, and theirs is a seventy-gun frigate. I must ensure you are safe and away by the time they come."

"Safe and away? Where?" She stared out the open ports. Water and night surrounded them on all sides, and not too far off a giant vessel loomed, cutting fast through the waves, its cannons' mouths breathing smoke. Silhouettes moved across its decks, working the guns, preparing to board Alanis's ship. Where the devil could she possibly go? She threw the sheet aside and pulled on her cut boots. A pirate attack was no time to be miss-ish. "Hoist the white flag, Lieutenant. I won't have us all murdered for my jewels."

Hopkins averted his gaze. He cleared his throat. "Beg your pardon, my lady, but jewels aren't the only prizes these villains are after."

She glanced at her nightgown. A warm flush pinched her cheeks. She wasn't a young chit fresh out of the schoolroom, yet in *that* area she was as green as a pea. "I . . . must get Betsy." She threw a cape around her shoulders and was about to leave when her maid burst into the cabin.

"Disaster upon us, my lady!" Betsy wailed, and a second broadside hit the ship. They fell to the floor. Hopkins's lamp crashed and lost its light. Betsy screamed. Alanis grabbed a

bedpost and hauled herself up. Hopkins lent Betsy a support-
ive hand and ushered them out the door.

They ran up the narrow companionways, swaying with the
sharp tilts of the ship. Someone collided into them.

"Sir," Matthews, the navigator, exclaimed. "Captain
McGee has surrendered. The Viper is boarding us. Make
haste! We can't hold them off."

Alanis started. "The Viper? The Italian they call Eros?" A
byword for infamy and vice, Eros meant cruelty, bloodlust,
and destruction. He sailed the seas, seizing one prize after another by valor, trickery, or the sheer terror of his name; his
legend hung over him like a thundercloud.

"I'm afraid so, my lady," Matthews confirmed. "We have
neither the men nor the metal to oppose him. The blackguard
hasn't raided private vessels in ages. He preys on fleets. We
didn't expect him to attack us. Nor did His Grace."

"May God help us . . ." Alanis murmured, recalling her
grandfather's words of warning. The Duke of Dellamore had
predicted a catastrophe. He was decisively against her sailing
to Jamaica, to join her fiancé, Viscount Silverlake. She could
still hear his harangues in her head. "Wartime is no time for
a young lady to be scampering about the world. I am needed
at Her Majesty's Court, and you cannot travel alone. If
Denton's boy wishes to make a name for himself, hunting
down pirates in Her Majesty's service, he shall have to do so
without you!" Sadly, Lucas Hunter, the distinguished Silverlake, *was* doing it without her while she pastured her days
away at home. She tried to reason with the duke, reminding
him that she was betrothed to Lucas since infancy, but he
would hear none of it. The solution to the discord came in the
form of trickery: Alanis exercised tears—so many tears the
duke had no choice but surrender. If her grandfather had
known her true motive for sailing away, nothing would have
broken his resolve.

"Get the boat ready, Matthews," Hopkins ordered, and to
Alanis he said, "Fear not. San Juan is but a day away." Before
the terror of being cast adrift upon the sea registered in her

head, he took her elbow and prompted her and Betsy toward the stairway.

The scene on deck was hellish. The mizzenmast was on fire. Pirates jumped off swinging ropes. Metal clanged. Guns blasted. Carefully paving a way amidst the fighting zones, Hopkins led them to starboard. Beyond the rail a tiny boat swayed precariously over black waves.

"Merciful Father in Heaven!" Betsy cried as she glimpsed at the boat.

"And the others? And Captain McGee?" Alanis inquired anxiously as Lieutenant Hopkins helped her onto the side step. Her gaze swept the battle-blazing deck. Acrid smoke burned her nostrils. Frozen to the spot, she watched the flames licking away at the masts and riggings. Twelve years ago, her parents died in a fire on her father's exploration journey to the East. Only twelve years old at the time, she was left at Della-more Hall with her younger brother, Tom. Now, as her father before her, her dream of sunshine and freedom was turning into a nightmare.

"Descend, my lady!" Hopkins urged. "*Now!*" He supported her arms as she took the first step downward. He cast her a re-assuring nod before five pirates rounded on him from behind.

Alanis shrieked. One of the villains grabbed Betsy. Another yanked Alanis back on deck. Flailing wildly, she craned her neck to see Hopkins vigorously fighting his attackers, but they were hauled away toward the area where the triumphant cutthroats, now in command of the helm, surrounded the *Pink Beryl*'s crewmen.

Squeezed together with Betsy, Alanis felt her maid's cold hands on her nape, twisting her long mane into a chignon and stuffing it inside the cape's hood. Alanis pulled the hood low over her eyes. "Cover yourself as well, Betsy."

Acute tension seized the smoky air. They were expecting the one man who could put a period to their existence—the Viper himself.

The pirates stirred and let him pass through their ranks. Containing her curiosity, Alanis huddled in the velvet folds of her hood and listened to his men greeting him in rapid Italian. The Viper stepped closer to survey his captives. A hum of dread passed among them. The confident pounding of his boot heels on the plank floor reverberated in everyone's heart. He halted. Alanis sucked in her breath, sensing him standing directly in front of her.

"*Giovanni, portami quella nel cappoto nero. Bring me the one in the black cape,*" his deep voice commanded, and a giant of a man with a black patch on one eye materialized before her.

Hopkins and Matthews bolted forward and were immediately blocked by sharp dirks.

"Leave her alone, you vile monster!" Betsy screamed fearlessly. "She is the Duke of Dellamore's granddaughter! He'll hound you for the rest of your days!"

The Viper assessed the maid, then instructed one of his men, "*Rocca, tu prendi la piccola serva. Rocca, you get the little maid.*" He turned and walked away.

All Alanis saw was a tall, dark, ominous shadow disappearing in thick swirls of smoke.

Dimly lit, the Viper's cabin boasted ample space and quiet luxury. Giovanni nudged her inside and locked the door. Alone, Alanis raised her head and looked around. It wasn't the sort of cabin one would expect a savage to reside in. Gilded, black lacquered cabinets lined the walls—a trademark of Venetian artisans. Elegant fauteuils and sofas upholstered in purple satin formed a sitting area. An ebony desk occupied the far end, heaped with papers and maps, and to her left loomed a four-poster bed, draped with rich purple silk. The large shadowed bed shot a tremor up her spine. She recalled Hopkins's warning how jewelry was not the only booty pirates were after. Was her fate to be ravished by the Viper tonight? Was this the reason she was brought here?

An old royal crest hung over the canopy, its black, silver, and purple matching the furniture. The insignia, although foreign to her, portrayed its family's prestige in partaking in the Holy Crusades—a serpent eating a Saracen. Apparently, the villain had no qualms decorating his cabin with any pillage, even if it displayed someone else's valor and magnificence.

The door opened behind her. Alanis's heart leaped with a start. The door slammed against its frame. She holed inside her hood, sensing a large body coming to stand behind her.

"*Buonasera, Madonna*," a low voice drawled over her shoulder. She remained silent and followed the sound of boot heels circling her. Tall sinewy legs in black leather boots stopped before her. "Remove your cape," he said. "Let's see the face you're so determined to conceal."

He was a large one, she realized, feeling very small and vulnerable. Thinking of the brave crewmen of the *Pink Beryl* who fought that night helped her muster her courage.

"Well?" The voice grew closer and huskier. "You've already piqued my curiosity on deck, hiding instead of gawking as the rest did." He smirked. "I assure you, I'm quite intrigued."

Alanis didn't stir. He sounded civil enough. His Italian-accented English was fit to be spoken in the queen's presence. Nonetheless, her heart thudded; her warm breath filled the hood.

"I don't intend to harm you, simply to have some conversation," he whispered to the hood. When she still refused to remove it, he cajoled, "I understand why you feel reluctant to reveal yourself, but speaking to a black cloak is somewhat tedious." He waited, his long legs braced apart, until suddenly, without warning, her hood was yanked back.

Alanis gasped. Her head shot up, causing the loose bun at her nape to spill glamorously to her waist, shiny and golden. Startled, she finally came face to face with Eros the Pirate.

Shock and confusion clashed in their gazes. The pirate's dark, glittering eyes narrowed thoughtfully, as though he *recognized* her and was flicking through his memory to associate the face with a place. The disturbing awareness was dulled by her private reaction to him, though. Alanis rarely paid attention to men since she was contentedly betrothed, but the tall, dark Italian standing before her had such staggering looks he could make a nun reconsider her vows.

A slow smile curved his handsome lips. "*Piacere*." He graciously inclined his raven head in a formal greeting. "What an unexpected pleasure."

Again she was plagued with the feeling he recognized her, but how could he? Surely she would have recalled seeing him before. His eyes alone were unforgettable: Intensely expressive, they gleamed in his deeply tanned face. Thick, glossy jet hair slicked back in a queue framed a tall brow, high cheekbones, a straight nose, and a strong square jaw—a warrior's face sculpted in bronze. A crescent-shaped scar curved from his left temple to his cheek, but she found it did not mar his handsomeness one bit. It added character to his countenance, which made him look even more intriguing. A pair of earrings pierced his left earlobe—a diamond stud and a golden loop. His shape was another attraction—that great height, a head taller than Lucas, and strapping physique radiated pure male power. His code of dress was reserved yet painfully smart, a trick of fashion Italians mastered long before the French assumed superiority in the field. His broad shoulders tapered to a wasp waist in a close-fitting black coat trimmed in silver. A snowy cravat frothed at his tanned neck. He was utterly compelling, and he was utterly dangerous.

Grinning, he looped one of her golden locks around his forefinger. "*Allora?* Well then? Have you nothing to say? Cat got your tongue?"

Alanis snatched her lock back. "What do you intend to do with my ship and crew? If you hurt my maid, or if a single Englishman dies tonight—"

A taunting spark lit his eyes. "Aren't you anxious to know what I intend to do with you, Lady Avon?"

"I do not give a whit what you do with me," she said through clenched teeth while her cold hands curled into fists at her sides. "As long as my personal companion is untouched."

"I see." His bold finger shifted aside one of her cape wings, exposing muslin frills. "So I may do whatever pleases me with you?" he inquired with a raised eyebrow.

"Certainly not!" She gripped back the cape wing to conceal her nightgown.

A knock rattled the door. "*Entra!*" he commanded, sustaining her apprehensive gaze. Four men came in, carrying her heavy chests. They set them down and departed, shutting the door.

"As you see," he crossed his arms over his chest, "all ship spoils go to the captain."

"I was under the impression you have long ceased to harass small vessels," she drawled scathingly. "Have you fallen on hard times?"

He laughed. "Fortunately, no, but you, my lady, are no doubt the most valuable prize I've ever acquired. The best of spoils."

Dismayed yet at the same time curious, her gaze followed his tall frame as he sauntered to the wine cabinet. His snug black breeches emphasized every corded muscle on his lean thighs. A curved, silver-handled dagger was strapped to his hip over a silk purple sash. It was an Oriental dagger—a *shabariya*. Her grandfather had one in his library. She recalled hearing once that Eros had been raised in the Kasbah of Algiers and was notorious for his mastery of blades. She also noticed in spite of her fear of him that the fiend dressed in the same colors of his cabin.

Crystal clinked as he filled a snifter with a bright amber fluid. "May I offer you a drop of cognac, my lady?" he suggested pleasantly. "Surely tonight's events have taken a toll on your nerves. A stiff drink should settle them down."

"You presume much if you think I will drink such spirits," she bit out caustically, "in the company of a bloody pirate, no less. Salute yourself!"

His eyes glided over her cloaked figure, making her feel extremely self-conscious. "The lady has a sharp tongue. I fear we must blunt it some with acid." When her temper flared visibly, an elegant jet eyebrow cocked with amusement. "*Va bene.* Suit yourself." He downed his drink, briefly shutting his eyes, as the acid charred his throat. He set the glass aside and continued perusing her with open appreciation. "Silverlake deserves to be shot for letting a woman like you sail alone when men like me roam the high seas."

"Silverlake?" How could he possibly know Lucas, she wondered.

"Yes, Silverlake." He started in her direction. "The blond pup you are engaged to, Lady Avon. The same one we shall pay a visit to in four days. The two of us."

Hope lit her heart. "You intend to hold me for ransom, then?"

"So eager to join the dashing knight in Kingston? How romantic." He smirked. "Yes, I do have it in mind to offer you back to Silverlake. For a certain price."

"His lordship will readily pay your price, Viper, whatever it is."

"Ah, now I remember." He came up in front of her, his supremely tall head forcing her to look up. "We haven't been properly introduced. So, allow me." He gallantly took her hand.

Alanis snatched it back, shooting him a look full of poison. "I know who you are."

Irritation flickered in his eyes, but he quelled it. He lowered his head closer to hers and whispered, "My name is not Viper."

"Your name is Eros."

He straightened up, saying nothing.

"So what is the price?" she asked. With the king's ransom of jewels stashed in one of her chests he should be able to procure half of Jamaica. How insatiable can a man be?

"I'm a reasonable man." He pensively rubbed his strong, clean-shaven jaw. "I only intend to ask for what is mine, something that is not measured in coin." The infuriating eyebrow rose inquiringly. "Are you measured in coin, Lady Avon? Gold doubloons perhaps?"

Her aquamarine eyes slanted wrathfully, granting her the look of a cat. "Beast," she hissed.

The black-hearted villain had the gall to tip his head back and laugh. "I'm certain you hope I am not, my lady, although . . ." His hand touched her face, causing her to flinch. Yet all he did was gently run his knuckles along the cream of her cheek, sending a suspicious shudder through her. "I shall be more than happy to live up to your expectations." He glimpsed at his bed, then recaptured her gaze. Humor and challenge twinkled in his dark eyes. "What exactly did you have in mind—rough ravishing or prolonged pleasure? I'm game for both diversions."

Alanis edged back. He followed, moving with an arrogant fluid swagger. A black leopard, she thought fretfully, graceful and deadly. When he caged her between his powerful arms and the wall, she barely managed to murmur, "Silverlake will kill you if you lay one finger on me."

"A serious detriment, to be sure."

Heart hammering, Alanis stared deep into his spellbinding eyes. Everything else faded into obscurity. His handsome face and the muscular breadth of his shoulders filled her view. Tension crackled between them, and for a brief moment she nearly forgot what he was.

He was thoroughly scrutinizing her face, admiring her naturally slanted blue-green eyes, the pert tilt of her nose, the soft roundness of her cheeks. His gaze settled on her lips— full, pink, and slightly quivering. Lust etched his irises. "You are beautiful," he breathed, fanning her lips with rich, titillating cognac fumes. "I think Silverlake's wrath is small punishment for a night spent with you, my lady."

Lud. No man has ever looked at her this way. *No man!* Not even Lucas, her betrothed, has ever told her that she was beautiful. When her brother was killed in a duel five years ago, she was nineteen and preparing for her coming-out. So her first debut into society took place two years later when her grandfather presented her at the French Court in Versailles while in France on diplomatic affairs. This man—*this pirate*—with his midnight eyes and granite face stared at her as though she were the most desirable woman in the world!

Noting her discomfiture, he smiled, and what a sinful smile it was. White teeth flashed in wicked contrast to dark skin, and Alanis experienced a deep feeling of sympathy for the women who fell into this rogue's net. This man was well aware of the power of his masculine allure.

"He is an idiot, your precious Silverlake," Eros drawled. "I think I shall be well deserving of sainthood when I return you to him unscathed."

Alanis swallowed hard. "You truly do not intend to harm me?"

Eros stood close enough for her to see the lines life had tilled into his skin. He was not as young as she had initially assumed. There was a hard, ruthless edge to him, yet something else as well, unexpected, which she hoped she was not imagining: a private code of honor.

"Harm you?" A strange look surfaced in his eyes. In an act of risqué, his thumb caressed the soft swells of her lips, its faint roughness startlingly seductive. His voice dropped to a gruff whisper. "A beautiful creature such as you was made for pleasure, Alanis. Not pain."

Stunned, she merely stared after him as he turned on his heel, strode to the door, and left the cabin, locking her inside.

CHAPTER 2

The pirates of the *Alastor* perked up when Rocca escorted Alanis to the foredeck the next day. They abandoned their chores and gawked as she traversed the sun-drenched deck in an ice pink gown with bolstered hips and far too deep a cleavage to remain calm in a sea of lecherous stares. She took shelter beneath her wide-brimmed hat, squinting against the radiant light, and reminded herself anything was preferable to dreary Yorkshire.

Eros sat on the foredeck railing, his long mane catching the breeze, as he wielded a dagger on an orange and spoke to Giovanni. He wore a white lawn shirt and black breeches with a purple stripe along the side seam. Black and purple, she smiled mockingly; the man certainly advertised his colors. She swept her gown's silk train off the plank floor and took the steps.

Giovanni noticed her first. He smiled broadly. "*Capitano, sono innamorato! I'm in love!*"

Eros ordered Giovanni to make himself scarce and greeted her with a gleaming white smile complemented with a disarming pair of dimples. "*Buongiorno, bellissima.*"

A strong flutter rippled in her belly. Not only was the blasted villain annoyingly handsome, but also the eyes glittering like gems in his suntanned face were the clearest, most unusual ocean blue eyes. Sapphires, she mused, somewhat dazed—a stone once believed to be the core of the earth and reflected by the sky. How could she have mistaken his eyes to be black?

His keen gaze raked her from head to toe, not missing an inch of face, bare ivory skin, or tastefully exhibited figure. And to her deepest chagrin, Alanis discovered she felt no less affected now than she had last night. She tingled, knowing this godless pirate, for whom the world was an oyster, found her—*beautiful*.

He grinned, munching a juicy slice of orange. "I trust you slept well . . . in *my* bed?"

So he couldn't resist asking. She leveled a glare straight into those confounding, ultrablue eyes. "I most certainly did not sleep in *your* bed, villain! Perhaps I will tonight, though," she riposted tartly, "and take pleasure in knowing I am depriving you of it."

"*Touché!*" His dagger sliced the air as he tipped his head. "My bed is at your disposal."

She eyed him hostilely, finding the suggestive gleam in his eyes contradictive to his gallant gesture. "You merit no thanks from me. Honorable men do not kidnap innocent ladies."

"Indeed they do not." He popped another slice of orange into his mouth. "The fools."

A tall wave broke on the bow. She skidded back, but Eros got soaked through and through. She laughed and licked salty drops of seawater off her lips. His boots landed hard on the plank floor. "*Mannaggia!*" he growled, wrenching water from his dripping mane. He glared at her, his eyes sparkling.

"I'm amusing you?" Not waiting for a reply, he peeled his wet shirt off.

She gaped. He had a stupendously beautiful body. Tanned, smooth of hair, and shaped in male perfection, it displayed supple strength obtained through years of a strict athletic régime. A golden medallion, large and lustrous in contrast to his burnished skin, dangled over his chest.

He threw her a cocky smile, setting her cheeks on fire, and sauntered to a table laid out for two. Crystal goblets, silver cutlery, and porcelain plates shimmered over a snowy tablecloth.

"Join me for lunch?" he offered and pulled out a gilded *chaise caré*.

She dithered. Verbal sparring was one thing, but consorting with a pirate? "I am not hungry," she lied, striving to keep her eyes off his powerfully wrought torso. It wasn't easy.

"You haven't had a bite to eat since yesterday, and it would be a shame if even a dram of beauty were to be lost. *E dai,*" he said sweetly, "I'm certain you've built up *some* appetite."

"I lost my appetite when I was captured by a rude pirate."

The indulgent smile disappeared. "You shall join the rude pirate regardless and keep him company while he eats."

"I will not," she articulated boldly. She hadn't escaped England to wind up dancing to a pirate's whims. Pivoting on her heel, she headed for the flight of steps. She managed two strides before a steely, tanned arm swept around her waist, pinning her back to a naked granite chest.

"Don't make me chase you," Eros whispered softly in her ear. "I'm endeavoring to behave like the perfect gentleman. Do not tempt the beast in me."

Her breath caught at the feel of his warm mouth moving in her ear. Realizing she liked it charged her with greater antagonism. She twisted around and gave his chest a hard nudge. "I will never sit at your table, not unless you strap me to a chair!" Yet the instant her hands touched his velvety, suntanned skin they jerked free as if singed by fire. She had felt his heart drumming, strong and steady, beneath cords of warm muscle.

Eros twisted his lips. "Strapped to a chair, eh? Don't put

ideas in my head, Alanis. I'm half tempted to strap you to my lap and feed you myself. I shall make it very clear to you. If you wish to keep enjoying my *gracious* hospitality, you shall have lunches and dinners in my company until I return you to your viscount. Now, will you sit at my table like a good girl?"

He released her and she staggered back, nodding obediently. He seated her and dropped into the opposite chair. "*Vino?*" He gestured at the green bottle gracing the edge of the table.

Giovanni appeared out of nowhere and seized the bottle. As he filled her glass with rich red wine, despite his black eye patch, he seemed more human to her than the dark Lucifer sitting across the table, his one brown eye lacking the diabolical fire of Eros's blues.

"I thank you," she said warily, and raised the glass to her lips.

Giovanni beamed. Unable to peel his one good eye off her, he let vast quantities spill into Eros's glass. Red wine gushed on the pristine white tablecloth. Eros caught Giovanni's wrist and pried the bottle from his fingers, snapping, "*Ma cosa fai, idiota? What the devil are you doing, idiot?* Have you nothing better to do than to make a pest of yourself?"

Giovanni grinned sheepishly. "No. Nothing."

Eros slammed his fist on the table and got up, radiating supreme annoyance. "Go—away!"

"*Va bene.* I got it." Giovanni chuckled. He sent Alanis another shy smile and walked off the foredeck, snickering loud enough for every sailor to hear.

"Are you always ill tempered with your subordinates?" Alanis inquired as Eros regained his seat. "If you keep this up, next thing you know, they'll be caballing behind your back, knocking you on the head, and making off with your ship." She smiled prettily.

"Isn't it impolite to wear one's hat at the table?" he inquired with a hint of a smile.

Arrant mutiny tilted her cat eyes. "Not when one is coerced to dine in poor company."

"This may come as a shock to you, but taking silly

maidens and irksome maids hostage is not my idea of
first-rate entertainment."

"Then, what is?" She winced, flaming obscenely red. "I
meant . . . why did you abduct me?"

He cast her a brain-muddling smile. "My idea of first-rate
entertainment is abducting silly maidens *without* their irksome
maids." He chuckled when she averted her gaze. "*Ma dai,*
come now. Don't sulk. You'll have your revenge on me yet. Besides, I'm famished. Remove your hat so we may finally eat."

Reluctantly, Alanis complied. A manservant dressed in a long
white tunic approached the table. He set down silver platters
heaped with fresh bread, colorful *antipasti,* and a covered bowl.

"*Ayiz haga tanya, ya bey? Would there be anything else,
master?*" he inquired respectfully.

"*Lah, shukran, Raed. No, thank you, Raed.*" Eros dismissed him.

"Was that Arabic?" she asked, failing to hide her admiration. Upon his nod she added with grudging respect, "You
speak many languages."

"*Grazie.*" He inclined his handsome head. "Kind of you to
notice."

"It was an observation, not a compliment," she muttered,
riled by his vainglorious grin.

"I choose to be flattered." He popped an oil-dripping olive
into his mouth, making her own mouth water. She never
tasted olives before. "*Allora,*" he pointed at the opulent fare
and began naming the dishes, "*zucchine e melanzane, pro-
sciutto crudo . . .*" He whipped the bowl's top off, uncovering
beef and spring vegetables cooked in wine. A waft of aro-
matic mist drifted her way. "Feel free to change your mind."
He selected a slice of crusty bread, dipped it in green olive
oil, scattered a pint of salt on it, and tore a bite. "*Salute!*" He
raised his wineglass and drank deeply.

Wretchedly, Alanis stared at the appetizing food and stoically
ignored the churning protests of her stomach. She was prepared
to starve to death rather than dine with a man of his sort.

He smiled perceptively. "Dinner is hours away, and your maid is lunching in my cabin."

"I'm not hungry," Alanis clipped stringently.

"I see. *Allora,* I give you permission to enjoy watching me eat."

She did watch him, thinking his table manners were as polished as a nobleman's. Yet he seemed determined to taunt her, savoring every bite, rolling his eyes, groaning with pleasure. Their gazes met over a sauce-dripping zucchini speared on a fork. Eros grinned. "Pity you've lost your appetite, Princess. There's so much to be shared. Ship's cook is a gifted Milanese. Worked for a royal family once. Are you certain you're not remotely peckish?"

She threw him a belligerent smile. "I prefer French cuisine." When a jet eyebrow rose at the deliberate provocation, she lifted her glass and prepared to do battle. Three years ago, she engaged in a similar debate with a French baroness, defending her true opinion, which was pro Italian, of course. So she had ample arguments up her sleeve. Today she was in the mood to play devil's advocate. Anything to annoy her host. "Italians have a lot to learn from the French."

Eros subsided onto his chair's satin upholstery and calmly sipped his wine. "Enlighten me about something. The English despise the French, yet they emulate and embrace everything that is French—French brandy, French food, French fashion. Why is that?"

"For the same reason the rest of the world does—it's the best! I imagine Italians may have had something to commend them once, but they lost the touch ages ago. I daresay the French outshine you in every quarter now. Even in art."

His blue eyes blazed. He was also smiling rapaciously, eager to crush the opposition. "You *are* aware that to settle the debate you will have to sample the food. By the bye," he studied the scarlet fluid swaying in his wineglass, "is the *Barbacarlo* to your liking? I personally feel it goes down very smoothly. What do you think, Princess?"

Her wine-glossed lips curled daringly. "If you are issuing an experimental challenge, you ought to provide French wine and food for comparison."

"That will not be possible since the only French object around you is the ship."

Intrigued, she glanced around. The *Alastor* was by every standard a formidable vessel, a floating fortress carried by vast, sun-bleached sails. "How did you acquire this French frigate? Unmistakably, 'tis a navy warship."

He looked impressed. "Very perceptive of you. The *Alastor* is indeed a French Navy girl. Used to be one of Louis's finest."

"I see," she said frostily, finding his allusion to the King of France as if he were one of his closest acquaintances daft. "*Louis's* docks were overcrowded, so he let you have one."

"Actually, I took it. A small matter of a private bet I had going with *Monsieur le Roi.*" He flashed her the infuriating grin again. "He lost."

"That's ridiculous. You run bets with the King of France as surely as I am on my way to the gaming hells in Tortuga!"

He was still grinning. The cad. "I pity the soon-to-be-impoverished pirates."

Ignoring him, Alanis concentrated on the scenery. How many sad winters had she longed for this breathtaking view? If she were doomed to go through life missing her parents and her brother to the depth of her soul, at least she would do so under a warm sun and as a free spirit.

"Have you visited this side of the globe before?" Eros summoned her attention.

"No, I haven't." Her tone turned sarcastic. "Have you?"

"I've been to many places, Princess, places that would fascinate you."

"Silverlake and I have grand plans to travel the world once we're married," she lied again, peeved by his cool superiority.

"*Davvero?* Would that be after or during the war? I regret having to put a damper on your plans, Princess, but it seems to me that your honorable Silverlake is more interested in fighting pirates than he is in fulfilling his duty to his lovely fiancée. It was very careless of him to let you travel alone in these waters when one is liable to run into French or Spanish warships."

"What would you know of honor or duty?" Alanis hissed.

"Very little, I imagine. Still, aren't you past the usual marital age of fine young ladies?" He studied her at length, then inquired quietly, "How long have you been engaged to him?"

"It hardly concerns you," she replied icily, rattled by the twist their conversation had taken. Though their engagement was settled ages ago, Lucas seemed determined to put it off, not giving thought to his restive fiancée sitting in wait at home. Sailing to Jamaica presented the perfect solution. She would finally have her taste of sunshine and freedom, experience the world she had read and dreamed so much about, and encourage Lucas to set a final wedding date.

"How long has he been stationed in Jamaica?" Eros dogged.

"Three years."

"Three years is a long time to be apart from the woman one loves." He held her gaze in laden silence, then leaned closer. "I know your opinion of me, Alanis. I have a rotten black soul, whereas he is a saint deserving of a pair of pretty white wings. But assuming Silverlake is the man you claim he is, why has this idiot left you behind? Does he prefer little boys or is he simply blind? If you were mine, *bella donna,* I wouldn't let you out of my sight for three days, let alone three long years. I'd keep you right where you belong—with me, at all times, and for the most part in my bed. And I would teach you better ways to use your quick tongue, *Amore.*"

Her tongue went dry. Gradually, coherency returned. "Why did you attack the *Pink Beryl?*"

"I was looking for you." Noting the terror in her eyes, his hard face softened with a smile. "Nothing like that. Finding you was pure luck. I stopped every ship en route to Kingston."

The tension eased from her shoulders. "Despicable wretch! Little wonder you're loathed by every man in the world. What were you hoping to catch? A poor victim to keep you company at meals while you feasted on your Milanese cook's treats? One who'd give you no trouble?"

"You call this 'no trouble'?" He chuckled and took a sip of wine. "If you must know, my sharp-tongued beauty, I was hunting for something of value to Silverlake."

"Something to barter with for that *thing* which is not measured in coin." Then she got it. She smiled triumphantly. "That *thing* isn't a thing! It's a person! Someone more important to you than gold, whom Lucas has captured and is holding prisoner, and given his honor won't allow Lucas to sell this man to you, you sought something to force his hand. Who is this unfortunate soul you are so desperate to set free? One of your cronies? A fellow picaroon?" she mocked.

"Now who would have guessed a blonde should have so much sense in her lovely head?" Eros remarked with genuine fascination. "I already regret having to forfeit you, *Amore*. Perhaps I should try to entice Silverlake with gold. One never knows until one tries."

Fear etched her eyes. "You wouldn't."

"Wouldn't I?" He smiled, his eyes daring her to challenge him. "With all this meat on the table, I'd still relish latching my teeth onto a choice area of flesh on your delectable body."

She stood up. "Insufferable beast! Find someone else to put up with your pitiful manners. I've had enough." With a scathing glare she left the table.

Eros bounded after her. He caught her wrist, and with a tug she pirouetted straight into his arms. She instantly recoiled. "Let go! You've had your lunch. Now let me return to the cabin."

He put a finger beneath her chin, tilting her face up to his. "You are more beautiful than I remembered, Alanis, and although I promised myself I'd leave you be, I find it . . . almost beyond my control. Three more days of this will turn me into a softheaded imbecile."

It took her mind several seconds to resume working. "*You remember me?* It's impossible! I don't know you. We've only met last night, for heaven's sake!"

"We *have* crossed paths, Alanis," Eros whispered, "and I can prove it. Dine with me during these three days we have together and I promise to tell you everything before we part company."

Alanis stewed in a mental caldron of curiosity and enmity for a long moment, enfeebled bit by bit by the potent plea in his bedeviling blue eyes. "Fine. Now release me. I . . . I am starving."

Chuckling, Eros did as asked and invited her to take her seat once again.

CHAPTER 3

It was not a good night to be an Italian prince. Cesare Sforza sank into a torn wingchair and scanned the cold, austere walls of Castello Sforzesco. Its splendor had been sacked. Efficiently. Brutally. Completely. Looted by his blood-sucking debt collectors. He had nothing. Worse. His days in his family palazzo were numbered.

A weak flame leaped on the hearth. Cesare's gaze fell on a shattered mirror leaning against a wall. Well built, raven-haired, clad in black from head to toe, his reflection sadly complemented his surroundings. Though in his prime, he looked finished: His white features were as cold as a statue's; his dark blue eyes held the glare his enemies labeled "the look of a savage beast at bay." Cesare smiled viciously. That which had earned him contempt and vituperation would win him glory and dominion in the end. One day soon he would find the scar-faced dog who had stolen the Sforza medallion. He would kill him and become the next Duke of Milan.

In the meantime, Cesare had to survive by his wits and cunning alone while the Spaniards looted Milan's taxes. He swore and downed a shot of cognac. It was the last bottle. The cellars' old treasure of wines and spirits had followed the sad path of the art and furniture. And now that the Imperial Armies were at the gates of Milan he had to flee as well, except where could he go? Every country with the Grand Alliance was a cul-de-sac for him because he openly sided with France. He did so after the emperor and the pope denied his *diritto de imperio,* his rightful claim to the Duchy of Milan. Should he go to Paris? He wondered. There were worse places to spend the coming winter, but what good was Paris for an impoverished Milanese prince? Also, one had to consider the unfortunate incident with the French heiress. Two years ago, Louis chased him off in disgrace, vowing that if Cesare ever neared a French woman again, he'd install him in the Bastille and lose the key. So he was married. It wasn't his fault that the bullnecked, pop-eyed pope refused granting him dispensation for annulment. If a man beat his wife, was it not a clear sign he had enough of her? Pity he hadn't poisoned Camilla after squandering her fortune. He was stuck with her, but the stupid cow had fled to Rome to cry to her uncle—who inconveniently was Pope Clement himself—what a wicked husband she had. Hence, he could definitely *not* go to Rome. He could go to Spain. Find a rich heiress in Madrid. Charm her, poison her, take her money . . . The idea appealed to him, but Spain didn't. He hated the sharp-bearded Spaniards.

Fast approaching steps echoed off the Great Hall's stark walls. Cesare drew his dagger, his lustrous, lethal old friend. "Who goes there?" he barked, squinting against the gloom.

Wrapped in a black cape, a diminutive man materialized in the feeble firelight. His voice was a raspy whisper. "I bring good tidings, *Monsignore.* Excellent tidings."

Cesare snorted and sheathed his dagger. Already bored, he muttered with the enthusiasm of a dead goat, "Tell me what you've learned, Roberto."

"I found him, *Monsignore.*" Roberto snickered. He put the tip of his finger to his left temple and carved an imaginary crescent scar.

Cesare shot out of his chair. "Are you certain?"

"*Si, Monsignore.* He flies the *biscione.* 'The viper that leads the Milanese to the field.'"

"I know that, *stupido!*" Cesare looked daggers at the spy. "Where is he? Tell me now!"

"I watched the *Alastor* sail from Genoa with the crescent-scarred man onboard. Though he didn't come ashore, I saw him with my own eyes, and he still looks—"

"I'm not interested in his looks, *stronzo!*" Cesare bellowed. He was interested in getting his hands on the medallion and then slitting the bastard's throat. His archenemy. *His curse.* "Tell me everything! Don't try my patience!"

Cringing under his master's fury, Roberto blurted, "He . . . he sailed to the Caribbean. What should I do now, *Monsignore?* Should I go after him? Merge with his shadow?"

Cesare sat. He had to think fast and craftily, exercise that killer instinct he had perfected on the baccarat tables. The King of France was the only man powerful enough to dispose of the dog, but to obtain Louis's assistance Cesare would have to give something in return. What?

Louis wanted Spain, so he put his grandson, Philip, on the Spanish throne and was waging war against the entire continent to keep him there. He wanted Italy, so he sent half his army to occupy it. Now Prince Eugene of Savoy, the supreme commander of the Imperial Armies, was threatening Louis's triumphs. There was nothing Louis wanted more than to eliminate Savoy.

Cesare smiled. He knew the exact method to capitalize on that. He looked at Roberto. "Yes. Go after the pirate. Merge with his shadow. I'll meet you in Gibraltar within two months. Find out where he goes, whom he talks to, whom he sleeps with. If you have to bribe, poison, or strangle someone to do so—do it. I want to know *everything! Capisce?* And . . . kill him, if the opportunity presents itself. I want the golden medallion he wears around his cursed neck."

Roberto flinched. "Kill the . . . ?" But when he saw his master's glare, he curtsied quickly, murmuring, "*Si, Monsignore.* It will be done." He crept away, his cape swelling behind him.

Smiling with satisfaction, Cesare lifted the cognac bottle off the floor. Soon he would have everything he ever wanted. He stretched his long legs and saluted the royal viper carved out of the stone wall. "Ah, Stefano. Though you must die, fear not, for death is bitter, but fame eternal."

CHAPTER 4

· Eros leaned forward in his chair, emerging from shadow into candlelight. He selected a red flower from the vase on the dinner table and tossed it into her lap. "A flower for your thought."

Alanis missed a heartbeat seeing his tanned, patrician face accentuated by the soft glow of the flame. She could no longer deny she took pleasure in his attentions. For the first time in her life she appreciated the power of femininity. Here was a man whom most of the world feared, but he endeavored to amuse her, to find favor in her eyes. Since their first lunch together the day before, he had become seamlessly amiable and courteous, behaving as a perfect gentleman. Yet despite his efforts, she wasn't entirely fooled: Eros was a predator— quiet, elegant, and lethal.

Absentmindedly she twirled the gilded lock arranged to fall over her exposed shoulder. "It would cost more than a flower to purchase my thought."

"Then perhaps the Malaga wine will do the trick. As the saying goes, '*In vino veritas*'." He refilled their glasses, his amused expression spiced with blatant masculine interest.

Alanis didn't fail to detect his appreciation of her low-cut bodice. His eyes were caressing her all evening. She pressed the wineglass to her warm cheek. "I had a different price in mind . . ."

A jet eyebrow lifted. "By all means, state your price. I'm in a venturesome frame of mind."

She took a sip of wine. "I was wondering about this person you're here to rescue."

He grinned. "You were? What would you like to know about her?"

A woman. Alanis's humor blackened. His mistress, no doubt. "Well, what is her name?"

Eros analyzed her well-bred smile. "Gelsomina," he replied. "Now tell me your thought."

She glanced at the scarlet petals nestling in her lap. "I was thinking of my fiancé."

"Ah." His smile frosted. "Already anxious to be gone from my company." He selected an orange off the silver fruit bowl, and using his dagger instead of a table knife, he slashed the skin.

"Silverlake is not informed of my pending arrival. I intend to surprise him."

"You will," he stated enigmatically. "Nevertheless, he should be grateful you ventured out to sea during wartime just to pay him a visit. Few women would brave the danger."

Alanis decided she didn't care to discuss Lucas anymore. She'd much rather interrogate her host. "Why do you target fleets? The risk is ten times greater, while the profit is very small."

"The immediate profit means little to me. I target French ships, navy and royal commercial lines alike, because they are Louis's strongest suit."

"You are fighting the French?" she asked incredulously.

He seemed amused by her reaction. "As you well know, the Continent, the high seas, and the Americas are in a state of war. One cannot live in the world and not partake of it. Personally I do not entertain an aspiration to the Spanish crown, but I find Philip's claim unacceptable. Louis cannot be allowed to control two-thirds of the Western world's power and resources."

"This is admirable," she murmured. It put Eros on *their* side. "But why should you single-handedly pit yourself against Philip's all-powerful grandfather, the Sun King, when you may join the Grand Alliance? Louis XIV has the means to crush a single man effortlessly."

He smiled. "I don't think the Allies will have me, and I am determined not to have them."

The man was a constant surprise. "You must be very brave . . . or very mad."

"Even the brave fall lured into fool traps and dupe themselves with high and noble ideals." Sustaining her gaze, he reached across the table and caught her hand. "I intrigue you, don't I?" he whispered. "Should we try to corrupt Silverlake with gold after all?"

Her heart flip-flopped. Slowly she pulled her hand free. "I have no idea why we should."

"I think you do, *Amore.* I think we understand each other very well."

The tension between them became too much for her, and she averted her gaze to the silvery trail of light washing the open sea.

"Allow me to tell you a story, then," he suggested. When he had her attention, he cleared his throat. "There was once in Pisa a rich judge, more endowed with intellect than with bodily strength, whose name was Messer Ricardo. But perhaps he was lacking in wits as well, for he shared the stupidity of other men who assume that while they travel the world, taking their pleasure first with one woman and then with another, their ladies at home are twiddling their thumbs. *Allora,* our good judge, because he was rich and prominent and believed he could satisfy a wife with the same sort of work he performed in his studies, he began searching for a woman possessed of both beauty and youth. His quest was surprisingly successful—Pisa is a town where most women resemble gecko lizards—and he married Bartolomea, the most charming young lady. With great festivity he brought his new wife into his home, but as he was a frail, wizened sort of man, he accomplished only one go at his wife on their wedding night, barely staying in the game for this one round, and found he had to drink lots of Vernaccia wine, eat restorative confections, and use a number of other aids to get back on his feet the next day."

Eros finished his wine, enjoying Alanis's slack-jawed expression. "Now this judge fellow, having formed an accurate estimate of his forces, resolved to teach his wife the calendar, namely, the days out of respect for which men and women should abstain from sexual coupling. *Allora,* there were the fast days," he counted his fingers, "the four Ember weeks, the eves of the Apostles, and a thousand other saints. Fridays, Saturdays, the Sunday of our Lord, every day of Lent, certain phases of the moon, and many other exceptions, thinking that one takes as long a respite from making love to a woman as one does from pleading a case in court."

She stared at him in shock. Yet even more shocking was the strange thrill she felt. "Well?"

"Our good judge continued in this fashion for some time, not without serious ill humor on his lady's part. One day during the hot summer, he decided to go sailing and fishing on the coast of his lovely estate near Monte Nero, where he could enjoy the fresh air. Having taken one boat for himself, he installed his lady and her ladies on another. The fishing excursion was delightful, and so caught up with his amusement, he failed to notice that his lady's boat drifted to sea. When all of a sudden," he paused dramatically, "appeared a galley commanded by Paganino da Mare, a famous pirate of his time. He caught the ship sailing with the ladies, and no sooner did he see Bartolomea than he desired only her. He decided to keep her, and since she was weeping bitterly, he consoled her tenderly, with words during the day, and when night came . . . with deeds. For he didn't think by calendars or pay any attention to holidays or working days."

Acutely aware of the fast beat of her heart, she inquired softly, "What did our judge do?"

"Having witnessed the abduction he was sorely distressed, being the kind who is jealous of the air surrounding his lady. To no avail he went about Pisa, lamenting the wickedness of pirates, although he had no idea who had taken his wife or where she had been carried off to."

"And Lady Bartolomea?" Alanis prompted.

"Lost all recollection of the judge and his laws. With great joy she lived with Paganino, who provided consolations day and night and honored her as though she were his wife."

She blinked. "That's it? The end? Her husband forgot about her?"

"No. Sometime later, Ricardo heard of his wife's where-abouts. He met with Paganino and artfully befriended the pirate. He then revealed his reason for coming and implored Paganino to take any sum of money for the return of his lady."

"And, of course, Paganino agreed," Alanis retorted, stabbing the dark pagan in front of her with an angry look. "For why should he regard her feelings when there's gold to be earned?"

"Paganino did not agree," Eros stressed. "Out of respect for her, he said to Messer Ricardo, 'I will take you to her and if she wishes to leave with you, then you may state the ransom price yourself. However,'" his voice thickened, "'if this is not the case, you'd do me a great wrong to take her from me, for she is the loveliest, most desirable, heart-robbing woman I . . .'"

Heat surged through Alanis. "What was Bartolomea's reply?" she hastened to inquire.

"What would yours be, Alanis?"

She hadn't realized just how devious he was until now. The point of the story wasn't to tell her what would or would not happen, it was to open her mind to possibilities, to choices, to the strange twists of fate. . . . "The husband had little to commend him and Paganino was mercenary. He did not truly love her if he was willing to accept gold as compensation for a broken heart."

"And if Paganino were to refuse the gold?" Eros prompted in a low, tempting voice. "You chose neither man, Alanis."

She looked away. "Pray finish this silly tale you've concocted—"

"I didn't." He smiled. "Giovanni Boccaccio who lived in Florence ages ago did, to amuse his remaining friends when the Black Death ravaged Italy. But since you've asked so graciously, I'll tell you the end. The lady said to her husband, 'Since I happened upon this man with whom I share this room where the door is shut on Saturdays, Fridays, vigils, and the four days of Ember or Lent, and here work goes on day and night, I can tell you that if you gave as many holidays to the laborers on your estates as you did the man who was supposed to work my small field, you would not have harvested a single grain. But as God, a considerate observer of my youth, willed it, my luck has changed. I mean to stay with Paganino and work while I'm still young and save the indulgences and the fasts for when I'm older. As for you, go celebrate as many holidays as you wish, for if I squeezed you all over, you couldn't come up with even a thimble of juice.'"

Blushing furiously, Alanis bit her lip. "Not very admirable for a married lady, was it?"

"The lady preferred her lover."

"Do you think so little of the sanctity of marriage, then?" she inquired.

An angry spark lit his eyes. "On the contrary," he rasped softly. "I bear the highest respect for the sacred vows of matrimony, but I'm not that much of a fool to enter this snare. Indulging in adultery is a common diversion for highborn married ladies."

"So you prefer assuming the role of the corruptor?"

"One can only corrupt she who wishes to be corrupted."

Interesting, she thought. Judging by his reaction, she suspected he'd been cuckolded once.

"Who is Tom, Alanis?"

His question took her completely by surprise. "*What? How* . . . who told you about him?"

"You did." He produced a suspiciously familiar journal from his coat pocket, flipped open the cover, and read, "'To my dearest Tom, who has the best place in my heart. I miss your sweet face and everything wonderful about you. As I bathe in sunlight, I recall idle days spent together on the banks of . . .' Your tears blurred the following lines." He glared at her reproachfully.

"My voyage journal!" Furious, she leaned over the table to snatch it from his hand, but he held it well out of her reach. "Give it back! It's private and you stole it!"

"My dear lady," he snarled. "Your *journal* puts Ovidius's *The Art of Love* to shame."

"How dare you! Ovid's book is . . . indecent. My journal isn't . . ." She pursed her lips. "You had the gall to read something private and you expect me to explain it? Where did you find it?"

"My men brought it to me. They found it in your cabin while clearing away the trunks."

"You ransacked my cabin?" Her eyes rounded in disbelief. "What were you hoping to unearth—secret missives forwarded to the French?"

"It was a mix-up. So who is he, Alanis? Your lover?" he demanded.

Her silent smile infuriated him even more; he seemed to take it as an admission of guilt.

"Poor Silverlake," he bit out. "A cuckold and not even married yet. And gullible me, here I thought you were an innocent little baggage, too pure to sully with my gory, wicked hands. You don't deserve the respect a professional courtesan does!"

The passionate resentment simmering in his eyes made her laugh. "One would think you were the one being cuckolded and not your enemy. Don't you find it absurd? Or perhaps you are jealous? Does it pain you to think me in love with another although you are not my betrothed?"

"I thank the Good Lord I'm not your betrothed," he muttered crossly. "I should give this to him, though, enlighten him as to the true nature of his bride to be."

"Please do." She laughed at his shocked expression. "You've no idea how silly you look, considering that . . . Tom is my brother."

That decked him. "*Your brother?*" He slowly slid the journal across the table.

She took it. "Tom is my younger brother. He died five years ago in a foolish, tragic duel."

Eros looked dully rueful. "My condolences. He was your only sibling? And your parents?"

"They died when I was twelve. My grandfather took us in." Why was she telling this pirate her entire life story? The answer eluded her.

"Must have been lonely," he remarked, his eyes not leaving her face.

"Not lonely. Alone. But I had Tom and Lucas when they were home away from school."

"Silverlake was acquainted with your brother?"

"They were famous friends. So you may imagine how idiotic you'd look presenting this bit of incriminating evidence of my infidelity to Silverlake." She smiled.

He stirred uncomfortably. "I never intended to. I apologize. Please forgive my rudeness."

"I forgive your rudeness. I do not forgive your reading my private journal! You had no right to snoop! You should have returned it once you realized the error."

"Perhaps I should have contained my curiosity," he admitted, not without a visible toll on his pride. "I'm willing to make it up to you. Tell me how."

She eyed him circumspectly. "Excuse me from dining with you tomorrow." Their last day.

Eros tensed. "No."

"You cannot choose the reparation that pleases you," she muttered.

"Ask for something else."

She considered the implacable set of his jaw, the resolute glint in his eyes. "No."

Annoyance crossed his features. "*D'accordo. Va bene.* You'll have your wish."

"Thank you." The less time spent in this ruthlessly appealing Italian's company the better, she told herself.

"Your grandfather seems very soft when it comes to his

granddaughter," he remarked after long moments of silence. "Does he know you read Ovid?"

The reason she was familiar with the Roman poet's works was her grandfather's eccentric views on female education. No refined English lady was allowed to read what she did. "You read Ovid. Why shouldn't I?" she pointed out tersely, annoyed that her cheeks were on fire again.

"Why indeed?" Eros grinned. "When the reason men prohibit women from improving their education stems from fear and stupidity? Women already wield so much power over us poor males, we are terrified that once you know everything, you'd have us completely at your mercy."

His comment quelled her belligerence, and she found herself smiling again. "I find it hard imagining you brought to your knees by a woman."

"You'd be surprised." The dark smile he sent her made her feel tingly all over.

Feeling shy and daring at the same time, she said, "Everything I heard about you concerns stealing, torturing, and murdering. Tell me one thing that is not a vicious rumor."

"Why do you believe they're but vicious rumors and not the truth?" he inquired, amused.

Disappointed by his smooth evasion, she replied, "I have had four meals in your company and I have yet to see you gnaw on raw organs or suckle fresh blood."

Eros burst out laughing, deeply, freely. "Is that what you've heard about me? And here you are, snatched from a world of decency and finesse and forced to dine with a cesspit monster."

"You are not from the gutters. You are exceptionally well educated, your manners—when it suits you—are excellent, your tastes are expensive . . ."

"Any person with a good eye can have a taste for the better things in life. My not being a viscount"—his hand sketched a flourish—"doesn't suggest I'm illiterate. Reading is a convenient method to pass time at sea, *Carissima*."

His softly spoken Italian endearment thrummed her heart.

"It's more than that," she said. "It's the way you carry yourself, it's—" She searched her brain for the right word. "Princely."

She could have sworn he flinched, but when he spoke, his voice was calm and even. "You deduced this after two days of observation? Alanis, prince or pauper, good or evil, it matters not in our world. The material point is what destiny has in store for us and what we choose to make of it. I chose my path, because this is what I am. A man whose loyalty lies with himself."

"And yet you defend the realm against French tyranny," she pointed out. Softly she recited, "'A bandit, as a lion, who roams the Lebanon. His home a sharp flint, and at the peak of a rock stands a leopard with spots as the keeper of his home, for he is a man of blood, a sorcerer whom even savages will fear.' You don't come from a world unlike my own, but you do live in a lonely place." The vulnerability she perceived in his eyes affected her as much as she evidently affected him. Eros chose his path as retribution against . . . something, and he seemed to her as caged in the world he created for himself as she was in the one she was born into.

He leaned closer. "You don't fear me, do you? But you ought to, Alanis. Although you see things others do not, you are too naïve to understand."

Her voice was a hesitant whisper. "Explain it to me."

"It's late." He rose to his feet and came to assist her out of her chair. "Your maid might put it in her head that I have wronged you abominably and come after me with her lethal tongue."

Taking his arm, Alanis sensed acute tension throbbing beneath his icy veneer. He would not meet her gaze, so cold and distant he'd become. Her eyes fell on the floor. "My flower."

He preceded her to it. When he straightened to offer her the stalk, their gazes collided. The transformation in him was swift and entrancing. The hungry look in his eyes, the potent craving he radiated—she saw a wild prowler on a nocturnal hunt, his instincts sharp, and his prey well within reach. They were caught in the moment before the leopard leaped to the kill.

He wanted to kiss her, feminine intuition announced. He would place his lips on hers as no man had done before, not even Lucas Hunter. Her heart beat wildly. Time stretched. She felt his pull so strongly her entire self awaited his kiss . . .

"Change your mind about dinner tomorrow," he implored softly.

Disappointed by his sudden withdrawal and angry with herself for feeling this way, Alanis replied pithily, "I should think not. Nothing good will come of it."

The sun set in the horizon, painting the sky a glorious halo of purple dusk. Tiny islands as surreal as a dream dotted the calm, cerulean surface. A cooler breeze swelled the sails, plucking twilight music over ropes and riggings. Laughter broke the silence. Eros tore his eyes away from the scenery and stabbed Giovanni with an irritated glare. "What are you laughing at?"

Manning the helm, Giovanni glanced at his captain and chuckled. "You. Can't remember the last time I saw you in such a rut, and all because of a little lady."

"*Stupido.*" Eros pushed away from the railing and crossed the quarterdeck toward a case of oranges. He selected a large one and slumped on a crate of ropes. "Haughty virgins are not my type. I cannot wait to be rid of her tomorrow, along with her noisy maid. I swear, I've never met a colder female in my entire life. My sympathy is with Silverlake."

"Mine isn't, and knowing you as well as I do, I'd say neither is yours. You have a beautiful woman sleeping in your bed, Eros, and the reason you are as sour as this fruit you are addicted to is you are not accustomed to rejection. Why won't she dine with you tonight?"

"Why don't you mind the helm instead of asking stupid questions?"

"*Va bene.* If you don't want her, and seeing that your plans to fight the French won't be getting me into any wench's pantalets in the near future, perhaps I'll ask Niccolò to stand in for me as I go ask the blond lady if she would take a stroll on deck with me this evening."

Eros's temper flared as a trail of gunpowder. "You'll do no such thing, Giova!"

"Why not?" Giovanni's one eye rounded innocently. "I'll behave."

"I said no." Eros gnashed his teeth.

Giovanni folded his arms across his chest, looking disgruntled. "When was the last time we had some fun, eh? Do you even remember what a female looks like underneath her petticoats?"

Eros stood. "You'll get your fun soon enough. Once we retrieve Gelsomina, we'll stop in Tortuga where you'll be able to explore under every petticoat roaming the island."

Giovanni watched Eros stride to a bucket of water to wash his hands. "I like blondes."

"There are blondes in Tortuga. And this one is not to be harmed. Do I make myself clear?"

"Who said anything about harming?"

"She is not for you, Giovanni," Eros accentuated ominously. "The discussion is closed."

Giovanni grinned. "Why can't you admit that you want her, Eros? Usually when a woman strikes your fancy, you go after her like a bull until you bed her and the boredom begins. What's special about this one? I know you prefer the experienced type, but if you want her, take her to bed and terminate the agony for the rest of us."

Eros paused. "She's not the kind one can simply take."

Surprise crossed Giovanni's fearsome features. "She got to you, didn't she? In all those fancy lunches and dinners she said or did something that flipped you over. What was it?"

"Enough. You've made your point. Now get your mind on the wheel before you sink us all." Eros stalked off the quarterdeck, leaving a very befuddled Giovanni staring behind.

Dinnertime passed and she was still plagued with a rotten feeling. Sitting at the open ports, Alanis stared morosely at the dark sea. Tomorrow she would reunite with Lucas. Why wasn't she ecstatically happy? She shut her eyes and let her head drop back as a cool night breeze lifted her unbraided hair off her nape. Why did she insist on fooling herself? She knew her affliction's name; she simply lacked the backbone to admit it. *Eros, you wretch. What have you done to me?*

The sound of a key entering the lock jumped her. The door opened. Formidable as ever, Eros stood at the threshold. His gaze swept the dim cabin. Betsy was sound asleep on a sofa. His bed was vacant. His gaze veered to the open ports, and her heart nearly plummeted to her feet.

His eyes glittered fiercely. "Put your cloak on," he whispered. "We'll talk on deck."

With trembling fingers she tied the black cape's ribbons at her neck, stepped into a pair of flats, and came to him. He closed his hand around hers and whisked her out the door.

Not a soul was in sight as she floated after Eros toward the night-shrouded quarterdeck. He positioned her at the rail overlooking the moonlit waters and stopped tall and shadowy in front of her. Untied, his long hair whipped without restraint in the sea breeze. His eyes reflected both yearning and reluctance. He ran his fingers through her long fair tresses, opening them like a fan over her shoulders, then gently cupped her face, murmuring, "*Sei bellissima.* You are beautiful. How is it possible you'll be escaping my clutches for the second time?"

Her whole body came alive under his touch. "Where did we meet before?"

His voice was deep and husky. "At a ball in Versailles three years ago. Your gown was the exact color of your hair."

"Gold brocade," she recalled with astonishment. "You were at a ball in Versailles?"

"You stood out in a sea of tired faces painted with rouge, white chalk, and false patches. It wasn't difficult to single you out as you circled the crowds with Madame de Montespan. I know the Madame. At the peak of her career she was Louis's mistress. I thought you were one of her young protégés. I thought you were a courtesan, Alanis."

"A courtesan?" She smiled wickedly. A woman of the

night. A temptress who brought men to their knees. The opposite of what she encountered in a mirror every day.

"I followed you around, plotting seductions in my head, until an elderly duke and a blond viscount stole you from right under my nose." He grinned ruefully. "I lost my chance."

"My grandfather and Lucas," she concluded with a smile full of wonder.

"They were extremely protective of you, which verified you were an unmarried lady, not a demimondaine. I knew I could never have you. Even if I had begged for an introduction, they would not have allowed it." His predator eyes gleamed, his teeth flashed sinfully white. "My reputation is not tolerated within a mile of an innocent débutante."

"Is it that terrible?" she teased. Then she frowned. "Why don't I remember you?" With his great height and very handsome head he was hardly invisible. "This is all quite astonishing."

His thumb caressed her soft lips. "You couldn't see me, *Amore*. You were guarded well."

"I see you now," she whispered, her gaze drawn to his mouth. A dark shadow outlined his upper lip. Her breathing thinned.

"Now you are mine." He bent his head and brushed his mouth across hers. She stopped breathing altogether. His lips felt soft and warm, and when she didn't recoil, they lingered, slow, tender, coaxing. She melted inside. Her eyelids sank. She felt his arms stealing inside her cloak, around her waist, pressing her to his torso. His heat, his scent—a musky blend of cognac, fire, and something else, more intoxicating than the sunny air or the salty breeze—tantalized her. Eros kissed her as one enjoyed a scoop of cream—thoroughly, unhurriedly. The tip of his tongue dampened her lips, seducing them to part for him. Though hesitant at first, she complied. Her tongue touched his, and a heady wave of pleasure swamped her. Primal, alien instincts urged her to explore him as unreservedly as he explored her.

Low sounds rose in his throat as her response gathered confidence, and their kiss deepened. His mouth was no longer tame but hot and needful. He tasted her, stroked her, pushed himself deeper inside of her. Their warm breaths mingled, becoming laborious.

"*Eros* . . ." She sighed, amazed how this strong, hot-blooded Italian, who only three nights ago had been a terrible enemy to fear and hate, had cast such a spell on her that her entire self responded to his kisses, to the feel of his large body crushing her to him. Nothing had ever come close to how she felt at that moment. She finally understood what it meant to be alive.

Kissing him passionately, Alanis's hands cruised up along his corded arms, over iron-hard muscles rippling beneath soft linen, and stole beneath the heavy fall of his hair. A profusion of cool silk spilled between her fingers. *Ah God!* How she ached to know everything about him, to keep him, consume him, engulf him with the warmth gushing from her soul . . .

Releasing a ragged groan, Eros tore his mouth away and dragged it along the curve of her neck. She was so caught up in the moment, so immersed in his effect on her, she didn't know how to object to the hand cupping her breast over the thin night-shift. His thumb flicked over her sensitive nipple. A sharp tremor shot through her, shattering the magic. *What has she done?*

She jerked free, shame and shock rounding her eyes. "What have you done to me?"

Breathing harshly, his lust-glazed eyes met hers. "What have I done to you?" he repeated, not quite grasping the abrupt change in her.

"You ruined me! Get away from me, you ravishing monster!" She pushed at his unmovable chest, frantic to escape him, to escape herself. How could she have lost her head and capitulated to a base fascination for a pirate? How could she have disgraced Lucas, behaving so wantonly?

"*Ravishing?*" His eyes lit up with a feral glow. He gripped her arms and pinned her to his chest. "I kissed you! And you kissed me back! I didn't do anything you did not want yourself!"

"I'm to be married to Viscount Silverlake! How could you do this to me?" The damnable blackguard made her want him with every fiber of her being, and now she felt empty and cold.

"Then don't marry him!" Eros countered resentfully, thwarted by the tears streaming down her face. "Alanis, you wanted this every bit as much as I did. You clung to me as a woman who had never been kissed in her life."

Smarting with humiliation, she sustained his incensed gaze. He was right on both charges. If he hadn't kissed her, she would have expired from curiosity and yearning. But for reading her sad inexperience with such careless ease, for making her crave him so wildly, she wanted to tear his beautiful eyes out. "I hate you!" she hissed, mostly because she knew she could never, ever have him.

"You think I'm not good enough for you," Eros rasped. "Not worthy enough for a princess of your noble birth to lust after. But you did, Alanis. You moaned and purred like a love-starved cat, and if this deck were my bedchamber, I'd have scratches on my back to prove it. One more night onboard my ship, *Amore,* and you'd beg me to keep you!" He laid into her with all the arrogance of a man who had had more women than he could begin to remember.

Alanis inhaled sharply. Perhaps because he was so close to the truth, or perhaps because he made it sound so cheap, her hand came up and slapped his cheek, all her hurt and fury condensed into one motion. "You—make—me—sick!" she spat vehemently, raw tears stinging her eyes.

Eros stilled, caught unawares by the intensity of her wrath.

Taking advantage of his momentary confusion, she gave his steely chest a forceful shove and fled as fast as her legs carried her, not daring to glance behind her once.

Eros touched his bruised cheek and stared after her as she flew across the deck, blond hair, white muslin, and black cape thrashing as wings in the breeze. When she vanished from sight, he balled his hand into a fist and slammed it hard into the dense wood of the railing. If words had the power to destroy, the guttural stream of Italian invectives torn from his throat would have sunk the entire French Navy.

CHAPTER 5

Eros trained his telescope on the horizon. "He's coming toward us."

"Are you certain you want to give her back?" Giovanni inquired.

Eros shoved the brass tube into his hands. "See for yourself who's onboard his ship."

Giovanni put his eye to the hole. A warship flying the English colors was approaching at full speed. "*Madonna mia!* He has Gelsomina onboard. We can't fire at him."

"But he can fire at us. His ship is a man-o'-war with weight of metal equal to ours."

Giovanni returned the telescope to his captain and glanced at the black serpent printed over purple ominously surfing the wind at the top of the masthead. "What are we to do, then?"

"Nothing." Eros shut the tube. A private smile tugged at his lips as Rocca escorted Alanis, dressed in sunny yellow silk, onto the foredeck. "Good morning," Eros said, unsmiling.

The instant they faced each other, Alanis relived their searing midnight tryst all over again: Moonlight, kisses, craving . . . then shame and guilt. Eros seemed trapped in the same moment.

"I imagine the reason I'm here is to spare us from getting blown out of the water," she said.

"You scare me sometimes," he whispered. "Your mind spins as rapidly as mine does."

"Don't flatter yourself." She took his telescope, turned her back to him, and scanned the horizon. "How much brain does one need to realize that I'm your best collateral? If Lucas spots me on your deck, he will hold his fire, and you shall have your moment with him. This is what you want, is it not? To haggle with the viscount as a common fishmonger."

His voice turned chillingly cold. "Considering the *aperitivo* I had the pleasure of sampling last night, I confidently expect today's transaction to go very smoothly."

His remark was so low she wasn't about to dignify it with a riposte. She concentrated on the English ship. *Lucas.* Soon they would wed and come to share their lives together, as man and wife. And after last night, she was better informed about what to expect. *Hopefully.*

"I suppose this is farewell." Eros's low voice filled her ear. Stark craving possessed her. Damnation! What was so intrinsically wrong with her that a blackguard should stir her blood with such wicked yearnings? "Last night when I kissed you, you called me Eros. I can't seem to get it out of my head."

Neither can I, she echoed bleakly. After today they would never meet again.

"I wish I could say we might see each other yet again," he spoke her thoughts, "perhaps in a future ball in France, but I doubt it. Louis is rather cross with me at the moment for stealing his frigates, and you are a soon-to-be-married *dame,* busy with producing blond toddlers."

"You say this as if you care," she mumbled stiffly, her eyes on the approaching ship.

"You say this as if *you* care." His lips scalded the delicate slope of her nape. "Do you?"

Yes. She shut her eyes. Pulling her wobbly self together, she turned to face him. The heat in his eyes unhinged her. "You're off to fight the French, then."

He was all suave Italian charm again. "Does a valiant soldier merit a friendly *adieu?*"

Inadvertently she glimpsed at his mouth. "I was not aware that we were friends."

Eros pulled her to him. "I have Santo Giorgio to watch over me, but no *ragazza* to shed her tears. Will you think of me from time to time, *Amore?* Shed a tear or two?"

"You have Gelsomina to shed tears for you," she retorted bitingly.

"It won't be the same." He stared at her mouth, his eyes heavy with desire. Her head fell back. One last parting kiss, she thought, waiting for the torrid taste of his mouth . . .

"*Ship on bowsprit, Captain!*" a voice hollered from the forecastle.

"Trim the sails!" Eros called over his shoulder, activating a disciplined commotion. Sailors climbed the ropes to furl the sails. Grappling hooks flew from one warship to another, bringing the vessels closer together. Alanis glanced at the warship approaching starboard. She wished she could stop time for one crazy moment, for one last parting kiss, but with Lucas came reality.

Eros looked grim. "Duty calls, my beauty." Sighing, he released her and marched off. His lionlike voice carried on the breeze as he fired orders, his strides establishing an air of authority.

Feeling cheated, Alanis took position at starboard where she secured a vantage view of the scene. It was not long before she spotted Lucas standing at the railing of the *Dandelion*. He was changed, she thought. The priggish lord was transformed into a dashing commander.

"Good God, Alis, it is you!" His green eyes expanded in a newly tanned face. "What the deuce are you doing here? Are you all right? Were you ill treated in any way?"

She had hoped for a warmer reunion. She sensed a large, annoyance-radiating presence at her back, and a crisp voice stated, "She was treated exceptionally well."

Alanis smiled. Eros sounded a little bit jealous. Deciding to tweak his temper, she called out cheerfully, "Hello, Lucas! I've come to offer diversions and support. I had the misfortune to be taken from my ship, but I'm in perfect form and dreadfully bored. And you are?"

"Splendid, but I do not much appreciate your coming here. It's wartime and the High Seas are polluted with scavengers." He shot the man at her back an intimidating glare. "I am shocked Dellamore allowed you this harebrained adventure. Kingston is hardly London, you know."

"Enough with the tear-jerking drama," Eros barked frostily and slammed both hands on the railing on either side of her. "Silverlake, we have business to attend to."

Alanis stiffened. She was facing her fiancé, yet every nerve in her body responded to Eros's closeness. She felt his jaw brushing her temple, felt his heat permeating her bloodstream.

"*Ciao pezzo di ragazzo!*" A ravishing hoyden in purple breeches and boots came to stand beside Lucas, her jet curls swelling, her blue eyes glowing. She threw Eros an orange and a kiss.

"*Gelsomina!*" Eros caught her gift and plunged into a torrential monologue in fluid Italian. Alanis studied his profile; he radiated such joy upon seeing this odd female. She knew he had come to save his mistress, but nothing had prepared her for *this*. The cad paid advances to her while he was in love with another, and she was brainless enough to fall for his dubious charms.

"Jasmine, I told you to stay below deck!" Lucas berated the woman at his side.

Ignoring him, she greeted Eros's men. Giovanni laughed and blew her a kiss.

"Silverlake, I have a proposition for you," Eros shouted. "Your fiancée for Jasmine. You'll never get a better deal than this."

"I do not wheel and deal with cutthroats, Viper. I have the authority to seize your ship and hang you, but if you wish to surrender, I might be persuaded to spare your Italian arse!"

Eros boomed with laughter. "Sorry to disappoint you, clown, but I never had a sovereign over my head before. I most certainly am not about to embrace one now."

"You will surrender, nonetheless. If not, you and your cronies will meet the scaffold!"

Eros curled an arm around Alanis's waist, making her catch her breath. "If this beautiful creature means anything to you, you'll release Jasmine right now. Or I shall be tempted to keep your delectable fiancée for myself and return for Jasmine in a less friendly advent."

Lucas lost his composure. "Let her go, Viper, or you'll pay dearly for this!"

"You obviously know of me, so you must also know that I do not make idle threats. Lady Alanis hasn't been harmed in any way, but if you insist on dismissing my offer, neither you nor her family will see her ever again. Believe me when I say that delightful thoughts cross my mind at the prospect." And in a flint-chipping voice he added, "Let Jasmine walk the plank, or you'll spend the rest of your life scouring the markets of the Orient for your golden bride."

Stabbing his arm with her nails, Alanis glared up at his stern face. "How dare you threaten me with slavery." And Lucas—she glowered at him—the blockhead was taking his principle of not negotiating with pirates to the bitter end. *Her bitter end!* She was not so dense she did not twig what was afoot here: He fancied the Italian tart! "My grandfather will slay you for this," she hissed, and glowered at Eros again. "He'll slay you as well!"

Unperturbed by her attack, Eros caught her wrist and wrapped her more firmly in his arms. "I wonder, Englishman, what would the Duke of Dellamore make of your lack of cooperation? I fail to see a brilliant office in your future. If I were you, I wouldn't antagonize Anne's advisor."

Lucas crimsoned. "Bloody bastard! I won't be blackmailed by the likes of you! If you do not release Lady Alanis this instant, you'll be hounded by Her Majesty's Fleet until you—"

"You'll have to do better than this," Eros cut him short. "I'm already pursued by every navy on the High Seas. Surely you don't expect me to balk at your uninspired threat."

Exasperated, Alanis called, "Let him have his girl and be done with it, Lucas!" If she didn't put her foot down, the two oafs were likely to stand there all day, exchanging threats.

"There's a sensible advice," Eros remarked. He smiled at her. "Desperate to escape me?"

"Do not even presume to think I'm on your side, villain. Now let go!" She tried to pry his steely arms off of her, but Eros only squeezed tighter, seeming to enjoy their embraced position.

"You're an overeager pup, Silverlake," he shouted, "unschooled in the ways of the world. I could let my entire crew taste this precious morsel, and you'd still be obliged to recover her. I'm offering you the sweeter deal. Grab it with both hands."

Lucas seethed. "I won't cower under your bloodstained flag! I won't relinquish Jasmine!"

The English soldiers seemed as amazed as the pirates, but not as aghast as Alanis. "*Lucas!*" She choked, mortified. She looked at Eros. The empathy in his eyes made her feel worse. That he should pity her was the worst humiliation.

He ran a finger beneath her eye and stared at the tears he'd collected. Fury lit his eyes. "*D'accordo. Va bene!*" he snarled at Lucas. "I'll keep Alanis for now, but don't expect me to give up on Jasmine. Cut the ropes!" he ordered his crew.

"Where the devil do you think you're off to?" Lucas yelled. "We'll settle this as it's done in the civilized world! And if you haven't the foggiest, I'll be happy to enlighten you!"

Her hope revived, Alanis hung expectant eyes on Eros. He blinked at the viscount, feigning utter astonishment. "My good man, are you by any chance suggesting a duel?"

"Indeed, I am, sirrah. So sharpen your cutlass and prepare to do battle!"

Eros gave a negligent shrug. "I didn't come here to tear you to shreds, but if you insist . . . " In Latin he said, "*A crown plucked from an easy summit brings no pleasure.*"

Loud cheers broke on the *Alastor.* Lucas bristled. "Latin or plain English, I suggest you put your metal where your mouth is!" Suitably, the *Dandelion* soldiers booed and jeered.

Alanis touched Eros's arm. "Please . . . don't kill him."

"I must accept his challenge, Princess. Your fiancé is a pig-headed fool, and I cannot leave Gelsomina behind. Don't hate me too much after today. Just remember that—" Sustaining her anxious gaze, he put the orange in her hands for safekeeping. "I'm doing this for you as well." He called to Lucas, "You have my answer, pirate hunter. We'll dance the plank, only be sure you don't fall off." And to the roaring delight of the Italian sailors he went to mount the board.

On the *Dandelion,* Lucas removed his vest and drew his rapier. He stormed with an elegant offensive maneuver, collecting cheers from his officers and crew. Eros was the first to leap onto the plank, his litheness once again reminding Alanis of a black leopard. Folding his arms across his chest, he called, "Are you ready to proceed, Viscount, or do I go below for a nap?"

Lucas ceased his exercise. "You may take a minute. To say your last prayer!" He joined Eros on the plank, causing the board to groan and lurch precariously. Flushing, he struggled to obtain balance while the giant pirate stood steady as a rock, looking amused. "You seem adept at this sort of thing, Viper, but so are monkeys."

"Enough of such compliments." Eros smiled. "Remember, this is a serious matter—your funeral." He withdrew his lustrous rapier and pointed it at the viscount. "*En Guard!*"

His lips pursed, Lucas crossed his sword with the pirate's. A hush fell on both decks. Then, thrusting lightning fast, Lucas performed a neat *volte-face*. The bluecoats hurrahed, waving their fists, but Eros parried fluently and forced the viscount to switch position with him.

Flailing wildly, Lucas cast anxious glances at the shark-infested waves splashing beneath the plank. Suddenly, his cravat was yanked hard, hauling him back to a steady posture.

"Going anywhere?" Eros let go of the lace folds, looking mildly interested. The *Alastor* deck raged with laughter, whistling, stomping, and hooting. Smiling graciously, Eros inclined his head at his enthusiastic audience, then faced the viscount again. Lucas's flustered expression was as splendid as Eros's broad, tempting smile as he offered, "Wish to yield?"

"Not before I send your loquacious mouth overboard!" He lifted his sword and struck. The duel turned lethal from then on. Eros thrust hard and fast, pressuring the viscount's rapier while using his bulkier frame to wedge him between the *Alastor* and the deep drop to the sea. Golden sunrays slivered off their scuffing blades. The board creaked beneath their dancing boots.

Alanis held her breath, watching them engage and disengage. She prayed for Lucas, winced when Eros escaped a near stabbing, and basically suppressed sheer panic. Her gaze clashed with Jasmine's, and they exchanged curious glances. Her adversary looked as anxious she felt. Alanis suspected

Jasmine was experiencing the same confusion of equally fretting over both duelers.

Wanting in practice, Lucas redoubled his agility, the price of which was a thick sheen of sweat on his brow. He moved gracefully, his blond queue wagging over his nape, his lean body hunching and bending to avoid the Italian's relentless strikes. His breathing thinned. Eros was steadily wearing him down. He must have faced deadlier foes than Lucas Hunter in his wretched life, Alanis surmised. Wielding his blade at an unbelievable speed, he constantly changed the rules and laid into the viscount without allowing him a moment to catch his breath.

Desperate to fell his opponent, Lucas aimed at Eros's knees, but the latter leaped over the blade with the grace of a cat and landed at the center of the board. Lucas lost his balance. With a loud whoop he landed flat on his backside. The Italians went berserk, guffawing loud enough to raise the devil; Giovanni was cracking up so hard tears were streaming down his cheeks.

"*Capitano,* show some mercy for the poor turtle!" he cried. His mates burst out laughing. The bluecoats didn't take kindly to the banter, and a verbal brawl erupted between the two decks.

Eros watched Lucas slowly getting up. "My offer still stands," he said. "Yield!"

"I'll see you dead first!" Lucas rasped, and with a guttural cry lunged at Eros. The pirate's reaction was blinding fast; his rapier shimmered as he screwed it expertly, pierced the viscount's palm, and knocked the rapier out of his hand. The blade soared high, flipping and flickering in the bright sunlight, before it dove into the sea. The viscount withdrew his dagger.

"Lucas, don't! He'll hack you to pieces!" Alanis cried out in terror. He could not afford to challenge the Viper with a knife! "Please, let him take his girl and be done with this madness!"

Lucas looked hurt, worn out, and desperate. His bloody fingers squeezed the knife's hilt. "Jasmine is a decent woman. She doesn't need to throw her life away on filth like you. She can have a good, respectable one in Jamaica. So leave her be, you bloody sea dog!"

A muscle twitched in Eros's jaw. "To be hung, imprisoned, or serve as your mistress? How inconvenient for you to have your fiancée show up so unexpectedly."

"Why don't you ask Jasmine what she wants?"

"I know where her loyalty lies," Eros replies. "Sheath your blade. She comes with me."

"Never!" Lucas charged with the knife. Eros gripped his wrist, twisted it behind his back, and relieved him of the dagger. He brought its tip to Lucas's neck. A drop of blood emerged on the viscount's damp skin. It trickled to his sweat-drenched collar, expanding on the white fabric.

Noting the savage glint in Eros's eyes, Alanis begged, "Eros! Please! Don't kill him!"

"Eros!" Jasmine cried out, her eyes wild with terror. "Don't kill him! *I love him . . .*"

Eros froze. He glared at Jasmine. "You love him?"

"Yes." Jasmine nodded, wiping her teary face with her shirtsleeve.

Alanis moaned with despair. Eros was sure to kill Lucas now. Yet to her utter amazement, the notorious pirate dropped the knife and released Lucas. He offered Jasmine a hand. "Come."

Jasmine started to mount the plank. Lucas roared. He dove at the dagger and slashed Eros's side, ripping his midsection. Blood spurted red and thick. Eros staggered, blue eyes burning. He dropped to his knees with a loud thud and toppled over, pressing his hand to his side.

"Dear Lord!" Alanis nudged the enraged pirates aside to reach the plank. Bloody knife in hand, Lucas was about to strike. "Lucas, don't!" she screamed. "You are not a murderer!"

Jasmine delved as a serpent between them, bracing her body as a human shield.

"Get out of the way, Jasmine!" Lucas barked. "Or I swear I'll kill you both!"

"Kill me, then, you cowardly bastard! He spared your life upon my request. What sort of a man are you to stab a man in the back? You! The noble viscount! You're a backstabbing knave!"

Giovanni and Nico drew their pistols and pointed them at

Lucas's back. Horrified, Alanis's eyes fixed on Eros. Her heart went out to him. "Lucas! Let them live! You've won!"

Reluctantly, Lucas dropped the knife. Her face run with tears, Jasmine sat beside Eros and gently put his dark head in her lap. "Don't just stand there, Lucas! Get him a surgeon!"

"There's no surgeon onboard the *Dandelion*. And just as well. Your *lover* will die as a dog, because that is precisely what he is."

His snarl proved conclusively what Alanis already suspected: He and Jasmine were lovers. This duel wasn't about her. It was about eliminating the competition—Eros.

Jasmine's eyes flashed murderously. "Eros is not my lover, you idiot! *He's my brother!*"

Alanis's jaw dropped open. Of course! How could she have been so blind? A brother and a sister, so much alike, both tall, dark Italians, damn-your-eyes beautiful with sapphire eyes. Everything clicked into place: Eros's efforts to rescue Jasmine, his willingness to spare Lucas's life because his sister loved him, and last, it dawned on her that his kisses, their moments together . . . He meant it. He must have meant it. And now he was dying.

Jasmine wept bitterly, her arm protectively draped over Eros's chest. "I need to get him off this board," she cried brokenly. "*Madonna mia,* he's losing too much blood . . ."

Alanis's tears were just as raw. "Jasmine, lower him on deck. I'll treat his wound."

Jasmine's head came up, hope brightening her eyes. "You will?"

"I'm no surgeon," Alanis admitted. "I've merely assisted our physician Giles in Yorkshire on occasion. Nothing fancy. Stitching, cleansing. But if there's no one else . . ."

"There isn't. Please help him." Jasmine stood up. Giovanni and Nico came to lend a hand.

Lucas blocked them. "My fiancée will not treat this vile man."

"Yes, I will!" Alanis countered. "I won't watch him bleed to death."

The viscount looked appalled. "Why should you concern yourself whether this blackguard bleeds to death, Alis? After what he did to you, you still want to help him?"

His attitude sent the pirates to their battle positions. Muskets and pistols were drawn. The Master Gunner gave out orders to load the guns. Dangling on ropes from the *Alastor's* masts, the pirate crew prepared to board the *Dandelion,* and then the best boys would carry the day.

"If you don't let me treat him, we shall all be swimming for our lives," Alanis warned.

"Please!" Jasmine implored. "Don't ask me to choose between my brother and you."

"We'll take him to Kingston, then." Lucas grunted. "My fiancée will not take one step toward this villain. She has suffered enough at his filthy hands."

Alanis looked at Eros. He was staring at her with the eyes of a wounded tiger. How could she let him die? "I never suffered at his hands. I will tend to him."

"Alis, what are you saying?" Lucas demanded. "You can't possibly treat this criminal!"

Alanis saw the terror in Jasmine's eyes. She knew that terror. Her brother was about to die. "He's lost too much blood already," she insisted. "If we wait until we reach Kingston, he will surely die. I refuse to see another man bleed to death and be told there is nothing to be done."

"You are thinking of Tom, aren't you? But you have no idea how evil this man is. Eros is a brutal murderer. He deserves to be hanged. I forbid you to come within a yard of him."

Her resolve was final. Because of his mad behavior, because he was besotted with another woman, he put them both at risk. It was time to assume command of her life and make her own decisions. "If Eros dies because you forced me to withhold treatment, I'll board the first ship home and tell my grandfather everything! He will not approve of your conduct and neither will your father *or the queen.* Do you wish me to state my case with Her Majesty?"

Lucas flinched. He sustained her glare, unsure whether

she'd pursue her threat to the end. She didn't blink. "Do as you please," he muttered. "You have my permission."

Not wasting another precious moment, Jasmine helped Eros up. Giovanni and Nico offered assistance, but to everyone's astonishment, Eros barked at his helpers and lowered himself to the *Alastor* deck. Grating his teeth with every agonizing gesture, he slumped against the railing.

Alanis knelt beside him. "Are you in a lot of pain?" she inquired softly, sweeping his silky black hair off his brow. Cold sweat dampened it.

"*Yes,*" he gritted. His eyes glinted feverishly blue.

"Good. It means you're not dying yet." His white linen shirt was soaked with blood. She had to rip it off to expose the wound, yet peeling the attached cloth was sure to cause him unbearable pain. "Jasmine, lend me your dagger. And give him something to bite on."

"*Just do it,*" Eros rasped through clenched teeth. "If I'm out when you're done, spill coffee powder over the cut. It should seal it. You'll find a pouch in my cabin." Though pain was visible in every line in his face, his mouth was set with stoical resolve. "*Do it, Alanis.*"

Considering the amount of blood he'd lost, Alanis was amazed he was still in command of his senses. She wiped her brow and very tenderly slashed his shirt. Blood gushed, so she pressed the ruined cloth against the open wound. *No panic,* she commanded herself. *You can save him.*

Eros watched her the entire time, his eyes heavy with pain, yet he didn't grunt. Nor did he flinch. He merely stared at her, his gaze obscure, his complexion gray, his body taut. Fighting the shaking, he gave only once to a sharp spasm. "Why?" he hissed. "Why are you . . . helping me?"

His question hung between them, challenging, personal. Why *was* she helping this ruthless pirate? He had done nothing to merit her kindness. "I hope your vigor lives up to your immortal name, Eros," she whispered with a smile. "Whatever my reasons are, you shall have to trust me."

CHAPTER 6

Soldiers patrolled the torchlit courtyard. Alanis left the window and came to her patient's side. Her hair was damp from a recent bath; a silk penoir hugged her body. She set the lamp on the bedside console and sat on the edge of the bed. With a light finger she swept his hair off his forehead. The heavy stuff spilled aside like cool silk, exposing his tanned, patrician profile. He made her think of Samson, the legendary hero whose hair held the secret to his great powers.

Eros groaned and stirred in his sleep.

"Sleep peacefully, Samson," she whispered. "You're safe with me." She put a cool hand on his brow to check his fever. Normal. The word made her grimace. Was it "normal" for the Duke of Dellamore's granddaughter to be succoring a notorious pirate? Was she insane?

His breathing quieted. Yet she was unable to peel her eyes off him. The man fascinated her. He had the mannerisms of a lord, the reputation of the Monarch of Hell, the body of a Greek god, the handsomest face, and when he was not pillaging— he attended balls at Versailles.

"Who are you?" she whispered. She glimpsed at the golden medallion resting on his chest. Gently she lifted it closer to the light. It seemed exceptionally rare. Shaped as a medieval shield, a cross divided it into four quarters. Two figures were carved diagonally: An eagle, its majestic wings spread open, and a serpent—the viper stamped on Eros's purple flag. The crest resembled the one in his cabin. At the bottom was inscribed: MORS ACERBA. FAMA PERPETUA EST.

She returned the medallion to his chest, and on impulse her hand glided down his torso. His warm, bronzed skin felt velvety soft. Cubically shaped muscles undulated beneath her palm.

Eros was sound asleep, but even in his weak condition, his potent personality radiated. She touched his arm, resting on the white sheet. It was thickly corded, as she well remembered, but shirtless the muscles felt larger, utterly masculine. She caressed the veined forearm below the elbow, marveling at the softness of his skin while recalling the immense power his hand could wield. His fingers were long and graceful. They gripped her. Her eyes flew to his face.

Brilliant sapphires glinted at her beneath heavy eyelids. "What the devil are you doing?"

"Wh . . . what?" she asked, her heart drumming in her ear. "I, eh, I was . . ."

Eros exhaled and eased his grip on her hand. "Where am I?" he inquired groggily.

"You don't remember?"

"My head." He groaned. "It feels . . . wooly. I can't seem to form one coherent thought."

"You daftly preferred draining one of Lucas's brandy bottles instead of taking laudanum. You are in his house, by the way, in my bedchamber."

He smiled faintly. "Now I remember. How does your fiancé feel about my commandeering your bed? Should we expect a squadron of guards to barge in on us at any moment?"

"He wouldn't dare. It would be the end of his naval career and quite possibly his life, if my grandfather got wind of it."

"And my ship? Did he confiscate her?"

"After Giovanni and Nico brought you here, your ship sailed away. Your sister stayed."

He nodded, still holding her hand in his. "Why are you helping me, Alanis? You should be begging Silverlake to hang me, not care for a strange pirate as if he were a wounded cub."

Not caring to discuss her reasons, she tried to free her hand. Unsuccessfully. "If you wish to scribble a complaint, I'll provide you with a plume and some paper," she offered sweetly.

"You cannot fool me." He slid her hand up his smooth chest and held it over his heart. "With all the venom in your tongue, you are as tenderhearted as they come. A romantic."

Alanis's heart missed a beat. "*A romantic?*"

"Obviously. Helping an injured stranger . . ." He shut his eyes ägainst a stab of pain, yet he was still smiling, his chest rising and falling beneath their laced hands. "Your hand feels nice."

She exhaled with relief. "You think helping you is a romantic deed?"

"I think it is a foolish deed. If I were your grandfather, I'd be spanking your bottom blue." One eye squinted at her. "Perhaps I should look into the matter when I'm improved . . ."

"You are not my grandfather. Besides, you know perfectly well why I helped you, to get back at Lucas," she added quickly before he jumped to the wrong conclusion.

"Really?" He opened his eyes, grinning. "You're right, Alanis. I am not your grandfather and you are not a child. You are a grown woman playing a very dangerous game with a pirate."

"A helpless, pitiable pirate," she pointed out while her cheeks bloomed with color.

"Well, this helpless, pitiable pirate is extremely grateful to put his life in such fine, delicate hands." Eros raised her hand to his lips and pressed a heated kiss inside her palm.

Heat coursed through her. She took a deep breath. Time to collect her delicate hand. "Your dressing needs to be changed, and I should paste some salve over your wound to help it heal."

He released her hand. "Where will you sleep? Here with me?" he asked hopefully.

Ignoring the question, she reached inside her medicine kit and took out a small bottle and several clean patches of linen. She peeled the fine linen dressing off and examined the stitches she had sewn hours ago. The bleeding stopped, and the skin was on the mend. She spread the white salve using her fingertips. The last thing she wanted to do was cause him more pain.

"You have a gentle touch, *Amore*. Unlike other females who've patched me up."

She continued to ignore him, so he grasped one of her wet locks and rubbed it between his fingers, as a tailor assessing the texture of a rich fabric. He brought it to his nose and inhaled its flowery scent. "Golden-haired girl, you could bring a good price in the *Souk* in Algiers."

She smiled. "I see you are determined to annoy me, though it is not to your best interest."

His white teeth gleamed wickedly. "I am determined to gain your attention, lovely nurse. There is a man around this wound, you know."

"I've noticed." She cleaned her fingers and gently retied the knot around the bandage.

"He may be helpless and pitiable at the moment, but he is still capable of appreciating the touch of a beautiful woman's hand." His fingers released her lock of hair and curled around her nape. "There's a saying where I come from," he whispered, drawing her head closer. "'Always beware of the Viper.'" He kissed her, as tenderly as she had dressed his wound.

His lips made her dizzy. By means of sheer willpower she managed to sit upright again. "I have a question. What does the Latin inscription on your medallion say?"

A distant look surfaced in his drugged eyes. "Death is bitter. Fame eternal."

She tried to decipher the look, but he looked away. "You should sleep. You will feel as a new man come morning. I left you a drink of water and this . . ."

Eros's head turned on the pillow. A water trencher and a glass were placed accessibly close on the bedside console, and beside them rested the orange Jasmine had flung him.

Alanis got up. The feel of his lips still hot on hers, she was eager to get away and hide in the adjacent drawing room, at least until he fell asleep. Her hand closed on the doorknob.

"*Alanis.*"

She turned around. His heavy-lidded gaze immobilized her. "*Thank you.*"

The next day Alanis went to confront Lucas in his study. Kingston's waterfront sprawled beyond open windows: a prosperous little harbor with ships coming and going, white-washed houses, palm trees, and a splendid turquoise sea.

Spending the next years of her life on this island appealed to her very much. She would simply have to adapt to the tropical climate. She snapped open her fan and was about to enter the den when loud voices quarrelling inside stopped her.

"You cannot hang my brother!" Jasmine raged. "He let you live because I protected you!"

"I am commissioned by the queen to sanitize these shores, and your brother will get his day at Gallows Point!" Lucas retorted harshly. "He held my fiancée captive on his cutthroat ship with all his cohorts onboard. God knows what she suffered at his hands."

"Lady Alanis happily volunteered to treat my brother's injury, Hunter. Besides, you did not give your fiancée much thought when she was tucked away in England. Why should it bother you now that she likes Eros?"

Alanis had to restrain herself from bursting in and giving them a piece of her mind.

"You may revere him as a god, but he is not," Lucas growled. "And while I sincerely doubt his humanity, I assure you he's all flesh and blood, of the worst sort, mind you, but mortal!"

"By God, you are still jealous!" Jasmine laughed. "Is it because of me or Lady Alanis? Do you suppose she's in love with him?"

Alanis held her breath, interested to hear Lucas's reply.

"For weeks you made me believe he was your lover. Then you side with him against me! He is practically a condemned man. There is not one power in the world that hasn't warranted his arrest. I cannot release him. And even if I could grant him a pardon, I absolutely wouldn't."

"I never claimed he was my lover. You *assumed* he was, as the rest of the world did."

"You didn't see fit to enlighten me as to the true nature of your connection. Did you enjoy making me insanely jealous?"

Blinking back tears, Alanis accepted the truth: They were more than lovers; they were in love. Neither sunshine nor freedom awaited her here, only heartache. Thank God she had taken the initiative and come here. If she hadn't, she would have wasted years waiting for Lucas to return and marry her. She had saved herself in the nick of time. So why did it hurt so much?

The doors opened. "Alis, it's you!" Lucas exclaimed upon seeing her. He looked extremely ill at ease. "I was on my way to find you and . . . Jasmine is anxious to see her brother. May she visit with him in your apartment while we converse in my office?"

"Can't see why not," Alanis replied coolly. "He is her brother. I only hope the sentries you posted outside will let her pass. It appears I am to reside in a prison."

"So long as you insist on nursing a dangerous criminal in your bedchamber, you shall have soldiers around you for your own protection."

He was either a hypocrite or an idiot. "Do you see a need to protect me from a wounded man who can scarcely keep his eyelids open?"

"I do." He sent Jasmine upstairs and invited Alanis inside his den. "The *Pink Beryl* arrived this morning," he announced, shutting the double doors behind them. He assisted her into the wingchair fronting his desk and took his seat behind it. "I had a long talk with Captain McGee. Devastation. Brutality. This is what your pirate is capable of, and you choose to champion him. What am I to think, Alis? What am I to tell your grandfather?"

"What an interesting question," she replied tartly.

"The situation is beyond the pale. I will not tolerate this kind of willfulness from you."

The venom in his voice appalled her. "You are changed. Yesterday I had the impression Jamaica improved you. I see now I was mistaken. Three years and you cannot find half a smile to greet me with. If you wish me gone, say so at once."

A guilty look surfaced in his eyes. He blinked and said, "Any word from my father?"

"The last time I saw the earl he was in excellent health. He sends his best."

"Thank you. We didn't part on the best of terms when I left England. He said he did not have an heir to spare and that if

I insist on making an impression in this war, I should do it properly alongside Marlborough. I imagine he deems me a poor legatee for his earldom, but consoles himself that at least his grandchildren will be half Dellamores."

The earl's disapproval was an old sore with Lucas. "His lordship is very proud of you," she assured him. "He speaks of your accomplishments to anyone who cares to listen."

His rueful gaze perused her appearance. The bright sunlight highlighted her aquamarine eyes so that they seemed to reflect the sea stretching beyond the windows. She had tiny pearls in her earlobes, golden locks spilling over a bare ivory shoulder. Her lace décolletage presented an alluring view of skin. "My, but you do look fetching," he admitted warmly. "Can't locate one hint of the ragamuffin who wrestled me for a seat on the old elm tree."

Her umbrage mellowed a bit, yet she couldn't decide if he regarded her as a man or as a friend. In many ways she considered him more of an older brother. She found him pleasing to the eye, but unlike the Italian upstairs, there was nothing pulse-quickening about him. "It is good to see you," she allowed frigidly. "Three years is a long time."

"Indeed it is, and we should make up for it. We have much catching up to do."

Perhaps all was not lost, Alanis mused. The island was lovely, and she always dreamed of living in a place such as this. She felt at ease around him, too; no danger lurked in dark corners.

Lucas smiled. "Tell me, was the voyage agreeable? I'm curious to learn how you obtained Dellamore's permission to come here. I scarcely believed it when I saw you on the pirate ship. If it hadn't been for your presence onboard, I'd have blasted the damnable villain out of the water."

She had no desire to get into *that* again. "Dellamore was very stubborn, and the war did not help my cause one bit. I had to explain that you and I would never be wed as long as an ocean runs between us, and that since you cannot abandon your post I must come to you. He is anxious for me to be married so that once he's no longer among us I won't be left unprotected."

"Your grandfather needn't worry. We'll be married soon and you'll sail back to England."

"I beg your pardon?" Alanis blinked. *Marry then leave?*

"Alis, do not tell me you're squeamish about marrying me. It was decided ages ago."

"I am not squeamish. I am wondering why I should wed you at all if I'm to be sent home."

"We live in perilous times, perpetually threatened by French and Spanish warships bent on destruction. It's too dangerous for you to stay, and I'm too busy to keep you diverted."

Alanis bolted to her feet. "That won't do, Lucas. I came to live here as your wife, not to be shipped home as a useless piece of luggage." She couldn't believe he intended to seal her fate so cruelly—locking her away in Drearyshire and throwing away the key. She would fight him tooth and nail, even cry off the engagement. "I won't stand for it!" she vowed. "I won't!"

"Calm down, Alis."

"I won't calm down. Not until you put this daft notion of sending me home out of your obtuse head. You of all people should know how I despise sitting in wait. I've waited all my life for the opportunity to see the world. I want to explore that which I have missed. I want to live!"

"Well, you can't live here," the viscount determined.

"Why not?" Her mind reeled, signaling a pending headache. It was a déjà vu of all the aggravations she had suffered over the years: when her parents left her at home to travel the world, when Tom left for Eton, and when the duke was busy with affairs of state.

Lucas set his jaw. "Why do you insist on defying me? Yesterday you made a spectacle of yourself volunteering to care for a pirate. Now you are acting as a flighty wench. I won't tolerate unruly behavior, Alis. I am to be your husband, and you will learn to obey me."

"*Obey you?*" She glowered at his pompous face, wishing she had something to throw at it.

"I am not an irrational tyrant. I am being quite reasonable, in fact, while you choose to defy me at every turn. The pirate you keep in your bedchamber is to be hanged tomorrow and you are to sail back to England as soon as the *Pink Beryl* is outfitted for the voyage."

"You cannot hang a man so severely wounded!"

"I can and I shall. Let me remind you the law: 'Any man who receives, harbors, comforts, or succors a criminal is guilty, as if he himself bore arms.' You should be grateful I do not charge you with high treason."

She felt nauseated. "Since when have you acquired the manners of a hangman, Lucas?"

"Since you decided to make an exhibition of yourself!" he barked.

She went utterly still. Disappointment choked her. She didn't recognize him anymore.

"I must hang him. If I don't, I'll be labeled an accomplice. Think of my reputation."

"Hang your reputation! I am not so green that I do not comprehend the true reason you do not want me underfoot. But let me enlighten you as to the nature of us women. We do not care for monsters who execute our siblings. I'm certain this rule applies to mistresses as well!"

"What am I to do, then?" Lucas frowned miserably.

"Figure it out yourself!" In a whirl of salmon-pink skirts she turned on her heel and left, slamming the heavy oak doors behind her.

Jasmine found Eros asleep amidst lavender-scented sheets and fluffy pillows. Warm gusts of wind swelled the muslin drapes screening the bright sunlight. She knelt beside the bed and kissed his cheek. His eyelids snapped open. The piercing glare mellowed once he recognized the sweet face smiling at him. "*Kitten.*" He smiled sleepily. "What time is it?"

"Noon, sluggard!" She strutted to the window, swept the drapes aside, and crashed into a chair, propping her booted feet on a table. "Were you planning on wasting the entire day abed?"

Eros grimaced. He pushed himself up against the pillows, cursing the damned light and the damned pain. "*Mannaggia.* I think my head is about to explode." He put his hands to his temples and kneaded away the pain. "Tell me everything. What are you doing with this imbecile?"

Jasmine examined the thick white bandage hugging his torso. "Hunter intends to hang you tomorrow. Nothing I say gets through to him. Do you suppose you'd be able to get out tonight?"

Eros sighed. "If I have to." He considered her for a moment. "You're coming?"

"If I have to."

His eyebrow rose. "And that depends on . . . ?" She shrugged. "Hmm. Guido tracked me down near Corsica, said you needed rescuing. He told me the pirate hunter captured your ship. Did Silverlake keep you a prisoner in one of his fortresses?"

"For a while. He wanted information leading to your whereabouts. Apparently, you are his prime target. When he realized the case was hopeless, he brought me here."

Eros swore. "Did he tell you he was engaged or did he let you believe he was in the market for a leg shackle?"

She smiled; her brother's perverse opinion of marriage was not foreign to her. "He did tell me about Lady Alanis. Their betrothal was arranged when they were still in the crib. He claimed they grew up together as a brother and a sister, not as sweethearts. I imagine it was foolish of me to nurture false hopes, but we fell in love. I believed he'd cry off the engagement and choose me instead. He was certainly in no hurry to return to her. I wonder why she put up with it."

"She didn't. So tell me, have you decided to give up your piratical existence in favor of a skirt of hoop? I'd rather you wreaked havoc on Viscount Silverlake than terrorize Frenchmen."

"I know you've always wanted me to pursue a quiet life, find a husband to look after me, and live in a nice home with children. I believe I'm ready to leave the unlucky Frenchmen to you now. Poor Louis has his hands full dealing with one member of the family."

Eros chuckled. "I missed you, Kitten. We've never been apart so long."

She sighed. "I miss you all the time, Eros, but even if I lived in Agadìr, you're never there. Aren't you tired of rampaging the high seas and fighting the King of France?"

"I never tire of pestering the King of France."

She laughed. "I've heard about your new sport, collecting Louis's frigates. How he must hate you now. He'll never invite you to any of his balls again."

"Of course he will. He adores me. I'm the only one who won't let him cheat at faro."

She shook her head, sighing. "Eros. You'll be two and thirty this October. Don't you ever dream of finding a woman to love, bear you children, and—"

"Let's talk about you getting married. Tell me about your new victim. He can't be all bad. Villains usually fence better than he does."

She felt a rush of excitement in her stomach. "Then, you don't mind if I—?"

"*Au contraire.* About time some other unlucky devil earned the privilege of pulling you out of the hot pan. I was beginning to despair I'd be straddled with the task forever."

She smiled, then scowled. "I should hate Hunter for what he did to you."

"Forget what he did to me. The question is—what does Silverlake have in mind for you? He's practically a married man, Gelsomina."

Silly tears sprang to her eyes. "What do you think I should do?"

"Don't be discouraged," Eros said gruffly. "I'm here now. I'll fix everything for you. If Silverlake is the man you want, you'll have him."

"How? You're a prisoner." She sniffed. "And Hunter will never defy his father. He won't leave his lady for a nameless hoyden."

"You are not a nameless hoyden!" Irritated, he concentrated on getting up. He stumbled to the dresser and splashed water into a porcelain basin. Only when his head was submerged in the cool water did the stiff muscles on his back unwind. He grabbed a towel to dry his face. "Leave Alanis to me. I'll handle her."

"He has a thousand soldiers at his command. Even with my help, how will you manage both Lady Alanis and slipping out tonight? This house is a damnable fortress."

He ran his fingers through his wet hair. "There must be a way. There's always a way." He ambled slowly to the window and gave a soft whistle when he glimpsed outside. "Difficult. Not impossible. It would be easier if you came along, but I'll manage. *Now may I have my hug?*"

She sprang into his open arms. "I missed you. I can't lose you, Eros. You are my one solid rock in the world. If it weren't for your courage and cleverness, I'd be dead sixteen years now, buried next to our mother and father in an unmarked grave in Italy. Nothing can come between us. You know that. Not even my love for Lucas Hunter. We are blood."

Eros kissed her teary cheeks. "I love you, too, *Amorruccio.* You'll always have me."

After the long embrace, he returned to the bed. He subsided stiffly on the pillows and shut his eyes. Jasmine dropped on the bed beside him. Lying on her stomach, she propped her elbows on the mattress and cupped her chin, crossing her boots in the air. "What sort of woman is she?"

One sapphire eye opened. "Who?"

She grinned. "Your pretty blond nurse."

He contemplated the ceiling. "During the four days I entertained Silverlake's fiancée on the *Alastor* I reached a few conclusions. One of them was that her betrothal to the viscount was not made in heaven. Perhaps with the right approach, I'll persuade her to give him up."

"I knew it!" She sat up. "You intend to seduce her. You'll make her fall in love with you so that she'd eagerly follow you anywhere. You'll ruin and cast her aside, as you do to all women!"

"I do not ruin women," Eros stated succinctly.

"Her reputation will not survive a liaison with you, Eros, and you bloody well know it. She was kind enough to help you. You cannot repay her with a nasty ruse."

"I won't harm her! Debauching haughty virgins is not my primary pursuit in life. Unlike your viscount, I've learned to master my amorous urges."

Jasmine eyed him skeptically. She had already surmised the lady had a soft spot for her unscrupulous brother. Yet as lovely as Lady Alanis was—and knowing Eros, he did not fail to notice—as a rule he avoided her kind, no exception. He would seduce her only to clear a path for Jasmine to wed Hunter. He would then jilt the lady, leaving her devastated. The idea did not sit well with Jasmine. Eros might not feel obliged, but she did feel indebted to the other woman. Damned if she let Eros crush the opposition in his high-handed way. "Lady Alanis comes from a powerful family," she warned. "Her grandfather is a personal advisor to Queen Anne."

"I know."

"So I urge you—reconsider. I don't think the duke will take too kindly to what you have in mind for his granddaughter. You have enough powerful enemies. You don't need to antagonize every monarch in the universe."

Eros turned cold, lazy eyes to her, the look in them chilling. "*I don't give a damn.*"

She recognized this look. Fleets ran away from it. "'Stefano Andrea,'" she whispered, "'he fears no one and does whatever enters his head.' Papa said that about you."

"Do not call me by that name," he bit out. "How many times must we go through this?"

"You call me Gelsomina," she reminded him gently.

"That's different."

She swallowed the sad lump in her throat. "I know you are past the point of caring which sin you'll fry for, but

please, Eros, don't hurt her. Not even your buried conscience
will live down an ugly ruse such as this."

After spending the day exploring the house grounds, Alanis
returned to her apartment. She found Jasmine in the drawing
room. Lost to the world, the female buccaneer sat on the
couch, admiring a gown of cherry silk that Betsy had pressed
for tonight's dinner. Annoyingly, Lucas had sent his butler to
inform her that a formal one was to be held and would include
fifty of the island's dignitaries. Alanis wasn't eager to plunge
into the local social scene, not while nursing a pirate in her
bedchamber, but as the saying goes—*la nobless oblige.*

"The hooks go at the back," she offered charitably.

Jasmine bolted to her feet, looking mortified. "*Caspita!*
Lady Alanis! I . . . I apologize." She struggled with the gown
in an attempt to put it right again. She wasn't making much
progress. "I cannot thank you enough for saving my brother's
life. I'm in your debt, and so is Eros."

Alanis smiled. Apparently, despite her swaggering independence, Jasmine wasn't all that different from normal females. She liked pink frills. Alanis wandered in and gently
rescued the gown from Jasmine's two left hands. "How is
your brother faring?" she inquired.

"Very well, considering. He did not much appreciate the
chicken broth you sent for his lunch, but the footman with the
bath amended his mood."

Alanis chuckled. "An ailing individual can hardly expect
to be served a savory meal sautéed in rich sauce. He should
be content to be alive to eat at all."

"He's asleep now." Entranced, Jasmine followed Alanis's
clever fingers as they worked their magic on the swishing
silks and frills. Alanis stepped forth and pinned the gown to
her front. Jasmine nearly swallowed her tongue.

"Hold this," Alanis instructed, fastening Jasmine's hesitant
fist around a bit of silk. She smoothed her hand along the
wrinkled front. "It requires a few minor alterations, but . . ."

"Lady Alanis—" Jasmine choked. "I cannot accept an offering from you. It is I who should reward you with gifts. Besides," she blushed, "it would go to waste on me."

"Oh, it's not a gift. I'll trade it for a pair of breeches and matching boots."

Jasmine stared at her as though she belonged in bedlam. "Breeches, Lady Alanis? You wish to dress as a man when you own a magnificent wardrobe?"

Alanis gave a shrug. She didn't so much begrudge Jasmine for conquering Lucas's heart as she did for the freedom she enjoyed. This outlandish female traveled the world as a free spirit while she had to read about the world existing beyond the golden bars of her cage. "Why not? I'd love to put on breeches and strut about without a care in the world."

"There are less gratifying aspects to dressing as a man," Jasmine lectured. "Being looked upon as a freak of nature for one, or having to stand up to male standards in man's world while secretly envying refined ladies who are the bane of one's existence."

Alanis stilled under the direct blow. Humor replaced her shock, and she sank on the couch, laughing. "The bane of refined ladies' existence is pretty Amazons who enjoy absolute freedom and rove man's world . . . and, of course, dour-faced matrons and overbearing men."

Jasmine smiled hesitantly. "You seem highly capable of handling overbearing men."

"Years of practice." Alanis prettily batted her eyelashes. "My world may twinkle to the eye, but the golden bars cast the luster. I require chaperonage to take a turn in the park."

"Indeed? Always?" Jasmine joined Alanis on the couch.

"Unfortunately, yes." Alanis sighed heartily. "We fine ladies must travel with our very own dragon to ward off licentious males."

Jasmine giggled. "How did your dragon react when you installed a wounded man in your bedchamber? I saw no scorching signs on the walls."

"My dragon is housebroken. Her snorts are worse than her blaze."

They both laughed. Jasmine said, "I can't say the same about the dragon in your bed."

Alanis jumped at the opening. "Tell me about him. What is he like as a brother? I've heard lots of stories about him, but from what I gathered these past few days he seems rather rational, deliberate, and highly intelligent. Not at all the mad monster people say he is."

"He's no monster. He's a great gun and a gentle, loving brother with the heart of a lion, but the traits you listed are exactly what makes him dangerous."

"Dangerous to the French?" Alanis subtly angled for more information.

"Dangerous to whomever Eros deems objectionable. Spain is on his blacklist as well."

"It seems your brother is determined to single-handedly rid our world of all its undesirable tyrants. Why doesn't he officially join the Grand Alliance? Surely it would be preferable to being tagged a pirate with a price on his head."

Jasmine averted her gaze. "It's hard to explain."

Now that sounded intriguing. Alanis was prepared to sit all day and listen to stories about the man with the heart of a lion. She glanced at the door connecting to her bedchamber.

Betsy walked in through the main door. Jasmine stood. "I should leave. Thank you again."

Alanis stood up also. "Don't forget the gown. I'll be happy to share Betsy when you decide to try it on. I think it was deliberately designed to exasperate. Wouldn't you say so, Betsy?"

Betsy nodded in agreement. Jasmine took the gift with a grateful smile. "Lady Alanis."

"Enough with the 'Lady' and think nothing of it. One should start somewhere." Amazing how of all people Lucas's mistress turned out to be a lovely person, Alanis thought. She was also Eros's sister and *that* enticed Alanis to befriend her even more. "If you'd like, we may call upon a local modiste and start you up at once. Within a week you'll have a whole new wardrobe."

"A whole new wardrobe?" Jasmine looked dazzled.

Alanis took her arm and escorted her out the door, away from Betsy's ears. Outside her expression sobered. "What are we to do about the hanging?"

"If Hunter doesn't change his mind, Eros and I must leave tonight," Jasmine whispered.

Alanis regarded her ambivalently. Should Jasmine leave, there would be no more talk of sending her home and she would have finally achieved her lifelong ambition. Yet Eros would be leaving as well. Tonight. *It was too soon.* Besides, didn't she deserve better prospects than a husband pining for the woman who slipped away? "Tell me what I must do to help."

Jasmine leaned closer. "I'll keep on trying to change Hunter's mind, but if you do not hear from me, please keep him occupied this evening while we make good our escape."

"All right." Alanis well envisioned what a dratted pleasure dinner was about to become.

CHAPTER 7

"Captain McGee, you must tell us the latest news from the forefront," Colonel Holbrook demanded across the table from Alanis. "How are our boys faring against those Frenchies?"

Alanis sighed with relief. Throughout dinner, Lucas scrutinized her as Lord High Justice while she smoothly charmed his peers and put a strain on his decision to ship her home. But she had nothing more to report on the subject of the latest French fashion.

"Well," the captain frowned, "our latest triumph was in the Milan Region. General Savoy was determined to have the strong bridgehead near Cassano and crushed Marshal de Vendôme!"

"To our first victory in Milan!" Mr. Greyson saluted and the men tossed back their wine.

"I keep telling you this Savoy fellow is not a bad sort, even if he is French," Holbrook said.

"Austrian," Greyson argued. "General Savoy is Austrian."

Captain McGee shook his bewigged head. "He's half Austrian, half French."

"His mother was French, Cardinal Mazarin's niece," Alanis recalled aloud, "but his father was an Italian prince. The Duke of Savoy in Turin is General Savoy's first cousin."

A hush fell around the long table. A woman publicly speaking her mind on politics was a gross *faux pas* and crossing propriety beyond the pale. Alanis groaned inwardly. If these people learned from talkative servants about the pirate in her bedchamber, a scandal broth would surge all the way to Yorkshire, Dellamore would send half the fleet to collect her, and she would lose all her freedom hereafter. To avoid another slip of the tongue she sampled the dessert cake.

The governor cleared his throat. "Ladies and gentlemen, you've all been invited to my ball tomorrow night. Now, in addition to celebrating the arrival of the accomplished granddaughter of the Duke of Dellamore, we'll be saluting this victory and many more to come. Please join me in another salute lauding our boys, Marlborough and Savoy, and the valiant troops they command on the Continent. May God bless them and keep them safe!" His salute was accepted heartily.

"What a bloody bullring Milan has become," Greyson lamented. "When the Vipers were in power, Milan was invincible. The Sforza dukes were fierce warriors, and the Visconti cunning to the last degree. For centuries these united houses put a chill in the hearts of their fellow princes."

Alanis bit her fork. *Always beware of the Viper.* What did her pirate have in common with royal Milanese dynasties that had ceased to exist ages ago? She wondered whether Eros and his sister were already gone. If only they stopped blathering, she would be in time to say good-bye . . .

"If Savoy vanquishes Vendôme in Milan, we just might win

this cussed war after all!" the old colonel declared, his scarlet cheeks attesting to the amount of wine he'd put away.

"Jonathan Holbrook, watch your ungoverned tongue!" his wife scolded. "There are ladies present. It is bad enough you subject us to your tasteless discourses. I refuse to put up with the sort of speech I must suffer in the privacy of our home. My dear Mrs. Greyson," she spoke to the lady at her side, "I insist we leave these warmongers to their port and cigars and take our cake in the next room. I cannot stomach another word on the subject of this horrid war." Lips pursed, she stood up, forcing the men to their feet and the women to follow suit. "Come along, ladies. We shall leave them to their port and have a better time on our own. Good evening, gentlemen."

Alanis's hopes to flee upstairs were dashed, and she had to sit for another hour until Lucas rescued her and they both saw the guests out. They went upstairs in silence. A bundle of nerves, she expected him to open the door and say good night. Yet to her dismay, he followed her inside her apartment. The foyer was dark; a patch of moonlight fell on the carpet. Her eyes flew to the bedchamber door. No bar of light shone underneath. Disappointment lanced her. Eros was gone.

"If you insist on keeping your pirate in this apartment, at least let me put you in another."

Alanis dropped her silk shawl on the sofa. "He's not *my* pirate, Lucas."

"Are you in love with him, Alis?"

His question numbed her brain. Then, with her best horrified airs she said, "Good Lord! The man is a worthless blackguard, lower than a lowly serf!" And intelligent and interesting and she wished he were here with her instead of Lucas, with whom she was stuck for the rest of her life. "Perhaps we should reconsider our betrothal. We could be making a dreadful mistake."

"Why? Because I said I'd hang your pirate? I promise I won't hang him until he heals. But you cannot seriously consider crying off our engagement, Alis. It would break my heart!"

"It would only affect your pride. I've yet to see a sign that you possess tender feelings for me. I think you have spent them all on Jasmine." *Hang him when he heals . . .*

"I do care for you, Alis, dearly. We have much in common and a solid friendship. I cannot see why our marriage should not be a success."

"Well, I can! Perhaps friendship is enough for you, but there is more to a marriage, much more. There should be tender moments and feelings running as deep as one's soul. There should be longing and excitement. What you describe is as exhilarating as cold porridge!"

Lucas opened his mouth, but she had more to say. "I have always been the docile girl who stayed at home while you went about your business. In your eyes, I'm as pure as snow and loved from afar, but never the . . . desirable one," she added uneasily. He'd never even tried to kiss her. In the past, she assumed he was well behaved. Now she knew the real reason: lack of interest. She recalled an old French saying of Madame de Montespan's: Woman's greatest ambition is to inspire Love. With Lucas she had clearly failed. On a whim, she said, "Kiss me, Lucas. *Kiss me.*" If his kiss proved half as ardent as Eros's, she might reconsider giving them a second chance.

The viscount blanched. Then, hesitantly, his lips touched hers. Shutting her eyes, Alanis concentrated on the feel of his mouth. *Nice,* she thought, but there was nothing interesting about his kiss, which defied the purpose of the experiment. He was going to be a gentleman about it and it would not do at all. She took an additional bold step and opened her mouth to his.

Lucas tore his mouth away. Alanis froze, feeling self-conscious and gauche. What had she done wrong? He didn't deem her worthy of an explanation, though. He opened the door and left.

Alanis remained standing alone in the darkness. She considered lighting a lamp but had no desire to encounter her reflection in a mirror. She had seen marble statues with more soul than the reserved ice queen she appeared to be. What was there to love? What was there to kiss? No wonder Lucas was reluctant. There was nothing sensual about her to inflame a man. She wasn't the spirited Jasmine. She was the cold swan from Yorkshire. Not even worthy of a kiss.

Sobbing silently, she became aware of an odd sensation: She was being watched. Her head came up. A broad-shouldered shape, outlined by moonlight, casually leaned against the window.

"You're still here!" she exclaimed. She was so glad to see him, it took her a moment to realize Eros must have witnessed her nightmarish scene with Lucas! Did he overhear her saying he was a worthless pirate? Did he see Lucas scorning her kiss?

Eros disengaged from the window and started toward her. Moonbeams poured over his tall, sculpted frame, delineating the fall of his hair. He stopped before her. "Come here."

Without hesitation she walked into his embrace. His mouth claimed hers, banishing every thought of undesirability from her head, and she was fire again, burning bright and raw. His lips moved hungrily, possessively; his head angled to merge with her mouth. She felt hot and shivery at the same time, intoxicated by his kiss, by the engulfing heat and scent of his seminude body.

Eros's mouth moved to her ear, breathing, "*Ti desidero, Alanis.*"

His sultry words filled her head. One didn't need to be fluent in Italian to understand. *He desired her.* She rose on her toes and slid her arms around his neck. "I'm glad you stayed."

"You look beautiful standing in my arms in the moonlight, *Amore.* I should steal you away, and together we'll explore the magical wonders of the world."

Unsure what to make of his vague proposal, she whispered, "Where would you take me?"

"The Arabian Sea touches a secret faraway shore where pearls are as copious as the grains of sand." His voice was deep and tempting. "There is a small town in Morocco called Agadir, where beaches are as white as snow with the most unusual purple sunsets you've ever seen."

"I've never seen a purple sunset. To be perfectly honest, I haven't traveled much."

"You should. One does not quite experience life until one experiences the world."

"I want to, more than anything. I'm afraid it is quite beyond my reach, though."

"Why? You're not a child. To my best knowledge you're past the age of twenty-one. There is no reason you shouldn't realize your dreams, Alanis. Life is too short to be wasted on regrets."

He had a strong point, but . . . if it were only that easy. She slid her hands along his muscular bare chest. "Is it true you grew up in the Kasbah of Algiers?"

He tilted his head from side to side. "Not exactly, but in many ways yes. Why? Want to visit the Kasbah?" He grinned challengingly.

She bit her lip. "Even if I had the freedom to travel the world, which I do not, I could never go there. It's a pirates' lair and much too dangerous."

"Dangerous, yes. Fatal, no. That is, if one knows his way around . . ." He grinned.

Alanis was struck with a sudden, wild craving to go there, to see it with her own eyes. "Do you also know your way around the Sultan's harem in Constantinople?" She smiled daringly.

"The Turkish Sultan is peculiarly possessive of his wives, but yes, I have stolen a few quick glimpses inside his harem. What else intrigues you, my inquisitive fair lady?"

"Are the taverns of Tortuga as shocking as people say they are? I hear the women there would take their clothes off and dance on a table in the nude for a few pieces of eight."

Eros burst out laughing. "Where do you hear these stories, Alanis? I wasn't aware innocent young ladies discussed shocking topics on social occasions."

"We sometimes discuss you as well, the most shocking topic of all."

"*Me?*" He splayed his hand over his heart, feigning bewilderment. "Must I assume it is my black character you and your little friends chew to pieces over tea and scones?"

"Have you been eavesdropping?" Alanis laughed, savoring the

feel of his arms around her. "You do enjoy a nasty reputation, Eros. You make delightful gossip material."

He cocked a jet eyebrow. "Such as?"

"Such as the fortified towns you held for ransom, the ships you plundered, the fortune of pillage you've accumulated, the men you killed, the women you . . ."

His mouth brushed against hers. "I admit there were women, but the last I came to know surpasses them all incontestably. Why do you resign yourself to a life you obviously deem small and insignificant? You're bright, exceptionally educated, and not lacking in spirit. Why seal your fate so ascetically?"

"My life is neither small nor insignificant." Nonetheless, his question touched the bleeding wound in her soul. "I'm not like you. I have responsibilities, loved ones I cannot let down."

"Do those loved ones always live up to your expectations?" He put a finger beneath her chin and tilted her face up. "*Bella donna,* no man in his right mind would refuse a woman like you. Silverlake is no less man than I am, but his heart already belongs to another. Who is he so anxious to please that he will marry you while he's in love with another?"

Startled by his perception, Alanis pulled away from him and stared out the window. Palm trees rustled in the breeze; wind chimes tinkled melodiously. She wanted to live on this island, but not when the only reason Lucas wanted to marry her was to please his father. The Earl of Denton would never absolve his son of marrying beneath him.

"You should get some sleep," Eros spoke beside her. "I'll stay here. I've spent too much time abed already. Rest assured I'll respect your privacy."

Oddly, she believed him. And she was exhausted. "I don't know what happened to Betsy. She was supposed to wait for me here after dinner."

"I dismissed her," he admitted sheepishly.

Alanis's lips curved. "No doubt terrorized the poor girl out of her wits."

"Harsh accusations, my lady, but I assure you, all I did was come out here."

"It was enough." She sent him a small smile. "No matter. I'll manage. Good night."

"Good night." His deep voice followed her as she disappeared behind the bedroom door.

She removed her gown, donned her nightshift, and slipped beneath the covers. Snuggling happily, she buried her face in the pillow and inhaled the musky, masculine scent enveloping her.

Someone knocked. "Come in," she called.

Eros opened the door. "Don't worry. I have every intention of keeping my word." He ambled inside and sat beside her. By candlelight his handsomeness made her heart beat a little faster. She pulled the sheet up to her neck, waiting to hear what he had to say.

"I've given the matter some thought and decided I'm up to the challenge."

Alanis sat up. "What challenge? You mean you wish to take me with you?"

"To the Kasbah, to Tortuga, to any spot that strikes your fancy. No strings attached."

She was speechless. And thrilled. "Why?"

"Because I've grown a fondness for pretty waspish blondes who read Ovidius." He leaned closer. "As they say in Venice, 'The time has come to squander gold and silver coins as if they were nuts.' Come with me. You won't regret it."

She sighed dreamily. "Traveling to Venice with an Italian sounds . . . delightful. After all, Italy is said to be the wonder of all wonders, the land of art and beauty. I would love to go there."

His eyes turned cold; his veneer hardened. "Italy is the one place I will never take you."

His distinct aversion to Michelangelo and Da Vinci's homeland, *his* homeland, triggered a host of questions in her mind, but she decided not to pry at the moment. "And the war? Shouldn't you be fighting Frenchmen?"

He smiled. "I think old Louis can spare me for a while. Don't you?"

Alanis pondered his offer. Sailing away with him for a few

months meant casting propriety to the wind. It meant relinquishing Lucas to Jasmine. It meant changing the course of her life—in favor of pursuing her dream. The idea had merit but was hardly the thing to do. However, hadn't she once said that if the opportunity arose she'd become an explorer of faraway lands? What grand prospects held her here? What such prospects awaited her at home?

"You *can* trust me. I'll be leaving at midnight tomorrow. You have a whole day to consider my offer." He blew out the candle and leaned very close. "*Buonanotte, bella donna.* Create a beautiful dream with me." He took her mouth in a slow, lingering kiss that twirled all the way to her toes, then got up and left the room, leaving her half wishing he hadn't. . . .

Alanis kept her word and took Jasmine shopping. It was a joint venture. Jasmine knew her way around Kingston, and she knew her way around fashion. By noontime Jasmine was outfitted for a whole new wardrobe and Alanis was in love with the town.

As the Silverlake coach entered the inner courtyard of Lucas's house, Alanis contemplated Eros's offer for the millionth time that day. She scarcely slept during the night, weighing the pros and cons. She woke up determined to sail with him, but as the day wore on, the more she thought of her grandfather the less she felt inclined to go. The coach stopped. Two footmen hurried forth to carry the numerous parcels. Pleased with her handiwork, Alanis watched Jasmine walk up the front steps in her new, sunny day gown. There wasn't a sign of the brassy female buccaneer.

Chambers, Lucas's butler, greeted them inside the house, looking impressed. "Good day, ladies. What a pity his lordship is out. You make a delightful sight, if I may say so."

"Thank you, Chambers." Alanis cast nervous glances at the top of the staircase and yanked her lace gloves off. "Has anything come to pass in our absence?"

"Nothing alarming, my lady. Although you do have visitors: A Madam Holbrook, a Mrs. Greyson, and a Miss Mari-anne Caldwell. They seem to be under the impression his lordship is harboring dangerous criminals in the house." He wriggled his eyebrows meaningfully.

"The Witches Council . . ." Alanis muttered, irritated. What remarkable timing they had.

"Pardon, my lady? I put them in the morning room. I trust I did the right thing?"

"Yes, Chambers, better to get it over and done with before the entire island is upon us. Please be good enough to serve us tea. Come along, Jasmine." She grabbed the ex-buccaneer's wrist before she managed a mad dash upstairs. "If you are to become a genteel lady, you should get acquainted with the less charming aspects of the business and have a clearer idea of what you are getting yourself into. 'Know your enemy,' my grandfather always says."

As soon as Alanis spied the two matrons and their young trainee huddled together on the burgundy settee, chattering actively, she experienced a strong urge to embrace Jasmine's initial plan and hide. They were bored-to-death busybodies with nothing better to do than to spy on everyone's lives and voice their cutting-edge criticism. Obviously they were here on a mission.

"Good afternoon, ladies." Alanis smiled. "What a delight-ful surprise. May I present my dear friend, Countess Jasmine. She's come all the way from Rome and hardly speaks a word in English. I trust you'll welcome her into your counc, eh, circle as you have embraced me."

The ladies tittered and curtsied. Mrs. Greyson exclaimed, "My dear Lady Alis! How lovely it is to see you again. We've met but once, yet I feel we've become dear friends."

"Hmm." Alanis smiled. "How lovely."

"Our visit today is of vital importance." Madam Holbrook plunged into the matter at hand. "A most distressing rumor has reached our ears. We came here at once to investigate."

"Indeed, we rushed here to save you before it was too late!" Marianne cried.

"Save me?" Alanis took her seat, cuing Jasmine to do the same. "Save me from what?"

"From *whom!* My dear, we strongly suspect his lordship is harboring dangerous criminals."

"Dangerous criminals?" Alanis gasped dramatically. "I don't believe it!" She cast horrified eyes at the chalk-faced Jasmine, hoping the poor girl would get the gist of it. "How dreadful!"

"Indeed it is." Mrs. Greyson huffed. "Quite shocking! Perhaps you'd be able to shed some light on the matter. According to our sources," she whispered, "the notorious pirate, Eros, and his promiscuous paramour are on the island in this very house. Now what make you of that?"

"Goodness gracious!" Alanis gripped Jasmine's hand, looking appalled. "Cutthroats, here?"

"Well, what is he like?" Marianne bubbled excitedly. "Is he handsome? May we see him?"

"Hush, girl. We are not here to pay a social call on a ruthless killer," Mrs. Greyson dourly reproached. "We are here to rescue her ladyship."

Madam Holbrook took the reins. "His lordship has an important mission to perform, and we salute him. However, you are genteel, unmarried females. Residing in a bachelor establishment without proper supervision while there are pirates onboard . . . why, that's blasphemous!" She shuddered. "Therefore, I've taken it upon myself, as the long extended arm of your grandfather, to ensure your reputations remain unblemished. I accept this responsibility neither lightly nor precipitously, and I am prepared to dedicate myself to the task as demanding as it may be. As it is written in the Good Book, 'Evil inclination is one of the worst things, since its Creator called it evil.' His lordship should exercise good sense and imprison the blackguards in the fortress!"

"Everyone expects the hanging, and his lordship procrastinates," Mrs. Greyson complained with palpable annoyance. "What is he about?"

"You must get rid of them at once!" Madam Holbrook huffed decisively.

Alanis scrutinized their flushed faces. They were not only ill-mannered snoops, they were bloodthirsty as well. Fighting the urge to kick them out, she realized no amount of good manners would see her through this inquisition without her losing her sanity altogether. Sometimes one had to put one's foot down to put wags in their places. "I'm afraid you were terribly misled. The villain you mentioned died by his lord-ship's sword yesterday. So if there's nothing else . . ."

"But there is!" Mrs. Greyson exclaimed. "We have all seen him. The big, dark man they carried wounded into the house. And there was a woman at his side, a heathenish thing, cov-ered in blood with an unruly mane of curls and wearing man's breeches!"

Alanis glanced at Jasmine, admiring her coiffeur. "Truly ladies, there must be a mistake. You must have imagined the entire thing. Perhaps the heat . . ."

"Heavens! To be labeled a liar!" Mrs. Greyson collapsed back, fanning her face. "Quick, Marianne, my smelling salts! I feel my faintness coming upon me."

Alanis was not deceived. "Do forgive my poor choice of words. I meant to say you must have witnessed another poor devil being carted away, but surely not—"

"It was Eros!" Marianne cried excitedly. "He had black hair and a powerful physique. I—"

"Hush, Marianne! Let Lady Alis enlighten us. It appears we have overlooked a great deal." A doubtful gleam appeared in Madam Holbrook's eyes. "Did you say a man *was* brought here?"

Alanis paused. It would take more lies to convince this shrewd hag no trickery was played.

Jasmine coughed discreetly. "*Un uomo?*" She looked thoughtful. "*Ah, mio fratello!*"

Alanis shot her a startled look, then hid a sly smile. "Of course. The countess's brother! What a charming man. Unfor-tunately, he was struck with a terrible fever on our way over and is presently ill disposed, but I shall be delighted to intro-duce him to you when he is improved."

"I don't believe this!" Madam Holbrook sprang to a battle

stance. "Lady Alis, you are leading us on a merry chase and I won't have it! I firmly demand satisfaction!"

Alanis defiantly rose to the matron's eye level. The other two came off the couch to uphold a united front with the madam. To bolster defenses, Jasmine joined Alanis. "I am sorry, madam," Alanis said, "but I can give you none. If you insist further, I shall be forced to see you out."

"Do not be impertinent with me, young lady! As your new chaperone, I demand—"

"I am not that young a lady, madam. I am four and twenty, which is too old to be in need of guidance. As for my manners, they are no more lacking than yours."

"I will not be dismissed—"

"You are not my chaperone, Madam Holbrook. Silverlake is my guardian, appointed by my grandfather, and the countess's excellent company will also keep me from harm's way. Now, I've answered your questions, and I must beg you to leave. I have a ball to prepare for."

The doors opened, and an unsuspecting Chambers walked in with the tea tray. The madam looked aghast. "I will not excuse such impudence! I demand to search the premises myself!" She took a precarious step toward the door. Quick to the rescue, Chamber swiftly stepped between the madam and the exit, embracing the silver tray to his well-tailored breast.

"This is Viscount Silverlake's private residence," Alanis said sternly, "and you've insulted him in every possible way. You are no longer welcome." She smiled coolly. "Good day."

Beaten but not entirely defeated, Madam Holbrook led out her troops with an occasional, "Why, I never—" while ignoring Alanis, who followed to confirm the council's safe departure. When they reached their coach, the madam voiced her final blow. "You have not heard the last of this, Lady Alis! Your rascally mouth will not go unpunished! What insolence! And from the granddaughter of the Duke of Dellamore, no less! I'm vastly displeased, vastly displeased!"

Chambers sealed the doors on another resounding "What

insolence!" and Alanis and Jasmine returned to the morning room to recover over tea and scones, utterly exhausted.

"It is yet early to change your mind," Alanis said. "Madam Holbrook is only a sample of what you are to expect."

"She was truly a nasty one. I was quite terrified. If they went upstairs and found Eros—"

Alanis grimaced. "I do not believe Eros is inclined to harming women, but it wouldn't have come as a shock to me if he had cut off their flapping tongues. I had the urge to do so myself."

Jasmine sighed. "You've said it yourself—the Witches Council. Thank God they mounted their brooms and winged away." They stared at each other and burst out laughing.

The Silverlake coach bounced on Windward Road toward the governor's mansion. Palm and coconut trees lined the road. An orchestra was playing a *cotillion*. Alanis felt restless. She was leaving with Eros tonight. She chose a fantastic adventure over a man who didn't love her and a life among poisonous serpents such as Madam Holbrook. She would not be gone long, and her grandfather . . . She would make him understand. Life was too short to be wasted on regrets.

Lucas stared at Jasmine. She sat in front of him, gowned in muslin with orchids arranged in her hair, a shy debutante. Alanis insisted she come to the ball. Once she was gone, Lucas would have no qualms asking Jasmine to marry him. She wished them Godspeed. She was embarking on a different adventure: She was going to see the world, and she was going to do so with Eros.

Alanis also dressed with extra care, deciding muslin was no longer the thing for a woman of adventure. She wore a glamorous gown of amethyst silk, which no French courtesan would balk at, and the amethyst set of jewels she had worn that fateful ball in Versailles when Eros first noticed her. In her reckless disposition she needed the powers of this stone, which the Romans believed warded off the wicked influences of Bacchus, the God of Revelry. One thing remained unsettled, though: Between the visit to town, the Witches' visit, relocating to new quarters upon Lucas's request, and dressing for the ball, she had missed her chance to inform Eros of her decision. She prayed he would wait until midnight. She would sneak out of the ball at eleven o'clock and take the carriage home. In the expected throng, nobody would miss her.

The ballroom buzzed with guests. There was dinner, dancing, and ample conversation, but nothing surpassed the thrill pulsing in her veins as she waited for the eleven chimes of the clock.

When at long last eleven o'clock came, Alanis was panting with tension. She slipped out, making sure no one was the wiser, and asked for her cloak. Out in the courtyard, she located the Silverlake crest with the driver nearby and urged him to take her back. There was no time to lose.

She was well ensconced inside the dark carriage when the door swung open and a cloaked figure climbed inside. "Return to the ball. It's a mistake what you're doing. Please trust me."

Alanis gaped at Jasmine's veiled face. "You know about this?"

"Do not go with my brother," Jasmine implored. "As much as I love him and bear him the highest esteem, he is not what you think."

Jasmine's subtle warning sent an unpleasant chill up Alanis's spine. "What is he?"

"Dangerous."

Alanis's hands turned icy cold. "Dangerous? In what way?"

"For one, his amorous conquests always begin with lust and end in tears. Not his tears."

"*Amorous conquests?*" Nervous laugher bubbled in Alanis's throat. "You are mistaken. It's nothing of the sort. Eros promised to show me a few interesting places on the globe. We have a perfectly decent understanding. No strings attached."

"I wonder how you'd feel about it in a month or so. My

brother is a sharp, handsome devil, and he'll turn your head as a carousel. If you are not already in love with him, you will be."

"Don't be so sure," Alanis clipped. "Eros is not the reason I am leaving. I have decided to cry off my engagement and follow my own dreams for once. You cannot begin to comprehend since you've always had the freedom to do as you pleased. But you should be delighted because it works out fine for the both of us. I want my freedom and you want Lucas."

"Please let me leave instead. You saved my brother's life and I'm in your debt, but more than that, I've come to consider you a friend. The rift between you and Hunter is my fault. When I'm gone, you'll be able to mend it and enjoy a good life together."

"It is much too late for that. I've made my decision, and I intend to pursue it."

Jasmine hesitated. "In that case, I wish you *bon voyage*. Eros will keep you safe. He's good at that sort of thing." She kissed Alanis's cheek and stepped out. "What should I tell Hunter?"

"Tell him the truth!" Alanis waved good-bye as the carriage clattered away.

Alanis hoisted her skirts and rushed upstairs, praying to God she was not too late. The door to Eros's room was ajar. Faint light poured through the crack. She took a fortifying breath and walked inside. The shutters screeched a weak salute in the breeze, the muslin drapes whispered softly, but there was no one in sight. Eros was gone.

She sank on the bed. A sole tear slipped her cheek. She was too late. Her last chance at sunshine and freedom vanished with Eros, as suddenly as it became possible last night. He must have slipped through the window and crawled on the roof. She couldn't do it in perfect health; Eros had twenty stitches in his side. And he didn't even let her say good-bye.

She wiped the tear and surveyed the room. She was so happy here last night, so hopeful. She must have dreamed the entire thing, for surely fate could not be so cruel. Her gaze settled on the bedside console. Lit by a candle, Eros's orange rested exactly where she had put it. "Damn you and your damned oranges!" She snatched the fruit and meant to toss it out the window. A note caught her eye. It was tucked under the orange. Quickly unfolding it, she read: *Old town. Until midnight.* "Damn you and your damned oranges!" Laughing, she raced out the door. She collided into Betsy. "Betsy! Thank God." Alanis grabbed her elbow and steered her along. "I need your help. Which one of our boys is around? Jamey Perkins? Robby Pool?"

"I reckon Jamey's in the kitchen, having a nip. Shall I summon him?"

"Tell him to meet me out front with the carriage. There is no time to lose!"

"My lady!" Betsy gasped, but Alanis shooed her to the kitchen.

"The coachman returned to retrieve his lordship," Jamey explained apologetically when he arrived with Betsy at the entrance, leading a saddled horse.

"No matter," Alanis exclaimed. Every minute counted. She could not afford to be late a second time. "Quick, take me to the old town. There's no time to spare."

"The old ruins? At this hour?" The two servants exchanged alarmed looks. "But the ghosts, my lady? The dead buccaneers?" Jamey reminded her fretfully.

"Do not ask questions. I beseech you, make haste," Alanis implored. "Help me up."

"Port Royal is on the other side of the bay. We'll need a boat." Jamey lifted her onto the saddle and mounted behind her, as he had held her as a child and taught her how to ride a horse.

"We'll find a boat, hurry! Take me to the wharf." Time was the enemy. She had now less than half an hour to midnight. "Betsy." She smiled at her anxious maid. "Please don't fret. I shall see you in England within a few months. His lordship will send you home."

"A few months? You're off with *him,* then? The pirate? What should I tell His Grace?"

"Tell His Grace whatever enters your head. I'll return soon."

"Oh, my lady!" Betsy wailed. "His Grace will have my head for letting you leave, and his lordship . . . and your clothes, my lady, your *jewels!*"

"His lordship will send everything home with you." Alanis's voice softened. "Please don't cry. I'll be fine. Give my love to His Grace." She waved farewell, and Jamey kicked his heels.

The wharf was quiet. Jamey assisted her into a fisherman's dory and took the oars. A warm breeze fanned her face as they made their way across the dark waters past Refuge Cay and Gallows Point, where she saw the gallows standing erect beside the waterline—a warning to all pirates. Hands clutched in her lap, she prayed time would prove generous to her quest. She was saying good-bye to the only world she ever knew. She was shaping her destiny and braving the world. She was putting her trust in a man she had known for less than a week—a pirate, a stranger.

They reached Port Royal, the infamous town of the buccaneers before an earthquake sent it to damnation. Her spine tingled. Jamey jumped ashore and helped her out of the dory.

"Would you like me to accompany you, my lady?" he asked timorously.

"No. Thank you, Jamey. You may turn back now." She smiled reassuringly. The poor man's hairs were virtually standing on end.

He frowned, weighing devotion against fear. Fear tipped the scales. Assuming his position in the boat, he said, "May God be with you, my lady, and keep you safe."

The old ruins emerged from the sand as a daunting headstone. She was mad; Alanis shook her head and started walking along the moonlit beach, cursing the damp sand for ruining her best pair of satin heels. Sunshine and freedom *indeed!* She was a reckless idiot! She scanned the night-veiled horizon. A ship awash in moonlight awaited her captain. Where the devil was Eros?

"Looking for someone?" a deep voice called.

Alanis whipped around. Eros was casually perched on a tall boulder. A pleased grin curved his lips as his eyes took in her appearance. Clinging to her neck by a satin ribbon, her cape hung low down her back, exposing her shimmering purple ball gown and the violet stones gracing the rises of her collarbone. Golden strands clung to her cheeks. A strong pulse throbbed visibly at the base of her throat, betraying the state of her nerves. She was out of breath and trembling like the breeze.

"I thought you'd left." She panted, causing her bosom to push above her low neckline.

"Still here." Eros hopped off the rock. He landed soundlessly on the soft sand and walked to her. His eyes gleamed in the moonlight. "So you found my note. Too clever for your own good." He came up in front of her, tall and dark, his jet hair catching the light wind. He splayed his hands on her small waist and pulled her to him. "Did you have a nice time at the ball?"

Heart pounding, Alanis stared into his eyes. "How long before midnight?"

He ran a finger along the graceful slope of her neck. "Not too long."

She frowned at his casual tone. Perhaps it was a mistake. Sailing the world still seemed a tempting endeavor, yet Eros was a stranger, a dangerous, unreadable stranger.

His large palm cruised up her spine and cradled her nape. "No changing your mind now, *bellissima*. You're coming with me." His mouth silenced her potential protests. His taste, his heat overwhelmed her. She wrapped her arms around him and sunk into his kiss. Dark waves broke ashore, spraying her skin. It was magic—sirens luring sailors to smash onto the rocks. *Magic.*

Snickering voices interrupted the kiss. "*Capitano,* did we come in a bad time?"

Alanis broke free. Five men were coming ashore; a boat lapped at the edge of the water.

"I think your physician is reluctant to release you." Nico's amused eyes boldly roamed her.

She burrowed against Eros, who shot Nico a debilitating glare. "*Star zitto, Niccolò!* And the rest of you—shut up as well!" He took her cold hand and started toward the boat.

"Wait!" Alanis dug her heels in the sand. She stared at the men—the company she was to keep henceforth. A chill ran up her spine. It *was* a mistake. She could not possibly go with them. She met Eros's questioning gaze. "Take me back, Eros. Please. I've changed my mind."

He stared at her. "Too late. I can't afford to lose the tide."

With one look he iced her blood. It was as if he had flipped and she was facing another side of him—a cold, unfeeling side. He was not the playful, wounded cub she had cared for two nights ago. "I will go by myself." She tried to unshackle her hand, but he only tightened his grip.

He marched ahead, dragging her against her will down the sloping beach. She struggled and protested to no avail. He scooped her off the sand and waded the short distance to the boat in his boots. His men exploded with laughter.

"Shut up, idiots!" Eros nailed them with a sharp look of warning. "Now row!"

CHAPTER 8

She was back in the black and purple cabin. Eros locked the door and slipped the key into his pocket. He contemplated her hostile face. Her skin glistened with seawater. Her golden hair tumbled to her waist, mussed and damp. Her purple gown shimmered in the soft lamplight.

"You look beautiful wearing my colors, *Principessa*. They suit you well."

"*Your colors,*" Alanis spat with contempt. "You take pride in these colors as if you were a noble knight fighting the Saracens in the Holy Land, when in fact you are an evil, base man."

A muscle throbbed in his jaw. His eyes betrayed the look of a wounded predator. He tore his gaze away and marched to the wine cabinet. He uncorked a cognac decanter and poured four fingers into a snifter. He tossed his head back and downed the entire glass.

Her voice echoed the frost in her eyes. "Take me back to Kingston or the entire fleet will swoop down on you and chase you to Kingdom Come. Do not presume for a moment that Viscount Silverlake will abandon his fiancée in the hands of a despicable pirate!"

Eros tipped the decanter over his snifter. "Are we discussing the same fiancée who up and left in the middle of the night because she preferred to travel the world with said pirate?"

"You know perfectly well I changed my mind at the last minute. You abducted me! You can hang for this!"

He shot her a hard look. "Why don't you swim back to Silverlake and tell him so yourself? I'm certain he'd see the humor in it, as I do. A word of caution—the Caribbean is infested with sharks. Better swim fast." He sauntered to the mirror and set his snifter on the dresser. He stiffly shrugged out of his shirt and examined his torso in the mirror.

The sight of his tanned, sculpted body still had the power to put her heart in a state, but his behavior tonight made Alanis question her heart's acuity. A large crimson stain blotted his white bandage. His wound must have opened when she jabbed an elbow in his ribs earlier. Eros swore and drained his snifter. She now understood his sudden attachment to the cognac. An alarm bell went off in her head. Drunken men tended to be vile and savage, but this pirate was vile and savage when he was sober. How would she deal with him smashed out of his wits? "I won't fix it this time," she informed him. "You cannot behave as a bully and expect kindness in return."

"So who asked you?" He splashed water into a basin and washed his face. Sleeking his wet fingers through his dark mane, he met her eyes in the mirror. "Make yourself comfortable. You are not going anywhere, Alanis."

She untied her cape and dropped it on a chair. "What do you intend to do with me?"

Eros tied his hair and caught her gaze again. "The *lowly serf* is taking you home."

Lud. "Home?"

"Home. England. Grandfather. Rings a bell?" He concentrated on removing his bandage.

She wondered if this nightmare was his idea of retribution for the silly things she had said to Lucas about him. Obviously he had overheard. "One remark doesn't merit the ruination of my life! I saved you from a hanging and from bleeding to death. The least you can do is set me free."

His irritation took the form of exasperation. "I can't set you free, Alanis. I wish I could. Regardless of your *low* opinion of me, this is not about getting even."

"Then what is it about?" she snapped, and instantly knew the answer. "You are doing this to help your sister." How could she have been so blind, so gullible? "You lied to me. You never intended to show me the places we talked about. The entire thing was a charade."

"I didn't force you. I offered a temptation and you took it. You were as eager to escape Jamaica as I was to get you out. You found the note and came after me, remember?"

"I trusted you!" How could she have misjudged him so? How could she have fallen for his false charm? He *was* ruthless, and not because he wielded swords and daggers better than most, but because he was chillingly clever, sly as a viper, and totally bereft of a conscience. "What sort of a world creates such an utterly ruined creature, destitute of any humanity?"

He bore her fury without flinching. "This world, Alanis. *This world.*"

"How sad for this world and how sad for you. Your world is not worth exploring. I'd be better off at home."

"I'm certain you would."

His answer only succeeded in reinflaming her temper. "You bloody hypocrite!"

Eros sighed. "She's my little sister. I'd do anything for her. *Anything.* She loves Silverlake, and you were in the way. Nothing personal."

"*Nothing personal?* It's personal to me, you bastard! It's my life, my honor, my dream you ripped to shreds. So don't you dare tell me it isn't personal! It's as personal as it gets."

He turned around and trapped her in his brilliant blue gaze. "So is kissing me one moment and becoming nauseated the next. I imagine we both had our illusions shattered tonight."

He threw her aback. Did he really take offense when she refused to go with him? She could easily explain what made her change her mind on the beach, but in a spirit of feminine revenge she chose not to. She whirled around and began pacing the room. She had to deal with her new predicament. Her grandfather would wring her neck, justifiably. And Lucas, he was her friend and she had treated him as an enemy, believing Eros to be her rescuer. She decided one last time to appeal to his sense of decency, although she sincerely doubted he possessed any. "Please take me back," she said, sounding exasperated to death. "I pose no threat to your sister's happiness. Believe it or not, I did wish them Godspeed when I left. I hope they marry. All I want is to enjoy a month of sunshine in Jamaica. Surely you have better things to do than to see me home."

"If I take you back, your fiancé won't have the backbone to marry my sister. He loves her, but he considers her beneath him. *As you do me.* Believing we eloped will induce him to wed her. He'll feel betrayed, rejected, dishonored. He'll consider marriage to her as proper payback." His tone softened. "She's in love with him, you're not. Why spoil it for her?"

He was right, and knowing her response to his kisses brought him to the conclusion made her feel even worse. She recalled the superlatives used by the Jamaican gentlemen to depict the Vipers of Milan: a fierce lot who put a chill in the hearts of their peers and cunning to the last degree. "How it must please you I played my part of ingénue perfectly in your clever game."

"It wasn't a game."

"Then why did your sister warn me you were not what you seemed? She implored with me to remain in Kingston."

His jaw muscle pounded. "Gelsomina knows me well. You should've heeded her advice."

"So you're not only a thief and a pirate, you're vain as well, which ranks next in turpitude with your other inspiring qualities." She resumed prowling his cabin. She halted at the door.

"You know the door is locked," Eros reminded her while examining the new dressing he had applied to his wound. It failed to stop the bleeding, so he dispensed with it altogether and fed his dagger to the candle flame. "And even if it weren't, what grand routes of escape did you have in mind? Swimming with the sharks or practicing your charms on my men? Believe me, Alanis, running on deck in this gown will get you the opposite attention of what you hope."

"There must be one decent fellow onboard your raft, *Charon.*"

"I wouldn't count on it. My men haven't had a woman in months. They'd be overjoyed to keep you onboard for a spell."

Cursing herself for being all sorts of fool, her eyes fell on his leather belt, casually draped over an armchair. It carried his brace of pistols. Daringly she drew one of the pistols and aimed it at the sinewy back standing at the mirror. "Turn—this—craft—around. *Now!*"

Eros dropped his dagger and turned around to confront her. Before her eyes he transformed from a tired, injured, slightly inebriated man to a night prowler. His expression personified cold restraint. He began stalking her, his brilliant eyes quietly assessing their prey. "Put the pistol down, Alanis. You don't know how to use it and you might hurt yourself trying to shoot me."

"I don't want to shoot you, but you brought this situation on your own head," she blurted, backing away. "You cannot shape my life to suit your needs. Whatever I do or wherever I go should be my decision and my decision alone." She glanced at the silver piece in her hands and moved a shaky thumb to cock it. She was not an experienced shot, but she knew how men used the blasted thing. Whether she'd have the nerve to pull the trigger was a wholly different matter.

He slowly advanced toward her. "You don't hate me enough to shoot me, so I suggest you put it down before you hurt yourself or force me to do something I sincerely don't want to do."

"You are absolutely correct. I don't hate you. *I loath you,*" she hissed, but what she really loathed was her wretched reaction to him. Even now, she still felt the rush his proximity always managed to stir. "Why did you have to be so low and deceitful? You used me. You manipulated my feelings. Are you truly heartless? You only pretend to be human?" Tears swam in her eyes.

Eros halted. His razor-sharp gaze shifted between her teary face and the pistol, trying to contrive a way to get it away from her without inflicting damage on either of them. He must have realized even nonviolent females were capable of making madcap decisions when they felt cornered. "If you put the pistol down, I'll reconsider returning you to Kingston."

"You're lying!" Her knuckles whitened around the silver handle. "You have no intention of returning me there."

"And you have no intention of killing me," he pointed out gently. "We both know that."

"We know nothing!" Hurt and disappointed, she recalled the incredible kiss they shared on the beach an hour ago. Labeling herself a fool was an understatement; her idiocy was beneath contempt. She raised her free hand to wipe her tears. Eros bolted forward. She panicked. Unable to shoot him, she turned around and, acting on impulse, shot the lock on his cabin door. An awful blast exploded in her ears; steely arms wrapped her from behind. Startled shouts sounded above deck. Wild-eyed, she stared at the smoky door. A hole the size of her fist appeared next to the lock. She had absolutely not a bloody drop of luck tonight.

"You wild, willful tigress! What the devil were you thinking?" Eros growled in her ear. He clutched her wrist and forced

the pistol out of her hand. He shoved its barrel down the back
of his breeches and spun her around to face him. He was furious; gripping her shoulders, he shook her so forcefully her
head fell back, and she was looking straight into his blazing
blue eyes. "You could have hurt yourself, Alanis, are you aware
of that? What if the bullet had hit metal instead of wood and
bounced off? You would have been killed, you silly, tempera-
mental baggage!" He clutched her chin and skimmed her pale
complexion down to her toes, making sure everything was in
one piece. Alanis gaped at him, surprised to find genuine concern in his eyes. How could one be despicable and considerate at the same time? "*Al diavolo!* I've a strong mind to tie you
up to a bedpost and keep you here until the end of the voyage."

Heavy boots scurried down the companionway. Somebody
banged on the door. "*Capitano,* what happened?" Giovanni
bellowed outside. His mates voiced their own concerns.

"*Nothing!*" Eros barked over her shoulder. He released her,
and she turned around to look at the closed door. An eye appeared in the hole, and someone outside gave a bark of laughter. She noticed that the peeping eye kept changing. The
curious gang of the *Alastor* was taking turns spying into the
cabin. Eros walked to the door, yanked the silk cloth off his
queue, and stuffed it inside the gap, blocking someone's eye.
"*Va bene,* monkeys, the joke is over. *Buonanotte.*"

"Good night to you, too, *Capitano.* If you need us, shoot!"
The snickering and backslapping diminished as boot heels re-
treated down the corridor, returning to minding their own
business.

Alanis was not so fortunate. Meeting Eros's angry eyes and
grim determination, her pulse quickened. Tonight she learned
how it felt to be a panther's quarry. With hair-raising resolve
he bounded in her direction. She shrieked and dashed away,
taking shelter behind a bedpost. Warily, she watched him
through the purple silk bed shades as he slowly closed the gap
between them.

Eros stopped at the bedpost closest to the one she was
clutching and put his hand on the sculpted pillar. "I'd love to

know what goes on in that tortuous female mind of yours. Why the devil did you shoot the door? Did you think getting past it would deliver you obstacle-free to Jamaica? Or perhaps you were unable to stomach my despicable lowly self's company for another minute? One word and I would have installed you in a private cabin. In fact, as soon as you hand over your purple stones that is precisely where you'll find yourself."

Alanis stared at him in astonishment. "You can't have my jewels, you greedy brute! You deserved having your door blasted. I wish I shot you instead."

He rolled his eyes to the ceiling, sending a silent plea for patience. He snapped two fingers together. "Come, come. Let's have the damned jewels and you're off to a separate cabin."

Her eyes narrowed into slits. "Never!"

"You can't keep them unless you care to spend the next three weeks locked up. And the same goes for your fancy plums. I won't have you parading the deck as a multicourse meal, drawing too much attention, muddling my men's already soggy brains, and snubbing me at every opportunity. I still have some of my sister's old clothes onboard. I think they'll fit." And at her appalled expression, he deliberately scanned her figure. His eyes lingered on her heaving bosom. A voracious smile expended on his lips. "You may find them a bit snug in some places, though."

Her cheeks turned cherry red. "No gentleman would dare speak of such matters."

Grinning from ear to ear, Eros folded his arms across his chest and leaned against the post. "I never professed to being a gentleman. Too many taxing restrictions. I, *tesoro,* am free to do as I please, including undressing unwilling females," he drawled, mentally licking his chops.

She gave him a disparaging look. "You may roll that lolling tongue back into your mouth. *You* may not be a gentleman, but *I* am a lady."

His grin broadened into a full-blown smile. "All the more interesting."

She assessed her situation, contemplating how to elude

him. Her back was to the wall, to her left was more furniture
with the open ports beyond, to her right his bed, and directly
in front of her was the devil himself. He took a step toward
her, his lips twisting in a wry smile.

"Looking for a getaway? There are hardly any hiding
places in my cabin. So why don't you hand over your pile of
treasures and we shall call it a night, hmm?"

"May the devil take you!" she muttered at his amused face.

"The devil and I are on best of terms. In fact, we're close
acquaintances. At times, it's hard to tell us apart." He came
closer, trapping her between his arms and the wall. She shiv-
ered. Not with fear. She was too agitated to be afraid. What
she felt, to her dismay, was a consuming need to touch him.
In the dim light, his skin looked as dark as chocolate, stretching over firm tendon.

Eros watched her. He must have sensed the charged air between them, for his grin vanished and in its stead searing
want darkened his eyes. He plunged his fingers in her hair,
luxuriating in its silken wealth. "What am I to do with you?"
he asked huskily, drawing her head closer to his. "You are
painfully beautiful and I'm very drunk. My due for sainthood
is hanging by a thread."

Heat surged through her wanton body. Her voice was a
faint, rugged whisper. "I know you are many things, Eros, but
I don't think you are a rapist."

He splayed his large hand on her neck and slowly ran it
along her bare shoulder, caressing her skin. "But that is the
problem, *Amore*. I don't think it would be rape."

She swallowed, cursing the familiar currents snaking
through her body. She now knew how Eve felt in the Garden
of Eden when inveigled by the serpent she took the forbidden
apple. She arched her neck and turned her head aside to shun
temptation. "It would."

"Would it?" the Viper whispered as he tasted her neck,
gulping the perfume clinging to her skin. Groaning softly, his
tongue and lips paved a trail of fire to the vulnerable hollow
between her neck and shoulder. Alanis stood still, fighting the

narcotic spell causing her eyelashes to sink languidly. She was battling two powerful enemies, not one: Eros and her crazy attraction to him. Succumbing would be the poorest choice she ever made. What were Jasmine's exact words? *His amorous conquests always begin with lust and end with tears. Not his tears.* She had to resist. If she cared to keep something of her ravaged self-esteem she must resist.

His thumb traced her soft pink lips. "Why did you change your mind on the sand tonight?"

She held his gaze, her breath shallow against his thumb. "What relevance has it now? You never intended to take me to the places we talked about anyway."

"Did you think I'd leave you with another man? Even if my sister hadn't met that imbecile, I would have done the exact same thing. Silverlake was not the man for you, Alanis, and deep down inside you know it." He caressed her lips with his, letting their warm breaths merge. Rich cognac fumes filled her head. *God,* how she wanted him to kiss her, but would he stop at that? "Tell me you don't feel as I do, *Amore,* and I'll let you have your own cabin tonight."

Alanis shut her eyes, anticipation of his kiss fogging her senses. *She wanted her own cabin,* an inner voice insisted, but her lips seemed incapable of uttering the words.

Eros leaned into her body. "You don't give a damn about him," he whispered sultrily to the curve of her jaw. "It's me you want, regardless of my black soul and pitiable lowly birth, and the curse of it is that I want you too." His white teeth gently grazed her jaw. "*Badly.*"

Alanis nearly melted to the floor. Heart pounding, she leaned against the wall, drugged by the rich musky scent filling the shadows, by the full-blooded male blockading her senses. She flattened her hands on his chest, slightly pushing, slightly gliding over his sinuous, velvety skin.

"I want my own cabin," she whispered, amazed at the self-preservation she still possessed.

"No, you don't." He caught her nape and locked their lips together. His tongue invaded her mouth, but the sensation was an

overall invasion. She whimpered in response, and before she realized what she was about she entwined herself around him, refusing to let go. He danced them to his bed and came down on
top of her. His kisses became softer, sweeter, making her feel she
was the treasure he'd been searching for his entire destitute life
and now that he had it he wasn't about to give it up. She writhed
beneath him, terrified of how she felt, of how *he* made her feel.

"Eros . . ." She caressed his cheek. His stubble felt as silky
soft as the stuff on his head.

He lifted himself on his forearms. His jet mane spilled
around her face; his eyes glittered as gems. "How did we
come to this, Alanis? Were we doomed to become lovers?"

New panic signals pulsed in her head. She wanted to kiss
him and caress him, but was she prepared to throw her life
away on a moment's craziness? "I think . . . this has gone far
enough."

"Don't think." He nibbled her lips, seducing her reason,
artfully kindling her desire.

A sob of yearning welled in her throat. The abyss in her
soul cried for him, eager to absorb him into the lonely chambers of her heart. She run her hands through his flowing black
mane and met the hungry strokes of his tongue with soft,
feminine purrs.

Eros moved aside, pulling her on top of him. He unclasped
her gown. Expertly, he unlaced her undergarments, then fastened his hands to her sides and dragged the garments off.

Heartbeats roared in her ears. She could scarcely breathe
or think as with incredible speed Eros removed the rest of
her clothing items one after the other, tossing them to the
carpet. When she had nothing on except her chemise and
modish short drawers, he rolled on top of her. He lay between her smooth, curvy thighs and ground his loins
against her softness. The rock-hard front of his breeches
squashed the frills on her drawers, exciting her in unmen-
tionable ways.

"*Santo Michele* . . ." he echoed her own muddled thoughts

as he pressed his hot mouth to a creamy swell of breast. His teeth found a firm nipple through the chemise's thin fabric . . .

Her nails stabbed his muscular back; her body arched beneath his, awakening to deep dark cravings. *This was no harmless seduction.* She had to call the insanity to a halt! Was about to . . .

Eros pulled away. Grating his teeth on a stream of Italian profanities, his forehead wilted on hers. He shut his eyes, breathing ruggedly. Alanis felt both relieved and concerned. "Eros." She framed his face with her hands. "Is it your injury? Is it bleeding again? Let me look at it."

He opened his eyes and regarded her opaquely, unwaveringly. He reached behind her neck and unclasped her necklace. Too shocked to move or voice a word of protest, she felt him removing her bracelet and earrings. When he had her entire small fortune, he sat up. He slipped the stones into his pocket and plowed the roots of his hair, bracing his elbows on his knees.

Alanis bolted up and glared at his profile. She felt chilled to the bone. Sensing her eyes on him, Eros raised his head. He seemed stunned at his own ruse. Cold as ice, her hand came up and cracked *hard* across his cheek. "Touch me again and I swear I'll kill you," she vowed.

A moment passed. Though she discerned shock in his eyes, his face tolerated her assault woodenly. He wasn't a man, she realized. He was an icicle. Stiffly he rose off the bed and went for the cognac bottle. He didn't bother with a glass. He gulped it down, shutting his eyes.

"There's a toll on the spirit for leading the life you do," she said quietly. "'Conscience, the torturer of the soul, unseen, does fiercely brandish a sharp scourge within. Even you yourself to your own breast shall tell your crimes, and your own conscience be your hell.'"

"What would you know about hell, about conscience, or about anything?" He let out a ragged sigh. "I did you a favor just now."

"*A favor?* You are a lying, petty thief. I hope you burn in hell!"

He met her glinting aquamarine eyes. "You'll probably get your wish."

She glanced at the medallion swaying across his chest. "You adorn yourself with beautiful emblems, but in your case the viper is a slithering, contemptible excuse for a man! You do the crests a great injustice keeping them around you. My sympathy is with their rightful owner."

His gaze veered to the antique crest. Its inscription read: FRANCISCUS SFORTIA DUX MEDIOLANI QUARTUS. His lips twisted derisively. "Yes, I stole the emblems from the *excellent nobleman* who is the current link in the illustrious dynasty. Does it shock you, my prim, delicate lady? Does this new piece of information put another blotch on my evil, base character?"

Alanis eyed him impassively. "Nothing you do will shock me ever again."

"Good. Then it won't shock you to put on a pair of my sister's breeches, because that is what you will wear for the duration of this voyage."

CHAPTER 9

The hired coach entered the gates of Versailles. Cesare hopped off and stretched his legs. It was a lengthy ride from Paris. Some time ago, Louis relocated his residence to this obscure village, thus forcing his entire court to move to the dull countryside. They came by the hundreds, though, and were *everywhere,* either gadding in the park or fornicating inside. He smiled at the ladies coming out for a stroll and wondered if Louis could be persuaded to forget the unfortunate incident. Sadly he had no time to spare for them now. The official receptions took place at the *Grands Apartments* in the north wing. Cesare knew exactly what to say to the court stewards barricading every inch of the way. The rule was that the more the king favored a courtier, the deeper the latter was allowed inside the palace. Knowing full well he scraped the bottom of this hallowed list of chosen ones, Cesare resorted to using crafty methods. He was walking down the *Galerie des Glaces* in a matter of minutes, confidently clomping his heels on the parquet floor.

Louis's inhospitable voice boomed from inside his chambers. "Get in here, Sforza! What is this great urgency you claim to know of? The only urgency that concerns the King of France is a threat to the permanence of the universe!"

"*Sua Maestà.*" Cesare hurried forth, bowing all the way to the king's silvery shoes. He rose with a flourish and smiled at the king. His gaze instantly located Jean-Baptiste Colbert, Louis's financial advisor, standing beside the blue satin throne embossed with golden lilies.

"I'm listening," the king muttered. His features, heavily powdered beneath a curly brunette wig, were old and wrinkled. His eyes looked tired and red. "What is the nature of your 'Grave Political Warfare Urgency,' as you put it, and artfully outsmarted my palace mediators?"

Cesare cleared his throat. "His Majesty, I would never have dared to impose unless—"

"Yes, yes, go on." Louis waved with little patience.

"I've come to offer His Majesty General Savoy and his privateer, Eros, on a single platter."

The Sun King's cloudy disposition brightened up. "Savoy, did you say?"

"Yes, His Magnificence."

". . . and that damnable pirate who has been pestering my navy?" Louis leaped off his throne with the dash of a spring chicken. "Speak up! Don't keep me pending on your next word!"

"Monsignor, since the fiasco with that bridge at Cassano—"

The king jarred. "What fiasco? It was a mix-up! Marshal de Vendôme outshone Savoy as he always does, and *Te Deum* was sung all over Paris for a week! It was a brilliant victory!"

For the Austrians, Cesare mentally corrected, who also

sung *Te Deum* in Vienna. "Sire, the emperor is taking over Milan—"

"Joseph is not an emperor. He's a blabbering idiot!" Louis paced up and down.

Cesare scrambled to get the right approach to his subject. "As the Prince of Milan, I—"

Louis came to a halt and cocked a painted eyebrow. "Prince, Cesare? Prince of what?"

Cesare ground his teeth. "I took it upon myself to investigate," he persisted. "As His Majesty is aware, my country is going up in flames due to that hawk, Savoy."

"Indeed he is, but you are not to worry. Marshal de France, Le Duc de Vendôme, is there to make mincemeat out of that ingrate! Did you know Savoy was my personal protégé? After his father's death, I took pity on him. He was a scrawny thing, slight physic. I destined him for the Church. The ungrateful miscreant took offence! He switched sides and stabbed me in the back! I offered him Marshal of France, Ruler of Champagne, but he spat in my face and joined forces with the English dogs. Now he is spilling French blood alongside that cur, Marlborough."

"Savoy is a sanguinary bastard! A disgrace to all Italians!" Cesare declared dramatically.

"*Italians?* What nonsense! François Eugene de Savoie-Carignan is French! If you Italians had a pinch of his fortitude, you wouldn't be disunited as you are today. I have yet to meet the Italian who'll bring this country together."

Irritated by the criticism, Cesare said, "The pirate I spoke of—"

The king's eyes narrowed on his visitor. "I know who *Eros* is, *Sforza*."

Cesare squirmed. "He is Savoy's right-hand man on the Barbary Coast." A well-crafted lie that would win him the richest princedom in Christendom.

"Eros is many things on the Barbary Coast," Louis remarked, refusing the bait.

"His Majesty, Eros the Pirate is to Eugene of Savoy what

Francis Drake was to Queen Elizabeth, only this time the target is not Spain but—"

"France!" Louis finished with a firm glare. "The Austrians have a *Modus Vivendi* with the Turks, and so do I, but the Maghreb corsairs continue to harass my navy and commercial lines."

"That's him, His Majesty! He controls them. Eros controls the Algerian corsairs!"

"No one controls the Algerian corsairs, not even their Sultan," Louis uttered with disgust. He glared at Cesare. "So how do you see yourself fitting into the larger scheme of things?"

Cesare bulked large to his full six-foot-four inches and assumed an air of momentous gravity. "My men are awaiting me in Gibraltar for further instructions, Sire."

"Indeed?" Louis puckered his lips. "Come now, know your facts. The Rock was captured by combined English and Dutch forces last year. Hasn't such disturbing news reached the prickly little ears of your industrious spies?"

Cesare disregarded the insult. "I have a plan, Sire. With His Majesty's aid in the shape of a warship, fully equipped, I will intersect the pirate when he returns from the Caribbean."

"How do you know he'll be back before this damned war is over? And how do I know that you do not seek my help in the guise of an ally when in fact you intend to use me to finance your petit personal war?"

Cesare's tongue went dry in his mouth; his face warmed. Yet as a practiced alley cat, adept at the art of survival, he recovered swiftly. "I'll stop him and use him to get to Savoy."

The cracks in Louis's powdered face quivered. "What a diversion you are, Cesare." He chuckled. "You make me want to laugh and cry all at once. Please, allow *me* to handle Savoy."

"And the warship, Sire?" Cesare prompted delicately.

Louis glanced at his advisor. "What is your opinion on this matter, Jean?"

"Well," Colbert said, "we've sent ships to hunt Eros down in the past, but he outsmarted the navy every time. He's cost us ten warships already, Sire, one of them was your favorite . . ."

"Of course, I remember!" Louis laughed heartily, surprising both Cesare and Colbert. "It was the matter of the frigate we had to settle. When he was in Versailles three years ago, we had a little game of faro going on, and he was winning, as he always does—that *voyou!* Didn't have the grace to lose to the King of France!" The king took a moment to calm his relived annoyance. "*Alors,* I suggested we end the game before I lost Versailles to that *diable,* but he proposed we raise the stakes. He wagered that he'd seize one of my frigates within a year. Needless to say, I laughed at his outrageous bravado and accepted. Three months later, I received a note from him, informing me that he renamed my flagship, my superior frigate, the *Alastor.*" Louis finished his story in good humor, as fit for a man so great he could afford losing pittance to a less significant being. "I was surprised he didn't name her *Le Roi Bouffon, The Jester King.*"

Cesare was too depressed to inquire what that dog had won from the king.

"Well, Cesare? What makes you believe that *you* can challenge Eros and succeed where my admirals have failed? He's an excellent tactician. He knows the Mediterranean as well as he does the back of his hand. You, however, have been known to drown in a bottle of cognac every so often. In other words, I have little faith in your ability."

Cesare's spirit shriveled and died. Louis eyed him thoughtfully. "Tell me what you really want. Surely you wouldn't risk your neck for the small profit of a warship. What is it?"

Cesare hesitated. Louis had backed him into a nice corner. "I want Milan."

The Divine Presence exploded with fresh laughter. "Is that so? How unexpected!"

Cesare could have smashed the powdered face. "Why shouldn't Milan belong to me? It belonged to my ancestors for over a thousand years. I deserve it. It's mine."

"No. It is mine," Louis corrected.

Cesare swallowed his fury. "But His Majesty needs a loyal, local sovereign who knows the people. I am that man. Command me to accomplish this feat for the glory of France."

"What about the small matter of the medallion?" Louis asked. "The emperor denied you ducal investiture because you failed to produce it and prove that you are the next Sforza in line. And since we both know who owns this medallion, I doubt you will ever be duke. Joseph is no less pernickety about following protocol than his late father was."

"The world is changing, Sire. By the end of the war, France won't need the approval of the Empire to establish a ruler of its choice. It will be the emperor who will seek His Majesty's approval on such matters. The Sun King shall rule the dawn of a new era!"

Gulping a lungful of air, Louis's chest expanded with pleasure. "Indeed he shall!" He took a moment to delight in the vision Cesare installed in his brain while contemplating the verdant horizon stretching beyond the windows. "Fine," he grunted. "You shall have your ship, and a hundred thousand gold *louis,* half of which you will receive upon fruition. However"—he pinned Cesare with his unyielding glare—"you will do exactly as I say."

Cesare almost kissed him, disgusting powder and all. "Yes? *Yes?*"

"Go to Algiers. Disguise yourself. I want no attention drawn to you or me. Find Eros's contacts, his allies, and his enemies. Speak to the Janissaries. They are easily bought since all they seek is revenue in the first place. If you must, go to Abdi Dey, Ruler of Algiers. His price should prove the most economical. Talk to the Raises, the leaders of the corsairs. Although their loyalty lies with Eros, they might prove useful just the same."

"Yes . . . *Sire?*" Cesare inquired humbly, not quite grasping the point.

Louis sighed. "Bribe them," he explained slowly. "They'll give you Eros on a platter."

"Yes, His Majesty!" Cesare's spirit soared sky-high. "I'll find him and kill him."

"And you will be the next Duke of Milan, under *my* investiture." The king summed up with satisfaction. "Just don't bring him here. The last time he visited Versailles, my new mistress requested my architect to build a statue of the God of Love with his quiver, bow, and arrows in Eros's image and place it in the park beside hers. A disgrace!"

A monumental understatement! Cesare churned with disgust. It didn't humor him one bit that his nemesis was invited to play faro with the king and flirt with his mistresses.

"Now off with you," Louis waved, "but remember—if you lose my gold on the baccarat tables, you might go after Eros anyway, for his retribution will be nothing compared with mine!"

CHAPTER 10

A vision of sunshine and freedom, the Island of Tortuga beckoned Alanis from across the lucid turquoise bay. A mild breeze carrying guitar music humbled the palm trees lining the shore. Taverns and brothels hid amid thick vegetation. Morosely standing at the railing, she cursed the odious man who promised to show her the world and selfishly went ashore without her. She was stuck on his dinghy while he and his cronies roamed Pirate Island to their heart's desire.

A voice hollered from the forecastle, announcing the change of guard. She saw Giovanni and four of his mates gathering to take the boat. She took a bold step forward. "Hello."

They gawked, not yet accustomed to ladies dressed as sailors, she surmised. Alanis rather liked her new attire. For a week she'd been residing in a small cabin and wearing Jasmine's old clothes. Swashbuckling on deck in boots and breeches, her long hair tied in a queue, she felt dashing and free. She regarded the men. "I'd like to go ashore. May I hop in your boat?"

Four jaws dropped open in stupefaction. The Frenchman, Barbazan, winked at his cronies. "I wouldn't mind staying on-board to entertain this sweet, delicate creature."

"You're not that brave." Giovanni chuckled.

"Barbazan knows better than to try and steal his captain's new object of lust." Nico, the hazel-eyed, honey-haired navigator, threw an arm around Barbazan's shoulders. "Don't you?"

Alanis cleared her throat. Matching their French, she said, "Well, are we going or not?"

Five faces crimsoned. Giovanni blurted, "To Tortuga? The captain will not approve."

Alanis didn't give a whit if the hypocrite exploded into infinitesimal bits of rage! "Eros is hardly in a position to lecture anyone on propriety, my friends. You're off to the taverns and the brothels, and I'm coming along." When they burst out laughing, she folded her arms across her chest and tapped the floor with her boot. "A fine body of men you are. Good-for-nothing jesters. I'm not interested in drinking, gambling, and womanizing as you do. I only want a quick peek around the island, nothing harmful." They laughed even harder. So she marched to the side step, set on taking the boat on her own. She seriously doubted her ability to work the oars, and after Eros's warning about sharks she had no real urge to swim, but she had no intention of letting technicalities hold her back. A bit of resourcefulness was all that was needed.

Behind her, she heard Barbazan say, "We can keep an eye on her. She's safe with us."

"*Idiota!* He'll slit our throats! He specifically told us to keep away from her!" Nico raged.

Alanis turned around and dazzled him with a smile. "I cannot think of anyone I'd feel safer with than you, Nico. What's wrong with us having a bit of fun, eh?"

Nico blinked. "Perhaps the captain will agree to take you ashore himself, if you ask him."

She had to bite hard on her tongue to keep from expressing her opinion of his captain. "He is never around. He went ashore a week ago and hasn't come back. How am I to speak to him? Should I send him a note, perhaps?" An idea popped in her head. She flung one leg over the railing. "Take me to him now. Otherwise, I'm jumping overboard and swimming there!"

Nico instantly grabbed her and hauled her back. She slithered free, yelling, "If you lock me in, I'll use the porthole! We shall see what's what when I meet you on the island within an hour."

"We've all seen what you made of his door." Nico grinned. "We believe you."

"Eros will butcher us like dogs!" Greco, the stocky chief gunner, warned.

"At least we're not yellow Roman dogs like you, Greco!" Barbazan snapped.

"Enough!" Giovanni bellowed. "We'll take her to Eros and let him decide what to do with her. But if you have any sense in your empty heads, you'll keep your hands to yourselves."

She was still grinning when they came ashore fifteen minutes later.

La Nymphe Rouge, the most disreputable establishment off the coast of Hispaniola, served the best liquor, catered to the worst blackguards, and offered a private room for captains on the second floor. The treacherous coral reefs circling the island protected their vessels from the watchful eye of the law, and they had the peace of mind to loiter leisurely, trade heroic stories of atrocities, elate over their ill-gotten gains, and devise lucrative raids on new targets.

"You look troubled, *Vipère.*" Lying on a divan with a pox-faced trollop in his lap, Captain Bolidar of *La Belle Isabelle* glanced at the large man sprawled on the scarlet sofa beneath the window. His booted legs crossed over the ledge, Eros was glowering at the sky.

Bolidar stirred the strumpet off his lap and grabbed a fresh wine bottle. He dropped into a chair across from Eros and re-filled their cups. "Let me tell you about my troubles, *mon ami*. Wine and women, the worst gods a man can worship."

"Which is why so many Frenchmen get married and grow vines, Bolidar." Eros swung his boots to the floor and reached for the wine. "At least find comelier habits to drain your purse."

Bolidar sighed philosophically. "Yes, you are correct, but if I were to socialize with the courtesans of Versailles as you do, my wealth would be depleted and I'd be reduced to beggary."

Eros chuckled. "Your fears of poverty didn't stop you from paying one of the tarts five hundred pieces of eight just to see her naked last night. Believe me, Bolidar, for this price you can have Queen Anne dancing in the nude on the deck of *La Belle Isabelle*."

"An ugly Englishwoman? How distasteful! I thought Italians had better taste."

"Ugly or not, Anne Stuart could certainly use the blunt. This war is digging a hole in her pocket, and she doesn't own gold mines in Panama."

The Frenchman gulped his wine. "So in which direction is the wind to carry you next?"

Eros hesitated. "East."

A broad smile curled beneath Bolidar's thin mustache. "Elusive as ever. But come now, *Vipère*, on which side do you stand in this war? Or is it *taboo* as well?"

"Obviously I needn't ask you which side you're listed on, *mon ami*." Eros smirked.

"Every *boucannier* south of the Bahamas has enlisted. With a Letter of Marque from my king I continue to do what I do best." Bolidar laughed. "But what of you? No Letter of Marque?"

"Is this line of questioning leading toward enlisting me into Louis's ranks?"

"Why not?" Bolidar pouted Frenchlike. "You're bound by no loyalty. You are a man with no country. You may pledge your allegiance to any king."

Whirling his glass, Eros studied the red fluid. "I was not born on the moon, Bolidar."

"You call yourself Italian, but there is no such thing, *mon ami.* There is no Italy. There are only Italian princes who hate and fight each other."

Cold disgust etched Eros's face. "While their country is being trampled and sacked."

"Ugh, you are depressing, *Vipère.* Think of the sweet prizes floating on the high seas."

A warm glow surfaced in Eros's eyes. He considered Bolidar. "To answer your question—I won't cruise in cahoots with you, *mon capitaine,* even if I do own a few of Louis's frigates."

"You read my mind, my quick friend!" Bolidar saluted. "But perhaps you'll reconsider?"

Eros downed the rest of his wine and put the empty glass on the table. "The answer is no," he stated flatly. "I will not shed my blood for Louis. Nor for anyone else for that matter."

Bolidar eyed him slyly. "You're in a foul mood, *mon ami.* If I didn't know you better, I'd say you have a woman on your mind. We Frenchmen are experts at sniffing such troubles."

"I hear Edward Teach is sailing these waters," Eros commented blandly. "Do you intend to crowd after him now that you have your king's blessing to hunt down English vessels?"

"Are you mad? He's Blackbeard! I was speaking of love. Why must we discuss this fat pig who sails a bloody man-o'-war? My sloop hasn't enough metal to crowd after him."

"Are there no men-o'-war on the high seas? Can't you take one?"

Bolidar looked beyond shock. "Take one? Just like that?"

Eyes brilliant with humor, Eros offered, "Think of her as a dory."

"*A dory?*"

"A dory. Like the fishermen's dories upon the beach."

Bolidar frowned in bewilderment. "Would you have me steal a dory, then?"

Unable to contain himself, Eros burst out laughing. "Do you make it a matter of conscience to steal a dory when you've been a robber and pirate, stealing ships and cargoes, and plundering all mankind that fell in your way? Stay here if you are so squeamish."

"Ugh . . . you make my head spin with your madness. Not every man who sails the seas has a death wish as you do. You are too wild, Eros. You do not know the meaning of fear."

"We have a different conception of fear, that's all."

Exasperated, Bolidar demanded, "What is so complex about fear? When a stronger enemy chases after you—you run away. You don't want to die. That is fear." He snorted with disgust.

"There are worse things to fear than death."

"Ah, yes? What?"

Eros caught the Frenchman's annoyed gaze but kept the answer to himself.

Isle de la Tortue, also known as Turtle Island, was a great nest of pirates. Ambling with the Italian sailors, Alanis fizzed with curiously. Crews of desperadoes from every nation swaggered about the curving streets, elbowing the inhabitants and trafficking their outlandish loot at half or quarter price to the wary merchant. After burdening their pockets with gold, they squandered it on gambling, carousing, and astounding the neighborhood with midnight brawl and revelry.

In this vulgar crowd of villains the pirates of the *Alastor* resembled a flock of good-natured lambs. Strolling amicably, they made Alanis feel safe and welcome in their midst. Darkness had yet to descend, and every ruffian was already jug-bitten. Loud voices ruled every alley—riotous jabber and coarse female laughter. A more terrible group of daredevils

Alanis could not have imagined than those who commanded her attention in this godless town. She loved it.

They stopped at an entrance to a frightful haunt, where the brass and wood sign on the door read *LA NYMPHE ROUGE.* Alanis peered inside. She was thrilled to discover that of all the hell-holes this one seemed the nastiest. She secured the red woolen cap serving as her disguise on her head and followed the men inside. A thick fog of smoke, sweat, liquor fumes, and cheap perfume assailed her. Bright lights pierced the opaque clouds. High-spirited music floated. Greco and Nico selected a table where two grimy men sat lethargically—one snoring, the other staring at an empty jug. The Italians hoisted them up and dumped them outside in the alley.

Seated, Alanis looked around with rascally delight. Judging by their colorful clothing and even more colorful swearwords, Frenchmen, Dutchmen, Spaniards, Portuguese, and a few grotty Englishmen crammed the spacious room, manhandling trollops, singing off tune, and basically regaling themselves warts and all. She smiled exultantly—success!

Giovanni waved over a bearded innkeeper to place their order of drink. Barbazan smiled at her. "You do not find this place offending, *mademoiselle?*"

Alanis met his admiring gaze. "Not at all. It has a certain, hmm, organic appeal to it, so to speak. In my disguise and with you around I feel perfectly safe to have more fun than I ever did in my entire life. Thank you for bringing me here, Barbazan. I know it may get you in trouble with your captain, but I'll always be grateful." She leaned forward and kissed his cheek.

He beamed. "Thank you, my pretty lady! You are a very courageous *demoiselle.* Not only because you do not fear my captain but also because you dare live your life as you please."

If only it were true, Alanis sighed. She met Greco and Giovanni's smiling eyes, but it was Nico who spoke. "We've decided our captain need not find out about our escapade today."

"I won't tell if you won't." She grinned and received a charming smile in return.

Their refreshments arrived—overflowing jugs of rum and

a platter heaped with sausages. To her delight, she was elected to propose the first toast. She was profoundly moved; these rugged sea-salts were truly good old birds. She gnawed on her lip, racking her brains. "Why don't we drink to"—she lifted her goblet high—"wine and women!"

The men blinked, exchanged amused looks, and then saluted the air. "Wine and women!"

Glasses clinked, rum gushed, and Alanis's heart welled with a private salute: To sunshine and freedom! She downed the bittersweet rum with the others.

Once slow warmth spread through her body, she smiled at the five pleased faces around her. "Won't you invite some of the, eh, ladies to join you? I wouldn't want to spoil your fun."

"No rush." Nico expanded in his chair, eliciting a coup of snickers from his cronies.

"Why should there be?" Greco mocked. "After you've had all the women on this island?"

Flustered, Nico crossed his arms over his chest and muttered sulkily, "I'm reloading."

Everyone boomed with laughter. Round-eyed, Alanis scanned their happy faces, not quite certain how to respond to such shocking candor, but with the spirit of the place, she gave Nico a sympathetic, straight-faced look and said, "Then by all means, don't rush yourself."

The table rocked with more laughter, and everyone drained their jugs. After a while, Greco said, "Niccolò, didn't you promise to tell us a joke?"

"*Si,* you're a fountain of jokes," Daniello encouraged through a mouthful of sausages.

Nico glanced at her. "I do know a new joke, but I don't care to offend the lady."

"No lady here, just friends!" Alanis stuffed her mouth with a sausage. It was heavenly. The crispy skin broke delectably between her teeth; the spicy beef sizzled on her tongue. She'd never fit into her purple gown again, but as it was no longer in her possession she didn't really mind.

Nico cleared his throat. "Where does an Englishman go

after jumping his wife?" He smiled puckishly. When no one volunteered an answer, he obliged, "Outside to defrost."

The joke was a winner; everyone hooted with laughter. Alanis merely gaped.

"No more jokes about Englishwomen," Barbazan scolded, looking awkwardly at Alanis.

She wished she understood why. She downed her rum and licked her lips.

"These are the only ones I know." Nico shrugged defensively.

She must have consumed too much rum because she suddenly got it. "Outside to defrost!" Lilting laughter filled her throat. Sitting among the lice of mankind, she was having the time of her life. Unfortunately, her head began spinning. She desperately needed a breath of fresh air before she completely embarrassed herself. Pushing to her feet, she said, "If you gentlemen will excuse me, I think I'd better take a moment outside. Won't be long."

Dragging the chair, she turned to leave, but a powerful dizziness assailed her. Nico bolted after her. He gently took hold of her elbow. "Allow me to escort you outside, *Madonna*."

The upstairs terrace of LA NYMPHE ROUGE had whitewashed walls and a canopy of stars. Darkness had fallen, and torches were lit throughout the town. Ships twinkled in the distance over black waters. The air had cooled, and a gentle evening breeze blew in from the sea.

"Have a seat." Nico dragged over a stool and crouched beside her. "Feel a little better?"

"Yes, thank you. I fear I overindulged tonight. I'm not in the habit of drinking spirits, but then, I'm not in the habit of having such a wonderful time either. Thank you."

"You're welcome, *Madonna*. I'm not used to having such a wonderful time myself."

She smiled. For all his bluster, Nico was an amiable fellow. Still, she could have used a moment alone. "Would you mind terribly if I asked you to return for me in a little while?"

Nico pushed to his feet. "Not at all. Take as long as you need. You're safe up here."

Alone, she rested her head against the wall and watched the emerging constellations. She wondered which was the Pole Star, the guide of mariners, and prayed it would always steer her new friends to safety. She inhaled the ambrosial fragrance of flowers and listened to the sounds of merriment floating around. She was half dozing when voices permeated her consciousness.

"When this war is over, I'll be rich and famous. My king will grant me a title for my efforts and retire me to a grand country estate. There, I will write my memoirs: *The Pleasures of the Enchanted Island.* I'll become the toast of Paris, and beautiful ladies will swoon at my feet!"

"Really? The toast of Paris? Take care Louis doesn't make a toast of you yet, Bolidar."

Her eyes flew open. Eros was here. She had no desire to run into him, not tonight and most definitely not on the island. Utterly sober, she scrambled to her feet.

"You mock me now," the Frenchman drawled, "but when I arrive at Versailles, you will lose all your advantage with the Grand Courtesans. They'll be lining up to meet Captain Bolidar. But do not let this upset you, *mon ami le Vipère,* for I will remember our friendship and save an ugly one just for you."

"Your generosity overwhelms me." Eros smirked. "Remind me to send you a note."

Her curiosity getting the better of her, Alanis crept along the wall in the direction of the voices. Light poured through an open door. Pasting her front to the wall, she peeked inside.

Eros's French companion stood in the center of the room, smiling at the man sitting on the red sofa next to the open door. "Don't look so smug, *mon ami.* It is true you have more luck with the ladies, but *morbleu!* I shall outdo you, despite your savage Italian charm!"

Alanis strained her neck to get a better look at the sofa's occupant. The glossy dark head was all too familiar. She turned around and pressed her back to the wall. Her heart thumped so hard she feared they might hear its wild cadence.

"Savage, you say?" Eros's voice came right beside her on the other side of the wall. "You may have a point there, my friend. Quite recently, I've been proclaimed a beast."

Bolidar laughed. "One of your *ex-charmantes,* no doubt. The broken hearts you leave behind overlap the dead bodies. You take your pleasure and then forget. As most of us do."

"Not this time, Bolidar. This time I had it coming."

"Aha! So you do have a woman on your mind. An unsuccessful campaign?"

"Not exactly." Eros didn't sound particularly inclined to share his stories with his friend. Nonetheless, something urged him to speak. His voice thick with wistfulness, he said, "A woman too beautiful for words, Bolidar, yet oddly ignorant of her charms."

Alanis nearly expired then and there. Of all the things to say!

"A beautiful woman is never ignorant of her charms, my young man." Bolidar heaved a sigh. "I advise you to practice caution."

"I've no intention of enmeshing myself in this confounded nuisance, so you may keep your advice to yourself," Eros grunted.

"*Ah, pardieu!*" Bolidar cried with exasperation. "She is a young lady. A noblewoman! I reckon she is very beautiful, eh? And fair?"

"She has the most beautiful light hair imaginable. And eyes like a cat."

Alanis slid along the wall to squat beside the open doorway and moon stupidly at the stars. A woman was singing below to the gentle cords of a Spanish guitar. The heady mixture blended in Alanis's rum-sodden head with Eros's words. She had eyes like a cat?

"Go downstairs, *Vipère.* It is you Cecilia is singing for. You've neglected her all week and stolen back to your ship every night. Now I think you must have a woman in your cabin to whom you are returning, perhaps one with eyes like a cat, hmm?"

Eros slipped his hand into his side pocket and scooped a

handful of cool gems. "No such woman," he breathed, keeping his hand in his pocket.

"If you are bored with Cecilia, perhaps I will convince her to take a turn with me on the beach. She is the prettiest piece on this island."

"You may take her to Paris for all I care."

Bolidar exhaled heartily. "I see you are determined to suffer tonight. I leave you to your sulk. *Adieu*." He sketched an unsteady flourish, then left for the revelry below.

Alanis leaned her cheek against the cool wall, sensing Eros's presence on its other side. Hating him when she was convinced of his indifference was much simpler. It was easy to write him off as a heartless wastrel who coveted her jewels and wished to humiliate her, but now she wondered if there was more to his behavior than she chose to believe. If so, why did he stop that night when he had her lying beneath him, eager for his kisses and caresses?

A quiver passed through her. Thank goodness he had put a stop to the madness that night. She didn't know what she would have done had he taken her beyond the point of no return. At least now she still had some dignity left, though no thanks to her appalling lack of self-restraint. He had indeed done her a favor. The only chilling aspect of his actions, which still left her horrified, was his aggressive strength of will—Eros was in total and absolute control.

Deciding not to risk exposure, Alanis pushed to her feet and quietly made her way through the shadows toward the sailors awaiting her below.

How did one despise a man who considered one too beautiful for words, who said "nay" to eager vamps and who stole back to his ship every night? Alanis wondered awhile later when she was sitting in the foggy room with her sailor friends. Nevertheless, she was committed to the task. Let him have her amethysts and ball gown. He could choke on them for all she cared. He was a despicable wretch and should be treated as such—with absolute and complete odium.

At least she had a taste of freedom; the voyage wasn't a total waste after all. In three weeks she would be back in England, pacifying her grandfather that being labeled a social disaster was not the end of the world. She wasn't altogether convinced she still wanted a husband, or ever did. Everything about marriage seemed to conspire against women: The nature of the nuptial contract was basically about giving up liberty, estate, and everything else to the man, thus tagging the woman a mere woman ever after. A slave. A husband owned his wife. If she had an affair, her lover was technically encroaching on her husband's property, but given the mercenary nature of men, the wronged husband was less likely to fight a duel than sue for damages. Her grandfather ensured that—married or not—his granddaughter would be well provided for after he was gone. So she didn't have to marry well to secure her future. *She could marry for love.*

The thought was so unsettling she had to take another swig of rum before returning to the *Alastor. Marry for love.* The memory of Eros's introduction to desire made her pulse race. For all his shortcomings—and the wretch certainly had quite a few irredeemable ones—he had made her feel . . . *Ah God!* He had made her feel that she was melting, that she would do anything for him, that she would close her eyes and lie still so long as he never stopped . . .

Her gaze fell on a tall, commanding figure coming to stand at the bar. A woman leaned into his strapping form, wrapping her voluptuous assets around him as a ripe vine. The damnable chit had a certain appeal. Alanis considered leaving but decided to stay put and damn his eyes!

"There goes Cecilia, trying her charms again," Daniello observed.

Alanis scrutinized the couple at the bar. Eros did have an air of boredom about him.

"Think he'll yield?" Greco elbowed his mate. "He's been avoiding her all week."

"I think he tired of her months ago," Daniello replied.

"She'll never tire of him," Giovanni contributed, "not after he rescued her from that rat hole and bought her freedom. She'll go on and on until we set sail."

"He should tell her he's lost interest and let the rest of us have a go," Nico muttered.

"I see your vigor has recovered, Don Juan!" Giovanni chortled.

Nico fumed. "Why are you always picking on me? Persecute someone else for a change!"

"No one is as interesting as you are, Niccolò. We're but a bunch of dull, gray men."

Despite her mood, Greco's comment made Alanis smile. The women of her acquaintance were all dull pots. If she were a man, she'd become a sailor.

A tall, dark shadow fell on the table. "What's up, shameless dogs? Don't drop into a bottle. We're cutting cable with the morning tide."

The men froze. Alanis bit her lower lip; he was standing right behind her.

Giovanni pulled himself together. "Join us, Captain. Greco, get the captain a chair."

"No need," Eros said pleasantly. "We were just leaving."

Alanis was suppressing nasty comments about dockside tarts when a firm hand settled on her shoulder. "Weren't we, my lady?" The rhetorical question was bolstered with an encouraging squeeze on her slender clavicle. She glanced up at him. He glared at her darkly.

Looking worried, the five sailors protested unintelligibly. An amused jet eyebrow rose as the captain of the *Alastor* scanned his men's concerned faces. "If anyone has anything to say, he should say it now. I've never been accused of biting a man's head off for speaking his mind."

There wasn't much to say, and they all knew that. Eros wasn't about to let her dally in taverns. Alanis had no choice but to go with him. He took her hand and ushered her away.

The private room on the second floor was brightly lit and vacant. Paintings of naked *filles de joie* were juxtaposed with gaudy divans, all looking quite shabby in every possible way. Eros led her to the scarlet sofa, which seemed the safest spot in the room, and slumped in the armchair opposite her. He selected a clean glass and filled it with wine. "Drink it," he commanded as he set the glass in front of her. Glumly he glared at her in silence.

Alanis glimpsed at the glass, then looked up. "Don't you think it's a little too late for that?"

"You drank with my men, you'll drink with me."

When pigs grow wings! She was silent.

An angry muscle beat in his jaw. His huge body negligently sprawled in the armchair, he reminded her of a spoiled boy having a tantrum. It suddenly occurred to her that the all-mighty Viper was—in Lucas's words—of dubious human material, but flesh and blood nonetheless.

"Rocca returned today," he mentioned offhandedly.

She summoned her patience. "What of it? I wasn't aware of his absence. Nor do I care."

"You'll care when I tell you that he returned from Jamaica, where I'd left him to keep an eye on my sister while we spent the week here. Congratulations are in order. Viscount Silverlake has finally taken a wife, by a special license they say. A mysterious Italian countess. Any idea?"

She smiled perceptively. What a cad he could be when the mood struck him—a very, very handsome cad. "Well, I wish them all the best, although I'm glad I'm not in their shoes."

His eyebrow rose. "Oh?"

Now she reached for her wineglass. Yanking the ridiculous red cap off, she said, "It seems that with food comes an appetite. I've developed a taste for shameless freedom and I intend to indulge it. I've decided that as soon as the right opportunity presents itself, I shall procure my own ship, hire a captain and a crew, and sail the high seas. Abundantly."

He was thinking. She wasn't surprised when he said, "Without stepping on toes, don't you think that for a lovely young female sailing the world alone is somewhat stretching it?"

"You mean perilous? Perhaps." She shrugged dismissively. "*But life is too short to be wasted on regrets.* I'd much rather spend whatever time I have left traveling the world, visiting foreign places, and pursuing happiness than dwell in boredom for three hundred years."

He grinned. "Sounds like a plan."

"Which I intend to set into motion." She placed her glass on the table and left for the open balcony, dismissing him outright. Up until now she hadn't realized the idea was taking shape in her head and becoming a full-blown intention. Voicing it aloud not only put skin and sinew on it but established resolve as well. If her grandfather disapproved, she would simply drag him along with her. Even brilliant politicians deserved a respite now and then.

The air stirred on her nape. "Before I pit myself against Louis," Eros's deep voice traveled over her shoulder, "I intend to make a stop in Agadir, Morocco. If you'd like, I can take you with me and return you to England a few weeks later than intended."

She turned to face him. His features were shadowed, his broad shoulders blocked the light spilling out of the room, but there was a suave, compelling quality about Eros that never ceased to rivet her. What an adventure it would be traveling to faraway lands with him. She hadn't truly appreciated the idea's potential when she had initially and quite idiotically decided to accept his offer a week ago. Of course, he hadn't meant it then. He did now, though. She knew he did.

"Your offer moves me deeply," she said in all seriousness. "Nonetheless, I must decline."

"You must?" he inquired, unable to disguise the shock in his voice. No doubt his immense confidence led him to anticipate nothing less than her throwing herself at him, showering him with kisses, and pledging undying gratitude from the bottom of her heart.

"Sorry." She smiled, enjoying every minute of it. "Your offer does have merit, though."

"But isn't this what you want? What you've just talked about?" he asked incredulously.

"It is," she admitted, wondering how far he would go to secure her consent. "But you know what they say—first time shame on you, next time shame on me."

Eros released a sigh. "I know you wouldn't believe me if I said it was night, Alanis, but I assure you," he paused meaningfully, "I have every intention of honoring this proposal."

She did believe him. Sadly for him, she had also acquired a taste for revenge. "Really?"

His beautiful tanned face was a paradigm of solemnity. "Really."

"Hmm." She put on a face of reconsidering his proposal. "I don't think so."

"Alanis—" He took a step forward, was almost upon her.

She prettily batted her eyelashes. "I *am* grateful, but seriously, what's the point in sailing so far away to see one single beach? It would be worse than not seeing anything at all. No, I thank you, but I shall wait for a better opportunity than this. We'll say adieu in three weeks when we reach England and go our separate ways."

His poise crumbled. If a week ago he hadn't truly been up to the challenge, she'd certainly rectified the situation—he seemed downright anxious for her to agree to come with him. So, the self-assured Viper wasn't completely in control now, was he? She did learn a valuable lesson that wretched night: Eros was a sharp devil, and she had to be twice as sharp.

His eyes glittered, as with acute concentration he ran his knuckles along her delicate jaw, entranced by the refinement of the bone structure. "You want to see the Kasbah," he breathed.

Their gazes locked. Eyes shining, Alanis curbed a huge smile and nodded. Once.

"I'll take you to the Kasbah of Algiers, *Amore*. And to Agadìr. Will you come?"

"No strings attached," she ascertained warily.

A wicked smile curved his mouth. "No strings attached."

"In that case, I wouldn't mind a short detour on my way home. We set sail tomorrow?"

"We do. But first"—still smiling, he slid his arms around her waist and pinned her to his flat torso—"we must seal this pact with a kiss." His lips touched hers and he kissed her with such bottomless craving, her resistance, along with her thoughts, melted away.

None were permitted to enter the fortress of Gibraltar without a special permission from the governor. Disinclined to expose his identity, Cesare took up his quarters at a Posade, situated on the neutral ground. He resided there for several days before resolving to enter the garrison in disguise and by stealth. His object in doing so was to procure a supply of money by a letter of credit he brought with him from Versailles. He rented a room at an inferior tavern in a narrow lane. Conveniently, it ran off the main street of Gibraltar.

One was unable to look at the place without feeling a sensation of horror: The smoky, dirty nooks as well as the estranged groups of Spaniards, dark Moors, and distant Jews personified his less than worthy life, Cesare lamented bitterly, but his fortune was about to turn. Soon, he would have the medallion, his enemy dead, and Milan—the land of his ancestors.

On his fifth day in Gibraltar he was having a jug of ale with a Moor named Bouderba, who having lived for some time in Marseilles spoke sufficient French, when a filthy-looking lad approached him with a message. Roberto had arrived. They met at the Posade an hour later.

"Tell me everything!" Cesare commanded impatiently.

"He's on his way to Algiers. But he is not alone. He has a woman with him."

"Why do you annoy me with petty details? So he took his whore along. She'll be his last."

"Not a whore, *Monsignore,* an English duke's granddaughter. An important duke."

"Highborn ladies are the worst class of whores." Cesare snorted. "Wait a minute . . ." He grabbed Roberto's shirtfront and lifted him to his eye-level. "Did you say an English duke?"

"I . . . I saw her," Roberto squealed. "A pretty young thing, blonde, delicious figure. They spent a week in Tortuga together."

"I don't pay you for your taste in women, *stronzo!*" His

face a mask of rage, Cesare shoved Roberto away from him. "The bastard is still in the game. Hasn't given up after all. Thinks he's snagged himself a piece of flesh that would link him directly to the War Council, to Marlborough and Savoy." He cursed. "*Va bene.* Let him have his day in the sun. He won't live long enough to pluck the crop of his labor." He pinned Roberto with a frosty glare. "We go to Algiers."

CHAPTER 11

The night was black, damp, and hot. A handful of lights glittered in the distance. Keeping his back to the coastline, Eros rowed methodically, a strange black headdress wrapped around his head. Alanis regarded his half-veiled face. He seemed more sinister than usual. Pensive, remote, tense. She sensed a terrible foreboding. Where the devil were they off to?

The three weeks spent crossing the ocean passed rapidly and uneventfully. She insisted on having her meals in her cabin, and Eros did not object, his inherent pride containing him from out-and-out begging her company. Spending most of the time on the quarterdeck with Giovanni, he went about the business of running his ship in his strict yet just approach. Sometimes she saw him sharing a joke with a sailor and was surprised to see how very much in awe his men were of him. However, for all her open display of aloofness, on the rare occasions their eyes linked from afar, she was always the first to look away. Eros invaded her thoughts day and night, becoming a puzzle she had to solve: Who was he? What shaped him into the man that he was? What were his aims, his ambitions, his dreams? What moved him? What touched his heart?

"Put the damned thing back on, Alanis," Eros ordered. "It's not my idea of comfort in this sticky heat, but it cannot be avoided."

She eyed him unsociably. The coarse black robe he made her wear swallowed her up, head and all, its tight facial veil coming up to her nose. She hated it, but the way he was, she didn't dare argue anything. She yanked the veil back up. "Where are we heading?"

"You wanted to see Algiers." He glimpsed over his shoulder at the coast. "The Kasbah of Algiers, princess, upon your command."

"Algiers," she murmured, while gently swaying with the boat. "The infamous dwelling of the Barbary corsairs, the Dey, and his court." She met his eyes. "Nico told me you're a wanted man in Algiers. He said the Dey was your sworn enemy ever since you broke ranks with him and joined the Europeans in the war. Are you absolutely certain you want to go there?"

"Nico told you all that? Fascinating."

"Nico said that for you, setting foot on the Dey's soil meant cruel and certain death."

"Nothing is certain in this life, Alanis. Or haven't you learned that by now?"

So it was true. He was a wanted man in Algiers. Then why hadn't the daft man told her there were such risks involved? "I don't want to put you in so much danger merely to entertain a silly whim I dreamed up. What if they catch you? They will torture you to death."

"*Si,*" he flashed her a maddening grin, "but what if they don't?"

He had a death wish! "I think we should turn back, Eros. This escapade is too dangerous."

"Of course it is." He shrugged his shoulders. "Wouldn't be much fun if it weren't."

"If they catch you, they'll get me too," she pointed out tersely, riled by his black humor.

He stopped rowing, letting the boat float languidly on the water surface. "Is that what's bothering you, Alanis? That something terrible might happen to you because you're with me?"

"Well, there's that." She shifted uneasily. "But as you once mentioned—I don't hate you enough to see you dead." There, she said it. She wasn't about to say another word on the subject. The vain man was already half-convinced she was unable to resist him. She had no intention of bolstering this vainglorious streak.

"Are you truly concerned about my welfare, princess?" he inquired gently. "Or are you worried you'd be losing your guide?"

She did care. How insane was she? She took a deep breath and composed herself, making sure she sounded as a reasonably concerned individual and not a niggling female. "Listen, I know Algiers was part of our initial agreement, but if entering the Kasbah may cost you your life, it is not worth it. There are other places I'd love to see. Let us return to the ship and—"

"There are times, predicaments, when one must gamble with his life to achieve a greater goal. I once made the mistake of valuing my life over the thing I cherished most in the world. I never repeated this mistake again."

If it weren't for the blessed veil, her mouth would have opened and her tongue would have dangled out. *Death is bitter, fame eternal.* What a demanding precept to uphold. What terrible event could have possibly honed Eros into becoming so hard?

They hit land minutes later. He jumped out of the boat and dragged it to the sand. A small island lay in front of the city, connected by a magnificent mole of solid masonry supported by arches. The entrance to the port was crowned with a battery bristling with cannon of immense caliber. The strip of beach was vacant. Alanis halted, awestruck by the amazing strength of the fortifications. A stronghold of sand on the edge of the desert, the Kasbah of Algiers was marked by the world for good reason, she thought. It emitted power. It was the realm of the terrible Dey, who was the first robber and merchant in his own dominions, a haven for castaways where others feared to tread, where night ruled and day surrendered. A city of mystery and enchantment.

"Mind your hair is concealed at all times, princess." He gently adjusted her veil, tucking in straying wisps of golden hair. "Are you ready?"

When she nodded, he tossed the lapel of his headdress over his mouth, took her hand, and moved swiftly toward the wall. Forgoing the strongly guarded marine gate, he circumvented the wall and climbed the hill. The sand was deep and the climbing tenacious, but seeming to know every grain of sand along the way, he led them to a secret opening in the wall.

Once inside the citadel, they meandered fast through the crooked maze of whitewashed alleys. Like a hawk, Eros maneuvered in the moonlight, taking the corners circumspectly, gluing their bodies to walls. A cat leaped from a rooftop onto a tin can in a distant yard. Alanis gasped. Eros put a hand over her mouth, whispering, "The walls have ears in the Kasbah, so be quiet."

They were on the move once again, running and pressing to walls until they reached a wide square. A stony well was situated at the heart of closed stalls, tents, and murky rostrums.

"This is the *souk,* the marketplace," Eros whispered. "It's dead now, but come morning it's colorful, spicy, and swarming with people . . . You'd love it. Unfortunately, I can't bring you here during daytime if I want to keep my head in place."

She totally absolved him of this shortcoming. His eyes lit up, as a young boy going to see a carnival for the first time. "One finds the most amazing merchandise here—stolen goods from the west and all the rubbish one can think of." He tugged on her hand and entered the aisles. "And one must haggle with the venders," he instructed in all seriousness, "or they get insulted."

She smiled behind her veil. All she saw were dark booths and empty lanes, but Eros must have being seeing a different sight, one her eyes were blind to.

"I remember the first time I came here," he carried on as they strolled hand in hand. "I was sixteen years old, had two Arabic words in my vocabulary, had never seen a marketplace before, not even in Italy, and this place seemed a muddled, dirty heaven to me. I loved it," he recalled, nostalgia thickening his voice. "Gelsomina was six years old, and she was terrified of the noisy, crude vendors. One moment I got distracted, and the next my sister was gone. I became frantic. I ran through the aisles, searching, until I found her standing there." He pointed at a nearby dais. "She stood transfixed, ogling a man who was speaking to birds. He was a parrot trainer, talking parrots. Gelsomina wouldn't budge until I bought her one of the vivid creatures." He chuckled. "She named him Zakko, and for years she tried to teach him Italian, but he was a stubborn old bird. I think he understood every word but insisted on crowing in Arabic just to be difficult."

She knew exactly how Jasmine had felt. Only her object of fascination wasn't a bird; it was a viper. For the first time since they met, she saw a glimpse of the boy he once was beneath the serpent's ruthless veneer. *It was happening again.* Her defenses were crumbling to dust.

Eros halted. "I should have become a salesman!" he announced, enlightened.

Alanis swallowed hard. "I'd buy all my spices at your shop," she whispered.

Their faces veiled, they stared into each other's eyes. "I nearly got my hand chopped off once for stealing an orange." His voice sounded huskier; the blue fire in his eyes burned brighter. She held her breath as he slowly removed the black cloth from his face. When his features were visible, she was startled by the grimness etching them. "I know you hate me, Alanis, but I swear upon my future grave I never intended to cause you any harm. I liked you from the start. Not just because you are beautiful, but also because sometimes, in moments like this—" A strange look appeared in his eyes, a perplexed look, as if he'd just discovered something rare and amazing. "Sometimes, I feel as if we have known each other for years. I never told this story to anyone."

His candor disarmed her completely. It was the first real moment they ever shared. No lust, no insidious motives, no banter, resentfulness, or fear. This was one soul touching another.

With hesitant fingers Eros peeled the tight veil off her mouth. He searched her eyes, trying to decide whether she would welcome or scorn him. She didn't know herself. Framing her face with both hands, he lowered his head and kissed her lips. His mouth felt warm, enticing, and full of promise . . .

Riders stormed into the souk. Eros pushed them into a crevice between two stalls and stood very still, merging their bodies with the gypsum wall. Tall, large, and hard, he nearly suffocated her. Yet she relished his closeness, his opulent scent, the feel of those slabs of muscle pressing against her. Her face was hidden beneath his headdress; her mouth was fastened to his neck. She gripped his firm waist, and it was all she could do to keep from ravishing him.

When the stampede rode off, Eros stepped back, swearing. He studied her face in the pale moonlight. "I shouldn't have brought you here. How stupid of me. Are you all right?"

She was not all right. What she had just experienced flattened against his body was worse than the shock of coming so close to danger. Pulling her veil back on, she cursed herself for being a wanton, boneless ninny. "I'm fine," she said. "It was . . . a little frightening, that's all."

He took her hand. "Come. We shouldn't be dawdling out here so long."

Moments later, they arrived at a small house. Eros knocked on the arched, azure door, and waited. A petite old woman wrapped in a dark mantle opened the door and charily stared at the cloaked figures on her doorstep. Eros revealed his face. *"Esalaam haleikum, Amti."*

"El-Amar! Blessed Allah!" The old woman's eyes widened with joy. She covered her face with her hands, saying a prayer. *"Tfadal. Come in."* She ushered them inside and latched the brass lock behind them. *"Merciful Allah! My beloved son is back. You are alive and well and you have come to see old Sanah again. Come, einaya, let old Sanah hug you and kiss you."*

Eros stepped forth and enveloped the old woman in his arms. *"I missed you, Amti."* His voice was thick with emotion, and although he spoke Arabic, Alanis understood—he was home.

Sanah glanced at Alanis. "*Yasmina, my daughter! You are back as well!*"

Eros switched to English. "No, *Amti*, this is not Jasmine." He drew Alanis to him. Smiling into her eyes, he peeled her hood off. "*Amti,* I'd like you to meet Alanis. She's my new protégé. Princess, I present to you Sanah Kuma—*La Maga.* The Witch."

"*Marhaba!* Welcome!" With a huge smile Sanah grabbed Alanis's hands, golden bracelets jingling at her slim wrists. Curiosity sparked her sage blue eyes. "Hello and again hello."

"I am honored to meet you, Madam Kuma," Alanis said, noting Eros's approval from the corner of her eye. "I'm afraid I'm at a loss for words." Indeed, she was. Sanah was remarkable— fine eyes shining with intelligence, skin as tanned and wrinkled as old leather, a thick mane of silvery white curls, and a smile full of Oriental charm.

"I am honored to meet *you,* Alanis, daughter of Christine." Sanah squeezed her fingers.

Alanis nearly fainted. Before she got a chance to ask Sanah how she knew her mother's name, the old woman slid a dev- ilish grin at Eros. "*Heya hellua giddan, ya eibni. She is very beautiful, my son. Inta baheb ha? You love her?*"

"*Hallas. Enough,*" he grumbled, casting a strange look at Alanis.

Sanah giggled, her mischievous eyes missing nothing. She led them into a parlor, where malachite candlesticks burned in small niches. Her turquoise silk caftan flowed behind her.

Alanis walked beside Eros through the arched hallway, breathing in piquant, herbal spices. "What did Sanah say about me that made you angry?"

"Nothing important."

"And how did she know my mother's name? *You* didn't know it."

He flashed her a heinous grin. "Sanah is a *vitch.*"

"Please, come in, sit down." Sanah invited her to be seated

on a low divan curving around a star-marked table. On the heart of the star a golden lamp discharged wafts of jasmine fumes.

After hanging their capes, Eros slouched beside her. As large as he was, he seemed very much at home sitting in Sanah's cozy little parlor. "What's this smell, *Amti?*" He grinned.

"I prepared *Harira* soup and *Tajine*. I'm certain you are as hungry as ever, *einaya*. I'll have dinner ready in a minute." Sanah rustled out of the room, her jewelry ringing cheerfully.

"What does *einaya* mean?" Alanis asked him.

"It's an endearment." He smiled. "It means *my eyes*."

Alanis caught his gaze, captivated by the midnight-blue hue of his irises. A thought crossed her mind—*if he were mine, I would call him einaya too.*

"What do you think of Sanah's house?" he asked.

She blinked and looked around. "It's . . . quite blue. Does it symbolize something?"

"Blue is a lucky color. Supposed to ward off the Evil Eye," he explained, looking amused.

"The house is wonderful," she whispered reverently. "Sanah is wonderful." This pirate who deceived her, who almost seduced her, and whom she labored to loath, brought her to the most enchanting place to visit an old woman he considered very dear to his heart. "Thank you for bringing me here tonight, Eros."

"The night is still young. Perhaps you won't feel so grateful when it's over."

"I know you came here at great peril, but I will never forget this night. I'm certain of it."

Eros lost his smile. He searched her starry eyes and swept a gilded wisp of hair off her lips. "This look in your eyes, *Amore,* it's worth all the perils in the world," he whispered gruffly.

Alanis sustained his intense gaze. A woman too beautiful for words but also a confounded nuisance he had no intention of enmeshing himself in.

Sanah returned with a tray laden with dishes. "You remember my *Harira* soup, *El-Amar?*"

"How could I forget, *Amti?* My palate is still on fire since the last time I ate it."

Sanah sighed and sat opposite them. "You made an old woman happy tonight, *El-Amar.*"

"I've missed our little talks, *Amti,*" Eros confessed with a smile. "It's good to be home."

Alanis felt her eyes becoming as misty as Sanah's. Evidently the lonely old woman loved the Italian Viper as if he were her son. She glanced at Eros, amazed at his transformation into a human. This was the villain who stole her amethysts?

Sanah looked at Alanis. "You are not eating, my child?"

"You have yet to fill a bowl of soup for yourself, Madam Kuma," Alanis replied.

"Oh, no, my child. I cannot eat. I am much too excited."

Eros chuckled. Leaning conspiratorially toward Alanis, he said, "Sanah must be pure in order to read into the crypt. If she eats, she won't be able to tell your fortune. Isn't it so, *Amti?*"

Startled, Alanis's eyes went to Sanah. The old woman smiled guiltily. "I've no secrets from you, *El-Amar,* you know them all."

"Not all." Wolfishly, he devoured a hefty spoon. Alanis considered her bowl of soup. The spicy aroma was rather tempting, so she decided to brave her palate.

"Tell me about my beautiful girl," Sanah asked. "How is Yasmina?"

"Very well, actually. Met some poor devil and forced him to marry her. The victim seems happy, though. Didn't mind in the least."

"*Married?* Tell me more. Who is this man? Is he honest? Do you approve, *El-Amar?*"

Eros nodded. "An English nobleman. They're very much in love—"

Alanis sputtered. Eros's gaze stabbed her flaming profile. She looked at him and knew exactly what he was thinking, but her throat, her tongue, the entire hollow of her mouth was on fire after tasting the spicy soup. She couldn't utter a single word, much less explain her sudden outburst. But the way he was glaring at her—she wasn't sure she cared to explain.

"*Amti,* would you kindly bring us some water?" he asked succinctly, his eyes on Alanis.

Sanah nodded and rushed to the kitchen. Alanis wiped her teary face, acutely aware of his glower. He leaned closer. "If you say one word that will spoil the old woman's happiness, you'll answer to me. Do I make myself clear?"

A tremor meandered up her spine. *Welcome Viper.* She glared at him. "Not that I'd ever do a spiteful thing like that, or want to, but you shall have to do better with your threats."

"Don't tempt me, Alanis. You shall find me a much more formidable foe than you think."

She smiled and looked away. Sanah returned with a water trencher and glasses. Alanis gladly accepted a glass, doing her best to keep the smile going. Eros was furious. Good.

"So, my sweet girl is married." Sanah sighed with pleasure. "How wonderful. I told her she would marry at twenty-two. She is still in the New World, yes?"

"I imagine she is," Eros replied.

"Ah, but she will come soon to visit old Sanah and tell me the good news in person."

"If you say so, *Amti.*"

Sanah served her *Tajine*—a stew of tender mutton—followed by dessert sweets dripping in honey and rose water. Gradually Eros's mood began to mellow. His stomach stuffed, he relaxed on the cushions. Alanis enjoyed every bite. Nothing was going to spoil her adventure, especially not him. Disregarding her stomach's protests, she reached for a thin, long black fruit.

"Carobs are very healthy. They magnify one's fertility. You should have some, *El-Amar.*" Sanah offered the plate of carobs to Eros.

Suppressing a cool smile, he graciously declined. Alanis gently put hers aside.

Sanah collected the dishes. "Would you like some coffee or tea?"

"Please, let me help you." Alanis began to rise from the sofa.

A hand on her thigh stopped her. "I'm sure Alanis would love to taste your famous coffee."

Alanis glanced at the masculine hand.

"And you will have some coffee as well?" Sanah hung expectant eyes on Eros. "Just this time to make old Sanah happy."

Retrieving his hand, he said, "You know I don't drink your coffee, *Amti*. I'll have a cup of your less famous cinnamon tea." Shifting his gaze to Alanis, he explained, "Sanah will read your fortune in your cup after you drink the coffee."

"*Aywah,* we'll drink coffee, smoke a Nargila, and tell fortunes," she determined cheerfully.

Alanis wasn't about to miss that for the world. "I will gladly have a cup of your coffee."

"Sweet, make it sweet." Eros nodded with a cool wink before Sanah left for the kitchen. Alone again, he asked Alanis cautiously, "Are you still enjoying yourself?"

"Yes, I am. Thank you."

"I should have mentioned in advance that offering to help the host was considered impolite, but since I didn't want to spoil the surprise . . ."

Stumped, she met his gaze. He was not mad, and neither was she. The man simply had two conflicting personalities. One was a vicious serpent, but the other—that's where the real danger lay. "*El-Amar* . . ." inadvertently, the name rolled off her tongue.

He smiled darkly. "What is it you're itching to know?"

Alanis paused. She wanted to know *everything.* "Why does Sanah call you *El-Amar?*"

"Easy question. She hated my pagan name, so she invented me another."

"Eros. In Greek mythology he's the god of—" She clammed up.

"Love." The humor in his eyes was spiced with male arrogance and with desire.

"It's hardly a common name." She looked away, annoyed with him for no apparent reason.

"You think I thought it up myself, don't you?"

She felt his maddening dimpled smile. "I wouldn't be surprised if you did."

"Sorry to disappoint you, *Amore,* but I didn't."

She shot him a scathing glare. "Was it one of your tarts in Tortuga, then?"

A flash of white appeared between his tanned cheeks. "No one from Tortuga."

"So you have conquests all over the world. Very impressive." She sounded like a shrew but was unable to contain herself. Her skin was crawling with antipathy. "So who was it? Zakko?"

"No." He was no longer smiling. "My mother."

"Your mother?" Of course he had a mother, why was she surprised? Eros was a boy once and his mother named him after the Greek god of love—the one the Romans called Cupid. She understood why a mother who adored her wild, blue-eyed son would name him after an adorable, cherubic toddler with golden wings. As a man, he was incomparable; he must have been just as endearing as a boy. "Why did your name bother Sanah to have invented you another?"

"Islam is a monotheistic, zealous religion," he explained. "Sanah is a devoted believer."

"Sanah is familiar with Greek mythology?"

"Sanah is special. She knows everything. She taught me a lot."

"How did you come to know her?"

"We met at the Souk. She offered to read the palm of my hand for silver, but I refused. We got into a heated debate about destiny and fortune, and the rest is history. She took care of Gelsomina when I was away at sea."

The more he revealed, the more intrigued she became. "Why *El-Amar?*" she whispered.

"In Arabic *El-Amar* means *The Moon.*"

"Why moon?" She held his gaze, unable to look away.

Eros raised a finger to his face and slowly ran it along the crescent-shaped scar slashing his skin from left temple to cheek.

"How did you get this scar?"

He didn't answer. He sank his long fingers in her hair and drew her closer. "I want to kiss you." His voice was a gruff, heavy whisper; his chest rose and fell against her breasts.

She stared into his deep blue eyes. His mouth was so close, his breaths fanned her lips. He was forcing her to consent, to say it. "*Kiss me,*" her lips moved in a whisper.

Sanah called from the doorway. "Help me with this wretched vase, my son."

Alanis searched Eros's molten irises—he was suffering as acutely as she was.

Exhaling, he dropped his hands and pushed to his feet. "Here, let me help you." He rescued Sanah from the heavy vase and arranged the plate, the coals, and the tobacco on top of the piped Nargila. Sanah served the coffee and tea, and Alanis rested in silence, waiting for her breathing to calm. She was beginning to suspect she was harboring two conflicting personalities as well—an intelligent, levelheaded woman and a besotted twit.

Eros brought the tip of the long pipe to his lips. "Apple scented!" Delighted, he puffed a chain of smoke rings. The long neck of the vase glowed, the water inside it bubbled, and sweet fumes evaporated from the colorful tube. He passed the pipe to Sanah.

"What a blessing I prepared so much food. I had a premonition I'd have guests for dinner."

Eros's mouth curved around the rim of his teacup. "You looked surprised when you first saw me on your doorstep, *Amti.*"

"Because you never drink my coffee, *El-Amar.* You want to be mysterious."

"I'm simply not that interested in knowing my destiny. Everyone dies in the end, never of anything pleasant. Besides, you know I don't believe in magic, incantations, evil-eye nonsense."

Sanah snorted. "You were cynical at sixteen, *El-Amar,* and you keep nurturing your morbid humor. Doesn't this unpleasant habit wear off with time? When you do find something you believe in, please let me know."

"Now who is being cynical?" he teased.

"All the same," Sanah said, "I know things, even if at times they seem vague to the simple eye. One should always look below the surface to see the *truth*." She glimpsed at Alanis.

Noting this glimpse, Eros said, "Sometimes, looking too deep may cause drowning."

"He who *fears* the truth risks drowning in his own obtuseness," Sanah lectured fondly.

"*The Truth* may also be the subjective perspective of a more complex reality," he declared, looking pleased with his witty response.

"*Everything* is subjective in life, *El-Amar*. The simple things are the ones that bring us the most pleasure. A man who complicates them is a fool."

"Simple or complex," Eros persisted, "not everything is worth the trouble of obtaining."

"How will you know unless you try, *El-Amar?* Stop punishing yourself, my son. Enjoy the good things Allah bestows upon you. Aspire to make your life worth living."

Eros threw Alanis a wary glance. Did the bizarre conversation revolve around her? She wondered. He looked away, and she continued to enjoy the extraordinary ambiance of apple-scented smoke and floating hints while sipping her coffee. She understood why Eros insisted Sanah sweeten it—it was strong enough to revive the dead.

He leaned toward Sanah and took her wrinkled hands in his. "You always had faith in me, *Amti*. Even when I was anything but deserving of your faith. *Shukran*."

"You are welcome, my son." Sanah's eyes glistened.

Alanis bit her lip; she hated it when he was like this—warm, candid, a bit gloomy. Made her want to do crazy things, such as hugging him tightly and never letting go.

"Now, we shall tell fortunes!" Sanah announced. "And individuals who keep their secrets to themselves cannot listen to others'." She gave Eros a meaningful glance.

"I'm staying," he declared stubbornly, and folded his arms across his chest.

"Alanis has as much right to her privacy as you do, *El-Amar*. Why don't you go talk to Zakko for a spell? His secrets are as interesting as yours are."

"That loudmouthed bag of plumes is still around?" Eros laughed.

"Regrettably. I won't mind in the least if you take him with you. That bird never shuts up."

"You may give him to Gelsomina when she comes to see you, as you are foreseeing." He made a face as he reluctantly got up and went in search of a bird.

"So, are you ready, my child?" Sanah waited for Alanis's nod.

"Absolutely." Alanis beamed and pushed the empty coffee cup toward Sanah.

"Let's see . . ." Sanah lifted the tiny cup, dripped water from the trencher into it, whirled it, and spilled the remains onto a saucer. She removed the conical lid off the oil lamp, discharging a waft of scented clouds, and leaned forward to concentrate on the markings. "Hmm. First, we tell the past. Then, we tell the present. And last, we tell the future."

Alanis braced herself. There were so many things she wanted to know, of course if one believed in that sort of thing, which she wasn't entirely sure she did.

"I see three fair-haired children—a little boy, an older sister, and a friend." Sanah wrinkled her brow. "A man and a woman die in a fire. An old man is mourning. His heart is broken." She glanced at Alanis. "Your grandfather never recovered from your mother's death. Christine meant everything to him. The old man blamed your father for taking his daughter away. He wanted him close and doing what he does—taking care of the people. Your father disregarded his wishes and sailed away with your mother. They died in the fire."

Alanis choked. Up to now, Sanah was right about everything.

"I like your grandfather. Strong character, honest, never compromises. An important man, influential but just. Has a soft heart for you. You admire him very much, I see."

"My mother died when I was twelve. He raised my brother and me."

"Let us see. Ah, another misfortune." Sanah sighed. "Your brother was foolish. He lost his gold and his life to evil men. You mourned him dearly. The older boy was a good friend."

"Yes, he was." Alanis wiped her tears and nodded to Sanah to go on.

"The old man is heartbroken. He feels he's neglected your brother. His death lies heavy on his conscience. Life lost its meaning. There is no heir to his family. He does not trust the fair boy to fulfill his duty to you. I see an ocean. The old man is alone. He fears he will lose you as he lost your mother and brother." Sanah raised her furrowed brow. "He has great hopes for you. He admires you and misses you deeply. He knows he made mistakes, but he is willing to change. He knows you will not marry the fair boy and will return . . . unmarried. And so you shall. You'll go back *unmarried*." Something seemed to trouble Sanah, but she wouldn't say what. "The fair boy was never yours," the fortune-teller stated. "Destiny has chosen another for you. He is close."

Alanis's heart lost a beat, but she banished her wicked conclusion immediately. "The truth is I am not entirely convinced I ever wish to marry, Madam Kuma."

"Please call me Sanah. Let me explain something to you, my child. Fate is prearranged, but a person may intervene and tip the scales of his fortune. Life will offer choices, but the ultimate decision is in your hands." She smiled. "That is the beauty of it. No one but you is responsible. Of course, there are other interventions and preventions but—" She pointed a finger at Alanis. "You have the power to create your own destiny!"

"I don't understand. If one's fate is preordained, how can one be responsible for it?"

"That is the question of all times. I have studied it for many years, and I still don't know all the answers. I will try to explain this in simple terms. If your fate is entwined with another's, then you will meet this person in your life, but what will become of this connection is up to you. If your union does not serve its purpose, you shall meet again and again in your next reincarnations until you fulfill your joint destiny. What you are doing now is asking your—let us say— guardian angel, using my talent as a mediator, to guide you in your quest for happiness. So you see, my child, I can tell you many things, but you may always change your destiny."

"Eros, that is, *El-Amar* does not believe in this idea, does he?" Alanis recalled Eros's stoical comments of earlier that evening. For him, life was a constant struggle.

"*El-Amar* is a skeptical man. He needs proof to believe. Life has shaped him that way. It was not always easy for him. He didn't have time to consider every single step, because his fight was survival. His life pushed him on. Nonetheless, he is changing now and he does not even realize it yet. But we digress. Let us go on before Zakko runs out of secrets, shall we?"

Smiling, Alanis nodded in agreement.

Sanah squinted thoughtfully at the cup. "I see a man. Your paths crossed before and will again. He is a powerful man whom people fear yet respect. You, too, have a strong fear of him, but also a weakness of the heart. You know little of his past. You sense secrets. There are two men inside of him— a serpent and an eagle—but he has one heart. You feel this man's heart, but you do not trust your feelings. He is unlike other men. He is singular."

Alanis inhaled sharply. "This man is a mystery to me," she confessed softly. "I don't know whether he is good or evil. Sometimes I believe he is both."

Sanah nodded cannily. "I will tell you a riddle, my child. Solve it, and you shall have the key to his heart." She hunched over the table, encouraging Alanis to lean closer, and whispered, "Where he loves, he does not desire. And where he desires, he cannot love. He may only wed at a specific place he can no longer go to. And nostalgia rules his dreams."

Goodness. Alanis felt a strong kick inside her chest. "But, I'm not certain I—"

"Risk your heart, Alanis, and you will know. I have something for you. One moment." She scuttled out of the room.

Alanis contemplated the orange light of the lamp. There were two parts to the riddle, two secrets. The first part referred to Eros's past with women, the second to his origins. Something happened to him at sixteen. It changed his life. His crests were important—serpents and eagles. Perhaps the man he stole them from was the key, an enemy from the past. It was gratifying to know she read him faithfully. There were two men inside Eros, and apparently her destiny was entwined with both. Sanah was right—she did have a soft spot for him, a rather large spot.

Sanah returned, dangling a golden chain with a pendant. "Here, my child. It is a good-luck charm to repel the Evil Spirit. Wear it around your neck." She offered Alanis the chain.

"You've given me so much already. I cannot possibly accept such a gift."

"Do you see the blue eye in the pendant?" Sanah pointed at the semiprecious stone. It was blue, marquis shaped, with a black dot in its center and resembling an eye. "It will keep you safe. Go ahead, put it on."

Alanis accepted the chain and slid it around her neck. "Thank you. I will treasure it."

"We will discuss your future now." Sanah raised the cup to the lamplight. "I see journeys, trials. Great fortune awaits you, Alanis, daughter of Christine, if you dare reach out for it." She lifted her eyes to Alanis. "If you dare risk your heart."

"What great fortune?" Alanis inquired with interest.

"I see a land of unrivaled beauty, a foreign land, and a man who will share your life on this land. He is an *Emir*, a leader among his people. Your grandfather will choose this man for you."

"My grandfather?" Alanis grimaced. What rotten luck! Was her fate to be married off as a peacemaker to a prominent figure in a strange country?

"Do not despair, my child." Sanah concentrated on the cup,

searching for promising clues. "He has a sharp, intellectual mind. He is tall, handsome, strong, virile, fair skinned . . ."

"Fair skinned?" Alanis's spirit sank like a heavy stone. Sanah's predictions were getting worse and worse—*Eros's skin color was as dark as bronze.*

"You'll share a special bond. You'll be very happy, very much in love, with four healthy, beautiful children. You will become deeply involved with your husband's politics."

Splendid! Her grandfather was about to set her up with another politician.

"Death will come for him, but you will save him."

Alanis didn't share Sanah's glee. She was too depressed to appreciate the good prophecies. A sensible woman would be ecstatic. She mourned the loss of a pirate!

Puffing out smoke, Sanah contemplated Alanis through the mist. "You may always change your destiny, my child. Fate has chosen a mate for you, but you do not have to accept him."

Alanis pondered that. If tonight proved anything, it was that her feelings for Eros ran much deeper than she had suspected. He had cast a spell on her, and she was unable to shake it off. But to give up her honor, her future with a worthy man of her grandfather's choosing?

Eros materialized at the threshold. "We should go, *Principessa.* It's almost midnight, and we have yet to get out of here."

Sanah sighed. "We'll stop, my child, but now that we have met, you may come and visit me anytime. Perhaps *El-Amar* will bring you again?" She cast Eros an impish smile.

Alanis regarded the man at the door, realizing her heart was beating much faster. 'The most handsome among immortals,' Hesiodus described the god of love. She wondered what sort of woman would end up with him? She resented her already. Of course, he might remain a lone wolf for the rest of his days. One should never lose faith. However . . . Supposing she solved the riddle and gained the key to his heart, would she use it? Would she say no to her grandfather's choice of husband and create her own destiny? Risk her heart with Eros?

Her bizarre mood didn't escape him. He frowned. "What did you say to her, *Amti?*"

"To know that you should have had a cup of coffee yourself. Now, you must be on your way. It is late and here in the Kasbah the walls have ears. I fear for you, *einaya.*"

When they were standing at the door wrapped in their dark cloaks, Sanah took their hands and joined them together. "God shall enlighten you, my children." She looked at Alanis. "The next time you come here, you will be with child."

Startled by Sanah's divination, Alanis murmured, "Good-bye, Sanah. I'll never forget you or this night." She leaned forward to embrace her. "And thank you for your gift."

Eros wrapped his arms around the tiny old woman. "I don't know when, but you know I'll be back, *Amti.*" He tenderly kissed her wrinkled cheek. "God is with you."

Sniffing, Sanah released him, but suddenly gripped his arm, fear in her eyes. "Beware, *El-Amar,* beware when the moon is in Cancer."

"I will, *Amti.* I promise."

"Now, go!" she shooed them out the door. "*Ruhu maà Allah!* Go with God!"

CHAPTER 12

Upon the British consuls making a complaint to the Dey, on occasion of one of his corsairs having captured a vessel, he openly replied, "It is all very true, but what would you have? The Algerians are a company of rogues and I am their captain."

—Marine Research Society

The walk back was taken in silence. Stealing a glimpse at the dark figure strolling beside her, holding her hand, Alanis inquired, "What is an *Emir?*"

Eros froze. She stumbled to a halt in front of him. His eyes gleamed sharply over the black headdress wrapping his face. "*Emir* is a prince," he said, his voice sounding cold and wary.

She was so gripped by the intensity he radiated she failed to notice the riders in black until he hauled her aside to stand with their backs against a wall. A shriek of terror rose in her throat, but he put his hand over her mouth. She stared frantically at the riders blocking the alley. They ruled the night, deftly merging with its shadows. A small hemp sac was tossed their way. Eros caught it and emptied its contents into his palm. Dirt clods—a secret message.

"Don't say a word," he whispered, as he moved them to a horse the riders offered. "Do exactly as I ask. And under no condition are you to take off your veil, *capisce?*"

Alanis bumped her head against his jaw, nodding quickly. He leaped onto the saddle and lifted her into his lap. They took off.

The dark labyrinth of alleys shattered all of her romantic dreams of the Kasbah of Algiers. Clustered walls hemmed them in. She had an eerie sensation of eyes watching them in every crack and window. Fear trickled along her spine. Seeming to sense her disquiet, Eros wrapped his arms around her, encouraging her to burrow against him. He rode hard until they reached tall arched gates. The gates opened, and they trotted into the courtyard. The riders dismounted and so did Eros. He swept her off the saddle, but before he released her he put his mouth to her ear.

"Remember what I said. Don't speak. Don't expose yourself. Don't look anyone straight in the eye. Keep your eyes fixed on the ground." He gripped her hand and marched straight toward the imposing, arabesque-imprinted portal.

"*Taofik!*" he roared as they barged in, ignoring the startled sentries at the entrance pillars. He yanked off his black headdress and halted to search the hall. Gold covered the walls up to the arched ceiling; polished tan tiles lined the floor. Nobody came to greet them. He started moving again, striding briskly as if he owned this covert palace, or at the very least had lived here before. They reached a lush chamber, furnished with leather divans and lustrous artifacts. Eros halted abruptly. He curved his arm backward to keep her behind him.

"Taofik!" he growled. "*Inta fin, ya calb? Where the devil are you, you dog?*"

A door opened, and a man ambled inside. Dark skinned, dark haired, dark eyed, wearing a gilt-embossed black tunic, he radiated dominance over this den of spoils. Alanis didn't doubt he was a nefarious corsair: His lust for blood was etched into every aspect of his appearance. On his hip, embedded with rubies, rode a short, curved *shabariya*—his Algerian dagger. A slow smile expended on his olive-tinged face. "*Marhaba. Welcome, El-Amar.* Do come in."

Eros remained rigid. "I speak French not to shame you in front of your men. I suggest you do the same." He flung the dirt sac into Taofik's hands. "Why am I here?"

"You are too angry, *El-Amar.* Is it so unthinkable that I should seek my brother out? My brother, whom I haven't seen for many years, when I hear he is in the Kasbah?"

"I've a strong mind to kill you for sending Omar to collect me off the streets. I cooperated out of respect for you—a respect you clearly do not feel for me."

"I meant no disrespect, brother. I apologize for the way I brought you here. I only had your best interest at heart. I have disturbing news. I believe you'll share my disquiet."

Eros took a step forward. "How did you know I was here?"

"The walls have ears in the Kasbah, and Sanah's house is watched over day and night. Did you know the old witch advises the Dey? He doesn't make a move without her guidance these days. You should thank Allah it was me who found you and not Abdi Dey's patrol."

"Sanah has always been an advisor to the Dey," Eros sniped with little patience. "Tell me what you know and we'll say *salamat.*"

"Why are you so hasty to leave? Let us sit and discuss it more calmly. Omar!" He clapped his hands, summoning a man who was invisible up until that moment. He invited Eros onto a bronze divan. "I trust cognac is still your poison, Italian?"

"Bad habits die hard." Eros descended the entrance steps and slouched on the divan.

Left standing as a wallflower in the shadows of the entrance pillars, Alanis realized he was protecting her by treating her as a slave. Practicing his earlier words of caution, she remained stagnant, shading her gaze though not entirely looking down.

Omar returned with a tray and set it down on a polished table between them. Taofik leaned forward to pour their drinks. "You look well," he said. "Success agrees with you."

"Not as well as it does with you." Eros smirked, putting his headdress aside.

"You know, it kills me to see you fighting for the other side now. Us enemies?"

Eros's mouth hardened. "I'm fighting for the side I always have—mine."

Taofik laughed. "At least you haven't changed. How long has it been—five, six years?"

"Eight."

"Ah, yes, I forget how eager you were to leave me, *El-Amar,* and go on your own."

"It wasn't your company I found objectionable, Taofik. It was the company you keep and the methods in which you operate. Dealing flesh offends my . . . delicate, Italian sensibilities."

"Delicate sensibilities!" Taofik roared with laughter. "You outdid me, *Rais.* Your name is more feared than mine ever was."

A genuine smile finally touched Eros's lips. "I sincerely hope not."

"Don't be modest. Your methods are more delicate than mine, but your aims are higher."

"You're wrong," Eros said. "I've no thirst for power. I leave it to those who relish it."

"Don't trifle with me, *El-Amar,* and don't fool yourself.

Your fleet is nearly as large as the Sultan's. Every day I am summoned by Abdi Dey to discuss how to deal with it."

"Amazing that with everything you have on your plate—the Sultan tagging you 'rebels and infidels against the Holy Law of Islam' because you ignore his agreements to cease your attacks on the French, your great losses at sea because it swarms with fleets fighting the War, and the Moroccan Sultan growing stronger every day—you still find time to worry about me."

"We have time for everyone." Taofik smiled, rubbing a giant ruby ring sitting on his little finger. "The Sultan's Janissaries bleed us dry. We worry about them as well."

Eros sipped his cognac. "I'm not interested in your preying ventures. You know that."

"But we cannot afford to have you blocking every attack against the Alliance. We're still at war with the Austrians, if you'll recall." Taofik lowered his voice. "Your strategies are clever, *El-Amar,* but you can't put up a wall around a certain peninsula and deprive us of the cities that have provided our best pillage for over two centuries."

"Then stop raiding them!" Eros rasped. "Did you think I'd let you sack Genoa?"

Alanis was startled by his ferocity, but Taofik didn't look surprised. "You can't defend all the Italian cities all the time, *El-Amar.* You're not their keeper. Think of the Barbarossa brothers. They didn't settle for pillage. They started off as we did, then took over Algiers and became its rulers. They went for the real power—the power obtained by ruling countries." His eyes thinned. "We could have been the strongest, the greatest corsairs of all times, you and I. We still can."

Eros smiled incisively. "Still entertaining thoughts of usurping Abdi Dey's seat? Is that the reason we're suddenly discussing the Barbarossa brothers and the size of my fleet?"

"Why don't you come back? It'll be as in the old days, only better. We'll be full partners."

"Algiers is a part of my life that is over," Eros stated. "My eyes are to the future."

"No." Taofik's eyes resembled whispering coals. "You're

returning to your past. I always knew you would someday. All the hate that kept you going when others, strong men, gave up . . . You had the devil on your tail. No one endures pain the way you did for no reason."

Eros's face remained as rigid as a bronze mask.

"This new generation, they don't have your wits. They don't have your character. They're spoiled, soft. They want the easy life, but they're too lazy to pay the price."

Eros downed his drink and rested the glass. "Why was I brought here?"

"You carry valuable goods aboard the *Alastor.* An English duke's property? In the past you shunned high-quality merchandise. You were always careful to be discreet. What changed?"

Alanis held her breath, waiting for Eros's reply. "Your point, Taofik," he clipped harshly.

"An Italian nobleman is looking for you in the Kasbah. He wishes to purchase your . . . goods, for an attractive price. He's also in the market for information concerning you, brother, and as you well know, such information is worth your weight in gold."

"Then perhaps I should eat more. Good night, Taofik."

A pair of strong hands seized Alanis from behind, and a harsh, mocking voice called over her shoulder, *"El-Amar!* I heard you were hiding somewhere in the Kasbah."

Eros bolted to his feet. "Let her go, Hani! Right now!" he growled, his voice leaving no room for negotiations. Nor did the pistol he suddenly held in his hand.

Hani burst out laughing. "What will you do, shoot us? You can't cast a stone at me so long as I hold this precious bundle in my arms." The bundle wriggled furiously, but Hani was as strong as an ox. "You took Jasmine away from me once. This time, she stays with me."

"Let her go, Hani. She is not Jasmine," Eros clipped menacingly.

"Is that so? Since when do you sneak into the Kasbah with a woman to see Sanah no less? Everyone knows you don't take your *whores* with you on your escapades."

Taofik barked a warning, but Hani shook his head. "No, uncle. I won't let you trick me as you did the last time. Jasmine agreed to stay with me, but you and the Italian dog schemed behind our backs and snatched her away."

"You'll give *El-Amar* his due respect and free Jasmine at once!" Taofik barked.

"What respect?" Hani snarled. "I'm your blood; he's nothing, a stranger."

"*El-Amar* is no stranger here. You know he is a brother to me."

"*A brother?*" Hani spat on the polished floor. "What brother? I'm your nephew, your flesh and blood. What is he? A worthless infidel, a former slave you took from the Bagnio."

"There'll be nothing left of you *but* flesh and blood if you do not release her this instant!" Eros took a threatening step forward. "This isn't Jasmine you are touching—but *my woman!*"

Alanis stopped fighting Hani and numbly stared at Eros. His face was taut with rage; his eyes glinted murderously. The cool restraint that was so much a part of his personality dissolved right before her eyes. *My woman.*

Hani turned Alanis around and peeled the veil off her mouth. "Hello, beautiful."

She glanced up. She knew it was a mistake the moment she saw his eyes. Swearing, he ripped the hood off her head. Hair as lustrous as spun gold spilled to her waist in all its glory. Her aquamarine eyes wild with terror, she stared at Hani, and she stared at Taofik. Carnal savagery burned in their eyes. Eros bounded forward, bellowing, "*Bastardo!*" A hand stopped him.

"No, brother," Taofik warned. "Hani is blood. I can't let you kill him over a woman."

Hani clutched her chin. "What have we here? A golden treasure, soft and priceless."

Taofik cackled. "I imagine this is your famous load, *El-Amar.* Don't tell me you've grown soft, coming to see Sanah for some fortune telling?"

"Let her go, Hani," Eros commanded. "She is not Jasmine.

My sister is happily married and living in Jamaica. You are too late. She has forgotten all about you."

"*Married?*" Hani's grip tightened on Alanis, causing her to wail with pain. Growling, he shoved her aside, drew his dagger, and hurled it forcefully at Eros, aiming at his chest.

"*No!*" Alanis shrieked, unable to perceive the catastrophe about to occur.

A flash of silver cut the air and stopped at Eros's chest. He didn't move. Standing exactly where he was, the palms of his hands pressed together, the dagger's bejeweled hilt protruding between his fingers, he was smiling vengefully. "Is that all you can do?" He flipped the knife in the air and caught the jewel-encrusted hilt. "Come on, idiot. Show me what you're made of."

Hani surged forward, a second knife in hand. Taofik stepped aside. Any interference on his part would insult one man and turn the other into a mortal enemy. Eros and Hani started circling each other, switching blades from hand to hand, jumping each other with false attacks.

"You're a dead man!" Hani snarled. "How sad for Jasmine, but how fortunate for my new blond bedmate." He plunged forward. Eros blocked the blow, knocking Hani's forearm aside.

"You're slowing down, pampered boy." He grinned, moving fluidly with his black cape swelling around his heels. "You've been lulling on your silky cushions too long."

"I'll show you who's been lulling on cushions!" Hani struck again, but his knife stabbed Eros's cape and twisted impotently in the ample folds. Moving fast, Eros ripped the cape off his shoulders and threw it over Hani, trapping him like a fish in a net while he moved with lighter ease. Furious, Hani wrestled to be free. He emerged wild eyed and disheveled.

"Filthy Italian dog! I swear I'll kill you tonight!" he raved.

They reengaged in the dance of death, wielding their sneaky knives so skillfully, Alanis scarcely saw their murderous glitter. Eros was taller and stockier, but Hani's rage fueled his prowess, turning him into a lethal opponent. He continued his provocations, thrusting again and again. Eros blocked his attacks and nicked his arm. A cry of pain tore from Hani's lips.

"Too bad for your shirt. It was so pretty." Eros smiled at the red stain expanding on Hani's ivory satin sleeve while the latter clutched his arm with bloody fingers.

"You'll pay for this, *El-Amar*," Hani gnarled, "with every moan of your white whore when I have her beneath me tonight." He laughed crudely, letting go of his arm and reengaging.

"I wouldn't make plans for later." Eros grinned. He switched his knife to his left hand. "No more jokes. Let's get it over with." He jumped Hani with the knife and seized his injured arm with his right hand, hurling him forcefully against the wall. Hani crashed hard, his knife hand twisted behind his back. Eros bent it up with such force the bone cracked. Hani growled. The knife dropped from his hand and he slumped against the wall, announcing his defeat.

Eros put his knife to Hani's neck. "Taofik, let me finish him off. You'll thank me one day."

"I appreciate your restraint, *El-Amar*. I'll take over now." Taofik stepped forth and turned Hani aside. The back of his hand cracked across Hani's cheek, leaving a vicious red cut with his ruby ring. "Your disgraceful conduct is unforgivable!" he spat with contempt, causing Hani's complexion to turn very red. "*Get out, stupid ass!*" He pointed at the exit. "*Out!*"

Alanis ran to Eros. Her heart leaped with delight. She checked him thoroughly and found he remained in his formidable one piece. Unable to resist the impulse, she grabbed his neck and pasted a loud kiss on his cheek. "You were absolutely splendid! I'm extremely proud of you."

He sketched a princely bow. "I'm humbled by your praise, *Principessa*. Now we must be off." He swept her hair and coiled it at her nape, looking pleased he was allowed this liberty. Her hood was torn, so he wrapped his headdress around her head, leaving a thin gap for the eyes.

Hani stumbled to the entrance, gripping his arm. When he reached the top step, he turned around and pointed a gory finger at Eros. "As you used to say—the world is a wheel.

Your day will come. In the name of Allah, I swear you'll pay for this!" Then he left.

"I apologize again, brother," Taofik said. "I hope you'll forgive and forget."

Eros raised an eyebrow. "Would you?"

Taofik smiled. "I'm glad you didn't stoop to his level. If you had, I would have had to avenge his death because he is blood, and that I would have hated."

Eros threw his cape around his shoulders. "We're leaving," he informed Alanis.

"I assume there's no point in trying to bid a price for this golden confection." Taofik's coal black eyes raked her cloaked figure. They settled on Eros, questioning. "Or is there?"

She shuddered, waiting for Eros's out-and-out refusal. He grinned. He assessed her glinting gaze. "The offer does have merit, to be sure. But not tonight."

Taofik escorted them outside to the *riyad.* "Omar will escort you outside the walls," he said as Eros mounted an auburn Arabian. "We must protect your golden property from thieves."

Sitting with Alanis in his lap, Eros said, "I pity the thief who steals this little baggage."

Taofik laughed. "Then you certainly have your hands too full to hassle us now, but do not forget what we talked about. You collect enemies like trophies. Be careful, *El-Amar.* Don't make the mistake of underestimating them." To Alanis his warning sounded like a threat.

"I'll keep that in mind. *Salamat,* Taofik." Eros kicked his heels and stormed into the night.

"May I assume you're still enjoying tonight's escapade?" Eros's deep voice broke the quietude of the night.

Alanis didn't want to talk. Moonlight pooled on the narrow earthy floor of the alley. They rode at a lazy trot with Omar nearby. Nestling in his arms with her cheek resting over his heart, she felt too content to spar with him. Eros seemed to understand. He tightened his embrace and rested his chin on her head, letting the night heighten every sensation. Shutting her eyes, she took shelter in the darkness to abandon her defenses in favor of this magical intimacy enveloping them. She savored the fluid motion of the Arabian, the salty Oriental breeze, the sounds of nighttime, but above all else the feel of him holding her as a man held his woman. *His woman.*

"Wakkefu wa istaslamu! Halt and surrender!" A voice barked at the foot of the alley.

Her eyes flew open. Eros reined in, causing the Arabian to toss its head and prance. Rows of riders blocked the bottom of the sloping lane, their black capes sewn with a red stripe at the seam. They were ambushed. "The Dey's Guard," he muttered between clenched teeth.

"Hani?" she inquired worriedly.

"Maybe."

The leader of the band withdrew a long, curved, single-edged sword. It chillingly reflected the silvery rays of the moon. "We're dead," Alanis whispered, as one by one the riders withdrew shimmering scimitars that seemed to have been whetted by Vulcan himself.

"Not yet. Hold fast." Eros gave Omar a signal, then with a guttural cry kicked his heels and charged ahead like a bat out of hell.

"Death to the infidels! Death in the name of Allah!" the leader of the band bellowed and burst forward, his pack of scimitar swinging soldiers following his lead.

Eros drew his pistol and shot the leader. Omar felled the second-in-command. The riders broke ranks, shouting and flinging their swords. The slope of the lane gave Eros and Omar the advantage of momentum and speed as they rode on, intent on gaining passage against all odds.

The clash was brutal, swords flying and slashing. A gleaming blade nearly hacked off Alanis's head, but Eros used his impetus to wrest the sword out of the man's hand. He swung it at the next assailant. Blood splattered warm and sticky. Alanis cringed against Eros, hugging his waist, trying not to hinder his movements. His breathing came in rough, short rumbles; warm sweat broke on his skin. Bodies fell on either side of them and got trampled under the metal hooves. Somehow they managed to forge a path through the terrible encounter while Omar stayed behind to delay the assailants. Eros sprinted ahead, cutting corners, daring the devil, until he reached a secluded alley. He hopped off the Arabian and swung Alanis to her feet. "Can you swim?" he asked.

"Yes, I can."

"Good. Take your *djellabah* and boots off." He ripped the black cape off his shoulders, peeled his shirt over his head, and dropped to the ground to pull off his boots. Alanis did the same, hastily ridding herself of the cloak and the boots.

"Come on." He took her hand and started running. In the distance, the roar of hooves grew stronger. He entered a pitch-black opening, a tunnel. The ground was slippery wet beneath her feet. Water trickled, echoing hollowly off moldy walls as it dripped into a distant pool.

"Where are we?" Her voice resonated as she hurried to keep pace with him.

"It's the *khettara,* the irrigation canals of the city. They lead straight into the open sea."

"Are we in the sewer?" she cried, the walls echoing her horror.

He chuckled. "No, *Principessa*. It's the city's water reserves."

All of a sudden, the ground dropped beneath their feet. They fell into the obscure bowels of the rock, deeper, deeper. Their drop ended swiftly in a big splash, as they plunged into a pool. The water was icy. Alanis sank like a stone, her blood frosting, until her feet touched rock. She kicked and rocketed for air. She came up sputtering and shivering with cold.

"Princess." Eros's deep voice filled the cavernous reservoir. "Are you all right?"

"Yes," she gasped, wiping water and wet hair off of her face. "Where are you?"

"Right here." He curved an arm around her waist and pinned her to his side. He swam on until they stood on solid rock. "We're not dead yet," he whispered, his breath sultry on her brow.

A shaft of silvery moonlight protruded through a crack in the rock. She gradually made out his grin in the darkness. He enveloped her to him. "You're trembling," he murmured, rubbing her back to stimulate the blood cycle. Sighing deeply, she hugged his waist and felt his body heat seeping into her limbs. A few hours ago he was the mean Viper; now, he was her knight in shining armor. She wondered how long it would last, the intimacy tonight's events have formed between them. Eros was good at that sort of thing—he made her trust him and then he flipped.

He indulged her for a while, stroking her back and holding her. His lips found her cheek. He moved his mouth to hers, murmuring, "I owe myself something."

"You considered selling me to that Algerian."

Deep laugher welled in his throat. "Not in a million years. You know I came here to fulfill your wish. Did you think I'd leave you behind? You're not for sale, *Amore*. You're mine. Only mine." The first touch of his lips was sublime; his kiss was a rare blend of gentleness and desire. She hugged his sleek neck and pulled him down closer. His caressing tongue burned upon hers. His taste was intoxicating. Her legs liquefied beneath her. She never wanted to let go.

Alas, they were not out of the woods yet. They still needed to take the oar boat back to the *Alastor*. Eros sensed her withdrawal. "We must move on, *mia bella*. I want you as far away from this place as possible. We'll finish this later," he vowed gruffly. "I promise."

Unsettled by his dark promise, she followed him through a crevice in the rock. The light of the moon seemed brighter after the swim via the dark reservoir, the deep sand warmer. She could not wait to be back on the ship, snuggling in a cozy bed.

Eros gestured to their right. "There's our boat." He took her hand and started running.

A movement caught her eye. "Look!" She pointed at the

three men emerging from the marine gate. Shouts pierced the night from the top of the mole.

"Push the boat into sea. I'll follow you." Eros turned away and charged at the soldiers.

Alanis ran to the boat, but when she saw the timber wreckage she tripped to the sand with a cry of despair. She glanced back at Eros in time to see him hurling his knife straight into the first soldier's forehead, executing him on the spot. Stunned, she saw him slamming his fist into the second man's face. The third proved wiser; he drew his scimitar and swung it. Eros ducked and lunged at him. They rolled in the sand, struggling fiercely. Eros sat up, the hilt of the sword in his hand. He raised his arm and buried the blade in the Algerian's chest. The second man began rising off the sand, his scimitar in hand. Alanis got up and raced toward him.

"Look out!" she shouted to Eros, and tossed a fistful of sand into the man's eyes.

Eros got up and charged at him. Steel met steel in a grating, metallic rancor. Eros raised his scimitar high in the air and with a forceful swing brought it down on the soldier's neck, hacking off his head. Alanis went utterly still. Eros's muscular silhouette stood beside the mutilated form of his victim, his hands still clutching the blood-smeared sword. Spasms of bile rose in her throat. She bent over and retched on the sand as fits raked her entire body.

She was gasping for air when he reached her. "Alanis, what happened? Are you ill?" He put a gentle hand on her shoulder. She jerked it off and pointed at the smashed boat. "Bastards!" he growled. At the gate, more soldiers were pouring out. "Alanis." He pulled her to her feet. Plastered with sand, he looked worn out, yet the fire in his eyes still burned. "We must get out of here, *amore mio,* or we will die tonight."

"What do we do now?" she asked, feeling scared and weary beyond belief.

"Now we swim. Take your shirt off. We're leaving now."

"*What?*" The last harrowing experience she would put up with tonight was stripping naked before him. "How the devil are we to swim such a distance?" She heard the Algerians shouting as they kept pouring through the gate, when all of a sudden, a loud explosion rocked the walls. A pillar of water gushed in the distance in a powerful jet not too far off the *Alastor*.

"*Porca miseria!* They're bombarding my ship!" He clutched her wrist with an iron grip and towed her into the sea. "Listen to me, you little baggage. We should be stripping down to our bare skin. Every piece of clothing will sink us like rocks once we get into the deep currents. Now, I know you wear something underneath. So take that shirt off, and no more arguments. This is no time to play 'miss prim and proper.'"

He didn't bother staring as she lost the shirt. They waded deep while tall waves crashed against their bodies, splashing their faces with salt water. Bombshells shrieked over their heads.

"Hold on to me!" Eros growled over the roaring waves.

"I can swim on my own, thank you!" Alanis screamed back.

"Not in these currents and not as fast as I can!" He forced her arms around his neck and dove headlong. His arms slashed the black waves with the force of an avenging angel, stimulated more by rage than vigor. She held on to his shoulders with all her might while paddling her feet.

The soldiers didn't follow into sea, entrusting the task of eliminating their fearsome enemy to the cannons. Far off, the *Alastor* awakened to the call of battle, firing enterprising broadsides at the immured city. They swam through gushing water pillars, defying the bristling missiles and the pitiless waves. Alanis was fast losing her remaining strength. Her arms fell numb. Her head spun with pessimistic thoughts of sharks and doom and never seeing her grandfather again. Her eyelids became heavy. The *Alastor* seemed to be getting farther and farther away. But just as her body gave, Eros gripped the *Alastor*'s side step and heaved them both up. Nico caught her arms and hoisted her up on deck. Grinning from ear to ear, Giovanni offered his captain a steady hand and pulled him right after her.

When she opened her eyes the world was swimming

around her. Men scurried on deck; the cannons continued to play fire. She was distantly aware of Eros's booming voice ordering the cutting of the cable and the unfurling of the masts, launching the *Alastor* in full speed.

Her knees buckled and she subsided against Nico, but a pair of strong hands peeled her away and swept her off her feet. She was vaguely surprised at the euphoric security she felt. Shutting her eyes, she let her head drop onto a broad shoulder and drifted into oblivion.

The first thing she saw was a naked body rummaging in an open trunk of clothes. Muscles rippled all over: powerful arms, a sinewy back, narrow hips, firm buttocks, and long muscular thighs. Smooth of hair, the dark tan turned surprisingly creamy white below the waistline. Slowly regaining coherency, Alanis realized she was lying on a soft bed, wrapped in a blanket, and gawking at a gloriously nude male. A matronly voice inside her head commanded her to look away, but her eyes refused to let go of the brain-melting sight before her.

He finally found items to his liking. He slipped on a pair of breeches and a shirt and tamed his hair in a queue. He went to the door and stuck his head out. "Get me some tea!"

She didn't expect him to turn around so abruptly, but he did.

"Enjoying the performance?" Eros smiled at her wolfishly.

Heat flooded her cheeks. She shut her eyes, but it was too late. The odious man burst out laughing. Her eyes snapped open. "What are you laughing at, you lout?"

Chuckling, he went to the wine cabinet and poured a full glass of cognac. He tossed back half, then came to stand beside her. "Here, it'll warm you up until the tea arrives."

Secretly grateful, she accepted the drink and pushed up to a sitting position. She sipped and eyed his grinning face. He didn't stay long to gloat. He returned to his trunk and selected a black silk robe and a lawn shirt. He tossed them in her direction. They landed over her legs.

"I suggest you get out of the wet clothes if you want to live for another adventure."

Alanis stared at the dry clothes. If he expected her to match his performance, he was sorely mistaken. "I had enough adventure to last me a lifetime."

"You can't stay in these wet clothes forever. You're totally *gelato.*" He smirked.

Alanis stole a glance beneath the blanket. Thank God she still had her clothes on, but her wet chemisette was frightfully transparent and pasted to her skin. She'd have to make a dash for the door with the blanket around her. She wished she could move.

"Don't be such a baby, Princess. I swear I won't look." When she adamantly shook her head, a dark smile formed on his lips. "If you refuse to put on dry clothes like a good girl, I shall simply have to do it for you."

Well, there was no getting around it. Groaning inwardly, she swung her feet to the floor. It took a huge effort to steady her wobbly legs while keeping the blanket secure around her wet body. She was mentally building up the stamina to take the first step when Eros's bare feet materialized before her eyes. "Where exactly do you think you're off to?" he demanded to know.

"I am off to die in my own bed, if you don't mind."

He smiled faintly. "I do mind. Can't you see you are too ill to walk all the way to your cabin? Who do you suppose carried you here in the first place? Besides, I have no desire to antagonize your grandfather. He's not the harmless pup Silverlake was. If you do make it to your cabin, you'll drop on your bed and stay in these wet rags until you die of consumption."

"So I'll make my peace with God and wait for the angels to come and take me."

"Have it your way." He reached for her. She swatted his hands but lost her blanket. Eros stilled. His eyes darkened at the sight of her full breasts seen through the clinging damp cloth. It did nothing to hide the firm, rosy peaks pricking it.

"Ugh, you hateful man!" She snatched the dry clothes off

the bed and pinned them to her bosom. "Fine. I'll do it myself, but you can't look! Go back!" She nervously waved him away. "Turn around! If you take one peek, I swear I'll shoot you and this time I won't miss!"

"You looked at me," he reminded her, but was already turning around.

"It's not my fault you parade your body for all to see as if it were . . ." She furiously fumbled with her wet clothes. "As if you were . . ."

"As if I were what?" he inquired with mild curiosity while keeping his back to her.

She couldn't come up with a single insult; her mind was still having trouble forgetting the sight of his magnificent, chocolate–vanilla male body. She cursed under her breath.

Eros tossed back his head and laughed. She seriously considered shooting him anyway. "May I look now?" he inquired meekly as his laughter subsided to simply annoying chuckles.

"Yes." She gritted her teeth and tied the satin belt across her navel. His linen shirt reached her knees, but his long, black-silk dressing gown spilled to her feet, cool and satiny, molding every curve like a second skin. She couldn't resist smoothing her hands along the purple and silver design embossed at the front. It was a robe worthy of royalty. Masculine and elegant.

"Comfortable?" Eros's deep voice came right above her head.

"Thank you for the generous change of clothes. I'll be leaving for my—"

"Wait for the tea." He leaned forward and yanked aside the damp coverlet. "Get under the covers. You'll feel better after you've had a cup of sweet hot tea."

Dilemma. Lying under his covers was definitely out of the question. On the other hand, she had a stack of questions she had mentally collected tonight. And she had a riddle to solve.

Eros sat in an armchair, nursing a glass of cognac. He seemed in the mood for conversing rather than intent on fulfilling his promise. She sat on the edge of his bed and reached for the cognac. The rich liquor spread a warm glow to her limbs. That and the warm dry clothes made her feel much better; in fact, she felt a kind of dreamlike sweet tranquility.

"Why did you befriend a man such as Taofik?" she braved her first question. "Anyone can see that he is evil. Even his warning to you sounded more as a threat than real concern."

Raed knocked. He entered with the tea, set it on the commode, and left. Eros got up and brought her a cup. When she refused to part with her cognac, he took the glass from her hand, spilled its contents in the tea, and fastened her fingers around the cup. He returned to slump in the armchair and sipped his cognac. "What if I told you I'm not all that different from Taofik?"

"You are not evil," Alanis stated flatly. "You have a soul, he doesn't."

"He's the craftiest bastard I've ever known. His company was a school for life."

"Why live in that inferno at all? What could have possibly made you go there?" She then inquired more delicately, "Were you a condemned criminal in Italy that you had to run away?"

Eros met her eyes across the room. "Criminal, no. Condemned, yes."

She thought about the riddle and the place he could no longer go to. "Sanah told me there were two men inside you—a serpent and an eagle. I had arrived at the same conclusion myself."

He gave her a sharp look. "Get some sleep, Alanis. It's been a long night." He walked to the ports and stared at the night. A cool breeze swirled into the cabin, swelling his shirt.

She got up and went to him. Something happened between them tonight. They connected, two spirits, unveiled. He couldn't brush it aside. She touched his shoulder. "Who are you?"

He shut his eyes. His voice was strained when he said, "I don't know . . . anymore."

"You were a slave in Algiers." Her hand slid along his arm. "Taofik said you were seeking your past and defending the Italian coastline. Are you trying to win your way back home?"

"*Mannaggia!*" He whipped around, jumping her. "You've a nosy tendency, Alanis."

"You interrogated me about everything—my family, my engagement, my past. Why is it so terrible I wish to know you better as well?"

The heat in his eyes made his blue irises glow against his bronzed skin. "Careful what you wish for, Alanis . . ." he murmured. His arms circled her waist and drew her closer. "What else did Sanah tell you about me?"

"Nothing." She squirmed uneasily.

"You didn't ask Sanah about us?"

She stared at his chin. "No."

He grinned. "Liar. Didn't Sanah tell you what was about to happen between us?" His hands delved into her damp hair and kneaded the taut muscles at the base of her scalp. Slow, circular motions. Her world spun, but this time she was floating on a cloud. "I should have brought my *tarocchi* cards." He ran the tip of his tongue over her parted lips, licking off salt. "There's one specific card that could save us buckets of coffee."

"What tarot card?" she murmured dazedly.

He put his mouth to her ear. His lips moved seductively, mouthing, "*The Lovers.*"

A slow burn of desire spread through her. She was powerfully drawn to him, but he scared her a little. He was brutal and devious, he hacked off people's heads, and where he desired, he could not love . . . She wasn't looking forward to finding herself trapped in an arranged marriage, but surrendering her virtue to a pirate would eliminate any hope of ever having a family of her own. No self-respecting gentleman would take a soiled dove for a wife, not unless he did the soiling. She took a step back, sadly shaking her head. "No, Eros. We cannot be lovers."

His jaw clenched. "If someone had told me a month ago

that I'd burn like this for a woman like you, I would have killed him. Go to bed, Alanis. The night is over."

She could not have agreed more.

CHAPTER 13

If perchance Glaucus had seen your eyes,
You would have become a mermaid of the Ionian Sea,
And the Nereids for envy would be reproaching you,
Blond-haired Nasaee and cerulean Cymothoë.
                                        —Propertius: *A dream of Cynthia*

The ruthless desert sun stalked their group of five as they rode across desolate, stony plains dotted with patches of scrub and stunted trees. The *Alastor* docked in Agadìr Harbor earlier that morning, but instead of going directly to his house, Eros loaded a train of camels with chests and three of his men and set out into the *Hammada,* the desert stretching all the way to the Atlas Mountains. He rode pillion with Alanis flanked by his arms.

He hardly spoke to her during the week they sailed from Algiers to Agadìr, exercising his turn to sulk. It was a sharp change from kissing her, caressing her, and whispering in her ear that they were meant to be lovers. She needed to somehow break the ice. "Where are we going?"

Silence. She was considering saying something else when she sensed the lightest brushing of lips against her temple. "To a small village called Tiznit, to visit my friends," Eros said.

Alanis craned her head aside and met his eyes. She couldn't decide what she saw in them. "Are you still . . . cross with me?" she asked.

As he sustained her questioning gaze, his expression softened. "No."

She was finally able to smile again. "So what does this village have to offer the traveler?"

"It's a surprise. You'll see." He clucked the camel, and they sped up ahead.

An hour later Alanis got her first glimpse of palm trees as pink walls heaved into view. A small, fortified village was etched into the flints, its houses perched one on top of the other. They took the steep trail toward it and were welcomed halfway up by eager young men in dark robes and headdresses. A ritual of greetings and inquiries as to the health of the tribe members and the state of the flock was enacted before any move to continue upward was made. When they arrived at the village, they were invited into the house of the Mukhtar, the religious elder and head of the tribe, and were received on the reception room's thick *kilim* rugs. They were immediately served with cool water, mint tea, and sugary dried fruit. Eros ordered his men to bring forth the chests and presented the Berber villagers with generous gifts. They were accepted with loud cheers.

"*Allora,* about that surprise . . ." Eros smiled at Alanis.

"There's more?" she asked incredulously. She was already enchanted with everything.

"Hanan." He beckoned one of the three girls serving them. "I'd like you to meet my friend, Alanis. She is eager to explore your lovely village. Show her around. Take her to freshen up."

He spoke English! Alanis's amazement multiplied when the girl said, "Certainly, *El-Amar.* I'd be honored to." She offered her hand to Alanis. "Welcome to Tiznit. Please, come."

"You speak English," Alanis said to Hanan once they were outside, walking along the rock parapet overlooking the breathtaking gorge below. Dry wind swelled her sailor shirt.

"My brother, Mustafa, is the house manager at Agadìr. He taught me. These are my sisters, Suhir and Nadia." Hanan gestured at the two girls accompanying them; like Hanan, they wore white tunics, ornate jewels, and colorful veils. "They are too lazy to learn how to speak English."

"You speak beautifully," Alanis said, and followed them inside a cool, cavernous tunnel in the cliff. When they emerged in the open, they were standing in a small valley encircled by tall, pink walls with the azure sky serving as a dome. A raging waterfall gushed off the opposite wall, forming a natural green pool at their feet. The three girls stripped naked, kicked off their sandals, and dove into the pool. Giggling, they splashed rainbow drops at each other.

"Join us!" Hanan called, backed by her sisters who chanted, "*Taàli, taàli! Come on!*"

Shading her eyes against the resplendent sun, Alanis surveyed the rocky walls. They did guarantee complete seclusion. One could bathe naked in this spot without a care in the world.

The water slapped at her boots, and Hanan surfaced before her, dark skin and long black curls, wet and glossy. "Come into the pool," the girl urged. "A *diffa* is to be served within the hour. Wouldn't you like to feel clean and fresh for the festive meal?"

Alanis smiled hesitantly. "Yes, I would." She pulled off her shirt and boots, and slipped out of her breeches and drawers. Snowy white and naked, she jumped into the pool. Her body sank like a gold nugget, happy to be back in its natural habitat. She came up for air, laughing. It was marvelous. "I love it!" she cried, a huge smile cracking the corners of her mouth. She swam toward Hanan. "What is the occasion for this festive meal, a local holiday?"

"The village will celebrate our engagement to *El-Amar*. My father is offering Suhir, Nadia, and me to him at this very moment. My sisters and I are very excited." Hanan giggled.

"Oh." Alanis lost her smile. A week ago he suggested they become lovers . . . She was going to roast Eros. *Slowly.* She stared at the sisters. "You seem so young, and there are three of you."

"*El-Amar* is a wealthy man. He should take many wives. My father is to be Mukhtar. He seeks *El-Amar*'s protection against the Sultan of Meknes. We are being offered as tribute." Her innocent gaze glumly raked Alanis. "Your hair is gold, your eyes reflect the sky, and your skin is the color of pearls. *El Rais* must have paid a lot more to have you."

Alanis's jaw dropped. "I beg your pardon?" Hanan looked away, so she gently touched her shoulder. "You are wrong, Hanan. I am not his wife. Are you being forced into this marriage?"

Hanan beamed again. "Not at all. It is a great honor and a pleasure. *El-Amar* is unlike any of the men in our village. He brings us gifts from all over the world; he speaks to us with respect, but also as a friend; and when you look into his eyes, they create magic. He is good and special."

He *was* special, Alanis thought, but Hanan had a very narrow impression of him. She knew him as a rich and powerful Moroccan Rais and had no idea who he really was. *Neither do you,* a grim voice asserted inside her head. But at least she knew there was much more to him than met the eye. What sort of father offered three young, naïve girls to a man like Eros? It was as cruel as serving sheep to a lion. Would Eros install them in his house away from their village and resume his life around the world? Or was *she* arguing against this union because . . . she was jealous?

"We must return to help in the kitchen," Hanan called from the ledge where the sisters were dressing. "You may stay. I will leave you a clean caftan and take your clothes to wash."

"You are very kind, Hanan," Alanis called back. She was glad to be left alone. She needed a private moment of peace and quiet, not to think of Eros and the raging emotions he stirred in her. The pool was so serene, a jewel in the desert, and she had been bathing in small tubs close to a fire all her life, watching hail pelt against her window. Swimming in the nude beneath a clear blue sky gave her the most unimaginable sense of freedom. *Eros made her dream come true.*

She swam toward the waterfall and stood before the vigorous flow. The water reached her pelvis. Clouds of spray swirled around it in a spectrum of color. Daringly, she stepped into it. A shriek of delight escaped her lips. She shut her eyes and let the thumping shower knead her sore muscles. *She was free at last.*

Noises penetrated. People were coming down the cliff passage. Alanis stepped away from the fall and was about to plunge deep into the green pool when Eros materialized at the opening. Fixed to the spot, she dazedly met his gaze. He appeared just as stunned. The voices grew louder. He signaled them to go back, but he remained. Slowly he turned around to watch her.

Alanis tensed. Her naked upper body was awash in sunlight, a glistening white contrast to the surrounding rosy red walls. Wet, golden hair snaked around her nude curves, almost reaching her hips, yet concealing nothing. She should have dived into the pool, but for some crazy reason she remained standing tall and proud, letting his hot gaze roam every nude inch of her.

His eyes glided leisurely over her milky curves; they caressed her breasts, her flat stomach, her rounded hips. He seemed terribly disappointed the rest was concealed beneath green waters.

Alanis was struck with a powerful arousal: her body came alive, her nipples hardened into tingling pebbles. A subtle rush of blood pulsated in her loins. She met his eyes. They blazed violently raw, wordlessly conveying how strongly she affected him and how feasible it was for him to take his clothes off, jump into the pool, and come after her. He took a step forward . . .

Alanis flinched. The illusion shattered, jolting her back to the lucid reality. Overcome with sudden self-consciousness, she sank nose-deep into the pool and willed him to leave.

Eros lingered for another excruciating moment, then spun on his heel and left.

Food was the last thing on her mind. Alanis sat on the warm parapet and let the afternoon sun dry her mane. *Ah*

God! How did one save oneself from such a fix? She glimpsed at her bare toes, amazed how carefree they felt, wiggling in the sand. They belonged to the brazen wench hiding beneath the white caftan. What the devil possessed her at the pool? She had always been a refined, sensible lady. How could she flaunt her body to a man? *A pirate?*

"Good afternoon."

Alanis looked up. "Oh. Hello, Hanan. Thank you for this lovely caftan." She ran her hand along the colorful stitches, reluctant to face the future wife of the man who made her body burn.

"*El-Amar* refused my father's proposal," Hanan said miserably, summoning Alanis's gaze. "He claims he cannot take a wife. His customs and religion decree that he may only wed—"

"At a specific place he can no longer go to." *And nostalgia rules his dreams.* He could not return to Italy, but he still adhered to an old Italian marriage protocol. She wondered about that, wondered if he was already married. However, one thing she did know with a certainty: He was a nobleman. "He is telling the truth, Hanan. A friend of his told me the same thing. His refusal has nothing to do with you or your sisters."

Tears filled Hanan's eyes. "He is the kindest man. He pledged his protection to our village regardless and assured my father he had personal contacts with the Sultan of Morocco."

Alanis's eyes warmed with understanding. "You love him, don't you?"

"He also said he could take only one wife." Hanan gave Alanis a tearful, accusatory look.

Alanis recalled the scene at the pool and reddened. "It is not because of me, Hanan."

Hanan sniffed. "But you are beautiful—like gold. And I've seen the way *El-Amar* looks at you. He will take you to his house, and he will make you his woman."

* * *

Alanis flipped the thin blanket aside and got to her feet. She was tired of lying on a thin pallet, imagining large hands on her body, but unfortunately not tired enough to fall asleep. She stole between the girls' pallets and crept outside. The rocky terrace was quiet. She sat askew on the parapet and collected the linen folds onto her thighs. Dark blue night studded with countless stars stretched above her in universal glory. A light breeze blew in her hair and swept one sleeve off her shoulder. She was alone at last. There was only the desert, the night, and she. She shut her eyes, inhaling the fresh midnight air. Tobacco smoke burned her nostrils. Her eyes flicked open.

"She finally noticed," a deep voice remarked in the shadows of the rocky wall.

"*Eros.*" She bolted to her feet. How did she fail to notice him—she, who always sensed his presence, his eyes on her, the vibrations of his ever-fluctuating temper?

He stood ten paces away, bare-chested, his back and boot heel propped against the rock. He appeared very large and daunting in the moonlight, with a black mood to match. Her first impulse was to flee this blue-eyed black leopard, but she decided to face him proudly. Bravely.

Eros tossed his cigar and pushed away from the wall. He crushed the burning butt beneath his boot and ambled closer, challenging her resolve. He sat down on the parapet in front of her and brought his booted foot up, resting his arm on his knee. "You may take a seat. I won't bite."

She doubted that. "I was about to leave. I only came for a moment."

"Liar." The black leopard eyed his prey. "You came up here for the same reason I did—you can't sleep. I wager a million gold *louis* our insomnia stems from the same frustration."

She stared at him woodenly. "I happen to sense a slight yawn coming so if you'll excu—"

He caught her wrist as she turned to leave. "Wait," he whispered. "Don't go. Stay with me for a while." His thumb drew slow circles on the sensitive skin above her wrist.

She stared into his eyes. *The man with the magical eyes.* "No."

He gently tugged on her hand, forcing her to stagger a step toward him. "Sit with me."

She looked away, fighting the craving stealing into her heart. "No."

Eros stood up. Again she was startled by how tall he was, tall and painfully irresistible. He released her hand, but before she enjoyed the wave of relief, he lifted her into his arms. He flung one leg over the parapet and regained his seat with her cradled in his lap. He was grinning at her.

After the scene at the pool, sitting in his lap was kindling to the way she felt—all at sea with an iron chain pulling her deeper into a gaping ocean. "Please let me go," she said.

He smiled into her eyes. "No."

Trying to wriggle off, she nudged at his chest. It was hewn of bronze, his skin warm and smooth. The urge to caress him was so strong she struggled harder to be free. "Let—me—go!"

"Stop fighting me or you'll send us both to perdition." He anchored her to his hard thighs and torso while her legs dangled over his knees. She glanced beyond them to the yawning valley below and hastily wrapped her arms around his neck. Their gazes locked. She was trembling, yet she wasn't at all cold. His jet eyebrow rose. "Surrender?"

"I don't have a choice, do I?" she replied snappishly, undone by their snug embrace.

"Who does?" Eros answered philosophically.

They sat unmoving, silent. She concentrated on the stars; he concentrated on her face. She was physically aware of him in every way. A floating jet lock tickled her neck, making her shiver. She felt his breath on her cheek and was dangerously tempted to turn her head aside and meet those soft, burning lips.

He pressed his jaw to her temple and stared ahead. "When I look at the stars, I almost believe in miracles," he whispered. "That we are not entirely alone down here. That there is a higher and nobler reason for everything we do. What do you think, Princess?" He met her gaze and was amused by her expression. "What's so shocking? Did you think despicable wretches didn't feel lonely sometimes? Well, we do, perhaps more than others. So we look at the stars and we see the Milky Way shimmering as a river of diamonds."

Alanis followed his gaze. What did he know about stars and beauty? He was a pirate, not a poet. "In Yorkshire," she said, "there are hardly as many stars to observe as here."

"In Yorkshire you see the Northern Sky. It appears less bright because you look away from the Galactic center, which has a huge population of stars, but you do see Ursa Major and Orion."

Nonplussed, she stared at him. "How do you know that?"

"I'm a seaman. I should know my way around the stars if I wish to reach my destinations. Look"—he pointed upward—"see the large square with its long arm?" She quietly nodded her head beside his jaw. "That's Pegasus. Andromeda and Perseus are right beside it. Ursa Minor is up there, and you can see Gemini, Orion, and Taurus. These stars know our secrets before we do."

She expected a volcano after the scene at the pool, not this amiable Italian who was all lazy charm and congeniality. She felt so vulnerable. A fierce need to rest her head on his shoulder and weep possessed her. Suppressing the urge, she inquired, "Which one is the Pole Star?"

"Right there." He pointed at a bright dot. "What is your zodiac sign, princess?"

"Capricorn," she murmured.

"Hmm. See the rough triangle to the left? That is Capricornus."

She studied his strong profile—tall brow, straight nose, handsome mouth. His earrings sparkled against his dark skin tone and inky hair. "What's yours?" she asked in a whisper.

"Libra. But we can't see it right now. Oh, there's Saturn."

"Libra, the dual man." She eyed the medallion resting over his heart. Eros finally noticed she was taking inventory of his person. She met his curious gaze. "What's your secret, Italian?"

He stiffened. A muscle pulsed in his jaw. "What makes you think I have one?"

"I know you do. I feel it."

"You know a lot about me, Alanis, but some things must remain hidden." He stared at her intently, and a lopsided grin appeared on his face. "I know *your* secret, though. During the course of my life I came to know a number of women, perhaps too many." He grimaced. "Now, there are *women* and there are *women,* but you are not a woman. You are . . . *una ninfa*—a nymph."

Lud. He spoke of women as if there were two kinds in the world—pure and evil ones. Yet he was unable to place her in either category, so he invented her a new one: She was a nymph.

Eros lifted a fistful of golden silk and let it catch the night breeze. "'Fountains and streams belong to the water nymphs,'" he softly recited Homer. "'On any glade or clearing one is sure to find the maiden daughters of Zeus indulging in their favorite activities of hunting and dancing, producing and raising heroes, and living in caves where water trickles constantly.'"

Alanis was unable to mask her raw feelings. "You refused to marry Hanan."

Eros considered her face. "Do you honestly believe it would have been fair to Hanan?"

"She loves you."

"She doesn't know me." He hesitated, then his voice dropped to a whisper. "You do."

Her heart beat wildly. "I know very little about you . . . I don't even know your real name."

His gaze bore into hers, full of enigmatic meaning. "There's a difference between knowing *about* someone and *knowing* someone. You know me better than you think."

Hold me, a desperate voice cried inside of her. She needed to feel his arms crushing her, not securing her from falling into the gorge. She was falling much deeper.

"If I kiss you now, I won't be able to stop," he murmured, "and you wish to return to your grandfather the same intact, pretty baggage he put on a ship weeks ago. So—go to sleep, Alanis," he suggested gently. "I'm entertaining my noble frame of mind right now. I cannot vouch for what will happen if you remain in my lap another moment."

Nodding wretchedly, she wriggled off him and dashed away.

CHAPTER 14

Alanis sensed a soft kiss on her cheek. Her eyelids fluttered sleepily, too lazy to open.

"Look ahead or you'll miss your first purple sunset," Eros said.

Her eyes opened wide. Gowned as a giant fireball, the sun was reclining into a dusky ocean while vividly painting the sky purple to inspire the world with her dying glory. A chorus of stars twinkled in the darkening skies. Alanis gasped with wonder. "How did you do that?"

He chuckled and tightened his arms around her. It dawned on her that she had shamelessly fallen asleep in his arms during their ride from Tiznit. She sat straight and stared ahead. Outlined by the purpling sky, isolated among date palms, a red fortress rose off the edge of a sharp flint.

"Welcome to my humble abode, Princess."

"That's your humble abode?" She looked at him and frowned. Lost in thought, Eros's eyes reflected the last rays of dusk and appeared just as wistful. Old pain and loss etched the very heart of those deep blue depths. She touched his cheek. "Eros. What's wrong? What are you thinking of?" What was it about this man that clawed at her heart and forced her to feel for him?

He stared at her with startling intensity. A look passed between them, more eloquent than words. He lowered his head and took her mouth with a slow, needful kiss. "I want you," he said.

A knot formed in her stomach. Only a day ago Hanan voiced her prediction of what would happen when they reached his house.

Eros urged the camel into motion, and they loped toward his house.

The *riyad* was lit with dozens of torches. As they entered the gates, a man in a white tunic exited the great arched portal. He was not alone. A golden leopard, light and swift, covered with black spots, leaped beside him as he came to greet them. Astonished, Alanis recalled, "His home a sharp flint, and at the peak of a rock stands a leopard with spots as the keeper of his home . . ."

"Greetings, Mustafa." Eros hopped off the camel and was rammed by the ecstatic leopard. "*Dolce, mia cara bimba!*" He laughed heartily and bent down to stroke the large cat. She purred with joy as she nuzzled his hand and rubbed her smooth body against him. He raised his eyes. "Mustafa, I present Lady Alanis. She is my special guest. You are to see to her every comfort."

"Welcome to Agadìr, my lady. It is an honor." Mustafa bowed. He offered her a spotlessly gloved hand and helped her dismount. "I'm the house manager. At your service."

Alanis smiled. "Thank you, Mustafa. I'm delighted to make your acquaintance."

Eros took her hand and led her up the front steps. A spotted missile lodged itself between them. Dolce raised her head and knocked their joined hands apart. Alanis shied away.

"Come here, jealous shrew!" Eros scolded. Alanis stiffened. "I was speaking to my cat." He grinned. He caught her hand and ushered her through a bottle green foyer supported by giant Roman pillars. His heels pounded arrogantly on the marble floor as they entered the portego. A golden-brown dome towered above their heads, promoted by Palladian windows to the height of several stories. Regal marble staircases curved on either side, leading to flanking halls, and a farther flight of steps rose to the gallery above the portego. A Venetian *fanò* lamp poured light over the sprawling marble spaces. Apart from tall vases bursting with flowers, Alanis noticed the house was empty. No furniture. No artifacts. Nothing. His home was an imposing cold crypt.

"This isn't an abode," she uttered with amazement. "It's a palazzo."

Eros laughed. "I've seen grander *palazzi* than this one, Princess."

"Have you really?" She cast him a perceptive smile. "Where? Venice? Florence? *Milan?*"

He smiled but said nothing.

She tilted her head back to examine the dome. Its clever scheme combined Oriental and Italian styles in a carefully judged equilibrium. "So which architect did you kidnap to do this?"

Eros's deep laughter resonated all the way up to the dome. "Regretfully, I must put another dent in your high esteem of me, *Principessa,* but I didn't kidnap Guarino Guarini to create this."

"Then who designed this house?"

He stroked his cat's small head. "I did."

"You did? Now where would a *Rais* acquire the architectural and mathematical knowledge necessary to design the scheme of such a palace?"

"At the University of Ferrara, I imagine. Come along. There's much more to see." He started toward the glass doors opening to the garden. Alanis halted abruptly. Another crest hung on the wall. The Latin inscription at the bottom read: GALEAZ MARIA SFORTIA DUX MEDIOLANI QUINTUS. Galeazo Maria Sforza, Fifth Duke of Milan. A third emblem.

"I want to show you the ocean," he whispered in her ear.

"If the crests are stolen, why are they so important to you?"

For a moment she could swear his pulse sped up. "Come. We'll talk outside."

The scent of almonds greeted them on the vine-run porch. A marble cupid spit water in a traditional Moroccan basin. They followed a tiled path lined with flower bushes and emerged on a loggia built at the edge of the cliff. Waves roared below. Alanis gripped the handrail and threw her head back, tossing her hair to the wind. "This place is lovely. It's a magical paradise."

Eros's eyes glided over her willowy figure clad in sailor's clothes. He stepped behind her and clutched the rail on either side of her. "*You* fill it with magic." He buried his face in her silky hair, inhaling its perfume. "I never had a golden nymph in my house before, and now that I do, I find myself help-lessly ensorcelled." He unclasped two buttons on her shirt and slid his hand inside. Warm and large, it came to rest on her smooth belly.

She sucked in her breath and clutched his wrist. "Eros, please don't—"

"You expect me to be calm after snuggling over me for two long hours?" He pressed his groins to her bottom and kissed her neck. "I'm on fire for you, *Amore*. How can you be so cold?"

Cold? He made her body hum. "Eros, please. You mustn't. We mustn't . . ."

"Come to my bed tonight," he whispered. "We'll have dinner in my chambers. I'll put you in my marble tub in laven-der-scented water, and while you enjoy a glass of Lambrusco, I'll wash every grain of sand off your body. *Personally.*"

Her mind liquefied at the image. "Eros, I can't," she mur-mured. "You know I can't."

"What are you afraid of, *bella ninfa?* That I'd hurt you? Treat you callously? How could I? A woman like you . . ." The hand inside her shirt slid upward and filled with her soft, bare breast. "There'll be no force, only pleasure," he said hoarsely and rolled her nipple beneath his thumb.

Staggering want assailed her. She shut her eyes and cov-ered his hand with hers. No ancient kingdom capitulated faster than she was about to before this mighty Roman conqueror.

"Say yes," his deep voice tempted. "Let me give you the

best kind of pleasure." Another hand unclasped the top button on her breeches and pushed inside.

"No!" She seized his hand and turned around. The look in his dark eyes immobilized her. It revealed more than hunger; she read defeat as well. Whatever withheld him from pursuing his seductions to completion thus far lost the battle. His iron grip of self-control was broken. Tonight no viper stood before her but a man who desired a woman, and she desired him as well, but did she dare? She'd be utterly ruined, and he was notorious for leaving a wake of broken hearts. She shook her head glumly. "No, Eros. You were right last night. I must go home . . . untouched."

"But you have been touched, Alanis. And so have I." In one fluid motion he scooped her up and started toward the house, the pounding of his boot heels echoing her drumming heart.

She struggled to her feet and skittered away from him. "You can't force me to do this!"

Eros looked as if she had thrown a pail of ice water in his face. "Alanis—"

"No." She backed away. "This is wrong. I wanted an adventure, but this has gone too far. You are a stranger to me. You want us to be lovers and yet you won't tell me your real name."

"You know my name!" he growled, although his eyes conveyed quite the opposite.

"Who's the liar now?" She finally understood what Jasmine implied when she said, *Eros is not what you think*. The Viper was only his façade. The tall Italian standing before her was someone she knew nothing about. "I know the old crests are important to you," she said. "I know you are not the monster you want people to think you are. Something happened to you when you were sixteen. It changed you and wrapped your heart with hate. It split your soul."

He took a deliberate step toward her. "I can make you want me, Alanis, so much so that life without me would seem cheap to you. That nothing but my touch would be

balm to the desperation of your love. If you challenge me—
I'll break you."

An unpleasant tremor coursed through her. "Why would
you want to break me? I am not your enemy. I want to be your
friend."

"I don't want to be your blasted friend!" He seized her
arms and pulled her to him. "I want to be your lover. I want
to bury myself inside you and make you mine. *I want you to
be mine . . .*" He kissed her roughly, savagely, unable to contain the volcano erupting from within him.

She tore her mouth away, but he wouldn't let go. Burying
his face in the crook of her neck, his breath was humid and
quick on her skin. She lifted a trembling hand and gently caressed his silky head. "Let me inside your life, Eros," she
pleaded next to his ear. "Tell me your name."

A moment passed. When his head came up, his veneer was
ice. "You want to know who I am? By all means, let me take
you on one final adventure—the *finalé.*"

The jet Arabian tore across the murky beach. Black waves
broke ashore in splashes of spray. A wall of rock rose to their
left, echoing the call of a rampaging ocean. Bleary-eyed and
anxious, Alanis clung to Eros's waist. She had serious doubts
about this madcap outing. She trusted Eros to protect her; she
did not trust his demons.

Fire flickered in the distance. Black tents blended with
the dark sands of the desert. Eros reined in and swung off the
saddle. He grabbed her waist and pulled her to the ground.

"Cover yourself," he sniped at her. "These people are not
what you're used to."

"Neither are you!" she sniped back, struggling with
another black robe he made her wear.

With a firm grip on her wrist, he marched into the obscure
encampment. They meandered between separate livestock
areas and large tents woven of sheep wool, their geometric
motifs identifying their dwellers as a Berber tribe of the Atlas

Mountains, desert traders and travelers whose movements were governed by the seasonal migration of their flock.

Aromas of roasted lamb drifted from the center of the encampment where a tall bonfire blazed. Men in dark robes sat on thick carpets, drinking, eating, and conversing in good humor. The women moved among the men, serving food and drink, their faces veiled.

"Stay close to me at all times," Eros commanded and entered the center of the *douar.*

As soon as he was spotted, men rushed to greet him and invited him to sit with the sheik. A head taller than most, with his black cape spilling off his broad shoulders, he reminded Alanis of a powerful warlock surrounded by his followers.

Eros made himself comfortable on the thick rugs and accepted a plate of roasted lamb and a cup of coffee. Alanis sat down beside him and surveyed her strange surroundings. He moved closer and adjusted her veil so that only her eyes were visible. "Are you hungry? Thirsty?"

She shook her head. The way she stared at him made him scowl. He looked away. She sat in silence while he conversed with the sheik. She followed his easy gestures, listened to his deep laughter, drank wafts of his musky scent on the ocean wind, and discovered the secret of her fascination with him— *Eros was life.* The life she never truly partook of.

The crowd cheered as a dazzling creature materialized in the firelight. Wearing a fiery red costume made of sheer scarves, she was a goddess born of the flame, her dark skin adorned with gold and glowing with the mystical aura of an ancient jewel. Flinging her long black curls over her shoulder, she fixed her eyes on Eros and smiled.

"*Leila,*" he called out in Berber. "*Dance for me!*"

Alanis's gaze stabbed his profile. Was *that* what he'd brought her here for? To watch this exquisite, sensual beauty—another one of his tarts no doubt—performing for him?

Leila served Eros with another seductive smile and whacked her gilded timbrels high in the air. A flute commenced playing an Oriental tune. Drums joined the flute, causing the shadowed ridge of mountains to throb with their mighty bangs. Leila swayed as another tongue of fire. Her red scarves soared on the night wind. Her face, her eyes, her whole body expressed the erotic abandon of the dance. The men clapped and cheered her on, and she, in turn, weaved her hands in invitation and shook her breasts to their roaring delight.

The drums went silent. Leila collapsed on the ground in a heap of flesh and veils. The flute trilled gentle notes. She gradually arched her body off the sand. She untied a ruby scarf off her hips and slowly caressed her shoulder with it, her eyes sending Eros a silent invitation.

Gnashing her teeth, Alanis glowered at him. To her surprise, his eyes were on her. He read her as fluently as she always felt his vibes. She was jealous and he knew it. He sustained her glare for another sizzling moment, then stood up and strode to the center of the ring. He lifted Leila into his arms and disappeared in the cluster of tents.

A gasp of anguish died in Alanis's throat. *He went with Leila.*

"I see you're wearing the silk scarf I gave you."

Leila unfurled a heavy woolen curtain over the tent's entry and took his hand. "Of course, *El-Amar.* I've been expecting you. I knew you would be back soon."

An oil lamp hung from the wooden beams supporting the tent. The rugs on the floor were scattered with herbs for health and luck. Eros dropped his cape on the floor and let her lead him to a cozy bed. She sat down and pulled him down beside her. "I missed you terribly, *El-Amar.*"

"Did you?" He smiled. "And how did you pass the time while I was away?"

"Doing nothing." She untied her filmy red veil. "Crying every night for you to return."

He laughed. "You are a natural born liar, Leila, but it is one of your various charms."

Laughing, Leila hurled the red scarf over his head and pulled him closer. "I'm glad you came to see me tonight. I was afraid you had forgotten about me and found someone else to please you." She eased her hands inside his open collar and splayed her bejeweled fingers over his chest. "No woman can please you as well as I can, *El-Amar.*" She lowered her head and ran her tongue along his jaw. Eros congealed. Sensing the change in him, Leila leaned closer. "What is it? Don't you want me to please you?" She took his hand and put it on her breast. When he did nothing, she snapped, "I don't understand. You are never like this, as cold as a fish . . ."

He gently peeled her hands off him and rose to his feet. "I'm sorry, Leila. You are very lovely, but I'm afraid I can't stay. *Salamat.*"

Leila sprang to her feet, her black eyes glittering murderously. "You leave me for another woman!" she screamed. "You found someone new!"

"I apologize, Leila. I'll send you a nice gift with one of my men."

"So it is another woman! I curse the Evil Eye on you!" She flung herself at him and clawed at his face. He clasped her wrists, but not before a sharp nail slashed his cheek. Leila jerked free.

Touching his cheek, he smiled sympathetically. "'Hell hath no fury as a woman scorned.'"

"Get out!" Leila heaved, pointing her finger at the opening. "Out!"

He lifted his cape off the floor, shifted the flap door aside, and left. Outside, he shook the herbs off his cape and flung it over his shoulders. Scowling, he headed back to the bonfire.

"Eros?" a voice called. "My dear friend, I cannot believe my eyes. It's really you!" A short plump man with a curly black mustachio slapped his arm and pulled him into a bear hug.

"*Sallah?*" Eros blinked incredulously, smiling. "What are *you* doing here?"

"We've spent a few weeks in Marrakech, visiting with

Nasrin's cousins and throwing away good money on things she'll never wear. Now we are on our way to board a ship in Agadìr Harbor."

"And it didn't occur to you to pay me a visit before you sailed home for England?"

"My dear fellow, had we known you were back, we would've called on you, invited or not. I heard rumors, though, that you were in Jamaica with Jasmine."

Eros rolled his eyes. "Is there anyone who is not informed about my every move?"

"Beg your pardon?" Sallah's bushy eyebrows knitted with curiosity.

"*Niente.*" Eros waved his hand. They started walking toward the center of the camp. "You are well informed, Sallah. I was in Jamaica with Gelsomina."

"And how is our sweet, beautiful girl? Getting you tangled up in her rascality again?"

"She did, but she has a new husband to chase her around now." He patted Sallah's bulging belly. "I see Nasrin is taking good care of you, my friend. Soon you will turn into a mountain."

Sallah boomed with laughter. "Nasrin's cousin, Farina, is to blame. The dear woman cooks better than your Milanese cook does. And my shrew is put out with me for overindulging."

"Stop complaining. I wish I had a wife like yours. Then, I'd resemble *Jebel Moussa* and be as content as a pig in shit."

"*Mountain Moses?*" Sallah laughed again. "Ah, Eros, if you wanted a wife, you'd be married now. How old are you? Thirty one, thirty-two?"

"Old enough."

"So what are you waiting for? Haven't you had enough women by now? Don't you know they're no good when you take them for an occasional tumble? A woman is like a good stew." He pinched the air with his fingers. "It needs to be cooked on a low fire. You need to tend to it, add expensive spices to make it richer and happy. Then, it thickens. It absorbs the qualities of the ingredients you poured in, until finally—" Sallah smooched the tips of his fingers. "Delicious!"

Eros burst out laughing. "I see you are still hungry, my friend."

Sallah looked offended. "I worry about you, and you repay me with your ridicule?"

"I humbly apologize," Eros said, still chuckling. "I know you mean well, but whom could I marry? A camp dancer such as Leila?"

"What about that Portuguese girl, Izzabu? She was a pretty piece."

"She still is," Eros admitted with a hearty sigh.

Sallah's bushy eyebrows drew together with distinct disapproval. "You amaze me, Eros. How vigorous you are to maintain a harem of your very own."

"As always, you exaggerate, but I shall take that as a compliment."

"You know what thy problem is, *huboob?* You consort with the wrong type of females."

"I know." A lopsided grin touched Eros's lips. "I should have married Nasrin myself. I've been saying that for years."

"Humph." Sallah eyed him superciliously. "You wouldn't last a day with a tough shrew like Nasrin. No, my friend, you need a woman from *your* world. One who will know your heart."

Eros's stunned look made Sallah smile with satisfaction. Fondly curling his well-groomed mustachio, he announced, "You should go home to Milan and marry a countess!"

Eros's face solidified. Very softly, he inquired, "What the devil are you rambling about?"

Sallah eyed his young friend as a mature bear eyed a wild, callow cub. "Forgive me, my friend. I often blabber idiotically and say bizarre things when I eat too much."

A distrustful look clouded Eros's eyes. "Let us move on," he suggested. They arrived at the bonfire shortly. "I shall see you both tomorrow, then," he said distractedly as his eyes glided over the gathering area with the focus of a hawk. "Convey my regards to Nasrin."

"Inform your Milanese cook that I'm on my way. These Berbers are out to poison me."

It took a damnable amount of time to steal her way toward the darker area of the camp where the livestock pens were situated. Alanis remembered all too vividly what occurred in Algiers when her hood was yanked off. She had no desire to provide these Berbers with another diversion tonight. She was not concerned about making her way back alone. She basically had to follow the coastline up north until she reached his home. There was nothing to it. She was an excellent horsewoman, and Eros could go to the devil he was on such friendly terms with.

How well he succeeded in revealing his true nature. He was a hard-hearted empty shell, corrupt through and through. There was nothing left of his soul. He was another Taofik, as he himself had proclaimed. *You should have listened when he spoke of himself,* Alanis slated herself mercilessly. *A man knows himself best.* Well, she had had enough. She was going home.

A hand fastened around her arm. "Where do you think you're off to?"

Her face was veiled in black up to her nose, but when she turned her gaze onto Eros, her slanted aquamarine eyes were glacial. *Damn you,* they spoke without a sound. *Damn you to hell.*

"Princess—"

She jerked her arm free. There was nothing more to be said.

When they arrived at Agadir an hour later, he escorted her upstairs to a tall, arched portal. He gallantly opened one of the wood and brass doors but didn't follow her inside.

"*Alanis*—" His apologetic voice stopped her beyond the threshold. She looked at him. His solemn eyes were perfect mirrors for the way she felt—wretched. Something broke inside of her. Shutting her eyes against a flood of tears, she slammed the door in his face.

CHAPTER 15

Warm sunrays spilled across her face. Smiling, Alanis sat up amid muslin drapes warmed by the sun and pitied those awakening to a dismal Yorkshire morn. Last night she heard a door slamming across the hall. Hence, her quarters had to be the ones reserved for the mistress of the house, but there wasn't one. The décor, although juxtaposing beautiful art pieces with turquoise vases full of larkspurs and lilies, gave no hint of a particular woman's touch. It was a lovely white apartment, free of Italian grandeur and not presided over by an old family crest. What sort of female did Eros have in mind for this bedchamber, she wondered.

A salty morning breeze welcomed her on the balcony. Seagulls screeched a friendly salute as they slashed the cloudless sky. A scintillating turquoise ocean broke in a splash of foam on the rough surf below and spread across a white powdered beach. Then came the stark beauty of the Sahara: sandy dunes, hot colors of desert . . . The supreme majesty of the Atlas Mountains stole her breath away. She appreciated why Eros chose to live in this fierce, primal land waiting to be discovered, but residing in an empty marble mausoleum with a wild predator as a pet seemed sad to her. *Lonely.* Nonetheless, she was leaving. She would not be made sport for him to ease his ennui. He had her blessing to devote himself to all the Jezebels in the area.

She returned inside and entered the bathing chamber. It was magnificent, with a luxurious marble basin large enough to accommodate a great plump sultan sunk into the alabaster floor. The wall was made of latticed gypsum; through it,

beads of sunlight glittered in lace patterns. She peered
through the holes. A mat of flowers, trees, and pretty pavil-
ions sprawled beneath her window. Roman statues from
Lixus or Volubilis adorned every corner, a reminder of the
proud owner's heritage. Thinking of the devil, she saw a
golden spotted body leaping up a set of stone steps. Trailing
behind, a glossy black head appeared. His dark masculinity
stood out in the sea of flowers, as it no doubt did anywhere he
roamed. The louse had a personal allure more potent than a
magnet. He seemed rather jolly strolling the gardens with his
wild cat, and why shouldn't he be? Last night he had indulged
in the abundant attentions of Leila, Queen of the Desert.

Eros halted and fixed his gaze straight at her. She jumped
back, but the latticed wall was designed to screen spaces reserved for women. He could only guess whether she was
standing there. Returning to her spying post, she rested her
forehead against the wall and peeped at him. The remorseful
look she'd seen in his eyes before slamming the door in his
face still tugged at her heart. He might be a worthless cad, but
he was not made of stone. He knew what he had done was unpardonable. He had justified her rejection. She could never
be his after that. *Never.*

After watching him wandering off, Alanis splashed her
face with cool water, combed her hair, and donned the matching negligee she had found folded on the bed the previous
night.

Moments later someone knocked. "Come in," she called,
and was startled by the flock of serving maids marching past
her, carrying mountains of chests. Mustafa brought up the rear.

"Good morning, my lady." He bowed handsomely. "I trust
you slept well?"

After drowning her pillow. "Very well. Kind of you to inquire." She followed the maids to the dressing room. They set
the chests down on the Nile-landscape mosaic floor and
started to unpack. Neither lustred silks nor gilt-stamped taffe-
tas emerged from the chests. Linen caftans, soft kid sandals,
and undergarments of modest simplicity were put in the

closet. Alanis smiled sardonically. Eros sent her local clothes, like Hanan's. The delightful pieces came not from pillaged ships but from the nearby souk. She'd appear exceptionally idiotic tossing them out the window. Besides, she had no intention of staying long enough to exhaust half the wardrobe.

"With the compliments of my master." Mustafa smiled. "I hope you will find everything satisfactory. Jenab will draw your ladyship a bath, and I will send up a breakfast tray. I strongly recommend remaining indoors. The sun is brutal today—even the pink flowers are suffering."

Alanis's eyes lit up. "Pink flowers in the sun? Mustafa, I must have my tea outdoors."

"Of course." Mustafa hid a smile and bowed graciously. "I'll return to escort you shortly."

An hour later, they were strolling among honeysuckle, rockroses, and ferns twittering with birdsong. They came upon a large terrace, where a sea green pool cleverly built at the edge of the cliff seemed to merge with the seascape. A white canvas pavilion stood at the end of their path.

Mustafa halted. "The *menzeh* borders the rose garden, my lady, as you requested."

The pavilion was charming. Instead of a roof, an overgrown trellis supported by the eaves provided welcome shade. In its background, a rose garden bloomed. A gust of air flapped the canvas lid open. She saw a bundle of gold and black spots slouching beside black suede boots.

"Eh, Mustafa . . ." Alanis glanced aside, but he had conveniently vanished. She stared at the pavilion. Eros was drinking coffee and reading a book. She was considering adopting Mustafa's dull suggestion to breakfast indoors when Eros raised his head. Surprised then curious, he leaned back in his chair and waited to see what she would do. *Hmm.* Returning to her apartment would suggest she found his presence unsettling. It was the last thing she cared to do. Furthermore, she needed to inform him of her decision to leave as soon as possible. Head raised, she took the path.

As soon as her toe touched the Berber rugs, Eros was on his feet. He pulled out a chair for her. "*Buongiorno,*" his deep voice spoke over her shoulder. She glanced at him. The uneasiness reflected in his eyes balanced the mad thumping of her heart.

"Good morning," she replied icily. The green-eyed leopardess raised her head and growled.

"I apologize for Dolce's ill manners. She isn't used to females other than my sister."

So he didn't entertain his lovers in his house. Was she supposed to be flattered? "What is your excuse?"

"I have none." He grinned, his eyes shining ultramarine in his tanned face. His jaw was smoothly shaven; his jet mane was combed into a queue. A rush of longing overcame her, until she noticed the angry scratch on his cheek. Contempt cooled her blood, and she sat down rigidly.

Eros sat opposite her. Blatant approval shone in his eyes upon noticing she wore one of the caftans he'd sent her—a white linen tunic embroidered with topaz. Washed to a shine, her hair flowed around her. Yet she found his reaction odd. Hadn't Leila's tender care quenched his lust that he should stare at her as though he contemplated spreading butter and marmalade on her cheek? On the scale of filmy red veils, Alanis stood depressingly close to the nunnery mark. She might have appreciated his interest if it weren't for the scratch. She couldn't bear to look at him.

An old volume lay on the table in front of him, titled *Dante.* The supposed pirate had excellent taste in literature, and knowing Eros he was most likely able to quote half of it. "'There can be no knowledge without retention,'" she quoted one of the Tuscan poet's famous lines.

"Show-off." He defiantly flashed his strong white teeth. He propped his elbows on the white tablecloth and cupped his face, a silly grin lifting the corners of his mouth.

What was wrong with him this morning? She frowned

speculatively and studied the warm glow of his irises. Clear as iolites, she concluded, canceling out high fever. The iolite gem was made legendary by the seafaring Vikings who believed in the stone's powers to filter the haze and glare from their eyes. Annoyingly, his eyes had the reverse effect on her.

Snapping his fingers and her silly thoughts with it, Eros summoned a footman. "What would you like for breakfast?" he asked her.

"Tea would be nice." She looked at the ocean. It almost compensated for the scratch.

He sent the footman to the kitchen and subsided in his chair. He laced his fingers over his flat abdomen. "I wish to repent. I, eh, seemed to have lost my head as well as my manners last night." His eyes came up, questioning. "I humbly apologize and beg your forgiveness."

Alanis considered his rueful gaze. "Don't concern yourself. Last night opened my eyes to the true nature of our association. Which is why I'd appreciate it if you put me on a ship sailing for England at the earliest convenience."

Alarm widened his eyes. "The true nature of our association? Alanis—" He leaned closer, reaching for her hand, but she pulled it back. He meant to say more, yet reined in his words, assuming any added word would only work against him. His eyes filled with remorse. "You've no idea how much I regret last night. If I could, I'd retract it to the point we reached my house."

"And then what?" she asked pithily. If she cared to preserve her sanity, she would have to erase the memory of him caressing her body on the dark, ocean-fronting loggia from her brain.

"Then, I would escort you to your apartment as a proper *gentiluomo* and say good night."

Understandable, she thought acidly, when one had been forced to rush it up with the Sahara Delight because of a confounded nuisance. "It's too late, Eros. I wish to go home."

"I wish you'd stay. At least for a few days."

She had a sudden urge to shoot him. "Whatever for? What

could possibly tempt me to stay? And why are you anxious for me to stay with you all of a sudden? You have Frenchmen to kill, do you not? And as I recall, you were quite adamant that night we left Kingston when you informed me that you had no desire to take me anywhere but home. What changed?"

His eyes were terribly serious when he said, "You have no idea." After a long pause of silence, he said in a lighter tone, "I'm expecting good friends to call on us this morning. They'll stay for a week. You'll like them."

"I've already met some of your friends. Sorry. Not to my taste."

"Look, they should be here any minute. They are a charming, worldly, warmhearted Jewish couple from London. Sallah is half English, half Moroccan, and he's my business partner. His wife, Nasrin, is a full-blooded Moroccan. She's all Oriental charm, the daughter of one of the finest jewelers in Marrakech, and a true lady. They have eight daughters and make an interesting divertimento. Please say you'll stay."

His Jewish business partner and his charming wife? Her interest was piqued.

The servant returned. With great care, he set down a teapot, a plate of warm scones, butter, orange marmalade, silver cutlery, fine Italian porcelain dishes, and a folded linen napkin in front of her. Eros delayed him with a commanding hand. "If you would rather have something else . . ."

"No, thank you."

He released the footman. "I don't eat heavy breakfast either," he remarked good-naturedly.

She eyed the tall mountain of peelings that appeared to have covered four large oranges piled on the plate before him and smiled wryly. "I see what you mean."

"*Bisogna mangiare quallcosa.*" He shrugged guiltily. "One needs to eat something."

She ignored his smarmy grins, stirring sugar in her tea. Eros resumed his staring.

"I have a confession to make." He smiled sheepishly. "I

asked Mustafa to persuade you to have breakfast with me out here. I was afraid you'd say no. I'm glad you consented."

"You should pay your man better wages, Eros. His crafty ways outshine Hassock's, my grandfather's man, who's legendary for his antics. Mustafa practically made me beg to have my breakfast outdoors. I was nowhere the wiser."

"I'll be sure to remember that." He leaned forward. The light wind swelled his white shirt, revealing his chiseled chest. She almost forgot what a cad he had been last night. Almost. "About my friends," he said. "I'd very much like you to meet them, and vice versa. And . . . I do want us to be friends, Alanis. I don't know what came over me last night."

Nor did she, but she had been frightfully tempted to yield. She almost felt grateful Leila's destructive shadow hovered between them now. Almost. "Friends share secrets," she said softly.

Eros's eyes turned opaque. "Give me time."

"I'll reconsider your offer when I meet your friends."

Looking hopeful, he resumed watching her every gesture. He watched her selecting a scone off the freshly baked pile; he watched her slice it through the middle, then spread it with butter. His hand reached out and subtly nudged the marmalade crystal saucer closer to her plate.

She dropped the scone. "What the devil is the matter with you this morning? You act as though you've never had breakfast with a female before."

"I haven't."

"I find this hard to believe." She averted her gaze to the azure seascape. "It's beautiful out here," she murmured distractedly.

"Very beautiful," Eros agreed huskily. "Forgive me?"

She met his hopeful gaze and sipped her tea. "I appreciate the garments you sent me."

"*Scusa?*" Eros blinked. He seemed muddleheaded this morning.

"Have I suddenly grown a beard?" she inquired with mounting vexation. "What is it?"

Two dimples appeared in his cheeks. "*Niente*," he answered affably, shrugging.

Her eyes narrowed. "Why don't I believe you?"

Eros grinned innocently. "I wouldn't know."

Unable to tolerate his pleased disposition a moment longer, she dropped her napkin and stood. "Coming here was a mistake. I should have breakfasted in my room." She left the table.

He bounded after her. His arms swept around her waist and pressed her back to his broad chest. He ran his face along her neck, deeply inhaling the floral scent clinging to her skin. "Don't leave just yet. I love having your company for breakfast. How did I ever manage without it?"

Her body's response to his was electrifying. She couldn't find the strength to break free from his embrace. But when his tongue licked inside her ear and his hand stole around her breast and squeezed, her resolve returned with a vengeance. "Take your bloody hands off me. Now!"

The instant he released her, she fled toward the house, hearing behind her a torrent of self-reproaching expletives. She nearly collided into the pair of strangers.

"Ah, goody! We're just in time for breakfast." The plump, mustachioed gentleman rubbed his hands with satisfaction. Long, elegant fingers closed on his arm with subtle yet lethal force. On one of them sat a large, oval diamond, the color of which matched the woman's silk sienna frock.

"You've *had* your breakfast, dear," said the tall, slender lady. Alanis instantly recognized the superb quality of her garments. An exquisite shawl threaded with gold covered her coal-black hair, revealing the silvery streaks at her temples. She radiated intelligence and warmth.

Her husband flushed. "What? Those few odds and ends the Berbers scraped for us hours ago? Hearing you, Eros might get the wrong impression that we've come from a banquet." He urged his wife onward and came to a sudden halt. "Can't believe my eyes!" His dark bushy eyebrows popped at the sight of the golden-haired young woman standing before them.

His wife noticed her as well. She shushed her husband and glided forward with a friendly smile. "Good morning. I'm Nasrin Almaliah, and the ill-mannered individual behind me is my husband, Sallah. Pleased to make your acquaintance." She swept an elegant curtsey.

"My pleasure, madam." Alanis returned the curtsy, feeling slightly timid. "I'm . . . Alanis."

"Lady Alanis," Eros corrected, materializing right beside her.

Nasrin's black eyes twinkled. "Why, my dear, you're English. How delightful. Sallah"—she glared at her shocked husband—"don't be rude. Come and meet Lady Alanis." She returned her approving smile to Alanis. "She's a charming young woman."

The gentleman approached tentatively, his large belly bouncing. Alanis stole a glimpse at Eros. The possessive look in his eyes, his arrogant airs—was he showing her off?

"Nasrin," he drawled warmly, brushing a kiss on her fingers. "You are as beautiful as ever, my genteel lady. Why do you put up with this gluttonous Jew when you can have me?"

Nasrin laughed. "That is one of the world's greatest mysteries, *El-Amar.* Well, Sallah." She looked at her husband with amusement. "Found your tongue yet?"

Eros's grin broadened at Sallah's bewilderment. "Sallah, allow me to introduce my friend, Lady Alanis. I told her all about you, so I'm counting on you to make a good impression, and"—He glanced at Alanis—"perhaps improve her impression of me as well."

"Certainly, certainly. Pardon my rudeness." Sallah gently took Alanis's hand and inclined his head politely. When he looked up, his eyes warmed. "My dear Lady Alanis, you have no idea how delighted I am to meet you. Indeed, the mere sight of you fills my heart with hope."

Alanis blinked at his odd greeting. Eros sighed. "You're an old woman, Sallah." He curled his arm around his friend's beefy shoulders and steered him toward the pavilion. "Come, *Jebel Sallah.* Let me treat you to another breakfast."

"By God, you're a shameless rogue, Eros," Sallah complained as they walked away. "You couldn't tell me about her last night?"

"Later, Sallah."

"What were you doing coming out of Leila's tent?" Sallah whispered incompetently. "For heaven's sake, what is the matter with you? Can't you tell a good thing when you have it right under your gentile nose? What else do you need—a knock on the head?"

Nasrin smiled at Alanis. "Men!" She rolled her eyes, and they both laughed. She curled her arm around Alanis's. "Let us join them before *Mountain Sallah* devours all the food, shall we?"

Annoyed at the numerous intruders, Dolce growled her displeasure and stalked away.

"Eros tells me you have eight daughters and live in London," Alanis addressed Nasrin once they joined the table. By now, the men were deep in war news and its impact on market prices. She didn't miss Eros's glances, though. The villain's mind was a busy, multiroute shipping line.

Nasrin opened her reticule and proudly produced miniature portraits. "This is my eldest, Sara. She's expecting our first grandchild. And this is Talàa. She's about your age. She'll be married in Passover." She lowered her voice, asking, "What brings you to Agadìr, my dear?"

Alanis lifted her eyes from the lovely faces and met Nasrin's curious gaze, but before she got a chance to embark on the abstract version of her story, a footman approached Eros.

"Nasrin, Sallah, what may I offer you?" he inquired.

"Tea will do for me, *El-Amar*. Thank you," Nasrin replied.

Sallah, whose mouth was already stuffed with a buttered scone, frowned thoughtfully. "I'll have runny eggs and potatoes and toast and strong Turkish coffee," he slurred his words, but the general idea was understood—he was hungry. Eros burst out laughing.

"May God have mercy on you." Nasrin sighed with exasperation.

"Hush, virago wife," Sallah scolded indignantly. "And you, too, rogue!"

"*Va bene, d'accordo.*" Eros chuckled, raising his hands in surrender.

Alanis observed the friendly couple, amazed how Eros had managed to snag himself such an excellent pair of friends who truly seemed to like him. He must have noticed her approval, for he smiled at them with pleasure. "I trust you'll be staying the week. You must be exhausted after looting every souk in Marrakech," he offered warmly.

Sallah looked at his wife. She nodded. "Of course we will!" he declared. "We'd love to."

As Sallah attacked his second breakfast, Eros locked his gaze with Alanis's. He made sure she would be staying as well, but her fleeting look at his bruised cheek was a message in itself.

"Well, do you intend to explain or must I bleed it out of you?" Sallah selected a cigar from a box resting on the library's tea table and scratched a match. Unlike the rest of the house, Eros's library was richly furnished with Berber pieces and decorated in dark green *djibs* work.

Pushing away from the brick fireplace, Eros ambled along the bookshelves. He halted at the wine cabinet. "Must you always stick your mustachio into other people's business?"

"We're partners, *ya habibi!* Your business is my business." Sallah puffed on his cigar. Two cushions away on the bottle green couch, a spotted bundle began coughing.

"What do you want to know?" Eros selected a Murano decanter and filled half a snifter.

Sallah's brow furrowed at the sight of his young friend reaching for cognac at such an early hour but kept his opinion to himself. "Tell me everything! Where did you find this lovely, fair Venus and what is going on between you? I know you are not lovers," he added pointedly. "The lady is seriously incensed with you."

Eros stared out the window. It gave onto an ancient olive grove. The women were chatting in the shade. "She wants to travel the world. She appointed me her guide and escort."

Sallah boomed with laughter. "Good God! Of all the people in the world she chose *you?* But how did it all come about? Out with it! My curiosity is killing me."

Eros's brooding eyes drew to the vision of flowing gold and catlike eyes resting against an old olive tree. "She's incensed with me because I took her to the camp last night to see Leila."

"*You did what?*" Sallah nearly came off the couch. "You took a sweet, well-bred girl to see that trollop taking her veils off? What is wrong with you? It isn't at all like you to—" He paused, his eyes rounding. "She was there when you hopped into Leila's tent for a quick toss? Where the devil was Alanis? Did you leave her with the Berbers at the bonfire?"

Eros evaded the glower. "I only stayed with Leila for a minute. I was making a point."

"Don't rub my ears with that. What point could you've possibly wished to make? That you can degrade Alanis to dust because you keep unsavory bedmates all over the world?" He shook his head. "I'm surprised at you, Eros. You used to handle rejection better than that."

Eros's eyes were dark, gloomy hollows. "She pressed the wrong issue." He came over and slouched beside the suffering cat. She snuggled close and put her dotted head on his thigh. "Sallah, you recall my telling you that Gelsomina is married? She married Alanis's fiancé."

Sallah's eyes narrowed shrewdly. "And you had nothing to do with that?"

"I intervened," Eros conceded, "but not for the reason you think. Gelsomina was in love with the Englishman. I had to get Alanis out."

Sallah looked beyond words. "So you snatched her away from her sweetheart, brought her to your lair in the desert, and when she didn't yield to your ruthless charms, you dragged her out at night to watch you seducing another female. Admirable." He pumped on his cigar.

Indignation and annoyance clashed in Eros's eyes. "Silverlake was not her sweetheart. She didn't give a damn whit about him. She wanted to come with me," he bit out vehemently.

"Did you say Silverlake? *The Pirate Hunter?*" Sallah choked, puffing out smoke as an erupting volcano. "Good God! And you approved?"

"Silverlake is a decent sort. Not my first choice for Gelsomina, but she seems to like him. He's a better match than I thought possible."

"What the devil are you blathering about? Jasmine is every man's dream. She's beautiful, spirited, intelligent. She could have had her pick."

Eros slammed his hand on the couch. "You don't need to list my sister's attributes to me! She should have married a king. Alas, she's not an only child."

"You're ruining my digestion, Eros. What's so terrible about you that Jasmine need be ashamed of her family connections?"

Eros fixed Sallah with a mordant glare. "*Allora,* for one, her brother is a professional killer, but also a selfish bastard. I should have left her in Italy. There were other options. She shouldn't have ended up in Algiers. It *is* an inferno, and I should have known better than to drag my little sister down with me into that pit of reptiles."

Sallah eyed him thoughtfully. Though they shared ten years of friendship, Eros's past was still considered taboo. No man was privy to the Viper's secrets. One thing Sallah knew with a certainty—his proud Italian friend was no peasant. "I understand," he granted. "You could have arranged for her to stay with a respectable family, but you wanted her with you. You love her. Sounds reasonable to me. Growing up with strangers, even respectable ones, is not always the best solution, my friend. I believe you made the right choice."

"I appreciate your good opinion, Sallah, but I disagree. I

deprived her of the better life. My responsibility was to do exactly the opposite."

"The gal is happily married. All's well that ends well." Smiling, Sallah blew out a cloud of smoke. Looking utterly miserable, Dolce coughed at the smoke cloud drifting her way.

"You're choking my cat, Sallah," Eros muttered. "Put that thing out."

Sallah crushed his cigar in an ashtray. "If I recall correctly, this Silverlake fellow was rumored to be affianced to the . . . Upon my word! Your blond Venus is the Duke of Dellamore's granddaughter! Queen Anne's personal consultant and a particular friend of Marlborough's!"

"So she is." Eros exhaled as he lovingly stroked the soft fur on Dolce's small head.

"You astonish me, Eros, how eager you are to play with fire. He who sleeps over a mine the match of which is already lit may consider himself in safety next to you."

"As is always the case, you exaggerate." Eros ran his hand along Dolce's delicate spine.

Sallah scowled. "You are digging yourself a grave, my friend, a deep, dark, unholy grave. Her grandfather will have your head for this. You can't keep a woman like her stashed with you alone in your private home. She's the sort you're not even supposed to look at."

An angry muscle bunched at Eros's jaw. "I can look at her as much as I want!"

Sallah smiled sympathetically. "I understand why you enjoy her company, but you have to take her back. You don't need this trouble. You have enough to go around as it is."

"She stays."

Sallah smiled. "So the unattainable has fallen. Who would have believed . . . ?"

Eros's dark eyes shot to Sallah's happy face. "What is that suppose to mean?"

Sallah chuckled. "It means, my friend, that I don't envy

you in the least. You're in for it now, *huboob!* You're finally about to suffer as the rest of us do!"

A thunderstruck expression hit Eros's face. Sallah exploded with laughter.

CHAPTER 16

"These are lovely." Alanis called Nasrin's attention to a pair of pointed red slippers put on display at one of the stalls. Agadir souk offered a variety of goods: rugs, lamps, spices and herbs, silver brooches embedded with stones, and animals. At one stand mint tea was being brewed; at another pottery was manufactured on sight. Family groups walked by, burdening their donkeys.

"The *babouches* are lovely," Nasrin agreed. "We should buy a pair for little Rachel. Sallah! Hand over your sack of coin and go check the camel sale over there."

Grunting, Sallah gave her a handful of coins and stalked away.

Alanis felt a hand lightly touching her shoulder. "You like these?" Eros asked.

She looked up. The warmth in his eyes dissolved her. She missed him. Dreadfully. But the lady had declined, so he kept his distance, only the effect was an agonizing void growing bigger inside her each day. His apartment lay opposite hers. She knew when he came, when he left, when he retired to bed. Sometimes, late at night, she heard his boot heels halting outside her door. Lying abed she'd listen, wondering what she would do if he came to her. He never did.

"You look beautiful, Princess," he whispered, his eyes sweeping her from head to toe. She wore a white caftan and a robe made of turquoise-dyed silk. Her aquamarine eyes shone over the filmy turquoise veil pinned to her hair. "I challenge the Sultan of Constantinople to find a single fair, cat-eyed nymph in his entire harem. You outshine all of his wives, *Amore.*"

Blushing, she lowered her eyelashes. Since the night at the camp he had changed; his harsh edge was gone, and now there was only this handsome Italian who conducted himself with the grace of a prince. It was hard to get used to him.

Eros turned to the vendor. "Rachid, how much for the red slippers?"

Rachid stated a price, and without asking for any abatement Eros reached inside his pocket. Alanis smiled. It was all very well, perhaps, for any gentleman at the souk to drive a bargain, but not for a man who had the bearing of a prince. A playful glint lit her eyes. She closed his fist. "A pirate once told me that one must haggle with the vendors. Otherwise, they get insulted."

A wide smile attacked his lips. "He did, did he?"

"But perhaps you'd rather inspect the camel sale with Sallah? I'll be fine with Nasrin."

His smile died. "I didn't come here to inspect camels. I came here for you. But never fear. I'll stay out of your way." He inclined his dark head and turned to leave.

On impulse she grasped his cambric shirtsleeve. "You are not in my way." She was tired of the cold war she was faring against him. In her heart she had forgiven him for Leila.

"Here." He dropped the coins in her hand. "Haggle your red slippers away from Rachid."

"Thank you." She chinked half in her pocket and offered a smaller sum to the vendor. The man glimpsed at the coins and shook his head, protesting loudly. Eros laughed.

"What is he saying?" Alanis murmured beside Eros's ear.

"He says he'd go out of business if all his customers were cheap misers like you and that the slippers are worth at least twice as much."

"Twice as much?" Alanis lifted one red shoe and stuck a finger in it. "See? A hole." She wiggled her finger at the astonished vendor.

"*Mish mumkin!*" He shook his head and took the shoe. After kneading the soft goatskin he handed it back with a mild, confident smile. The hole had mysteriously disappeared.

"Fine." She put another coin on the scale. "That should be enough."

Objecting, the vendor exhibited his plain tunic and pointed at the five little boys wrestling in front of the stall. Alanis smiled at their youthful faces, but they stuck out their tongues at her. Eros began translating Rachid's words. She stopped him. "I understand. He is a poor man with five children to feed." Genuine concern clouded her eyes. "Eros, perhaps I should pay—"

"Don't believe everything he says. I know Rachid. He is a successful merchant. Go on."

The negotiations continued, yet once Rachid realized how attached she had become to the red slippers he refused to set a reasonable price. She gave up the effort and collected the coins. "Your babouches are too expensive for my taste, sir. Good day." She left in search of Nasrin.

Eros propped his elbow on the counter, his eyes following the turquoise silk drifting away. "You've lost, Rachid. She's a tough little dealer."

"She's a pretty dealer." Rachid's eyebrows lifted inquisitively. "Do you want to buy her the babouches yourself, *El-Amar,* or do you want me to get her back?"

Eros gave him a dark smile. "Get her back."

Rachid bent over the counter and yelled at the top of his lungs, "Pay as you will, *Lalla!*"

Alanis halted. When Eros saw her brilliant smile, he tipped his head back and laughed. Smugly satisfied, she returned to renegotiate. Two additional coins sealed the bargain. Rachid's eyes twinkled as he wrapped the slippers. "She is charming, *El Rais.* My compliments."

"Thank you, Rachid." The men warmly shook hands.

Alanis investigated Eros's face. "You were cheating!"

Eros looked shocked. "*Io?* No, no." He pointed his thumb

at the grinning vendor while whispering behind his hand, "Rachid was cheating."

"You were both cheating!" Her shocked smile split into peals of laughter, infecting the two men. "I'll never do business with you again. With either of you!"

Chuckling, Eros accepted the parcel and took her hand. "*Andiamo, Principessa.* Let's get something to eat. *Arrivederci, Rachid!*" He saluted the vendor and started off.

Hand in hand, they continued down the busy alley. She was in high spirits and still smiling.

"Thank you for the slippers," she said brightly.

"*Prego.* Don't mention it." He squeezed her hand. Truce was declared; they were friends again. He seemed just as pleased. He wore his hair loose today, and it whipped at his shoulder blades, making him appear larger and utterly compelling. A silver-purple thread adorned his shirt cuffs, his lethal *shabariya* was strapped to his hip, and a silver-handled pistol was shoved barrel down the front of his breeches. A pirate–prince. She looked at the parcel he carried—his gift for her. The caftans she would leave behind, but not the babouches. They would be her memento of Eros in the years to come. She offered him back the remaining coins. He looked amused. "Keep them. In fact, I should have given you something nice days ago. I'll rectify that tonight."

"You don't have to give me presents, Eros." She wasn't a kept woman. Not *his woman.* Buying her funny red slippers was one thing, but showering her with expensive gifts men bestowed upon their mistresses was quite another.

"I want to. I know you've always had every delightful treasure women crave, Alanis, but surely if I put my mind to it, I'll find one little oddity your grandfather hasn't given you yet."

She met his solemn gaze. Gently, she said, "I'm not a difficult person to please, Eros, but I think you should save your gifts for others more . . . appreciative than I."

A muscle throbbed in his jaw. He understood. "I'm hungry," he said after a while, radiating his good mood and vigor once again. "Let's find something interesting to exercise our jaws."

A sharp movement in the crowd caught Alanis's eye. A scrawny-looking boy not older than ten snatched a watermelon off a busy fruit stall. He managed two paces before the large fruit slipped from his bony arms and crashed to the ground, squirting juice, black seeds, and red fleshy chunks. Mayhem ensued. The vendor became aware of the theft and rallied his colleagues. They set into pursuit after the boy. Standing at the village well, Alanis and Eros avidly followed the scene. The livid vendors caught the boy and hauled him to the stone platform.

"What will they do to him?" Alanis inquired apprehensively.

"What they do to thieves. They'll chop his hand off."

"*Chop his hand off?*" She gripped his arm. "Eros, you must do something. Help him."

The boy squealed as one man restrained him while another wrapped a rope around his wrist. They secured the boy's hand to the stone ledge, positioning it for the chopping. Terrified, Alanis's eyes fixed to the small hand as it strained against the rope, trembling.

"Eros!" Her fingernails dug into the steely muscles on his arm. "Do something. Please."

"Not yet," he stated with maddening calm.

She glared at him. "Are you waiting for the knife to grow dull or the boy to save himself?"

"That would be preferable. Either way, the boy needs to learn his lesson first."

"And what lesson would that be? That stealing is bad? How can you be such a hypocrite?"

"The lesson is not to get caught the next time." He left her side, disappearing in the crowd.

Bristling, she marched straight into the gathering mass, intent on offering her coins for the boy's hand. The mustached man who secured the rope hoisted a huge butcher's knife. "No!" she cried, desperately pushing to the fore. Someone shoved her, and she fell. Her knees and hands hit the stone-flagged ground a split second before the knife came down on the ledge, splitting chips of stone in every direction. She braced herself for the harrowing sight of the mutilated hand.

The little hand hadn't been severed. The boy had vanished. Uproar broke. People shouted, searching around for the boy, but there was no sign of him anywhere. Alanis exhaled with relief.

"Come on." Eros grabbed her hand. He had the scrawny thief hoisted over his shoulder. They forged a path through the tide of people until they reached a secluded alley. Eros peeled the boy off his shoulder. He gave him several coins and a pat on the head to send him on his way. The boy cast him a sunny smile, his black eyes alight with awe, then sprinted off.

Stunned, Alanis stared at the dark-headed pirate at her side. "You saved him."

He slid her a lazy glance. "So I'm not the rotten bastard you think I am, or was I moving too slowly for your satisfaction?"

She held her bruised hands, not quite sure how to apologize. He gently took her hands and examined the cuts. "We should rinse them in cold water," he said. "Let's return to the well."

"What you did for the boy, it was the kindest thing. Thank you." On impulse, she stood on tiptoe, lifted her veil, and touched her lips to his. Eros caught his breath. He moved closer to prolong the contact with her mouth, but she drew back. Reluctant to meet his gaze, she started walking, her heart beating wildly. He drew alongside her, and they continued in silence.

When they reached the well, Eros insisted on rinsing her hands. His gentle touch reminded her how much she had hungered for it. She peeked at his stern profile. "The little thief was very fortunate you were in the souk today. Do you suppose he learned his lesson?"

Eros examined her hands. Clean of dirt, the bruises seemed less severe. "He won't wake up tomorrow to discover the world is a nice place. He must learn how to survive it. He had to taste his fear to better protect himself in the future, avoid mistakes, and always be prepared."

He spoke from his own experience of the tough school of life he graduated, she concluded. For him, the world was a hard, ugly place where only the strong prevailed. She remembered the story he had told her in Algiers about stealing an orange. "You once found yourself in a similar predicament, didn't you? You knew the terror the boy was suffering."

"When I was a boy, I had no idea there was such a thing as hunger in the world."

Alanis blinked. He was constantly confirming her suspicions regarding his origins, but who was he that he had lived such a sheltered childhood, one so above the ordinary? "So it happened to you when you were a little older. It still honed you in some way."

Eros came to a halt. He looked frightfully serious. "What are you talking about?"

She had the vague impression he was thinking of a different incident. "You told me they had caught you once in Algiers stealing an orange and had intended to chop off your hand."

"Oh, that. I had a dagger in my sash when they caught me stealing that orange. I spent a few long minutes bewailing my bad luck before it occurred to me to cut the rope."

"Why did you leave Italy, Eros? Surely your life there could not have been much worse than the difficult lives these people must endure."

"You think life in Italy is easy because it is a rich country? I envy these people, *Amore*. They are content people with simple needs and simple lives. We should all be so blessed."

"Wasn't your life simple where you grew up?"

"Simple?" He smirked. "Where I come from, war is business and a way of life. Wait here. I'll be back in a minute." She saw his broad back disappearing among the opulent fruit stalls, but in her mind she saw galloping warhorses, villages on fire, the barbaric hordes raiding Rome. He couldn't have referred to that. He had spoken of Italy's more recent history:

ambition, treachery, avarice, inner strife settled with the sharp edge of the sword. What role had Eros played in his country's gory past? She thought of his emblems and knew it had something to do with Milan.

Eros reappeared with a ripe melon. "Let's find a quiet corner, shall we?"

They took a turn into a whitewashed alley and sat down spartanly on a flight of steps. Eros broke the large fruit over his knee, scooped out the seeds, and offered half of it to Alanis. She removed her veil and tried to dig out the juicy flesh. Eros simply buried his nose and teeth in it. Scented juice trickled off his chin and oozed along his neck. She smiled at his smudged face.

"Your technique is inspiring," she remarked with amusement.

His eyes sparkled. "Eat! So that I'll make sport of you as well."

"Aye, aye, Captain!" She sank her face in the sweet cup and devoured a cool, sugary bite.

"You look much better," Eros observed, choking her with laughter. "Do you forgive me?"

Her laughter died. "For Leila?"

"I couldn't touch her that cursed night we rode to the camp. I took her to her tent, then left. Ask Sallah. He was there. Kept me for an hour, haranguing me on the benefits of taking a wife."

Her pulse accelerated sharply. He couldn't touch Leila. "I forgive you."

His juice-dripping face brightened up. "Thank you. Now tell me about Dellamore. Tell me about your home. I want to know." Genuine curiosity lit his eyes.

"Well, it's rather dull, I should say. Dellamore Hall is a massive Gothic thing, surrounded by hills and forest. There's a fish pond, where I swim on occasion during summertime."

"Go on," he urged, brushing a yellow seed off the tip of her nose.

She frowned, finding his interest bewildering. "Last winter

we had pheasant poachers, but the sheriff popped them off. The culprits are now poaching rats in prison."

He looked relieved. "Bless the good sheriff."

"Don't jest." She playfully slapped his arm. "I've yet to tell you about our grand library."

"Aha!" He smiled broadly. "The famous library. English bards and Greek philosophers."

"And a Roman poet or two . . ." She pouted thoughtfully.

He laughed. "Our friend Ovidius! No library is complete without an interesting Roman."

"There is such a thing—an interesting Roman?" she asked in all seriousness. In retaliation, he pressed her melon cup to her face. She gushed with laughter. "Tell me about your home."

His expression shuttered. "My home doesn't exist anymore."

She searched his deep blue ocean eyes, wondering which demons dwelled there. "Please."

He sighed. "There's nothing to tell. The lowly serf had a hamlet once and now it's gone."

"Eros." Her fingers closed gently around his wrist. "Tell me one thing about your home."

He stared at her hand. "The land that was once my home guzzled the blood and the souls of those I loved along with everything else that mattered. Gelsomina is everything I've left of it."

She felt his buried pain so strongly her heart welled with sadness. "Is this the reason you keep your house empty— because it cannot replace the home you've lost?"

A vulnerable, bewildered look etched his eyes. "Yes."

"No wonder you live so wildly and fully, as if there are no tomorrows." She felt a sudden need to hold him and provide what little solace she could. She leaned closer and pressed her lips to his. He remained as still as a statue and quietly submitted to her kiss. So she wrapped her hand around his nape and ordered in a whisper, "Kiss me."

Only then did Eros respond.

* * *

Someone knocked on her door. Alanis knew it wasn't Nasrin. Her long fingernails rapped lightly. Nor was it Mustafa's distinct scratch. This particular knock was an outright command to open the gates and surrender the fort. She opened the door.

"*Buonasera*," Eros greeted her in his easy manner, his forearm leaning on the gilded beam. There was nothing nonchalant in the way he stared at her. "May I come in?"

"Cer . . . certainly." Alanis stepped back to let him pass. Eros straightened away from the door frame and entered. Immaculately dressed in a blinding white lawn shirt and black breeches, he sauntered into her room. There wasn't a hint of purple in his entire heart-stopping appearance.

Her gaze followed his tall, dark frame as he moved about her bedchamber. He propped his shoulder against a brass bedpost. "A white palace for the white princess." His lambent blue eyes swept the bed, then found her gaze. "You're leaving me in two days. Only two nights to go."

She nodded, unable to speak. How could she leave him? *She was in love with him.*

"Then you mustn't leave without these." He slipped a hand inside his pocket and produced the bit of purple missing from his attire. He extended his hand to her view.

"My amethysts." She stared at him in shock. He was erasing that horrid night in his cabin. She wanted to tell him to keep the stones, the gown, anything to remember her by.

Daunted by her tears, Eros said, "It was never my intention to steal your jewels, Alanis. I only took them because I didn't want anyone else to steal them. They were always yours. And . . . I also have the rest of your personal effects here. I'll send them up first thing in the morning."

"My personal effects?" She murmured, too overwrought to grasp his meaning.

"Rocca brought the trunks to Tortuga," he explained. "Your maid helped him."

"You have *all* of my things here? Why didn't you tell me? Besides, Lucas would have—"

"Silverlake is nothing to you, an acquaintance," Eros bit out tersely.

"Sending my things home would not have put a strain on his marriage to your sister, Eros. And you are not what I'd call a confidant."

His eyes glinted. "You put *yourself* in my hands and you worry about your gowns?"

"I am not concerned for my gowns. I am concerned about your reasons. Tell me the truth."

"*Va bene,* the truth. I wanted you to feel free to travel anywhere you pleased. And I didn't tell you because I didn't want to alarm you. You thought I was a pirate, if you'll recall."

"I still do."

"No, you don't. You know I haven't practiced piracy since I left Taofik, and even when I did, looting a lady's trousseaux was never my style. For your information," his expression turned cynical, "since Taofik knew I was versed in war he always sent me after navy vessels. I was what you'd call his War Dog, the one they sent where no one else cared to go."

The harshness in his eyes filled her with empathy. "So how did you make your fortune?"

"Nothing admirable. As you well know, Spain and France haven't always been on the best of terms, and since I had personal scores to settle with both sides, I dealt their pillaged weaponry to one another. There was a time when I found it amusing. I got bored of that eight years ago."

"So you left Taofik."

"I got bored of him as well."

"You were sixteen years old when you arrived in Algiers. What personal scores could a lad have to settle with great powers such as France and Spain?"

His eyes turned cold. "*Personal* scores."

A chilly sensation crept up her spine. A sarcophagus was less arcane than this man who had martial and architectural education at sixteen, who had private vendettas to settle with empires, and who had royal Milanese crests hanging at every corner.

He came over and offered her the jewels. "The princess I

spotted in Versailles wore purple gems to complement her beauty. Allow me?" he inquired huskily.

Alanis turned around and swept her long tresses off her nape. He circled her neck and put the cool necklace on her collarbones. His fingers felt warm and gentle, but his touch scalded her. She shut her eyes and enjoyed his caress as he latched the two ends together. The necklace felt foreign on her skin, its pear-shaped diamonds and amethysts belonging to another woman in another world—the one who hadn't visited Algiers, who hadn't bathed in the pool in the desert, whose heart was free. Yet she wasn't a woman any longer, she smiled. She was a *ninfa*.

Warm lips touched her nape. "I . . . wasn't entirely truthful before," he admitted gruffly. "I collected your trunks because I . . . wanted you to come with me."

Alanis turned around. "You did?"

He lowered his eyes. "Let me have your wrist." As he clasped the bracelet she had a sudden vision of her standing before him wearing nothing *but* her jewels.

The latch clicked. He handed her the matching earrings. "I was wrong," he breathed. "This princess doesn't need gemstones to enhance her beauty. She glowed dressed only in sunrays."

"Good evening!" Sallah exclaimed as Eros seated Alanis on the cushioned divan curving around the dinner table. The pavilion glowed with candlelight. Soft breeze blew in from the sea. "We were beginning to despair of you two . . . Ouch!" He glared at his wife. "What was that for?"

"Sorry, dear. Did I kick you?" Nasrin asked innocently. "How awkward of me."

"This wine comes from the southeast marches of Ancona." Eros uncorked a green bottle and poured for his guests. "It is one hundred fifty years old and has a secret ingredient."

Alanis followed the soft dance of light and shadow on his face as he offered her a glass. An Englishman would hesitate to call Eros "civilized," but in his Italian way he was the embodiment of poise and sophistication, and his every nuance thrummed her heart. "What is the ingredient?"

His eyes gleamed. "If you have sensitive tasting buds, you should be able to identify it."

"A challenge." She smiled darkly and sipped the red elixir, letting it brand its taste on her tongue. "Has a distinct sweetness, but also a sour tang, suggesting green forests and wild berries picked after the rains. Raspberry!" she ventured a guess and delicately licked a drop off her lip.

"Right you are. Rubus it is." His eyes settled on her glossy lips, transmitting his thoughts to her with sharp alacrity. It was no longer the wine but the haunting flavor of his mouth fogging her reason—an aphrodisiac far superior to merlot or raspberry.

Sallah and Nasrin exchanged glances. Deciding to clear the heavy innuendos thickening the air, Sallah cleared his throat. "I propose a toast in honor of my favorite cook—to Antonio!"

The diversion managed to engage everyone's laughter, except for Nasrin. She sighed.

Dinner was served. The main course was the *mechoui:* A slowly roasted lamb, falling apart with tenderness, and served with the traditional couscous, which was undisputedly Antonio's masterpiece—a vegetable piquant soup on a bed of semolina flakes. Though eager to sample the dish, Alanis soon discovered what a very messy business the couscous was. Her fork kept losing the grains on the way to her mouth. The sauce had a way of seeping up her sleeves. She resolved to secretly study Eros. His fingers pinched a heap of grain and applied gentle pressure in shaping it into a ball. He was about to pop it into his mouth when he caught her staring. Smiling, he slid along the curving length of the divan and commanded in a whisper, "Open your mouth."

She glimpsed at their dinner companions. Sallah was wolfing down hot kebabs to Nasrin's evident vexation. "We'll make a spectacle of ourselves," she admonished in a whisper.

His thumb traced the contour of her lips. "Open your mouth to me, *Amore.*"

Her lips parted. She was a little disappointed when instead

of a kiss she tasted salty grains. He brushed a grain off her lip and slid back to his former place. She shut her eyes. Suddenly two whole nights seemed awfully long. His coming to her no longer posed the worst evil, but rather her coming to him, slipping into his bed, and crawling all over his body.

Nasrin leaned closer. "Take heed, dear. I've seen them come and I've seen them go. Do not follow the sad path of so many who have fallen from grace. He must surrender before you do."

Embarrassed by her transparency, Alanis asked in a whisper, "What should I do then?"

"Nothing. Men are innate hunters. Make the chase easy and they lose interest. However, it is very important to accurately assess your hunter's prowess. Small fish prey on sponges. Yours is a full-blooded predator. Give him a worthy chase to exercise his predacious skills."

Alanis glanced at Eros. He wasn't merely a predator but a magnificent blue-eyed one, and she had no wish to suffer the dismal fate of a sponge. "What sort of predator was Sallah?"

Nasrin smiled. "A devious one. We were introduced when he came to visit his mother's relatives in Marrakech. His father was an English earl's accountant. I saw no reason to refuse his attentions. He made me laugh, bought me outrageous gifts, and became my best friend. By the time he declared himself, I was utterly smitten and eating from the palm of his hand."

"Sounds romantic." Sadly, Eros didn't let her come close enough to be his friend. Only his eyes spoke to her in a language she partially understood. "How did they become good friends?"

"Ten years ago they met in the souk in Algiers," Nasrin whispered. "*El-Amar* was scouting for an honest tradesman to export his goods. He didn't trust his Algerian associates. Sallah spoke Ladino and had contacts in Spain. He was perfect as a partner. *El-Amar* was young, dangerous, volatile. The Raises were terrified of him. His reputation held that he neither feared nor trusted anyone and that he was capable of executing one of their own if he only suspected betrayal. I

Take A Trip Into A Timeless World of Passion and Adventure with Kensington Choice Historical Romances!

—Absolutely FREE!

Enjoy the passion and adventure of another time with Kensington Choice Historical Romances. They are the finest novels of their kind, written by today's best-selling romance authors. Each Kensington Choice Historical Romance transports you to distant lands in a bygone age. Experience the adventure and share the delight as proud men and spirited women discover the wonder and passion of true love.

Get 4 FREE Books!

We created our convenient Home Subscription Service so you'll be sure to have the hottest new romances delivered each month right to your doorstep—usually before they are available in book stores. Just to show you how convenient the Zebra Home Subscription Service is, we would like to send you 4 FREE Kensington Choice Historical Romances. The books are worth up to $24.96, but you only pay $1.99 for shipping and handling. There's no obligation to buy additional books—ever!

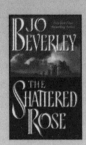

Save Up To 30% With Home Delivery!

Accept your FREE books and each month we'll deliver 4 brand new titles as soon as they are published. They'll be yours to examine FREE for 10 days. Then if you decide to keep the books, you'll pay the preferred subscriber's price (up to 30% off the cover price!), plus shipping and handling. Remember, you are under no obligation to buy any of these books at any time! If you are not delighted with them, simply return them and owe nothing. But if you enjoy Kensington Choice Historical Romances as much as we think you will, pay the special preferred subscriber rate and save over $8.00 off the cover price!

We have 4 FREE BOOKS for you as your introduction to
KENSINGTON CHOICE!
To get your FREE BOOKS, worth up to $24.96, mail
the card below or call TOLL-FREE 1-800-770-1963.
Visit our website at www.kensingtonbooks.com.

Get 4 FREE Kensington Choice Historical Romances!

▶ *YES!* Please send me my 4 FREE KENSINGTON CHOICE HISTORICAL ROMANCES (without obligation to purchase other books). I only pay $1.99 for shipping and handling. Unless you hear from me after I receive my 4 FREE BOOKS, you may send me 4 new novels—as soon as they are published—to preview each month FREE for 10 days. If I am not satisfied, I may return them and owe nothing. Otherwise, I will pay the money-saving preferred subscriber's price (over $8.00 off the cover price), plus shipping and handling. I may return any shipment within 10 days and owe nothing, and I may cancel any time I wish. In any case, the 4 FREE books will be mine to keep.

NAME_____

ADDRESS_____ APT. _____

CITY_____ STATE _____ ZIP _____

TELEPHONE (_____) _____

E-MAIL (OPTIONAL) _____

SIGNATURE_____

(If under 18, parent or guardian must sign)

Offer limited to one per household and not to current subscribers. Terms, offer and prices subject to change. Orders subject to acceptance by Kensington Choice Book Club. Offer Valid in the U.S. only.

KN116A

PLACE
STAMP
HERE

Ił.ıllłłı.ı.ıIłıınılłIıılıılłIıılıılıılıIılıIłıIıılılıIıIł.ıll

Zebra Book Club
P.O. Box 6314
Dover, DE 19905-6314

confess I was adamantly against the partnership at first, but Sallah assured me that *El-Amar's* heart was in the right place. When I met Jasmine I understood what he meant. The twenty years' difference of age didn't deter them from becoming fast friends. Later, when Mulay Ismail, the Sultan of Morocco, bestowed upon *El-Amar* the ownership of the royal mines in Agadìr, Sallah exported the raw materials outside the Medina. They made each other very wealthy."

"Why should the Moroccan Sultan hand over his mines to Eros?" Alanis asked.

"For a host of reasons. Sallah claims *El-Amar* is a special favorite with the King of France and that he served the Sultan as *mendoub,* an occasional ambassador at the French Court. Thanks to him a relationship of amity and respect ensued between the two nations."

Alanis was impressed but not entirely surprised.

"The best story Sallah spins is that thanks to his contacts in Algeria, *El-Amar* obstructed an assassination plot against the Sultan. He's no angel, my dear, but he's better than you think."

"Let's have some music," Eros suggested. He summoned one of his guards. The young man sat down on a stool, adjusted his guitar, and began singing a tender Italian love song.

Alanis sipped her wine and let the guard's melodious voice transcend her thoughts to stars, oranges, and moonlit kisses. Inevitably her gaze veered to Eros. He stared at her, hiding nothing; stark hunger, which seemed to run as deep as his soul, manifested itself in his expression.

When the song ended, Sallah was snoring loudly. Nasrin poked his belly. "Sallah, dessert."

"What? Oh. Never mind. I'm too sleepy." He helped Nasrin up, ignoring her protests.

"Good night," Alanis said. She usually retired with them, but tonight she wanted to sit with Eros for a little while longer. Arm in arm, the loving couple made their way to the house.

When they were out of earshot, Nasrin hissed, "What was that about, jackal?"

"The boy needs help, or he'll never get it right. Thought I'd give him a hand."

"If you think he'll declare himself because you coordinated a perfect setting, you don't know your partner by half. He'll exhaust every trick in the book to avoid a wedding before bedding. I only hope Alanis can resist him. She's madly in love with him, you know."

"Eros's head is not exactly up to the mark, either," Sallah grunted.

"I know perfectly well where he keeps his thoughts."

Sallah looked at her askance. "I hope you didn't teach her any of your shrewish tricks."

"Let me teach you a shrewish trick. Sleep alone tonight!" She marched ahead briskly.

Emerging from the shadows into the golden haze of the table lamp, Eros refilled their wineglasses. "You seem to be enjoying Nasrin's company," he remarked.

"Yes, I do. She's wonderful." Alanis smiled and reached for her glass. She felt the warmth of the wine she had imbibed over dinner flowing in her veins, easing her tension.

"I agree. So," he whirled the red liquid in his glass, "would it be presumptuous of me to say that changing your mind about staying the week was not a bad idea?"

She took a sip of wine. "I enjoyed the week."

"Then stay another."

Her eyes met his. He looked utterly serious about his suggestion. "Alone with you?"

"Alone with me."

They both knew precisely what would happen if she remained in Agadìr alone with him.

Eros set his wineglass aside and edged closer. "Stay with me because you want to, Alanis, because you want me and I want you. Let's terminate this agony, *Amore*."

The heat of desire flowed between them, a glow as powerful as a magnet. She let out a shaky sigh. "I'm not the courtesan you thought you spotted in Versailles, Eros. I can't be yours and then another's. I'll belong to one man only for the rest of my life. If I stay here a little longer, my life will be over, but if I leave, yours won't. Now who do you suppose has more to lose?"

"We have the same to lose," he replied quietly, searching her eyes. "What do you think I'm made of? Do you honestly believe nothing can faze me? That once you leave, I'll jump the first petticoat that comes along? You think the lowly serf is totally bereft of feelings."

She caressed his cheek, aching for him. "If I thought that, it wouldn't be difficult."

His warm, wine-scented breath preceded the hungry assault of his mouth. He embraced her fiercely, drawing her into prolonged, passionate kisses. She didn't fight the flames; she let their slow burn raze her. Perhaps if she were beyond reason, the choice would be out of her hands . . .

"Come to my bed tonight," he breathed heavily. "I go mad wanting you."

She shut her eyes and rubbed her cheek against his. She wanted to break his queue and sink her fingers in his silky hair. She wanted to whisper in his ear that she loved him. She wanted to yield to him right there in the dimly lit pavilion overlooking a dark, roaring ocean. But she couldn't. It would be a mistake she would spend the rest of her days paying for.

"Don't hate me for saying no," she begged softly, "because in spite of your complicated ways and deep, dark secrets, you are the man I want. I'll miss you more than you'll ever know . . ."

She felt him stiffening against her. "It unpleasantly sounds like an ultimatum, Alanis."

She tilted her head back and sought his eyes. "You are asking me to give up *everything* for you, but you won't even tell me your real name. You say you have feelings, but you won't tell me how you feel. You want a submissive, uncomplicated bedmate, Eros, who'll never meddle in your affairs and your past, and for that you have others. You don't need me to take their place."

"If you weren't so busy counting faults in me all the time,

you would have realized weeks ago that the only woman I want, Alanis, is *you!*"

"Prove it," she whispered vehemently, "because I'd rather miss you than end up hating you."

Frustration and rage battled across his face. He understood what she was asking of him but seemed incapable of surrendering it. He stood up. "You want to leave? Leave. I'm positive the excellent aristocracy will line up when you return to England unattached. You'll find your man for life, who wasn't designed with so many defects, who'll treat you better than a *cortigiana*—as to my deepest regret you feel I treated you. I wish you all the best."

She watched him marching away through eyes brimming over with tears.

CHAPTER 17

Man once I was, and my parents were of Lombardy.
                                    —Dante: *Inferno*

"Knight to b6. Check. And say farewell to your queen!" Sallah lifted an ivory knight with a flourish and knocked aside the sculpted jet queen. "Your turn," he informed the shirtless, barefoot, unshaven heathen sitting across from him in the dappled shade of the olive tree. Eros's luck in the game was consistent with the color of his chess pieces and with his mood.

"This cursed, bellicose game!" he ranted mean-spiritedly and raked his fingers through his thick long mane. He leaned forward, planting his hands on his knees, and tried to concentrate.

Smiling, Sallah stuck a smoky cigar between his teeth. "You're only saying that because you're losing, *huboob*.

About time you paid me back for all the games I lost to you this week."

"Shut up, Sallah. Let me think." Eros forcefully rubbed his beard-roughened jaw, fixing his sharp gaze on the chessboard. Defeat loomed; the jet king was cornered.

"You're in a foul mood today. Anything to do with our blond Venus holding gudgeon in her ivory tower?"

"Haven't noticed."

Sallah harrumphed. Alas, his previous night's plotting had backfired. Beauty and the beast were more at odds than ever. "You do recall we're leaving tomorrow. The *three* of us."

Eros didn't bother lifting his eyes off of the board. "I'll be leaving shortly as well."

"So she'll go her way and you'll go yours."

"So it seems."

Sallah leaned closer and asked delicately, "Why are you giving her up?"

"Shut up, Sallah!" Eros bellowed and slammed his fist on the chessboard, scattering the pieces. He got up and went to stand at the handrail overlooking the ocean. Turquoise and gold, the splendid scenery conjured to mind the crux of their chat. Yet Sallah had no doubt Alanis dwelled in Eros's head without any help from the view. The man was turning into a pitiful wreck.

"Good God, man. What is wrong with you? Why is it so difficult?"

Corded muscles stiffened on the broad bronzed back, but no word was voiced.

"You are in love with her. Marry her."

Silence. Sallah half expected the handrail to be torn from its hinges and thrown at him with the force of a raging blizzard. Instead, Eros turned to face him with bloodcurdling calm. "I'll fry ten times in hell before I do that," he drawled icily, his gemlike eyes simmering low.

"Yet the more she denies you, the more you want her. This isn't going to go away, you know. If you let her leave, you'll curse yourself for being every kind of fool." He hauled himself to his feet and joined Eros at the rail. His young friend was in a dire need of a heart-to-heart talk. "I know it isn't insatiable lust for women putting you off the idea of making a real home for yourself, Eros, but living with demons for the rest of your life is an inferno of your own making. Surely a sweet little thing who presses her body to you at night and smiles at you come morning can help ease the torments of the past. Now, I am not making light of the burden of responsibility that caring for a wife and babes entails, but it is the essence of life, my friend. Where would I be today if I didn't have Nasrin? I'd be a bitter old man. Why would you wish that on yourself?"

Eros lowered his eyes. "What you and Nasrin have is special. Few are as blessed as you two are."

"You can have that with Alanis. She's a rare beauty, both of body and spirit. And deny it or not, there is a special bond between you. It could be the start of something for life. What more can one possibly want?"

"She's leaving."

"You know what you have to do."

Eros glared at him. "Why would I want a nosy, straight-laced aristocrat who thinks she can rule me?"

Sallah chuckled. "In your case, I'd say it is you who feels this way. Because you want her so badly, you'd do anything to please her. In my case . . . well, last night I considered divorcing my shrew, but when I took that delectable woman into my arms—"

"Spare me." Eros sighed. "Besides, I have pressing matters to attend to. This war is coming nowhere near conclusion. Louis is pouring more men into the field. Marlborough is hampered by lack of men and money in the Netherlands. Savoy is countermaneuvering against Vendôme in northern Italy, trying to join his other cousin, Duke Victor Amadeus, in Torino."

Sallah stirred. "Do you mean to tell me that Savoy is Vendôme's cousin as well?"

"*Si.*" Eros grinned wryly. "But rest assured he's loyal to your allied forces. Unfortunately, he can do very little since . . . Milan is completely under French control now."

Sallah gave his tall friend a gimlet eye. "So when will *you* join Savoy in liberating Milan?"

Eros stiffened, then exploded again. "What do I care about Milan? I should be getting back to sea!" He pushed away from the rail, picked up a jet knight, and tossed it for Dolce to fetch.

Sallah dogged after him. "What do I care about Zion? What do I care about the Holy Land? It's in my blood. That's what it is!"

"I have nothing in my blood," Eros muttered angrily, "but if Louis wins this war, we shall all end up his vassals, paying him tribute for the rest of our lives."

Sallah fixed Eros with a grave look. "Before you go out saving the world, my friend, why don't you save yourself first?"

The sun was sinking, and so was her heart. She was leaving tomorrow on the evening tide. Standing at the balcony, Alanis stared at the crimsoning sky and fought the tears threatening to emerge. Yet her heart wept for him, for her, for what could have been, might have been, if only he gave her a reason to stay, a sign, something beyond lust, something from his soul.

Someone scratched her door. "Come in, Mustafa!" she called and walked inside.

Mustafa looked as sour as a pickle. One would think she murdered his entire family. So she was leaving his master. It wasn't entirely her choice. "Good evening, my lady. I'm afraid one of your chests got lost in the storage room. Would you care to accompany me to identify it?"

"Certainly," Alanis replied and followed him out the door.

The house was quiet as they meandered through obscure marble halls. Sallah and Nasrin were most likely having dinner with Eros. Her heart cramped. What if she stayed with him? He may not feel as she did, but he wanted her passionately. What precisely was she rushing off to?

Mustafa halted at the end of the last corridor and gestured at an imposing portal. "This is the storage room." Alanis found it resembled a doorway to another kingdom. "It is well lit inside, my lady. You will have no trouble finding your misplaced chest." He pulled open one of the giant mahogany doors, and she went inside. The door slammed behind her. She jumped, appalled at his shocking ways. She turned to survey the room and forgot the reason she was there.

Crammed among giant, black marble pillars and lit by great brass lamps hanging from the ceiling, a parade of riches unfurled before her. What Mustafa described as a room of miscellany was in fact a treasury chamber stacked with carpets, tapestries, and beautiful pieces of furniture. There was an armory section amassed with weapons of the finest manufacture, a stock of fabrics shimmering in all sorts of colors, and scores of coffers filled with gold coins and gems.

Alanis passed the chests, drawn to the art collection displayed deeper inside the chamber. Her eyes widened on a portrait of Caterina Sforza, on the magnificent *Madonna and Child,* the *Virgin of the Rocks,* the *Archangel Michael,* and the *Lady With An Ermine*—the portrait of one of the Sforza dukes' notorious mistresses. A bronze statue of Marshal Trivulzio stood on a gilt-festooned commode. Beside it, framed in gilt, the model of the *Duomo,* Milan's cathedral, rested on a sofa heaped with yellowing paper pads of engineering designs. If she dared question the artist's identity, her doubts dispersed once her attention shifted to the last masterpiece down the row: The portrait of the artist himself—Leonardo da Vinci.

If Eros wished it, his house would be decked to the rim! *The lowly serf had a hamlet once and now it's gone.* "A hamlet, ha! Who the devil are you?" she exclaimed, irritated to the tips of her toes. Her gaze fell on a remote corner. Another crowned crest of vipers and eagles imprinted on a shield rested on the floor against the wall. When she came to examine it up close, she noted it wasn't as antique as the other insignias. The viper wasn't black but dark blue, the devoured Saracen ruby red. The gold on the crown still sparkled. This was a new device, she realized, and instead of a duke's name, four letters were inscribed at the bottom: SF—AD.

"You amaze me," Eros's deep voice sounded right behind her shoulder. "Of all the things here, *you* notice a rotten piece of metal."

Alanis all but suffered a fatal apoplexy. She whipped around and almost collided into his bare chest. "Eros." She pressed a hand over her fast-drumming heart. "What were you thinking creeping up on me? I very nearly died of shock."

"I'm not the one creeping into private chambers," he grunted, looking defensive.

"How dare you accuse me of creeping? It was that conniving man of yours who lured me here to locate my misplaced chest." An operation that had obviously been a ruse, but for what purpose? She glanced around. "Did you rob all mankind to accumulate this . . . fortune?"

The muscle in his jaw clenched. "You'd be surprised, but the lion's share of what you see here I actually bought. And most of it already belonged to me when I bought it!"

"You're drunk." She moved away from him and from the heady cognac fumes clinging to his skin as some spicy, female-head-turning cologne. He wore nothing except flowing black silk pantaloons laced disturbingly low beneath the muscular wings of his waist. "I didn't expect to find you here," she confessed. Had Mustafa acted on his own or on his clever master's orders?

"I know." Eros's lips curved. "I watched you come in. You didn't notice me because you were too busy taking inventory."

She hadn't noticed him because he was barefoot and furtive. "Why aren't you at dinner?"

"Why aren't *you* at dinner?" His eyes glinted in his hard face. "Was another evening with me too much for you to stomach?"

"I wasn't hungry," she bit out. "And besides, what are you so enraged about?"

"You cat-eyed witch." His fingers closed on her arm and pulled her to him. He wound her shiny blond hair around his free hand and forced her to look up into his eyes. The desperate need she perceived in them worked on her as magic. She was the witch? This blue-eyed savage owned her heart. He put his cheek to hers, his breath shallow in the whorls of her ear. "Do you think that by leaving me you rid me of your curse? You're a heartless demoness, Alanis, but tonight I'll exorcize you from my soul once and for all."

Feeling lightheaded by his words and closeness, she smoothed her hands up his chest and embraced his neck. She felt weak, excited, desperate to keep him. She shut her eyes against the bristly feel of his cheek and simply held him, her heart echoing his.

"What would it take to keep you, *ninfa bionda?* Which part of my soul do you want?"

"I don't want a piece of your soul." *I want a place in your heart.*

His head came up. "Take your pick, Alanis. Whatever you see here is yours."

"I don't believe you." She disengaged from his hold. "I know now you were the one who lured me here, but not to purchase my favors as you would a whore's. You are too clever to think it would work with me. So what is the test? What am I missing?" She investigated his eyes. He was very tense. "You truly outdid yourself, stealing Leonardo da Vinci masterpieces . . ."

"These paintings were commissioned by *my family!*" he growled, his eyes ablaze. "I could have entire frescoes uprooted if I wanted to, including *The Last Supper!*"

Her throat felt dry. "Your family is the Milanese House of Sforza," she concluded quietly. She touched the medallion dangling over his chest. "This is yours. And that"—she pointed at the crest in the corner—"what you call a rotten piece of metal, also belongs to your family, as the other crests do. Why did you put this particular one out of sight? What do the letters stand for?"

"They're initials," he spoke at last, his throat taut, "of the heir who never became a duke."

Her heart went wild in her chest. "SF—AD. What is the heir's name?"

He stared at her bleakly, the lost boy inside the thirty-two-year-old man. "*Stefano Andrea,*" his Milanese accent rolled smoothly off of his tongue, as rich Lombard wine.

Alanis held her breath. She knew the answer before she asked, "And this name is—?"

"Mine."

CHAPTER 18

Eros studied her carefully. "Now you know."

Alanis nodded, awestruck. "You are His Royal Highness, Prince Stefano Andrea Sforza," she murmured. "The lost duke of the largest, richest princedom in Italy—Milan." Milan's history was a tale of blood, she recalled. Though it possessed naturally strong frontiers, was conceived in grandeur, and accumulated great wealth and power, Spain and France destroyed it. In a volatile world engaged in continual struggles, not even the formidable Sforza and the cunning Visconti could save it from ruin. Their supreme abilities went to waste, along with the natural strength of the land, and their successor turned renegade, a godless animal of the seas, a desperado. Yet even as a desperado, stripped of his name and consequence, she had fallen in love with him.

"You're impressed." He condemned her with a glare. "You see the prince protocol requires you incline your less privileged head before."

Or in other words, she thought, *You don't see me.* "I see a man who is better than what he wants people to see, better than what he himself wants to believe. I see the man I . . . could love."

"Sheath your claws. Stefano Sforza doesn't exist anymore. He's a rotten piece of metal on the floor of the storeroom." He moved away, losing himself among the crowded artifacts.

"Eros, wait!" she desperately called to him and heard one of the giant doors closing with a bang. She felt a rush of terror, as a mouse caught in a trap. She had asked for a sign from his soul, and he had given it to her. Only now he wanted nothing to do with her.

The way she felt she should have been weeping. She thought about her parents, about Tom. Was she destined to remain loveless and alone? *You have the power to create your own destiny.*

Yes, she would wield this power, Alanis decided. She would fight for the man she loved. She left the chamber and searched the endless marble corridors. There was no sign of him anywhere. She ran into Mustafa on the first-floor gallery. He gave her a sly smile.

"My lady, did you find your . . . misplaced chest?"

She wasn't in the mood to play mind games with him. "I am looking for your master."

"*El Rais* went out for a nightly ride on the beach. Should I inform him you wish to speak to him when he returns?"

Was he off to Leila, she wondered. After her clear-cut rejection last night why shouldn't he seek a willing female? "Please do. It is imperative I speak to him tonight, no matter the hour."

"Yes, my lady. I will deliver your message personally, no matter the hour."

"Thank you, Mustafa." She nodded gratefully and retired to her apartment. She would wait for Eros there. She would know when he returned to his chambers. But what would she do then?

The air was hot and humid. Needing to cool her body and her head, she lit a night candle and carried it into the bathing room. There was no need to summon servants with water buckets. The large marble basin was constructed in the ancient Roman lead-workers' method, with three bronze spouts protruding from the wall: *Aqua Frigida, Aqua Tepida,* and *Aqua Calida.* She turned the tepid valve and watched as water filled the basin. She poured in scented oils, shut the valve, and stripped naked. Cool serenity engulfed her when she reclined in the tub. The sound of trickling drops echoed off the whitewashed dome. The candle at her side created a tawny glow around her. She occupied her time in performing all sorts of toilettes done only in the Temple of the Good Goddess, but as she lathered her skin and hair, images of Eros kept haunting her mind. She imagined the taste of his mouth, the feel of his hands caressing her nude limbs. Swearing, she plunged to the bottom of the basin and rinsed her hair. The desire she had been tamping for weeks pulsated through her veins, driving her insane. She lost track of time as she lay in the tub, yet all the while a single thought pounded in her head—*Go to him!*

A door slammed in the hall. Alanis emerged from the basin and toweled herself hastily. It had to be close to midnight. Her hands shook, as she combed her hair and put on a fresh caftan. She sat at the vanity table, meeting her gaze in the mirror. As a clock, her pulse beat at the base of her throat. Tick tock, tick tock. *He was not coming.* She stood up. The more she thought about it, the clearer it became: She had to go to him. Life was too short to be wasted on regrets.

She cracked open one of her trunks, the one containing her wedding trousseaux, and dug out a bridal *chemise de nuit.* The whispery silk was so terribly delicate she feared she might rip it in her haste. She removed the caftan and slipped the nightgown over her head. It sashayed to her toes, cool and satiny, molding her curves in a sensuous caress. She inspected her image in the mirror. The pure silk made her look naked; the dusky peaks of her nipples were all-too-visible.

Her nerve faltered, but a stronger voice spoke in her head. *Don't be a spineless prude! You want him. You can make him yours. He shared his secret. He let you into his sanctum sanctorum.*

Now she had to show him how she felt. Eros was all fire. She had to become fire as well.

Not wasting another precious moment, she left the bed-chamber. Raw tension twisted her stomach, as her bare feet crossed the dimly lit corridor toward Eros's imposing doors. She felt as nervous as a thief on his first nightly venture. Eros was a handful when she thought him a pirate. A Milanese prince was downright daunting. She commanded herself and pulled one door open.

The silvery walls of the antechamber reflected the glimmer of a single night candle. Alanis slipped inside and was welcomed by a low roar. She shushed the leopardess sprawled on the cool marble floor with a brave pat on her spotted head and crept around her large body.

Eros growled something in Arabic. She froze. Her heart beat like a Berber drum. She took a deep breath and materialized beneath the Oriental beam. Open to a wide terrace, the spacious room was submerged in shadows. Linen drapes billowed in the late-night breeze, inviting gentle drafts of air. Her gaze fell on the enormous bed situated to her left. Made entirely of silver, its engraved backing panel and posts softly reflected the glow of the moon.

"*Eros,*" she whispered, her heart in her throat.

A movement caught her eye at the far corner. A large figure lounging in a wingchair, half facing the terrace, half facing the entry, raised his head from supporting hands. Though she barely made out the plains of his face, she felt his eyes gliding over her, the eyes of a tiger.

"*Com'è capriccioso il cuore di una donna. What a fickle thing is a woman's heart,*" he murmured to himself. "Has the lowly serf become worthy all of a sudden? Last night I wasn't up to your standards. What changed?"

His bitter smirk unnerved her. Mustering her courage, she moved forward in slow, feline steps. "You did. You told me who you are. You confided in me. Tell me what happened,

Eros. Why did you leave Milan? What became of the rest of your family?"

Light sparked at the tip of a match, revealing his fierce tanned features. He radiated bone-deep fatigue, which she suspected wasn't entirely physical. He slammed an empty glass on the table beside him and lit a candle. His medallion was thrust there, a tangle of gold and memories. Gruffly he said, "You didn't come here to talk. Not in this bit of nothing that exhibits your liver."

His ruthless restraint was disconcerting. She hadn't expected a wall of ice. "You don't have to be crude. If you want me to leave, I will, but we must talk first. We can't leave it at that."

"Don't play games with me," he warned harshly. "I'm no fool to fall for your artless wiles. I've dealt with professionals you don't hold a candle to, Alanis, creatures far more sophisticated, ten times more experienced in the art of duping a man than you'll ever be."

"Nor do I aspire to be. I'm not one of your . . . little friends with a price on her affection."

"You're worse, Alanis," he breathed roughly. "You're out to steal my soul. *A harpy.*"

She halted, horrified by his cold accusation. "Why? Because I care for you? Do you think so little of us both that you believe yourself undeserving to be loved for artless reasons?"

He stared at her as if she had gutted him with a knife. "Get—out!" he rasped slowly. He bolted to his feet. "Go back to your dull world and leave me in peace. *Leave me in peace!*"

Startled by his fury, she assessed his taut features and the savage glint in his eye. He looked as ominous as a Spartan warrior carved in bronze, but under his indestructible veneer, lurking deep in his eyes, she saw what she never imagined she would: *Fear.*

Someone—a woman—hurt him in the past, and her betrayal sowed this irrational sentiment in him, a man who showed no signs of fear up to now, not even of death. *That* was his secret, and it related directly to the man he once was: Prince Stefano Sforza.

Fortified by her insight, she advanced forward. "I remind you of someone. Who was she? Do I look like her?"

Eros stiffened. Unable to meet her gaze, he muttered, "You're off course. If you knew what you were talking about, you'd see the absurdity of your assumption."

She came up in front of him and touched his chest. His pulse sped up beneath her palm. She ran her hand along his warm torso, caressing the hard, well-formed muscles. "Tell me."

He didn't blink, though her hand must have felt like a shock of ice. Terrible pain etched his eyes. She nudged him lightly, and he dropped into the chair. She moved to stand between his thighs and delved her hands into his thick, black hair. She tilted his head back to meet his gaze. In her hands she held the face of a man, but the eyes staring up at her were those of a lost boy.

The air between them crackled in a silent battle of desires and fears. The pull between them went beyond passion, beyond friendship, beyond any human bond she'd ever formed. Staring into Eros's eyes, for a space of a heartbeat, she found a part of herself that was missing her entire life, though she wasn't aware of its absence. What was it between them—destiny, insanity, *love?*

The feeling terrified her, and she sensed it terrified him as well. And yet, he wanted her to seduce him; he wanted her to want him and to make him believe it. "You know why I'm here." She smiled softly. "You said it last night. I want you and you want me. So if an ungrateful guest may still change her mind . . . I'd love to stay here with you, for as long as you'll have me."

His eyes burned with longing. He caught her hips and buried his face in her flat abdomen. "*Stay,*" he exhaled haggardly, his fingers kneading her flesh through the silk. Alanis hugged his broad, sun-kissed shoulders and surrendered to the thrum of anticipation. Tonight, there'd be no lonely hours drenched in unbearable yearning. Tonight, she would share her ache with Eros.

He pushed to his feet, melding their bodies together. She felt his blood pounding as though he were an extension of herself. "I want you to stay with me for a hundred years," he confessed.

"There must be total honesty between us. Your past, your feelings, they cannot be secrets."

"I'll tell you everything you want to know about me, Alanis, but I warn you—some of it, *most* of it, you won't find charming in the least. If you have any qualms about living with a man of my sort, this is the moment to withdraw and sail home with Sallah. I want no regret later on. But . . . if you decide to stay with me," his voice softened. "you become mine. In every way. No dashing off. No damning tears. *No regret.*"

No regret, the hardest commitment of all. She remembered Sanah's words, *Risk your heart.* In a voice thick with emotion she whispered, "No regret." She pressed a soft kiss on his shoulder, tasting salty skin, then kissed the strong pulse at the base of his throat. "Make love to me."

She felt a sharp spasm slice through him. He shut his eyes and rested his forehead against hers. "You'll never regret this night, *Amore.* I swear to you. I'll never give you any reason to regret it." His mouth found hers, soft and familiar. The tip of his tongue teased her to respond, yet curbed the pace, savoring the rush, stoking the flames. *An introduction.*

Eros. Eros. She purred in response. Her body felt faint, hot, restless. She leaned into him, losing herself in his opulent kiss, in the heat of his skin. She was butter in his hands, his passion washing over her in a blaze. The sounds in his throat made her think of a starved tiger, growling. She would not flit away from his desperate clutches tonight. He made sure of it. With every kiss, with every caress, he eliminated her fears, her shy inexperience. When he took her hand and led her to his bed, she stumbled after him in intoxicated silence, ready to follow him anywhere.

He lit the candle on the bedside table and swept her long, fair tresses off of her shoulders. "I want to see all of you tonight," he murmured. He looped his fingers around the thin straps of her nightgown and tugged. The pure silk cascaded along her body and pooled at her feet. He inhaled sharply. "I've dreamed of you coming to me like this, climbing into my bed, but you are lovelier than I imagined, *ninfa bionda*. I've never wanted a woman the way I want you."

His words warmed her to her curling toes. She reclined askance on his bed and caressed the vacant space beside her, her blue-green cat eyes conveying the silent invitation, *Come to me*.

Eros gazed down at her graceful nude body gilding his bed as a Greek goddess. He pulled the string of his pantaloons loose, and the black silk spilled to his ankles. Her pulse quickened. *He* was beautiful. His eyes were electric blue; his jet hair flowed wild and copious around his shoulders. The nightcandle's soft glow accentuated the sculpted sinew on his body. Tall, broad-shouldered, and fully aroused, he made her blood roar. He lowered himself onto the bed and lay down between her thighs. "Say it again," he whispered. "What you asked me before."

She framed his face with both hands. "Make love to me, Eros. I want you so desperately."

Groaning, his mouth captured hers. She tasted dark, moist hunger in the velvet strokes of his tongue—desire that made her body shiver. He dragged his mouth along her neck, toward her breasts, and sucked an erect nipple into his sultry mouth. Lightning shot through her.

"You're so responsive, *tesoro*," he murmured breathlessly and reclaimed her mouth. They rolled and entwined on his bed, exploring one another's bodies, as pickpockets feeling for coin on gullible victims. Intoxicated by his scent and the velvety expanse of his large male frame, she needed to touch and be touched in complete abandon, much to his delight. His hands and mouth were everywhere—on her breasts, on her hips, gliding smoothly on her skin.

Heady with desire, she explored his body in kind, attuned to his low sounds, learning how to pleasure him, where his secret sensitivities lay. It was a tantalizing game, making her weak with wanting, but mostly Alanis enjoyed staring into Eros's eyes and discovering each time anew how much he desired her, how deeply she moved him.

"This is what I've dreamed of." She flattened him on his back and crawled him as a cat, her mouth hot and wet on his smooth skin. She flicked her tongue over a flat dark nipple.

"*Santo Michele.*" He shuddered and rolled on top of her. "It'll be over in two seconds if you kiss me like that. Allow me to direct this assault, and I'll let you lead the second, *va bene?*"

Smiling, she arched her body beneath his. "There'll be a second?"

"If you're not too sore, a second and a third and the more the merrier, because unlike certain judges . . ." His hand sailed up her satiny thigh. "I'm exceptionally diligent, with no regard whatsoever for Fast days, Saint days, Lent days, or any days, and even more assiduous at night."

She laughed. "You are an arrogant cad. I pity the poor woman who will end up with you!"

Dimples appeared in his cheeks. "I'll be sure to convey your sympathy to this future saint. I only pray she'll be as charitable as you." Her laughter caught when his hand slid in between her thighs and cupped her intimately. He held her startled gaze in thrall as his fingers opened her to his gentle strokes, bringing forth a flow of warm moisture. He exerted precise rubs, shooting fire to her brain. He dipped one finger inside of her, then another, agonizingly, wonderfully deeper.

She moaned and rolled her hips with his hand. *Dear—God.* She was dying of sweet agony. A guttural cry for release spiraled up her throat, but he swallowed it with open-mouthed kisses. He pressed his thumb against her knob and flicked his middle finger inside her tight warmth.

Alanis did cry, blinded by her body's raging call for fulfillment. "Eros, please. *I can't—*"

"Neither can I," he admitted hoarsely. She felt new increasing pressure, and suddenly it was his rock-hard flesh pushing into her, filling her, stretching her, *tearing her apart!*

"Eros, wait!" she cried, but it was too late. He surged all the way, burying himself fully. His groan of pleasure vibrated in her ear. Panic paralyzed her. The pain was unbearably raw. She couldn't move. She couldn't breathe. Belatedly it occurred to her that while his strapping body made her heart flutter, a certain part of his anatomy could cause her serious damage. He started moving. She wriggled beneath him. "Stop, Eros, *please!* I cannot bear it. It's too painful."

He went absolutely still. His breathing was arduous. Beads of perspiration gathered on his brow. His eyes were the color of molten desire. "Don't be afraid. Don't cry." He kissed the salty drops clinging to her cheeks, kissed her soft, swollen lips. "There'll be no more pain. I promise. Only pleasure."

She soulfully searched his eyes. She felt profoundly consoled by his concern. The smarting was gradually ebbing, and she could feel the subtle beat of his flesh inside of her. He planted his hands on the bed and lifted himself up, locking elbows. He withdrew slowly, his eyes asking her to trust him, then slid into her again, grating his jaws inch after excruciating inch.

She keenly followed the play of emotions on his taut features and forced herself to breathe, to concentrate on how he made her feel. He was saturated with pleasure that was also torture, and something awakened inside of her. Subtle at first. Then it intensified, coiling in her female maze of sexuality to tingling tremors. On instinct, she lifted her hips to his, matching the rhythm of his disciplined thrusts. She linked her hands behind his neck and pulled him down to her.

"Better?" Eros inquired, as he rocked them gently, erasing the memory of pain.

"Yes." It felt better and better as he drove in and out, teaching her body to move in perfect accord with his. She enveloped him intimately, luxuriously, caressing him inside of her. The feel of him was . . . *beyond anything now.* His hips moved faster, lancing her with shocks of pleasure.

"*Brucio per te, Amore.* I'm burning for you . . . burning inside of you." Jaws clenched, he pushed harder, his eyes revealing his fight for control and the need driving him to the edge.

Violent tremors seized her, *and she was getting so close,* but it was not enough. "I—*can't.*" Her body begged for release. She moaned and clawed, trying to conquer the illusive pinnacle.

"Don't fight it." His gaze riveted hers; his hips pounded harder and faster. "Let it happen."

She felt so taut, so damned blocked. Ecstasy beckoned her at the end of a long, obscure tunnel, but was impossible to grasp. "*I can't . . .*"

"You can." He curved an arm beneath her waist and hoisted her up to straddle his thighs. She clung to his neck, as his hands anchored her to his loins and showed her how to dance to his lovemaking. They kissed and coupled in a trance of passion, connected in body and soul. With each thrust the pressure inside her intensified, spurred, threatened to burst, drained her strength, and just when she felt she was coming apart, roaring pleasure shot through her like a cannonball. She cried out, her mind dissolving into a million slivers of light, and sagged against him. *Bliss.*

"*Al diavolo!*" Eros tossed his head back, his long mane whipping his shoulder blades, and spilled his seed inside of her. Utterly spent, he collapsed on the bed, his heavy body crushing her to the mattress, his head nestling in the crook of her neck, his breaths coming in short gasps.

Slick with sweat, they lay still, hearts thumping chest to chest. Time stilled for an eternity. Floating in an afterglow, Alanis listened to his harsh breathing, to the slowing beats of his heart, and knew she would never regret coming to him tonight, no matter what the future held in store for them. How many of his former paramours could boast to such a night of rapture as well as to strolling hand in hand with him in the marketplace in Algiers, discovering a world of mysteries?

After a while she was convinced he had fallen sleep. His breathing was quiet, his body lax on top of her. Burying her face in his hair, she confessed in the softest of whispers, "I love you."

Eros stiffened. She wasn't certain if he'd heard her or not because he didn't utter a sound.

"How are you feeling?" Eros's deep voice filled her ear. His large hand swept blond locks off her brow. He enveloped her tightly, spoonlike, his warm torso supporting her back.

Alanis wasn't sound asleep but rather contentedly nodding on and off. The sky was grayish blue in the horizon, striated with orange hues, signaling the break of dawn. She rolled to her back and met his eyes with a smile. They were the clearest, brightest sapphires in the early light. Her heart swelled at the sight of him, so real and handsome beside her. She would give anything to encounter this particular sight every morning henceforth to the day she died. "I feel wonderful," she whispered, brushing aside the cool jet veil covering his cheek. "How are you feeling?"

"Happy," he admitted, smiling bemusedly. He leaned over and kissed her. It was a lover's kiss, intimate and languorous. When it ended they continued staring at each other in silence.

"Eros." She stared at his chest. "Are you married?" She sensed a smile forming on his lips.

"No."

"Have you ever been?"

He was still grinning. "No."

Do you want to be? She looked up at him anxiously. "Do you have any . . . that is, do you suppose you might have—?"

"If the question is do I know of any bastards I might have spawned—the answer is no." He looked amused at her concern. "My, eh, former bed partners took care of the business."

She nodded with a slight blush. No children. "What was your first time like?"

He blinked. "*Scuza?*"

Her smile broadened. "Your first lady love. Who was she?"

"And this is important to discuss right now?" When she nodded, he rolled to his back and tucked his hands beneath his head, staring up at the bed canopy. "She was a chambermaid at the house of the Duke d'Este where I was educated since the age of twelve. I was fifteen years old. She was ten years older. Her name was Alessandra. She came into my bedchamber one night, and I . . . indulged her." He cast Alanis a candid smile. "Nothing inspirational."

"Who was the woman who betrayed you? The one who made you hate women like me?"

His smile disappeared. "You don't waste time warming to the subject, do you?"

He started to rise off the bed, but she stopped him with a hand on his shoulder. "I'm sorry. You don't have to answer. We agreed on 'no secrets,' but you do have a right to your privacy."

His gaze pierced her. "You're assuming I fell in love once and the object of my admiration broke my heart, but you're wrong, Alanis. I was *never* in love and there was *no* such woman."

He got up and splashed his face with cool water. He strode to the open balcony and leaned against the frame, his eyes fixed on the horizon. His naked body was strong and beautiful against the backdrop of an orange-gray sky. He was shutting her out, she realized, as he always did when he found her questions too probing. Nevertheless, she felt an absurd elation. *He has never been in love.* She was stirring in open sea! No ghost ships on the horizon.

She was about to reach for her nightgown when Eros spoke, his deep voice laced with his soft Italian accent. "It was two days before Christmas in the year of our Lord 1689. The season was ice cold, and the city of Milan was dark and troubled. Ordinarily, my father attended Mass at the church of San Francesco the next morning. He never lived to attend it."

Alanis let go of the nightgown and leaned back on the pillows, pulling the blanket over her.

"I was returning home from Ferrara, where the Duke d'Este, who was family as well as an ally, contributed to my princely training." He sighed, running his hand through his hair. "I went to live there, because it was customary for a future duke to be trained by someone other than his father. I spent fourteen hours a day working with fourteen different tutors. I studied philosophy, art, science, astronomy, languages, and what not, to take my place among my peers someday. I had a master for fencing, a master for riding, a master for dancing. In tournaments I gained honor for the Viper banner, but mostly I studied the Art of War." He turned around. "Because in Milan power is everything, and it can only be attained and maintained by a strong duke."

"No wonder you became a Rais in Algiers and universally feared," she whispered. "You were primed to take your father's place as another fearless sovereign, a Viper of Milan." And no wonder he was a personal favorite with the King of France and enjoyed free access to Versailles. King Louis must have known young Stefano Sforza since childhood. "Didn't you spend any time at all with your family while growing up?" she asked.

"I did. During the holidays I returned home, and my father took me around Lombardy and Emilia and the other provinces to familiarize me with what was to become mine someday. Those were the best and the hardest times." He smiled wistfully. "My mother always complained she never saw me and that my father forgot I was merely a stripling and not one of his seasoned captains. My father was a tough-to-the-bone Lombard Duke, made of rock. Unlike me. I was my mother's son, a spoiled baby, though people often said I was a spitting image of my father."

She returned his smile. She hadn't been wrong about him.

Eros had a sensitive, tender core that only an affectionate, devoted mother could nurture. He was a much-loved child.

His expression sobered. "The evening I entered Porta Giovia I knew something was amiss. The Spanish troops outside the city were checking every passer. You must understand, Milan has been occupied by the Spaniards for over a hundred years, but they let my family maintain its prestige and employed my father as their peacemaker and tax collector in the area. It saved them costly efforts in establishing a new system. My father hated serving them as a puppet. He had a dream: one united Italy, too strong for French, Spanish, or any looter to pillage when his coffers were empty. Like the Italian League created by Francesco Sforza and Cosimo de' Medici, he formed secret societies, operating with the sole aim of bringing all the Italian states together. Naples, Piedmont, and Bologna were beginning to embrace the concept, perhaps more concerned with securing constitutions from their absolutist sovereigns than with any great nation aim in mind, but they did refer to the peninsula as Italy." Eros sighed, leaning his head against the engraved beam. "Someone informed the Spaniards. It was my uncle, Carlo, my father's younger brother." He swore. "When I entered the Great Hall, Gelsomina ran to me in tears. The Spaniards were detaining my father in the Tower. I rushed there and found Carlo with the Spanish officers. When he saw me, he laughed and said, 'See what I brought you? Not only *Il Duca* but the Count of Pavia as well. Now you don't need to worry about a vengeful heir.' They grabbed me and . . . slaughtered my father before my eyes." He shut his eyes, old pain plowing his face. "Things happened rapidly after that. I broke free, slit my uncle's throat with my dagger, grabbed my father's medallion, and fled. A death warrant was issued against me, and I wasn't sure which of our allies I could trust. Venice was hostile. The others lay low. No duke in Italy was about to jeopardize his relations with Spain by harboring the fugitive young Duke of Milan, not even the pope. I was on my own. There was not enough time to rally the Milanese battalions, and even if there were, I couldn't challenge Spain without the backing of at least one of the other major powers of the peninsula. Staying in Italy would have cost me my life. So I took Gelsomina and rode that night to Genoa, where we boarded the first ship that raised sail."

"You were sixteen? Jasmine six?" she asked. Eros nodded grimly. She could envision them, a brother and a sister running for their lives in the dead of night, scared, betrayed by their family and friends, powerless against the wrath of Spain. "How did you end up in Algiers?"

"The old-fashioned way. Algerian corsairs raided our Genoese galley. I was thrown into the *Bagnio,* the dungeon where they kept the slaves. Gelsomina was sold as a scullery maid to a rich family. But I convinced one of the Raises, an individual you've met, that putting me on their wall to fortify it against the Spanish cannon was a poor allocation of resources. My capacity for destruction was greater than my tolerance for brick." He smiled mirthlessly. "Taofik appreciated it. He knew exactly how to cultivate this useful aspect of my nature. Then I met Sanah. I retrieved my sister and put her in the old woman's safekeeping. The rest you know. The noble *Principe Milanese* became an utterly ruined creature, destitute of any humanity."

Alanis winced at his use of her old words. "You are not destitute of humanity." Half of him was a viper, a ruthless survivor, and the other half was a lost prince consumed with nostalgia.

"I did ugly things for Taofik. Things that would make your skin crawl."

Their gazes locked in silence. "Why didn't you go back?" she asked quietly.

"Go back?" He smirked cynically. "Go back to what?" He came to sit beside her and ran his knuckles along the creamy curve of her neck.

"You have *diritto de imperio* to rule Milan. Lay a claim with the Holy Roman Emperor."

"Don't be naïve, Alanis. Joseph won't give Milan to me

simply because I demand it. The whole world is wrestling over it. Besides, what gave you the impression I want Milan back?"

She frowned. Something was missing from the story. He wasn't telling her everything. "What happened to your mother?" she inquired curiously

"Sharp as always." He smiled bitterly. "My mother . . ." he spat the word out like a curse, "was Carlo's mistress. My father didn't trust his brother. He knew that traitor was itching to replace him. My mother and I were the only ones who knew about the New League. She sold out her husband and son to clear a path for her lover to the princely seat."

Alanis sucked in her breath, incredulous. "How did you find out? What happened?"

"My father was a proud man," he said impassively. "When we were held in the Tower and it was becoming clear we would not be leaving it alive, he didn't even try to get the Spaniards to spare us. He did ask his brother to take care of his wife and daughter. Carlo laughed. He said my mother was in his apartment, waiting to celebrate their success. Rest assured I didn't take his word for it. I checked. She was there. She locked herself in and wouldn't open the door even to my six-year-old sister, who banged on it with crying hysterics, asking for her mother."

Horrified, she murmured, "Your father must have done something to make her hate him."

"You don't understand!" he growled. "My mother sentenced *me* to death!" He hit his fist against his bare chest where his heart pounded. "Not just my father. I was his heir! I was next in line! In Italy, a usurper obviates the fear of vengeance by extinguishing the line of princes who ruled the land formerly. When my mother plotted my father's downfall with Carlo, she signed *my* death warrant and she knew it! What sort of a mother sentences her own son to perdition? What can a sixteen-year-old boy do to deserve such hatred from his own mother?" He sighed. "Alanis, I was my mother's son. I adored her. She meant *everything* to me, more than my father ever did," he confessed, his eyes glinting much too brilliantly. "I would have given my life for her."

Shaken, she took his hand and kissed it. "What happened to her?"

She had never seen him look so cold as when he said, "I don't know and I don't care."

Silent tears trickled along her cheeks. No wonder he became so tough and spread hell wherever he roamed. She couldn't begin to imagine the ravaging need to strike back at anyone and anything and somehow tear the pain out of his soul by making the entire world pay for his torments. The mother who gave birth to him, who coddled him and named him after the god of love, turned out to be his Judas. A noblewoman, virtuous and refined. *Like her.* A harpy.

"Who else knows the truth about you—Sallah, Giovanni?" she inquired.

"They know nothing. Only you do."

"And your sister?"

"She thinks her mother is dead."

Alanis hugged him tightly. He felt as frigid as a glacier and remained so well after she enveloped him with warmth and affection. How could a mother fail to love a son such as him? He was brave, affectionate, clever, and gifted in so many areas. Inside his hard shell blazed a strong, generous spirit ready to move mountains for those it loved and sentient to other people's misfortunes. She willed her heat to seep into his limbs and melt the frost encasing his heart.

It took awhile, but eventually his arms came around her and he squeezed her ardently. She rested her head on his shoulder. Her lips moved in a whisper. "You are not alone anymore."

She knew the worst was over when his hands began exploring her body beneath the sheet. Warm lips followed, and before long they were kissing and caressing each other as desire blazed between them again. Eros laid her back and fastened his hot, mobile mouth to her breasts.

"Isn't it my turn to assume command?" she asked breathlessly.

"No serious campaigning this time. I don't want to bruise you too badly." He kissed her navel and moved lower. When she tried to dislodge him, he blocked her. "Lie still." He parted her legs and she felt his warm mouth on the inside of her thigh. Then he licked inside of her.

Her brain burst into flames. She sat up, dazed by the indescribable, unspeakable pleasure his mouth had fleetingly given her. "What are you doing? Do it right."

He smiled darkly. "I am doing it right."

She licked her dry lips. "How would you feel if I did the same to you?"

His jaw dropped. "You would?" His torrid gaze lost any trace of amusement when her hand curled around his erection and her thumb caressed the velvety crown. He cringed with a groan. "I'm a weak male, Alanis. Don't tempt me to commit villainy."

"You are a villain, Eros." She kissed his neck. "Might as well live up to your reputation."

"You'll hate me later," he warned, but was already pushing her onto her back.

She wrapped her legs around him, draping her arms around his broad shoulders. "I hate you already." She smiled, enjoying the feel of his heavy body lying on top of her.

Eros lifted his head. A lopsided grin twisted his lips. "No, you don't. *You loath me . . .*"

CHAPTER 19

Sunlight flooded the bed. Ensconced in a warm cocoon of muscular limbs and velvety skin, Alanis opened her eyes and looked at the dark head sharing her pillow, hiding from daylight. A smile spread across her face. Her pirate. Her lover. Her friend. She slid out of his snug embrace and donned her nightgown. She wanted to bathe and dress and make herself

beautiful for him. She cast an admiring glance at his powerfully sculpted, tanned back and left his apartment.

She bathed hastily and inspected her image in the dressing
room mirror. With the exception of the high color in her
cheeks, she didn't detect any marks on her body. *Amateurs
leave marks,* Madame de Montespan had informed her once
while drawing her attention to an ugly teeth mark on the
Countess de Créqi's powdered neck. So there was no evidence
of her exploits now, but there could be, in three to four months.
A sudden image of a soft, cherubic infant with a wisp of jet
hair and dark blue eyes nestling in her arms liquefied her
brain. *Eros's baby.* How would Eros react to her having his
child? As one reacted to a tight noose squeezing his windpipe.

She needed to talk to someone—her mother—and the natural substitute was . . . Nasrin.

Moments later she was knocking on Sallah and Nasrin's
door. Nasrin answered the door with a sleepy smile. "Too
much Lumbrusco," she apologized. "Sallah will sleep till
noon, but if you will allow me a moment, I'll join you for tea
in the pavilion."

Alanis smiled weakly. "That would be delightful."

Nasrin frowned. "Is something the matter, my dear?"

Alanis sustained her questioning gaze. "I shan't be sailing
home with you today."

"Oh?" Nasrin's eyes sobered with a vengeance. "I should
have known! The shameless rogue! Couldn't keep his hands
off you, could he? Well, we shall see about that. Sallah!"

Alanis seized her hand. "Please don't wake Sallah yet. I
need to speak to you in private."

Nasrin considered her apprehensive eyes. "Certainly, my
dear. I shall see you in a bit." She sashayed into her apartment, shutting the door softly behind.

They met in the pavilion shortly after. A footman served
them a pot of tea and some juice.

"Well?" Nasrin asked. "Was it everything you'd dreamed
it would be? My eldest, Sara, had the look of one who had

expected a sweet on her wedding night and received a radish instead."

Alanis laughed softly; her cheeks flushed, and her eyes sparkled a bright aquamarine.

Nasrin sighed. "You needn't answer. Your eyes speak for you. But bearing in mind whom you've set your cap at, I'm not certain whether it is a good or a bad thing."

"Why?" Alanis sensed unpleasant tension coiling her nerves.

"Because you love him," Nasrin replied very motherlike, "and although I confess *El-Amar* is a prince in a world of ordinary man, he is a . . . an unattainable one."

If Nasrin only knew . . . "Why do you say he is unattainable?" Alanis asked bleakly.

"Because he abandons every woman he beds. Now, I sincerely believe you have crawled under his skin as no other had succeeded before you, but I've known him for many years, and to in effect infiltrate that particular heart seems a hopeless quest to me."

Eros's admission of never being in love didn't delight Alanis anymore. "Where he loves, he does not desire. And where he desires, he cannot love," she murmured. He was incapable of loving and desiring the same woman. His mother's betrayal had scarred him for life. He'd lost his family, his home, his dreams and ideals, the liberty to go by his name, and above all else his faith in womankind. In his eyes, women were either pure—the sister he loved—or dissolute—the women he desired. The question now was, What was she to him? "How does one prevent conception?" Alanis blurted the question before her nerve failed her.

"*What?*" Nasrin set down her teacup. "Oh no. This is not for you to know at your age. You need to beget a healthy brood of your own before you earn the privilege. That vigorous devil you adore so much can well bring himself up to scratch. You are not a member of his harem. You deserve better than a bitter brew every morning henceforth until he locates his courage. You are not without friends. Let Sallah have a word with him. He can act on your grandfather's behalf."

Alanis adamantly shook her head. "He doesn't want a wife. Nor does he want babies. I will not become a hateful burden. I'm not without pride. Besides, have you ever known Eros to do anything he didn't want to do?"

"Then you must sail home with us."

"No."

Nasrin stared at her pointedly. "You cannot live with him as his concubine."

Her friend had a point, Alanis admitted privately. If Eros proposed, she wouldn't be sitting here glumly, considering the use of unnatural vices. "What am I to do? Give him up? I can't leave him. I am in love with him. He is the best man I know, and last night . . ." She took a deep, calming breath. She would not succumb to tears. She had made her bed, and she would sleep in it. "He asked me to trust him, and I will, while minding my responsibility to myself. I won't give birth to a fatherless child and subject him to a life of ridicule and pain. At least if I protect myself, when I do return home, I'll still possess an ounce of hope for a normal future. These women's ways, will you teach me?"

"The herbs do not guarantee absolute protection. You are a healthy young woman, and *El-Amar* . . ." Nasrin snorted. "He will keep you occupied. What will you do if the herbs fail you?"

"Naturally, I will have the baby. The effect of these herbs isn't permanent, though, is it?"

"No. You may quit the herbs anytime, but then your body will be exposed. Also, you must drink this vile brew daily, first thing in the morning, and keep drinking it so long as you keep spending your nights with him. I had eight daughters vowing it would never happen again, but it does. Are you certain you wish to go through with this? It could become a way of life."

Alanis took a moment to consider her situation. "I am certain."

Nasrin nodded. She left the pavilion and returned with a pouch of herbs. She dropped a few leaves into a pot of steaming water she'd asked of the footman and poured brown brew into two cups. Pungent vapors drifted. Alanis wrinkled her nose at the obnoxious smell.

"I'd like to impart a bit of Hebrew wisdom, if I may," Nasrin said. "Our Sages of Blessed Memory teach us about the roles of women in man's eyes. 'Two women. This was the way of the generation of the Great Flood: one for procreation and one for delight. She who is for delight drinks a bitter cup to be barren and is adorned as a bride and feeds on delicacies, and her equal is rebuked and desolate as a widow.' They advised women to strive to find wholeness as wives and mothers *and* as adored lovers. Remember, my dear, a clever woman knows how to make herself indispensable to the man she loves and always remains a little bit out of reach."

"I understand." Alanis smiled. Married to Lucas, she would have become the undesirable wife. However, the woman who ventured into the Viper's lair last night . . . Her pulse quickened. Feeling more self-assured, she raised her cup and clinked it against Nasrin's. "Bottoms up!" She consumed it in one swift swallow. *Bitter.* She immediately gulped a full glass of orange juice.

"A word, if I may."

Eros's crisp voice nearly yanked Alanis out of her skin. She exchanged startled glances with Nasrin. How long had he been standing there? Alanis had a strong suspicion that if he had witnessed their private talk, an explosion was pending. Why was she feeling so damned guilty? She was doing him a favor. He should be bloody grateful.

"Good morning, Nasrin." He nodded courteously. He stared at Alanis. "Shall we?"

Impeccably dressed, wet hair tied in a queue, he was his old self again, but his eyes—their feral blue glitter singed her. He took her hand and led them to a small fountain hidden among honeysuckle and palm trees. "You were gone when I woke up," he said. "Something the matter?"

She freed her hand and stepped to a fragrant flower bush. "I needed a private moment."

"A moment with Nasrin." The harshness in his voice made her look up. A muscle beat in his jaw. "The regret in your eyes is heartwarming, Alanis."

"I do not regret last night," she admitted quietly. "Do you?"

The accusing glitter dimmed, and he was staring at her with bedroom eyes again. He sighed and pulled her to him. "Only that it's over." He embraced her quietly, strongly.

So he hadn't witnessed her heart-to-heart with Nasrin. He was worrying about her regrets. She wrapped her arms around his waist and rested her head on his shoulder. She believed in him. She believed in *them*. Somehow, they would make it work.

"*Bimba*, why did you leave my bed without waking me?"

"I did need a private moment. Alone."

"I would have liked to wake up with you beside me, with sleepy eyes and a head too slow to protest against what I had in mind for its body. I have it on good authority that this sort of awakening brightens up one's entire day." He lifted her chin and sought her solemn eyes. "I will stand by my word, Alanis. You won't regret last night. I promise." He kissed her softly. "Let me show you the beach today, and perhaps you'll start believing in me . . ."

Two warships cruised vigilantly along the winding coast, a French and an Algerian. Rocky desert cliffs lined the shore, but little else. Hani paced across the French deck, too agitated to sit at the Italian's table and not really invited to. "We should have found his house by now," he muttered impatiently. "Taofik said it was a giant red fortress, impossible to miss."

Cesare eyed his coconspirator. The time to dispose of the worthless pest was in the cards, but not yet. Not before they located Stefano's home. Philosophically he murmured, "'Patience is a virtue, possess it if you can. Rarely in a woman, never in a man.'"

Hani stopped pacing. "Are you implying I have no virtue?"

Cesare dabbed a lace napkin at a corner of his mouth, his expression a blend of disgust and pity. "*From a zero comes nothing but zero,*" he said in Latin; it was a particular proverb of his.

Incensed by the cryptic insult, Hani raved, "Just remember our contract! *El-Amar* is yours, but the blond woman is mine! She returns to the Kasbah with me."

Mounted on graceful Arabians, they raced along the white-powdered shoreline, defying the splashing froth, the salty breeze, and the radiant sunbeams whipping at their faces. Alanis was living her beach dream. She was free. She was in love. Life was . . . *almost* perfect.

"Let's turn back!" Eros called, his long mane flogging his bare back. "There's a secluded cove beneath the house's promontory. We can hide there for a while."

"What about Sallah and Nasrin?" Alanis called back.

"They can spare us for an hour or so. Their ship sails on the evening tide."

"In that case . . ." She turned around and kicked her heels, daring him to an out-and-out race. He was a magnificent centaur, but she weighed considerably less and easily sailed past him, laughing exuberantly. She dismounted at the opening to a shell-embedded tunnel and dashed inside. She shrieked as his hands grabbed her and spun her around. "I won," she panted, smiling.

"I want to make love to you right here, right now." Eros's gruff voice filled the tunnel.

She ran her palms up his chest, feeling his heart pounding beneath hard, shapely muscles. Dark stubble outlined his upper lip. She rose on her toes and flicked her tongue over the soft swell, tasting salty ocean mist. He caught her head. Their kiss went deeper, slower, longer.

"I want to *devour* you." His Italian *R* rolled on his tongue. He nudged her against the wall and unbuttoned her shirt. He palmed her breasts, squeezing, shaping, rolling her nipples between his thumbs and forefingers. He bent his head and licked an erect nipple to screaming sensitivity.

"Eros . . ." She wormed between him and the wall. He undid her breeches and slid his hand between her thighs. His fingers pressed into her, bombarding her senses. Tidal heat waves surged through her. His rapid breaths filled her ear, and she could hear her own shallow gasps as he kept stroking and teasing her. She stepped out of her breeches and gripped his hard buttocks. "I want you. I need you now." She felt dizzy with a need so powerful her knees were quaking with it.

He groaned. "*Diavolo.* You deserve better than this, but . . . I'm so hard for you." He pushed a hand between their grinding bodies to unfasten his crotch. His erection sprung out, steely hard and smooth against her belly. He curved an arm beneath her bottom and hoisted her up. He came inside of her in a swift thrust. Alanis cried out. He felt *so good, so right* as he rocked her with the fury of a man possessed. She clung to his neck, walking the opposite wall, giving contrast to his pounding hips. His rhythm was ruthless, ravaging, unbearably arousing.

Sight-dimming pleasure ripped through her. "Yes," she cried. "Yes, yes . . . Don't—*stop!*" She convulsed violently, her inner muscles clenching around him, milking his release.

Eros bowed his head in torment and growled as rapture overtook him.

Alanis had no idea how he managed to carry them both, but when she opened her eyes they were sprawled on the sand in a small cove surrounded by rocky walls. They lay tangled together, sweaty and spent, listening to waves crashing ashore. She felt at peace with the world.

"I'm exhausted." Eros smiled at her weakly.

Her face warmed. "You must be wondering what happened to the demure female you—"

"Are you serious?" He propped his head on his fist and grinned. "You think I'm so stupid I didn't know what you were made of?" His gaze roamed her slender legs and recaptured her eyes. "You are fire, *Amore.* White-hot, golden flames shaped as woman. With eyes of a cat."

She bit her lip. "Is . . . is this the only reason you lured me to your bed? Because you found my body . . . appealing?"

"*You* lured *me* to my bed." He smiled incredulously and rolled onto her. "I've never been so deliciously seduced in my entire life." He kissed her sensually, leisurely.

She refused to let his teasing and kissing distract her. She put a firm hand on his chest. "So this is merely an attraction, what we have between us?"

"If this is merely an attraction," he said in all seriousness, "why did I hesitate the night we left Kingston? I had you beneath me just as you are now. And I stopped."

"I was about to stop you, regardless."

"I didn't want to ruin your life, Alanis."

Her heart missed a beat. "And now that we are lovers—you believe my life is ruined?"

"I still think you'd be better off without me." He smiled. "But to answer your question—I do not think your life is ruined. Things have changed. Which is why I want you to write a letter to your grandfather. He deserves to know that you are safe. Sallah will send it to Dellamore."

"Are you mad?" She nudged him aside and sat up. "My grandfather will send half the Fleet to bombard Agadir if he gets word that his granddaughter is . . . You of all people ought to know that unmarried granddaughters of dukes do not take lovers."

Eros sat up beside her. "If you don't let that old man know where you are, within three weeks you'll start crying to me to take you home, and I won't, Alanis. I give you fair warning. Last night we made promises, and I intend to hold you to yours. You're staying with me."

"Then what am I to tell my grandfather in this letter?"

"Tell him you are with me."

Another test—*with whom?* Her grandfather might react more tolerably to the news that she was with Stefano Sforza, the lost prince of Milan, but bearing in mind Eros's insistence on secrecy and his distinct aversion to grasping females, she dared not tell her grandfather the truth.

She felt his eyes on her profile. "You are ashamed of your feelings," he bit out frostily.

"Why don't you write this letter yourself and I shall simply sign it?" she offered blandly.

Eros stood up. He walked to the edge of the water, scooped a handful of shells, and flung them at the waves. "I'm not sure what you expect of me, or what you think I'm capable of at this point in time, but—" He turned around to face her. "I want us to be together. We don't have to remain here all the time. We can travel. I'll take you anywhere you want, show you all the places you dreamed and wrote about in your voyage journal."

She winced. "Don't remind me of *that*. Your reading my private journal doesn't stand to your credit." He was offering to fulfill her dream, but it wasn't enough anymore, not from him. Returning to the matter at hand, she said, "You are assuming that once I inform my grandfather of my whereabouts all will be well. It won't. He will not tolerate my living with you out of wedlock. He will either declare war against you or force you to marry me." She waited . . .

"I can't marry you, Alanis. Not as he'd like me to. You shall have to choose between your former life and a life with me. This is how I live my life. Split in two. I do what I must to survive, and I carry Milan in my heart." He waded into the water and dove underneath the waves.

His wife was ready to chew his head off. Sallah eyed Nasrin as she entered their apartment, black eyes flashing, and marched straight toward the coffeepot a servant had delivered while he had still been snoring. He practiced his meekest tenor, "May I have some coffee, too, please?"

Nasrin stabbed him with a seething glare. "Serve yourself."

With an indignant grunt Sallah slid off the bed and came to pour himself a cup. He needed a strong swig of coffee to clear his head and bolster his nerve before tackling this unpromising mood. "*Ahh.*" He sighed as the heavenly brew coursed down his gullet, reviving his vigor. "So, m'dear, how may I be of help? Anything I can do to fix this crisis?"

"You did *enough*. I suggest you contemplate on how you will *undo* it, jackal."

"Something tells me this has everything to do with our lovesick friends."

"Lovesick friends. Ha! *My* friend is lovesick. *Yours* is concerned with putting out the fire in his loins! What do you suppose they've been up to since yester eve? Since your meddling?"

"The devil he did! That splendid fellow! All it took was a strong word of advice and the feminine fort of resistance disintegrated to a pile of rubble. I tell you, Nasrin, he's my hero. Not even your shrewish guidance held head to his prowess. So, when's the wedding?"

She gave him a baleful look. "When you have finished clapping yourself on the back, you may want to ask him that yourself, because I don't think there will be a wedding. You should not have meddled, Sallah. Whatever you said to him gave him the key to accomplishing what he was unable to do on his own merit. He thinks he has snagged himself a highborn demirep. You know he is incapable of loving any woman romantically."

"Eros is lonely. He needs her. Perhaps with time desire will grow into love."

"I dread to think what will become of her in a few months. He will destroy her."

Sallah scowled. Had he misjudged Eros's feelings? He could have sworn it was true love tearing his friend apart, but Eros thrived on extreme emotions, and there was nothing like a difficult challenge to get those Lombard cannons up and roaring. "I'll have a word with him."

"Alanis asked us not to interfere. I gave her my word that we won't."

He sighed. "He is playing with fire. He is not even fully appreciative of the danger he's courting. The Duke of Dellamore is a powerful man. Sooner or later, word will reach Dellamore, and Eros will be hunted down as a rabid dog. He can't keep her with him in the desert forever."

"What should we do, Sallah?"

"There's only one solution, and Eros won't like it one bit. She must return home with us."

Eros emerged from the ocean in a sparkling splash. Tapering to a lean waist, his muscular chest glistened with seawater. His sapphire eyes shone in his face. He wrenched water from his glossy jet mane and cast Alanis a pearly smile. "Come swim with me, *ninfa bionda!*"

Lounging against a boulder, her toes wiggling in the sand, Alanis stared at the naked pagan standing waist-deep in the scintillating water and brooded over his last statement. He couldn't marry her. *Ever.* What would she ultimately tell her grandfather? What would become of her?

He sent a spurt of water in her direction, but only a drop landed on her toe. "*Dai,* come into the water with me. I promise I won't make a pest of myself." When she shook her head, smiling defiantly, he waded a step forward. "Or I'm carrying you in myself."

"All right, tyrant!" She removed her shirt hastily, self-consciously, aware of his hot gaze missing nary a thing, and dove into the azure ocean. She surfaced before him, slick and golden, feeling like a veritable nymph. "You rang?"

"*Anima bella, beautiful soul,*" Eros murmured in Italian, as he held her waist and pressed her slick breasts to his sun-warmed torso. "'*For you I must burn, in you breathe, for I've been only yours, and if I am deprived of you, it pains me more than any other misfortune.*'"

"One day," she whispered, "you'll have to speak your heart in a language I understand."

"One day." He flashed her a wolfish smile and slurped up her face with his tongue.

Grimacing, Alanis pushed him away and tried hard not to

laugh. "That was disgusting! I'm not your luncheon, tiger. And you promised you wouldn't make a pest of yourself."

His dimples gave a grand appearance in his cheeks. "I lied."

"Another disgusting habit of yours."

"I'm a disgusting individual." He enveloped her in his arms again and sank them chin-deep in the water, wrapping her legs around him. He kissed her. "But you like me as I am, don't you?"

"Very much."

His eyes clouded. "What happens when I cease to be an interesting puzzle? When you are bored with desert dunes, Italian food, and me?"

Her heart melted, realizing this strong, arrogant, beautiful Milanese prince who was the toughest man she knew worried she might abandon him. No one ever worried she might leave them. It was always the opposite. The ones she loved left her. "What happens when the novelty wears off?" she countered. He had had so many women, and they had all fallen from grace . . .

"I imagine we shall simply have to take it one step at a time."

Without formal marriage vows what he suggested went against her entire upbringing. She was terrified, but so was Eros. Yet the way he smiled at her, the warmth in his eyes, encouraged her to believe anything was possible. She circled her arms around his slick neck and kissed his crescent scar. "You didn't tell me how you got this brutal scar."

"*Spagnolo stupido*. Tried to stop me the night I fled the Tower in Milan."

"And this scar has characterized you since—*El-Amar,* the corsair." His life had split in two—before and after. "I can't help thinking about your poor sister, Princess Gelsomina. She must have been petrified seeing her brother's face ripped open, bloody, having to ride throughout the night, away from the only home she had ever known and loved, her safe haven.

And you, sixteen years old, carrying her on your lap with your face in shreds."

"My soul was in shreds, Alanis. Believe me, it hurt more."

"I believe you," she said quietly. "And yet—"

A jet eyebrow lifted. "What?"

"Your mother. Perhaps you don't know the whole story. No one changes his spots from one day to the next without a justifiable cause. If she was the affectionate mother you claim—"

"Alanis," he mustered his forbearance, "my mother is not my favorite subject."

"I know, but if she's alive somewhere, you may find answers . . ."

"I don't give a damn whit about her answers! If our paths should cross again someday, I'll do what I should have done years ago." His eyes blazed with resentment. "I will kill her."

She searched his eyes. Sixteen years and still he burned. "I don't believe you would. If you didn't do it then, you won't be able to do it in cold blood. You may have the equanimity to chop strangers' heads off but not to slay your own mother. You don't have it in you, Eros."

"What about my father? Doesn't he deserve to be avenged?"

"Your life is not a Greek tragedy. What happened to your father was terrible, but you killed your uncle and got away. If you really want to right your life, concentrate on healing, on creating a future for yourself. Return to Milan. Take back what you've lost. Free your people from the bondage of the French and the Spaniards."

Eros pulled away from her. Staring at the far horizon where the ocean melded with the sky, he said, "Have you read Aeschylus's story of Agamemnon—the Greek commander who returned home from the Trojan War to be murdered by his wife and her lover?"

Frowning, Alanis replied, "I did."

"Agamemnon had a son, Orestes. He was a boy when his father died, but when he came into manhood, he became aware of his obligation—to kill his father's assassins, a duty preceding all others. Only Orestes knew that killing his own mother was an abomination in the eyes of gods and men. His holy duty was linked with a vicious crime. The man who sought to walk in justice had to choose between two iniquities: betraying his father or becoming his mother's assassin."

"Orestes's dilemma is a moral one, Eros. Yours is emotional. It isn't the same thing." She saw she wasn't getting through to him, so she asked, "What did Orestes do?"

"Orestes consulted the Oracle at Delphi. Apollo was clear on the matter. Kill the two who killed. Avenge death with death. Spill blood over spilled blood. Orestes had no choice except to dispel the curse on his house, take revenge, and pay with his own damnation."

"His own damnation," Alanis murmured, feeling chilled.

"'Appease, the god commanded me, the raging dead,'" he quoted. "'For he who listens not to the cry of his dead, will drift alone forever, bereft of shelter. No flame will blaze for him in the altar, no friend will greet his face. Contemptible and desolate will he die.' So, Orestes killed his mother, and for years he roamed the earth, haunted by his horrors."

She finally understood. He thought himself damned, so he punished himself by pursuing a life of violence, residing alone in an empty marble tomb in the desert, enjoying the occasional attentions of high-class prostitutes, fighting a king he was also fond of—the king who was tearing his country down—but building nothing for himself.

Eros sighed. "When Orestes's spirit tired of suffering, when he lost everything men value, he sought Athena's advice. The Goddess of Wisdom absolved him. She convinced Alastor, the Goddess of Revenge, that he had atoned for his sins. Orestes and his descendants were free at last of the curse on the House of Atreus."

"You believe that by killing your own mother you'd avenge your father's death and dispel the curse on your house? Aren't you tired of suffering? You were unable to kill her sixteen years ago. Let it be. If she truly is a harpy, then she deserved what she got in the bargain—no family, no princedom, no lover. There was no shame in letting her live."

He kept his eyes on the horizon. "That is not what I am ashamed of."

So there was more, something he wasn't ready to share with her yet. She put a hand on his cheek, asking him to look at her. "Forgive yourself," she whispered. "Your mother may have committed the unpardonable, but you loved her." And in a softer voice she added, "*You still do.*"

He shut his eyes, his Adam's apple moving. He looked so vulnerable she pulled him to her and kissed his eyes, his lips, his cheeks, wanting to heal all his torments. He crushed her in his arms, as if trying to absorb her into his heart. His mouth found hers. It was the headiest kiss, two souls reaching for one another. Her veins flowed with warm honey. *I love you,* her heart said.

He stared at her. "I pounced on you earlier. I'd like to make it up to you. Are you game?"

A quiver swept through her. "Yes," she whispered.

Eros carried her ashore and laid her on their clothes. He stretched out beside her, dropping soft kisses along her neck and breasts. "You are so graceful. I love touching you, tasting you."

She smiled up at him. "You are an Italian . . ."

"*Sì.* And the one thing Italians have abundantly is imagination." He took his time exploring her body, learning its secrets, showing her things she didn't know about herself. He was astute, thorough, and for a man who lived by the sword, incredibly sensitive. His command of her body astounded her. He simply needed to stroke or squeeze her gently in a strategic place and her body tingled, bucked, and shuddered. He aroused her senses to the edge of endurance.

"Eros." Her tongue was hot and messy in his ear. "Let me torture you a little. *Please.*"

A shudder raked him. He sighed, grinned, and nodded. "Be gentle with me." He rolled onto his back and lay still as she applied her newly acquired knowledge of his body into making him writhe as she had writhed beneath him. She ran her nails, her lips, and her hair over his skin and felt him straining and pointing. He had many scars but was still unbelievably beautiful. *Perfect.*

Growing bolder, she glided southward, kissing the hills and valleys on his hard abdomen, tantalizing his loins with her warm breath, and fastened her soft lips around his heavy rim.

He jumped. "*Santo Michele.* Are you trying to kill me?" He was on top again, the muscles on his arms swelling, as he suspended himself above her. "Alanis . . ."

She stared into his dark eyes. "So you may touch me, but I'm not allowed to touch you?"

"You may touch me as much as you want, *Amore,* just . . . not yet."

"Why?"

"Because . . ." He eased onto her, big and heavy, and positioned himself between her thighs. "I'm mad for you. I nearly lost my control earlier. I don't want you to think it can be like this with other men. I want to go slowly, explore every beautiful inch of you, pleasure you, but if we keep on mating like crazed rabbits—which is exactly what will happen if you use your mouth on me again—we'll miss out the best pinnacles." He took her mouth in a devouring kiss and drove into her. The rush of pleasure made them groan in unison. She locked her legs around his hips until he was so firmly embedded, he became a part of her. He withdrew and thrust again. *Hard.* She moaned, hating herself for moaning, but was unable to stop. He put his large hand on her belly and rubbed, exerting subtle pressure, intensifying the friction of his rhythmic invasions. He did exercise restraint, but she was fast spiraling out of control, about to tumble into oblivion.

She gripped his arms, quivering, begging. He increased the speed, guiding her, pushing her toward her climax. "Don't hold back, *Amore.* I am taking it slowly, but as a woman you may find fulfillment in swift succession as many times as you want. *Don't hold back.*"

She was incapable of holding back. The sun could have set

and she wouldn't have noticed, she'd sunk so deeply into sensation. Like a pulse, his thrusts vibrated through her. She dissolved beneath him, around him, discovered ecstasy, and begged for more.

Lost to the world, they made slow, indulgent, narcotic love in the sun, drunk by feel and taste, absorbed in each other, soaring and crashing with the waves. They were forged as one in the blaze of passion, every roll of hips taking them into profounder levels of sensual awareness. Eros's essence fused in Alanis's head with the scent of the sand, with the radiance of the sun, and with the call of the waves breaking ashore in gusts of spray—as intoxicating as potent drugs.

And while in the throes of the long-drawn-out delirium that went on and on and on, in the deep recesses of her liquefied mind, she came to a decision: She would love her fierce Milanese lover with all of her heart and soul and hope that one day he would reciprocate her love.

Concealed behind a remote boulder, a pair of eyes burned bitterly. Cesare swore. He was sweating as a pig, his body on fire. He hadn't expected the English duke's granddaughter to turn out to be a saffron-haired beauty with long, creamy limbs. Watching her with Stefano fried his nerves. The bastard would pay for this, with pain, blood, and humiliation. He would squeal as a swine roasting on a stick, begging for an early tomb.

"It's been two hours," Roberto droned, his beady eyes hanging out of their sockets. "How long does he intend to go on? Even the Greeks didn't give Olympic medals for humping."

"Shut up, *stronzo!* You're salivating on my boots." Shutting his telescope, Cesare shoved the pest aside and produced a lace neckpiece to wipe his perspiring brow. He couldn't recall the last time he felt such rampant lust. It left him shaken, his breeches painfully tight. He would do this blond *caramellina. Soon.* He'd do her so thoroughly she'd forget Stefano ever existed.

Roberto rose off the ground, dusting sand off his shoddy garments. "What now?"

Cesare smirked. "Now we bring on the *bêtes noires,* the despicable beasts."

"We should be getting back." Eros sighed. "Beside the fact that I can eat a horse, Sallah and Nasrin will wonder if I have done away with you."

Alanis was already pulling on her breeches. "I could drink a bucket of cold juice."

"Listen," he brushed sand off her cheek, smiling conspiratorially, "we'll have lunch with our departing friends, send them on their merry way, and then take a long nap in my chamber."

"As long as it includes a bath." She finished dressing and was ready to return to the house when Dolce came trotting through the tunnel, a cook's neckpiece tied around her spotted neck.

Eros chuckled. "I think we've been summoned to lunch. Mustafa has a bizarre sense of humor." He patted the feline's small head. "*Vai,* go to Antonio. Tell him to keep the food warm."

Dolce licked his hand and obediently darted into the tunnel.

Alanis laughed. "She's a clever one, isn't she?"

"Dolce is very intelligent," Eros agreed proudly. "Also possessive, spoiled, and more discriminating in her tastes than a Roman princess."

"Where did you find her? You must admit she's not an ordinary pet."

"She found me. She was a tiny thing, starved and dehydrated. I think her mother died and she got lost. The Sahara is the leopards' natural habitat, but water and food are sparse. I took her in, and when she was stronger, I rode with her to the Rif. She followed me home. I considered finding her a mate, but keeping two wild cats in captivity seemed too cruel.

I hope she'll catch a whiff of a healthy male one day and follow him to the wilderness."

Alanis slanted Eros a sardonic smile. "Can't you see Dolce already thinks she's found her mate? And looking at you," her smile broadened, "I can't blame her."

Eros curled his arm around her waist. "You think I look like a large, speckled cat?"

"Actually, you remind me of a blue-eyed, black leopard. A very dangerous beast."

He gave her waist a tight squeeze. "*Allora,* this dangerous beast has already staked his claim on a golden nymph, so Dolce will have to find someone else to lock tails with."

Their shared laughter was interrupted by a meaningful cough. They spun around and froze. Algerian corsairs and French soldiers filed through another passage in the cliff, aiming French carbines straight at them. One of them, Alanis recognized, was Hani, but the leader—a European nobleman judging by his looks and clothing—stepped forth, and her eyes widened in disbelief. She stared at Eros, who looked stunned, then stared at the stranger. Except for minor details such as Eros's scar, tan, and hair length, they looked *exactly* alike, two drops of water, as identical as twins. There was one distinct exception, though; the stranger's vivid sapphire eyes were cold.

He smiled rapaciously. "*Saluti, Stefano. It's a pleasure to see you after so many years.*"

"Get out of here, Alanis!" Eros rasped. "*Now!*"

The stranger trained his pistol on Alanis and switched to English. "*Dai,* Stefano, introduce me to your beautiful companion. Sixteen years in the wilds and you have become a savage." He smiled at her. "You do know his name is Stefano? Usually he finds relaying such information futile because he never stays with one female long enough to bother with introductions."

Eros glared at the stranger and fired a salvo of warnings in Italian. The man only laughed.

"Eros, who is this man?" Alanis asked in a whisper, her legs rooted to the spot.

He glanced at her, and she read tension in his eyes. "Cesare is my cousin. Carlo's son."

"*Si*. The resemblance is chilling, isn't it? One may think we're brothers and not cousins. A strong possibility, considering your mother was a whore." Cesare laughed crudely.

Hani materialized at Cesare's side. "What are you waiting for? Let's take them and get out of here before his entire army will come pouring down the hill!"

Cesare's jaw clenched. "Shut up, *idiota!*"

Eros fixed his eyes on the French soldiers. "So you went to Louis. Predictable. How much did he pay for your country and soul? Not more than a few thousand *livres,* I presume."

"More than you're worth," Cesare spat. "Knowing I'd be the next Duke of Milan delighted him so much it put him in a spendthrift mood."

"Louis is never in a spendthrift mood. The old cheapskate must have sent you to collect his marks from me from the last time we played *vingt-et-un* in Versailles. He always was a poor sport."

Cesare's complexion reddened. Eros smirked and folded his arms across his chest. He was stalling, Alanis decided, hoping their lengthy absence would trigger alarm at the house.

"So what do you want from me?" he inquired. "The reason you haven't killed me yet?"

Cesare tensed. "*Il medaglione.*"

Eros threw his head back and laughed. "Poor cousin. After all those years they still won't let you have Milan without proof of my death. I understand why you went to Louis."

Alanis glimpsed at his bare neck. The medallion had to still be in his bedchamber on the table where he had left it last night.

"Louis was more than happy to oblige," Cesare sneered. "He doesn't seem to like you as much as you believe he does."

"Louis loves no one except himself," Eros stated, "and France, but he considers himself and France to be one and the same. He probably didn't think you'd find me. Out of curiosity, was he the one who put you up to seeking my enemies in Algiers?"

"They, too, proved helpful. It appears you have no one in the entire universe, Stefano. Everyone wants you dead. Now hand over my medallion, before I—"

"You'll never have *my* medallion, Cesare. It belonged to my father, to the *rightful* duke of Milan. And it will remain in the rightful hands."

Becoming restless, Hani stepped closer to his associate. "Let's take them and go!"

"Not yet," Cesare hissed. "Not before he hands over what I want from him."

Eros took advantage of the distraction and nudged Alanis aside. "Go, *now!*"

"She moves, you die." Cesare trained the barrel of his pistol on Eros. "Your call, *bionda.*"

"*Yallah!* Let's go!" Hani insisted. "He'll give you what you want later."

"I don't need to listen to the opinion of a filthy monkey!" Cesare bellowed. "I think you've served your purpose." He aimed his pistol and fired. Hani collapsed, clutching his bleeding torso.

Eros turned to Alanis. "Get out of here! There's no point in both of us dying!"

Terror in her heart, she stayed put and whispered, "We go together."

Eros stared at her in shock, then shoved her away from him, barking, "Go back to England! Forget about me! Let your grandfather marry you off to a stuffy nobleman! You never meant more than a diversion to me, you silly, sniveling tart!"

She stared at him through eyes suffused with tears. "He'll take you and I won't be able to find you . . . I'll never see you again . . ."

Eros gnashed his teeth. His eyes burned with anguish. "Then it was not meant to be. Now go, Alanis, *please . . .*" he pleaded in a whisper. "*Go!*"

She gave him one last glance, carving his image in her heart, then turned around and ran. She heard terrible blasts, shells shrieking past her head, splinting shards of rock, but she kept on running through the tunnel until she reached her horse. She hopped on and galloped up the hill, hoping against all odds that by the time she reached Giovanni, it wouldn't be too late . . .

Alanis rode through the gates, yelling at the guards to get down to the beach and help Eros. She handed her reins to one of them and dashed toward the separate billets of the crew, shouting Giovanni's name at the top of her lungs. Giovanni, Nico, and Rocca rushed forth. She explained succinctly, urging them to hurry. They didn't waste time. They grabbed arms and horses and tore through the gates. More men gathered. Mustafa and Sallah came running down the front steps.

Alanis repeated her concise explanation, panting, crying, terrified out of her wits. "Sallah, let's go down there. I saw a ship's stern beyond the promontory. I'm afraid Cesare will take him away and we'll never see him again. We'll never be able to find him."

Sallah steered her out the gates. They raced down the steep hill, kicking up a cloud of sand. In the distance, men and horses hovered at the mouth of the tunnel, few going in, others coming out. Pistols in hand, faces drawn, Niccolò and Giovanni approached her. They shook their heads.

"*No!*" She dashed into the tunnel and emerged on the hidden cove. Hani was sprawled on the sand, dead, surrounded by footprints. Her whole body shook. Eros was gone.

CHAPTER 20

Her first impulse was to drop to her knees and cry, but she had to keep her wits about her. She had to rescue Eros. She raised her head and found Sallah and the men watching her glumly.

"Prepare every accessible ship," she ordered Giovanni. "We set sail at once."

Hours later she stood at the quarterdeck railing and viewed the barren coastline crimsoning under the setting sun. How did this come about, she wondered. She was in command of the *Alastor*, in charge of its cutthroat crew, and making fatal decisions concerning Eros's life.

This pirate is extremely grateful to put his life in such fine delicate hands. You have no one in the entire universe, Stefano; everyone wants you dead.

She shut her eyes and said a silent prayer. "I won't fail you," she vowed. "I won't."

Nico materialized at her side and gently patted her shoulder. "Don't worry. We'll find him. There is not one man among us who won't give his life for Eros. We owe him everything."

"There is still no sign of an Algerian or a French ship?" She glanced at him, but he shifted uneasily and wouldn't meet her gaze. "What?" she demanded. "Tell me now."

"The wind has weakened and they had a head start. We're sailing in a blind chase."

She pushed away from the railing. "We need to hold a concilium. Find Giovanni, Greco, and anyone else who may contribute an intelligent idea. We'll convene in Eros's cabin."

Moments later she was plowing the carpet in the luxurious black and purple cabin.

"Our best recourse is to sail to the Kasbah," Sallah stated. "For a while now the Dey has been hot after Eros's head. I'll call on Sanah. She might be able to tell us something."

"The King of France is involved in this as well," Nico said. "We mustn't rule out France."

"Or Milan," Giovanni added. "You did say this man, Cesare, is a Milanese?"

Alanis nodded. "But there's a war in Milan. If I were Cesare, I wouldn't risk venturing into the fire zones. I'd take my captive to a place I knew well, somewhere private, where I'd keep him secreted for a long time until I got what I needed from him. I'd avoid Algiers and France as well, because I wouldn't want the Dey or the King of France interfering with my plans."

"Italy isn't the largest country in the world," Nico said, "but it's a lot of territory to cover."

"I warned Eros he was playing against too many sides all at once." Sallah sighed. "It could be the Dey, deciding to eliminate one of his enemies, or Hani acting on his own, or the French, or Cesare . . ." He stared at Alanis quizzically, no doubt wondering what it was she wasn't saying.

"He could be anywhere," Alanis summed up, feeling the tight squeeze of panic.

"I know someone who may be of assistance to us." Nasrin's voice drew all eyes to her. "His name is Sidi Moussa d'Aglou. He is a blind old fisherman who lives up the coast in the caves near Safi. It's a few hours' sail on the way to Algiers. We can stop en route to see him."

Alanis sent her a grateful smile, but Sallah looked slightly uncomfortable. "Sidi Moussa is a diviner, m'dear, or what others would call a quack. The Moroccans invite him to poke around their wells when they dry up, and even at that I'm not convinced he's any good."

"Sidi Moussa is a holy man," Nasrin insisted. "Besides, you were the one who started this business of consulting soothsayers and seers. Where's the harm in stopping by his cave to ask him? My sister told me that last year he located a missing camel by fingering its metallic harness. We can let him touch *El-Amar*'s medallion. Perhaps he'll locate him for us."

Alanis saw Nico and Daniello rolling their eyes, but no one openly ridiculed Nasrin's idea, except Sallah. "That's sheer idiocy," he raved. "It will cost us precious time in getting to Algiers and doing some serious reconnaissance."

Nasrin glowered at him. "So when we consult your quacks it's intelligence work, but when I suggest someone who's respected from here to Tangier, whom the entire city of Marrakech—"

"Tell me more about this man, Nasrin," Alanis asked. Time was running out.

"He's the sweetest man and very wise," Nasrin assured her. "My sisters and I used to visit his cave on the beach when my parents took us to the seaside during the roasting Marrakech summers. He shared his fried fish with us and told us stories about foreign lands no one around these parts ever heard about. He's special, I tell you, and he has the divine gift of locating lost individuals by touching metals they were in the habit of wearing."

"You mean lost camels . . ." Sallah murmured, and gained another glower from his wife.

"What do you want us to do, my lady?" Nico inquired gently. "Do you wish to consult with this Sidi Moussa d'Aglou?"

Every eye settled on her. She wondered how Eros would accept this new situation. She fingered the heavy medallion nestling inside her bodice. It was Cesare's objective in coming after him and the crux of Eros's whole life's tragedy: the entitlement to rule the Duchy of Milan, a privilege he didn't even want anymore yet was reluctant to forfeit altogether. *His curse.*

She knew Eros would welcome death before relinquishing his father's heirloom to Carlo's son. She, however, wanted him alive, and medallion be damned. If she could get to Cesare, she'd negotiate Eros's return for the medallion. She raised her head and said, "Sidi Moussa first."

That night, the *Alastor* dropped cable off the coast of Safi. They embarked ashore in two boats and came upon a company of fishermen cooking dinner on an outer fire set on the sand. Nasrin made the introductions, humbly offering fruit and blankets brought from the *Alastor.* The fishermen received the gifts and invited the odd group of strangers to share their coffee and fried fish. Once they relaxed around the fire,

Nasrin encouraged conversation, mentioning *El Amara*—the Red City, Marrakech—and gesturing at the caves.

"She is telling them she's from Marrakech," Sallah whispered next to Alanis's ear, "and is asking them to please point out the cave of Holy Sidi Moussa, a man she has great respect for and visited often with her sisters as a child. Let's hear if they know him."

The fishermen consulted each other. One of them spoke. Nasrin nodded at Alanis. "They trust us. Sidi Moussa still lives in one of the caves up ahead. They will take us to him."

Led by the friendly fishermen, they made their way toward the amorphous openings in the cliff. A frail-looking man, old and wrinkled, sat quietly by his fire, playing his flute.

"We come with the blessing of God, *Sidi Moussa*." Nasrin sank beside him and crossed her legs. She offered her hands for greeting and examination. A smile animated the old fisherman's wrinkled face, his eyes—a pair of lights of indistinct color—shone. He spoke to her warmly.

"He's asking about her sisters and her parents," Sallah translated. "My wife will be in high spirits tonight. No one has asked about her parents in years. They've been dead for a decade."

The old man listened attentively to Nasrin's story, nodding his head and asking questions. She stood up and came to Alanis. "I need *El-Amar*'s medallion."

With trembling fingers Alanis removed the heavy gold chain off her neck and handed it to Nasrin. Nasrin sat down beside the old fisherman and put the medallion in his leathery hands. He rubbed the engravings with deep concentration, murmuring to himself, calling upon the Divine One to enlighten him. "*Ah!*" His indistinct eyes glowed with uncanny awareness. He spoke to Nasrin with a knowing smile, moving his hands in the night air, pointing north.

"Sallah—!" Alanis clutched his thick wrist, hissing next to his ear, "Translate!"

Sallah frowned. "He said that in Berber. We'll have to wait for Nasrin's translation."

It took more time, but finally, Nasrin got up and approached them. She looked ambivalent. "Sidi Moussa referred to the medallion's owner as The Emir with the Split Soul."

"Sallah! Did you hear that?" Alanis cried. "What else, Nasrin? Where did they take Eros?"

"It gets even more peculiar. Sidi Moussa says the Emir is not yet arrived at his destination but that his road leads to a special city—an eternal city—and a black pit of despair."

"*A black pit of despair?* In an eternal city?" Alanis's heart cramped with dread. Dear Lord!

"What special city?" Sallah asked in a practical tone of voice. "It could be anywhere—Algiers, Paris. Makes my head throb with possibilities."

"There's more," Nasrin added uneasily. "The road, Sidi Moussa says, is one of many long, winding roads, all leading to the same place—the city that all roads lead to." Her eyes filled with remorse. "I'm sorry, my dear. I didn't mean to lead us on a—"

"Wait!" Alanis sensed the tiny hairs on her nape standing on end. "The eternal city that all roads lead to . . ."

Nasrin's frown deepened. "This makes sense to you?"

Alanis turned away from them and stared at the black ocean. *The eternal city that all roads lead to . . . And a black pit of despair.* Fixing her gaze at the stars, she breathed, "Rome."

CHAPTER 21

Crisp winter wind welcomed them outside the somber confines of Castel Sant'Angelo. Her hand tucked in Sallah's elbow, Alanis followed him onto the marble bridge poised over the Tiber River and sent a silent plea to the protective goddess, Roma, begging her to reveal where in her city she secreted her beloved. After three weeks of searching every possible incarceration pit and still no clue of Eros's whereabouts, she was becoming desperate.

"That was one futile venture." Sallah sighed beside her. "Only a simpleton would install a prisoner such as Eros in the dungeons of a castle as conspicuous as City Hall. Unfortunately for us, this villain, Cesare, is anything but simple minded."

"Simple-mindedness doesn't run in their family. We have to be shrewder, Sallah. We can't go on like this, stumbling in the dark while Eros is paying dearly for our incompetence."

"Damn, but this is despairing. Not that I mind dragging my feet from dawn to dusk, from one pit to the next, or bribing every nasty jailor in Rome, but it's taking a dratted amount of time, and God knows what horrid hospitality his cousin is extending, or if he's still alive . . ."

"He's alive," she stated emphatically. "And he is here. I feel him." She could not lose hope. Not now. Not ever. Not until she saw his . . . She was incapable of completing that thought.

"Of course he's alive!" Sallah exclaimed with a heartening smile. "And I don't envy his jailors in the least. Did I tell you about the time he came to see me in London and was put in the Tower under charges of espionage? The fools suspected he was a Spanish agent. As if a Spaniard would have the eyes of a northern Italian prince!" He chuckled.

"Sallah, when I told you the truth about his origins you claimed to know nothing about it." She had to tell him and Nasrin. Three minds were better than one. The only details she omitted were those concerning his mother's betrayal.

"I had strong suspicions. I knew he was a nobleman. One cannot miss that about Eros. Also his Milanese crests were telling, although I was too cowardly to come out and ask him. He knew all the salacious tidbits about the monarchs, the princes, and the high-ranking generals on the continent. It implied more than a casual interest in politics, but it never occurred to me he was Stefano Sforza. You see, I understood him. I knew the man that he was."

"Is," Alanis corrected.

"Is. And I didn't need to know more. I'm glad he confided in you. He needed someone he could trust, who isn't his younger sister. Someone strong enough to be there for him in his hour of need." His black eyes warmed. "You're but a wisp of a girl, Alanis, pretty and fragile looking as a fairy, yet you're all heart, sharp as a razor, and strong. I think in you he found his match."

"Not so strong," she admitted in a quiet, hollow voice. She was dying inside.

"Come." Sallah curved his arm around her shoulders. "We'll cross the river and walk to Piazza Navona. I'll treat you to a cup of hot chocolate. That should cheer us up."

As they strolled in silence across the ornate bridge, Alanis absorbed the sprawling sights of the city: Grand palaces and piazzas commemorating cardinals were juxtaposed with monuments in honor of gods and emperors. This was Rome of Caesars, legions, and gilded eagles, of popes and princes, power and decline. London she found inspiring, Paris breathtaking, but the Eternal City humbled her spirit. With Christmas in the air, Rome was garlanded in red, green, and gold.

"Which foul dungeon is next on Nasrin's list?" she asked. Nasrin had trouble breathing in closed places, so she was in charge of researching and coming up with bright ideas akin to the one that had brought them here.

Sallah produced a crumpled piece of paper and frowned at it. "Catacombs, columbarium, necropolises. The list is endless. There's a whole subterranean city constructed beneath our feet."

"I dread to think of Eros buried alive in a sinister Jesuit tomb." She stopped at the midpoint of the bridge. "This is no good, Sallah. We need to narrow our search. Were it London, we'd be pulling strings, trying to enlist the help of influential people, so why not here?"

Sallah took out a cigar. "We don't know anybody here. Whom can we turn to? Family?"

Alanis stilled. "My family?"

He pumped the tip of his cigar to a red glow, looking

pensive. "Your grandfather is not the relative I had in mind, although he's an influential man. I understand your reluctance to appeal to him. You're afraid he'd order you back to England and insist you leave Eros to save himself."

"He will." Alanis's blue-green eyes etched with sorrow. "Whose family then?"

"Eros's."

"I don't know if there are other Sforza about beside Jasmine and Cesare, and I'm afraid that if there are any, they might also be in cahoots with his vile cousin."

"His mother's family, then. Royalty marries royalty. His mother's branch should be just as high up. Somebody should know something."

"This is not a good idea." She knew Eros wouldn't appreciate any help from that direction. "Sallah, we don't need anonymous relatives. We need an accessible, neutral figure who can pull rank, has currency everywhere, and knows this city inside out. Someone like the pope."

They stared at each other in utter stupefaction, then burst out laughing.

"We're idiots!" Alanis exclaimed cheerfully.

"You're a genius!" Sallah threw his cigar and smothered her with a bear hug.

Staring up at the sky, her heart welled with hope, and she gave silent thanks to God. It was Christmas, after all, the season of miracles. "We'll go to him straight away!" she announced. "He won't be able to refuse lending his help to rescuing a royal Italian prince. He'll find Eros for us."

Sallah coughed. "Ugh . . . I assume that when you say 'we' you mean 'you,' and that you have a solid idea on which pretext you will approach the pope on behalf of a man you are not related to. You are an unmarried young lady, alone in a foreign land . . ."

Her heart sank like a rock. "I have no pretext." Her connection to Eros was not something mentionable in the presence of the Holy Father.

Sallah's brows knitted. "Then we shall have to find you a credible excuse."

"Perhaps you should be the one to go," Alanis encouraged. "You are a gentleman, you are Eros's business partner, and you are his closest friend. It is as good as family."

Sallah shook his head. "I cannot call upon the head of the Catholic Church, my dear. I will not genuflect before him. I will not kiss his hand or cross myself. I'll brave the lions in the arena, but I won't renounce my faith. Not even for Eros."

Alanis nodded grimly. "I respect that."

Sallah curled his mustachio. "The duty of saving life overrides the Sabbath laws. Do you suppose it overrides lying to the pope?"

"I will lie, if I must," Alanis said slowly. "For Eros."

Sallah grunted. "Then so be it. I have a plan that will get you admitted."

They spent the entire day looking for the individual they needed to legalize their scheme. Their hunt proved amazingly successful—a good omen—and they returned to the hotel on Rione Campo Marzo to dress. Alanis took exceptional care with her toilette, anxious to make the right impression on His Holiness, and secretly titivating herself for Eros as well. It was a silly notion; he was not likely to be waiting in the Pope's apartments, but she was thrumming with him, catching whiffs of his heady scent as she rummaged through her trunks.

Sallah and Nasrin escorted her in a closed carriage to the ensemble of St. Peter's basilica, the greatest of all basilicas, and left her in Piazza San Pietro between the imposing, colonnaded arms. Snow flurries floated in the air. Towers, castles, offices, and libraries encircled the area, but she had eyes only for the regal cathedral soaring before her. She prayed His Holiness, Pope Clement XI, would prove as omnipotent as the aura of his great dominion.

Tears and fears surrounded her on all sides as Alanis

registered at the secretary of the Vicar of St. Peter's front desk, signing her name and specifying her reason for requesting audience. Evening was falling, and the colossal spaces of the edifice seemed to have absorbed the outside frost. Taking a seat in a hall crammed with endless callers, she mentally went over the particulars she had discussed with her clever friends on their way over. She had to be especially careful with what she said if she wanted this to work, while—to save her soul—lie as little as possible.

A vision of poise and virtue, she sat still for hours, kneading her hands, rehearsing her lines, watching the file shorten at an impossibly slow rate, and praying for Eros . . . Hours passed.

"Madonna." A tap on her shoulder jumped her. Her eyes flew open. She must have nodded off. What time was it? Midnight? A priest in a scarlet cassock stood before her, his expression serene. "Please come. His Holiness will see you now."

They traversed long, frescoed passages lined with giant marble statues created by masters. Sculpted opuses designed to put mortals in their places canonized previous popes, freezing life into their faces. Divine inspiration reigned supreme, the *spettacoli grandiosi* intended to bring Catholics into the fold and strengthen their faith, to reunite heretics with the Church, and to shed the light of God on unbelievers. Somewhere in this realm of godliness existed a ceiling more beautiful than the sky, painted by Michelangelo. For some reason, the thought inspired her.

Surrounded by cardinals and other high-ranking priests, dressed in gilt-embossed ivory, the pope sat on an elevated throne in a spacious, frescoed chamber. It was fundamentally an office. A senior secretary gestured her forth, and she gracefully knelt down to kiss the hem of the pope's robe and his ringed hand. "*Sua Santità,*" she murmured, her eyes lowered, and crossed herself.

The pope made the sign of the cross over her head, murmured a blessing, and waved her up. His eyes instantly went to the golden medallion swaying between her breasts. "Admittance on a short notice is highly unorthodox." He spoke fluent English, proving his famous linguistic aptitude. "People come here from all over the world and spend months waiting for an audience. Do you know why an exception was made on your behalf, Donna Sforza?"

Her pulse accelerated at the mentioning of her false title. She had trouble deciding whom she feared more—God, for deceiving his envoy; the pope, if her lie was exposed; or Eros, who was bound to hear of it eventually. For lack of a reply, she inclined her head reverently.

The pope read the brief in his lap. "You are the Duke of Dellamore's granddaughter. I had the pleasure of meeting His Grace when he visited Rome fifteen years ago. I was Secretary of Papal Briefs at the time. He made a considerable donation to the Vatican Library. As I recall, the duke is an ardent student of Roman philosophy and political science."

"Yes, he is, His Holiness," Alanis replied, her eyes still lowered.

"He is also a patron of ancient art."

"Indeed, His Holiness. Ancient Roman art is his favorite."

"As it is mine," the pope remarked with pride. "His Grace came here after the anti-Roman Catholic revolution in England, consequent to which he lost favor due to his being a Catholic."

"My grandfather is a member of the Whig Party, His Holiness. His views do not coincide with those of the pro-Church of England Tories. He is Queen Anne's personal consultant." She was glad she belonged to a family that supported the right side, at least on this occasion.

"Providentially, Queen Anne is a Catholic and things are back in order." The pope smiled. "You are well informed about your grandfather's politics. Also unorthodox, for a female."

"We are very close, His Holiness. My grandfather raised me after the untimely demise of my parents. I have often assisted him in his correspondence."

"While paying close attention." He studied her keenly. Was he trying to decide if this odd creature before him was worthy of the late Duke of Milan's princely son? She wondered. "Tell me about Prince Stefano. Your husband has been presumed dead for sixteen years, Madonna."

She was prepared for that. "After the murder of his father, Duke Gianluccio Sforza, The Good Lord rest his soul, my husband had to flee Milan. He has been living overseas ever since."

"Prince Stefano was sixteen years old when the Spaniards murdered his father. One would assume he outgrew his youth. Why has he not come forth to lay claim to his royal birthright? He has a binding commitment to a million Milanese! His regions are being crushed under a rampage of foreign powers! Has he no concept of virtue or honor that he neglects his responsibilities?"

That Alanis hadn't expected. "He is aware of his responsibilities, His Holiness. In his heart, my husband has not forsaken Milan." No matter how strongly Eros negated it.

"Then, where is he?" the pope demanded. "Why does he procrastinate?"

Alanis swallowed hard. "Stefano Andrea is a prisoner," she replied quietly, aware that her voice was faltering. "He is incarcerated in Rome by his own cousin, Cesare Sforza."

The pope's eyes flashed. "Cesare Sforza is imprisoning the rightful duke of Milan?"

"I have come to seek His Holiness's help in locating my husband."

"According to this marriage certificate," he tapped on the document in his lap, "you were married in the Catholic Church, St. Jago de la Vega, on the Island of Jamaica three months ago."

"Correct, His Holiness," she responded, sensing heat flooding her cheeks.

"Tell me, Madonna, among your pursuits as a politics expert and a secretary, are you by any chance familiar with Lombard Law?"

Her heart jolted. "No, His Holiness."

"Well, you ought to, because your marriage certificate isn't worth the paper it's printed on."

Alanis paled. The master forger had mucked it up. "His Holiness?" Her voice quavered.

"Lombard Law decrees that the Royal Prince of Milan is lawfully married *only* after the Archbishop of Milan performs the ceremony in the *Duomo* of Milan. Therefore, if Prince Stefano passes on or wishes to break the vows of matrimony you took in Jamaica, you'll have no legal claim to his name, his titles, or his worldly possessions. Your marriage will be annulled."

Lombard Law. Another piece of the riddle was solved. "His Holiness," she whispered, her throat clogged. "If Prince Stefano passes on, I will have no interest in any worldly possession."

The pope considered her carefully. "Your heart speaks for your husband, Madonna. Cesare Sforza is a disgrace to his family's august name—treachery, adultery, vice. He has committed every sin. You did well in coming to see me. Be assured that I will make my inquiries. Prince Stefano Sforza will be found, and returned to you."

Cesare detested caliginous, gruesome tombs of places where sinister shadows crept over walls, where dripping waters echoed off low ceilings, and where barred cells whispered madness.

Deep gloom accompanied him as he descended deeper and deeper into the fetid bowels of the earth, his boot heels thudding on the rudimentary sandstone. On either side of him funerary beds holed the walls. He was prowling a damned grave. Carrying a lamp in one hand, he pressed a handkerchief to his nose and hastened his pace, eager to be out in the open. Had he the stomach to bring himself down here more often, he would have obtained the Sforza medallion by now. He calmed himself with the belief that Stefano was breaking. As tough as his cousin was, no man could endure torture, starvation, and captivity in a place such as this forever. Sooner or later, Stefano would capitulate, and Cesare Sforza would become the next Duke of Milan.

Intense darkness greeted him inside the last chamber. Raising his lamp high, a tortured figure came to light. The wrists were heavily shackled, crucified to the sidewalls, the feet fettered to the ground. Brutal marks and grime covered the ragged sinew on the large, naked body, the testament of Roberto's fine touch. "Stefano," he summoned the living carcass's attention, "you are saved. Your vacation here is over. Where you choose to go next is entirely up to you."

He let the words sink into his prisoner's dimmed awareness, but as moments ticked by and no reaction resulted, Cesare stepped forth and yanked the wilted head up by its short hairs. Black valleys sunk beneath the eyes. Gaunt bones protruded through pale skin. Black beard swathed the lower part of the face. And still the battered eyes refused to open.

"I know you hear me," Cesare rasped, "and it is in your best interest to cooperate. Trust me when I say you do not have the stamina to withstand forever the pain the means at my disposal can inflict upon you. You will either die or break. And since time is of the essence, I will not spare you as I have until now. Tell me where you hid the medallion, and I shall release you."

After what seemed like an eternity, the prisoner's lips moved. Cesare hated having to lean closer, especially when the carcass smiled, as it uttered the barely audible words, "Jesus will whisper it in your ear before I do."

Cesare seethed. "Idiot! Why do you resist so long? You can't take that piece of gold to the other life. Let it buy you a clean, painless death in this one. A soldier's death."

The sunken eyes remained shut. "Kill me, Cesare, as I killed your father."

"I don't want to kill you!" Cesare roared. "I want to keep you here until there's nothing left of you but rotten bones even rats bulk at. Where is the Sforza medallion?"

The eyes opened a fraction. "I'll take my medallion to Elysium and await you there."

Swearing, Cesare dropped the head. His fool cousin was a glutton for punishment. It would take subtle persuasion to get the bastard talking. "Have I mentioned your wife is here in Rome?"

Victory! The prisoner's head slowly lifted. Deep, brilliant eyes fixed on Cesare.

"Ah, I finally have your undivided attention. The pretty blonde means something to you. Splendid. Now, we'll simply need to find out exactly how much you value her well-being."

The sunken eyes glittered fiercely. Cesare went on, "I admit, I had no idea you married the chit. Makes things more interesting, wouldn't you say?" He circled the chained stiff, pressing his lace handkerchief to his nose. "It seems blondie has brains as well as a luscious bottom. Went to the pope, and now the entire city is being combed for you. So you see, as much as I want to, I can't keep you here much longer. Soon you'll be greeting both our fathers. However," he halted behind the prisoner's shoulder, "if you deliver the medallion, I promise to leave blondie alone."

"*Va all'inferno!*" his prisoner hissed, rattling his chains.

Cesare narrowed his eyes. "Are you protecting her because she has the medallion?" Or did she not mean as much as he had hoped to his cousin? He wondered for the first time whether he'd be able to establish himself in Milan without the damned medallion. The emperor would give him the brush-off, but Louis, although fickle and treacherous, could be trusted to play his role in the destruction of his rivals. All in all, he could no longer keep his prisoner alive. He withdrew his dagger and put it to his cousin's throat. "You fought well, Stefano. But your fate was in the cards. Say hello to my father when you meet him. And tell the bastard that his son is a better man than he was." His voice sounded rough to his own ears. His fingers tightened around the bejeweled hilt but refused to hack. No less surprising was his prisoner stiffening under the cold steel. *Stefano did not want to die.* Strange, Cesare thought, after weeks of complete apathy.

Still, he didn't care to dwell on the change in his cousin's mental state when surrounded by thousand-year-old remains. He'd send Roberto to finish him off. Sheathing his dagger, he strode to the entrance, anxious to be off. He fixed his cousin with one last glare. "Your title, your princedom, your prestige . . . They should have been mine in the first place." He whirled on his heel and marched off, missing the new burn of life in the eyes following his retreating back.

Even more astonishing to Alanis than the arrival of the envoy from the Secretary Office of Papal Briefs only three days after her interview with His Holiness was the small mounted army in the red uniforms assembling in the piazza below her hotel window. She skimmed the missive gripped tightly in her trembling hands for the third time: HIS ROYAL HIGHNESS, PRINCE STEFANO ANDREA SFORZA IS INCARCERATED IN OSTIA ANTICA AT THE BORGO.

Alanis left the window and came to stand with Sallah and Nasrin, who were ogling the three strangers crowding her hotel suite's lavish foyer—the Papal Captain General, the official envoy, and the hotel manager, who was there because the excitement provided excellent publicity for his hotel's image. "Will you accompany me?" she asked her friends.

Sallah gave a snort of satisfaction. "Of course."

They collected their coats and took off. A magnificent carriage bearing Pope Clement XI's coat of arms waited at the entrance to the hotel. They climbed inside and settled on the soft, red velvet seats. Carriage and horses clattered off the piazza's San-Pietrini cobblestone driveway.

As they left the Aurelian Walls, taking the old Ostia Road, the view changed from brick and marble buildings to green hills lined with pine trees. Hands clasped in her lap, Alanis stared out the window and wondered about the ill-boding feeling in the pit of her stomach. Nearly five weeks had passed since Eros's capture. She couldn't banish the terror gnawing at her heart.

The carriage stopped in front of an imposing brown bastion. The soldiers secured the area, and their carriage lurched onward. The captain met them at the gate. "I urge you to wait outside, my lady. The cells here are considerably less salubrious than those in Castel Sant'Angelo."

"My . . . husband is imprisoned here, Captain," Alanis said. "He's been here for weeks now. I will accompany you inside."

"As you wish." The officer gave a curt nod and proceeded through the gate.

Alanis felt a gentle arm around her shoulders. "We'll do this together, as before," Sallah's warm voice assured her. She met his kind eyes and smiled gratefully. They entered the bastion.

A fortified ravelin enclosed the rotund keeps of the Borgo. Various escutcheons of popes and cardinals were plastered everywhere. A moat with a scarp ran along the outer limits, as well as merlons and casements constructed to fire grazing shots. A Latin inscription carved above the entrance read BEWARE OF DECEPTIONS. HOPE IS IN THE FORTRESS. FREE YOURSELF FROM FEAR.

Alanis's fears multiplied. Armed sentries in unidentifiable uniforms watched them warily as they filed in but made no move to block their path. The bastion's interior was shadowy and cool; high openings in the thick walls let in light and air. She linked both hands through Sallah's arm and burrowed against his side. Her heart beat ferociously. The captain and his soldiers halted to equip themselves with torches before they descended the steps of a narrow, winding tunnel. It led to a dark pit. The first vibrating shriek of misery jumped Alanis out of her skin.

"Steady now," Sallah soothed and squeezed her to him. "It won't be long."

She wanted to jump into his pocket. Her nerves were strained so thin she missed her step repeatedly. Voices from ancient times seemed to murmur their names, throwing out cries of defiance to death, or were they living voices beset with madness and despair? Another Latin message warned those who inclined to linger: DO NOT TOUCH O MORTAL. RESPECT THE MANES.

The walls became small niches, sarcophagi and chests, a storehouse from Hades. Dust rose off the sandstone, making the air even less bearable than it already was. The place reeked of death, not only of those who had chosen to be buried here over a thousand years ago but also of recent death. Alanis was a breath away from snapping when intense darkness welcomed them into a small chamber. Heavy chains lay on the bloodstained floor. Someone—Eros?—was held down here until recently. The soldiers exchanged pessimistic glances. Alanis wasn't aware of the grimy jailor guiding them until the captain addressed him sharply. The man cringed, guilt and terror rounding his eyes. The captain's barks broke him, and he whimpered pitifully.

Alanis had never seen Sallah looking grimmer than when the captain turned to face them, his expression inauspicious. "To my deepest regret . . . His Highness is dead. The jailor claims the prisoner died last night. They threw his body into the Tiber this morning."

"*No!*" Alanis's shriek of angst reverberated throughout the tunnels, carrying pain wrenched from the soul. Afterward there was nothing. Only blackness.

CHAPTER 22

At one time Rome, which made the good world,
had two suns, each lighting up its road:
the way of the world and the way of God.
                                        —Dante: *Purgatorio*

The nightmares were as bad as the cold waking hours. Consciously Alanis was unable to summon more than a hazy image of Eros, but in her dreams she saw him vividly— beautiful, strong, glistening with seawater. Only it never lasted, liquefying the moment she reached out to touch, disappearing between her fingers, fading as ocean mist. And she was cold. *So cold.*

Seven days came and went in one continual flow, and even more than cold, she felt gray. The glow in her heart was snuffed out, leaving emptiness and depression so bleak she ceased to be a person. The season was icy cold and gray in Rome. The streets were vacant most of the time; the chime of bells announcing the hour a sole testament that inside homes, shops, palaces, and churches, life beat on. Yet in the dark chambers of her heart only despair lurked.

She had no idea what she should do now, nor did she have the mental strength to decide. She was only capable of sitting at the open windows, watching rain pour heavily.

Sallah and Nasrin came by her suite when darkness fell. The temperature had dropped sharply, and she was no longer able to hear the beat of rain. Was it snowing? She had no idea. Nor did she care. She cared about nothing.

"Goodness! You're residing in a glacier." Suppressing a shudder, Nasrin rushed over to shut the windows. "You'll catch your death sitting here day and night, not sleeping, not eating. You cannot go on like this. You are a young woman. You have years to look forward to."

That was the problem, Alanis thought. *The years.*

Warm hands settled on her shoulders. "Come downstairs and have dinner with us," Sallah suggested. "It won't take the sadness away, but it will remind you that you are still among the living. It will make you feel better."

A lamp was lit in a far corner, its sharp glow causing Alanis to squint. "I'm not hungry, Sallah. You go. I do not feel fit for company at the moment."

"You never do these days." Nasrin sat down beside her and patted her hand. "Mourning is a healthy process, my dear.

One needs to weep for the demise of a loved one, otherwise one is never free of grief. But there are rules for grieving and rules for living, and after observing the seven days of mourning one rises up and resumes the business of living. Torturing your body and spirit won't bring him back."

Alanis covered her face with her hands. She felt so . . . *bleak*. She had failed the man she loved. "How did we do this to him? We let him rot in that pit for a whole month . . ."

"So now you're blaming yourself for his death." Sallah grimly glanced at his wife.

Alanis raised her head, tears burning her eyes. "One day, Sallah! We lost him in less than a day! And yes, it is my fault! No matter how you see it—I'm to blame! I killed him! He would be alive today if not for me. I followed him as a noose around his neck, when all he wanted was to be free!" she cried, unable to keep her emotions bottled up a moment longer.

"That's utter nonsense," Sallah muttered. "When I casually mentioned to Eros that he had no business keeping a woman of your noble background with him, he sent me to the devil."

Alanis shook her head. "I wheedled my way into his life, scrambled his head, forced him to reveal his identity to me. Cesare wouldn't have gotten to him if we hadn't gadded like imbeciles on the beach that morning. *I distracted him while he should have been safe . . .*" She sank to the carpet and sobbed, her body quaking, her soul lacerated by anguish. She wanted to die too. She didn't want to go on living in a world that had lost its brightest sun. She wanted to lie in a dark grave and feel nothing. Be nothing. She wanted to die and be with Eros . . .

"My dear child!" Nasrin knelt beside her and enfolded her in her arms. Rocking back and forth, as a mother rocked her babe, she soothed and murmured, kissed and sighed, offering every consolation possible. *"Don't cry, my soul . . . Don't cry . . ."*

Alanis wept uncontrollably, shedding more tears than she had during the past seven days. The reality that never again would she feel him, touch him, see him, was dragging her down a bottomless black pit of gloom where only madness awaited.

It took a long time, but ultimately her sobs subsided and she was able to lift her face again. She looked terrible. Yet, surprisingly, she felt better. Lighter. She was even capable of meeting her friends' eyes and offered a nod of reassurance. Alas, she was not dead yet.

Nico and Daniello joined them for dinner at the hotel's exclusive restaurant. They were saying good night in the grand foyer when a clerk accompanied by a grimy lad approached them. The clerk motioned the boy forth, and the latter stuck out his hand and offered Alanis a stained missive. He clutched his tattered bonnet and waited, his eyes wide and anxious in his smudged face. Not knowing what to make of this bizarre scene, Alanis accepted the note and unfolded it.

"Well," Sallah pressed, "what does it say?"

"I don't know," Alanis murmured. "It's written in Italian." She skimmed the page, trying to decipher the foreign scrawl. She read aloud, "*San Paolo Fuori le Mura. Via Ostiense. Venga da sola. Sorella Maddalena.*" She raised her head. "Nico?"

"San Paolo outside the Wall. Ostia Road. Come alone. Sister Maddalena," Nico easily translated. "There's a convent outside the Aurelian Walls by that name. It's on Ostia Road, near the bastion where they kept Eros. You can't miss it. It has tall campaniles, and—"

"A convent?" Alanis's eyes came aglow with new hope.

"It's a trap." Sallah scowled at the boy. "Ask him who paid him to deliver the missive."

Nico did as requested and immediately translated. "He is an urchin from a local orphanage. Sister Maddalena teaches them daily. She asked him to deliver the missive and gave him a sweet for his efforts. But it rained all day and he had trouble finding the hotel. He insists you come alone. Sister Maddalena was adamant about it. Would you like us to accompany you, my lady?"

"Absolutely not," Sallah declared. "You are not rushing off at this hour in this weather after a scrawny imp who emerged from God knows where, on behalf of who knows—"

"I must go, Sallah." Alanis asked the clerk to send someone to her suite to fetch her cloak. "Nico and Daniello will escort me in a closed carriage. I'll be perfectly safe."

Nasrin intervened. "You are forgetting, my dear, that Cesare Sforza is still out there. He may know you have the medallion. I think Sallah is right, for once. You mustn't go."

"I'm going," Alanis stated resolutely. "I have nothing to lose."

"But what have you to gain?" Nasrin said, then added in a whisper, "Eros is gone."

Alanis fixed her with a resolute glare. "I did not see his body. Did you?"

Deep slush covered the ancient Via Ostia. San Paolo Fuori le Mura towered up ahead, its brownstone campaniles white against the dark blue sky. Alanis opened the carriage window and stuck her face out in the nippy night wind. She had lost the only man she ever truly loved—could love—and she needed to find some answers, even at the cost of risking her own life.

As soon as the carriage stopped, Nico hopped off and went to ring the bell at the iron gate. Daniello assisted Alanis out of the carriage and escorted her to the entrance. A hatch opened at eye level, revealing a pair of eyes. "Lady Sforza to see Sister Maddalena," Nico informed the quizzical eyes. Alanis lowered the fur-lined hood off of her fair head and stepped forward.

A metal latch was unbolted, and the gate opened. "Only the lady," the nun insisted.

"I'll be fine." Alanis patted Nico's hand. Alone, she entered the immured convent. The old edifice was built around a frosted rose garden, surrounded by four wings of open arcades, their sculpted pillars spiraling in a mosaic and marble weave. She followed the nun down the moonlit passage, trying to recall if last winter was as cold as this one—was it her fear looking for a place to hide? A cloister was a peculiar choice of place for a secret meeting, even for a nasty piece of work such as Cesare Sforza, but why did the nuns let him inside their refuge?

They entered a murky corridor. Smoky torches hung on the dank walls high above their heads, providing little light and less warmth. The nun walked briskly, undaunted by the screechy, hairy rodents scuttling along the stone-flagged floors. Not so valiant, Alanis endeavored not to step on their thin tails as they rapidly crossed her path. The hollow echo of her strides resounded in her heart. Perhaps whoever summoned her here wasn't Cesare. Perhaps a mysterious hand was reaching out from the darkness to extend her benevolence. Perhaps . . .

The corridor ended in a curving flight of steps. Alanis raised her skirts and climbed in the nun's footsteps. On the top floor, the nun proceeded toward a heavy door. She halted before it, knocked, then opened it and motioned Alanis to enter. Alanis paused. Whatever lay beyond this door would change her life. For the better or worse, she squared her shoulders and walked in.

Stark ocher walls surrounded her inside the dimly lit chamber. A tawny lamp cast a patch of light on a remote bed. A veiled figure sat hunched and stilted beside it, throwing a thin, long shadow on the floor. A modest figurine of the Crucified hung over the bed. Alanis forced her gaze to the silent bed. A man lay there, thin, white, deathlike, his dark hair cut short to his scalp, his ashen face swathed with a black beard. A white sheet covered the entire length of him. Alanis shuddered. She was staring at a corpse. "Sister Maddalena," she said warily. "You sent for me?"

The veiled shape turned her head. "Donna Sforza. Thank you for coming." Her voice was soft and feminine, her countenance peaceful. Framed in a linen wimple and a flowing black veil, sea blue eyes shone large and expressive, personifying the radiance of the Mother of God—the source of light in this somber place. Deep compassion glowed in the mature nun's fine patrician features, compensating for lost beauty. "Please. Come. Sit." The nun patted the stool beside her.

"Sit beside a stranger's cadaver?" Alanis's gaze flitted over the sprawled corpse. Who was this man? He didn't remotely resemble her pirate. And this nun—how did she know of the search for the Prince of Milan? And why did she bother to locate his supposed wife? Apparently, information traveled fast anywhere, especially in a giant institution such as the Catholic Church.

Disappointment crossed the nun's brow. "You do not recognize him?"

"Should I?" Reluctantly, Alanis glimpsed at the man. His features were indistinct from her spot, but she didn't need an eyeglass to know it was not Eros. "Sister, there's been a mistake."

"There is no mistake," the nun insisted firmly. "If you are who you say you are, then you should take another look." She returned her gaze to the bed and took the man's limp hand in hers. A brutal hemorrhage ring circled his wrist; the fingers looked battered and black. The nun held it reverently in her hands, then raised it to her lips and kissed it.

Alanis drew back. There was something awfully familiar about the hand. *This couldn't be!* She was imagining things. Her mind was so beset with grief, it was prepared to believe anything. Stifling a sob, she spoke to the nun, "This man is not Stefano Sforza. Give him a proper burial. I'll pay the costs for your trouble."

"I found him in an underground chamber in Ostia Antica, locked in chains."

Alanis's heart gave a forceful kick. "The jailor said they had thrown his body in the Tiber."

"They threw someone else in the Tiber. I switched them. This man is alive."

"You made the wrong switch!" Alanis choked, gutted with disappointment—or was it rage at the cruel vicissitudes of fate? *Why?* Why couldn't this man be Eros, alive? Why did she have to lose him in the space of a day, a night? So many whys, so many goddamned whys . . .

Unable to withstand this a moment longer, Alanis collected herself and turned to the door. What was she thinking coming here? Was she to be accosted by every Tom, Dick, or Harry to identify some poor, nameless vagabond from now on? She should return to her grandfather, to England. That's what she should do. She felt so cold, so utterly cold and alone . . .

"You are making a grave mistake," the nun warned.

Clutching the folds of her cape with one hand, Alanis grasped the doorknob and turned it. "There is no mistake," she murmured. "This man is not Eros." She pulled the door open.

The reclining man released a faint groan, murmuring something. Alanis spun around. *Eros.* Her knees folded. If this was a cruel joke, if someone above decided to torment her . . . Yet the voice. The hand. The hair. The long limbs. With a sudden certainty she knew it was Eros. *It was Eros.* And he was alive. She had refused to believe because she had been—still was—so afraid . . .

She stumbled forward, taking one step, then another and another. *Eros!* A thick, guttural cry tore from her heart. She vaulted to the bed and dropped to her knees, heaving over the still form. "Eros," she whispered. She touched his gaunt cheek tenderly, afraid to believe, too many darned tears blurring her vision. His skin felt warm beneath her palm, his scent was familiar, the thin, rawboned, bearded, battered face the most beloved face in the world. He resembled the ghostly image of the man he once was. She had to convince herself it was he. *She had to be brave to believe!* "Eros," she murmured. "Can you hear me?"

His eyes opened a fraction—stunning sapphires, slightly glazed, tired. He smiled at her faintly. "Princess . . . what are you doing here in Rome?" His voice was barely audible, yet it was his voice, making her weak with love. Their gazes met, and she was no longer cold. She brimmed with warmth and happiness. *A creature of light.* She held his groggy gaze, entranced, the contact of their spirits as strong and as direct as it has always been—two people very much alive.

"You're fine," she said, bemused, smiling, tears rolling down her cheeks. "You are alive."

"*Ugh . . .*" Eros uttered a feeble protest. "*Mezzo morto.* Half dead."

"Not even a quarter inch." She would probably go to her grave smiling like a sot. Leaning forward, she pressed a soft kiss to his bruised lips, letting her eyelids droop for a brief moment of pure intoxication. Eros kissed her back, very weakly but actively. She thought her heart would explode. "Thank you," she whispered, "for being alive."

A muffled laugh escaped his lips. "You're a silly baggage, Alanis."

"Very silly," she agreed. "I came here to tour the town and found you instead."

His eyelids sank. "I should have known." He exhaled haggardly. "Silly, silly baggage . . ."

A feminine voice said, "You must take him away from here. Tonight."

She had forgotten about the nun. Straightening up, Alanis met the large, sea blue eyes. The elderly nun seemed pleased. "How did you know who he was?" Alanis asked with amazement. "How did you know where to find him? And why did— *who are you?*"

Sister Maddalena's eyes sparkled. "I know Rome, and I have spies everywhere, even in the Papal Office. There aren't many well-kept secrets there. One needs to know whom to listen to, where to be. Once in a lifetime one hears of a miracle, so one investigates and one finds his miracle. As I said, it happens only once, so one must be very attentive or one loses his miracle."

Was she smiling? Alanis couldn't say, but she was the oddest nun, and there was an air of completion about her, and peace. Alanis's eyes narrowed. "You know him?"

"I do."

The woman intrigued her. "And does he know you?"

The nun lost some of her serenity. "He does." She glimpsed at Eros. "He's asleep now. He needs his sleep. He's been to hell."

Alanis frowned. "Why must I take him from here tonight? He seems too ill to travel."

"His cousin is dangerous. For now, Cesare believes him to be dead, but you are a well-known figure in Rome, and people talk. Cesare will realize the deception soon."

"The deception?" Alanis didn't quite follow.

A glimmer of triumph shone in the nun's eyes. "I switched him with a dead body the night before you went to Ostia. I knew it would be best if people thought he was dead."

"You've had him here for a week? Why didn't you at least inform me he was safe?"

"It had to be believable," the nun stated. "He has too many enemies."

Alanis stared at her askance. The eccentric, regal-looking nun had secrets she didn't want to share. "All right. I have two of his men waiting outside. We'll take him out of Rome tonight, but I still think he's too ill to board a ship." She glanced at Eros's pale face.

"On that we agree. Take him to the country," Maddalena suggested. "Go to Tuscany. I'll give you directions to a house belonging to his family, a safe house. It is one of the few his noble folk haven't commandeered yet. The man in charge, Bernardo, was his father's man."

Now that was too much. "How do you know all that? And how come you care so much about him?" Alanis had a flash recollection of the nun taking his hand and kissing it.

"So many questions." The nun smiled. "Do you also interrogate Eros all the time?"

"Yes." Alanis pouted guiltily. "Otherwise, how is one to learn anything? In my experience, secrets have a nasty way of surfacing in the least convenient moment."

Maddalena seemed amused and interested. "Where did you meet him?"

"Aha." Alanis smiled. "Now you are intrigued."

"Tell me."

Following a vague hunch, Alanis said, "I met him and his sister in Jamaica."

"Gelsomina." Maddalena beamed. She inhaled sharply. "Is she pretty?"

Alanis gave the nun a gimlet eye. "Very pretty. With long black locks and eyes of sapphire blue. Her smile is like the sun, and she wears breeches. She married an English nobleman who turns into an imbecile when she is around. I think Eros sees that as his only redeeming quality."

"Thank you." The nun turned aside, and Alanis saw her brushing a tear off of her cheek. A crooked smile touched Alanis's lips. Sister Maddalena was Eros's mother. *The Harpy.*

She didn't look like a harpy. She was a sad, penitent woman who missed her family very much; it was evident in the expression in her eyes, in every line in her face. Beyond doubt Alanis knew that a woman who loved her son as much as Maddalena seemed to love Eros was incapable of cold-bloodedly sentencing him to death, not now, not ever, regardless of what Eros chose to believe. She had a quality about her that did remind Alanis of Greek tragedies—a heroine fated to destroy the thing she loved best and spend the rest of her life paying for her preordained sin. What *had* occurred that night in Milan? Alanis dared not ask. Not now. "Does he speak to you?"

Maddalena's eyes were mirrors of misery. "He ignores me."

Alanis felt a stab of compassion toward the older woman. Maddalena's cool serenity, her grace and wit, her hidden frailty, and the loneliness reflected in her large eyes touched Alanis's soul. "I have a confession to make . . ." She heard herself say. "We are not married."

Maddalena looked disappointed. "You never married? Not even outside of Milan?"

Alanis shook her head. The nun smiled, and Alanis knew from which parent Eros inherited his dark, lazy smiles.

"You are in love with him," Maddalena stated with satisfaction. "Good. He deserves to be loved by a woman such as you. Rome has been in an uproar since you went to see the Holy Father. Thanks to you, I knew where to find him. You saved his life."

"Why are you here in Rome, of all places?" Alanis asked, uncomfortable with the direction of the conversation, especially now that Maddalena knew about her lie.

"I am a Roman. I feel less lonely here than I did in Milan."

On an unspoken agreement they had put everything on the table—amazing, and moving in an extraordinary way. "What was Eros like as a boy?" Alanis inquired with a curious grin.

A motherly smile lit Maddalena's face. "Sharp as a devil, wild, handsome as Leonardo's *Michael,* with eyes full of mischief. He wrapped me around his little finger."

Alanis gave a soft laugh. "He's good at that sort of thing."

"He was good at everything. That was the problem—nothing was good enough."

Alanis frowned. "What do you mean?"

Maddalena sighed. "He expected too much of himself. He had to be perfect, just like his father—a great duke. Milan always came first, except for his family. He adored his little sister."

"He still does." But he could scarcely speak about his princedom. *For the same reason.*

"I have something for you." Maddalena reached inside her pocket. "And then you must be off." She extended her hand and offered Alanis a ring. An exquisite viper embedded with tiny diamonds, black ambers, and a pair of amethysts for eyes snaked around a huge oval diamond.

Startled, Alanis met her gaze. "But I am not his wife."

"You will be."

Alanis's heart leaped, but she said nothing; she really was uncomfortable with the subject.

"It was my engagement ring," Maddalena whispered. "It belonged to Bianca Visconti, the wife of Francesco Sforza, the first Sforza duke. Put it on."

Alanis shied away. "I'm sorry. I cannot accept this ring. It wouldn't be right."

"It is a good ring, untainted," Maddalena assured her

humbly. "It was designed by a Jewish jeweler called Menashe Ish Shalom. His name means—'man of peace.'"

"I am honored you chose me to have it," Alanis replied in earnest. "But I must decline."

Maddalena nodded. "For now."

Braving one final question, Alanis asked, "Why did you call him Eros?"

Eros stirred. Alanis crouched beside him. The sight of his face instilled her with euphoria. "I must take you away from here. Do you feel strong enough to travel?" she asked softly.

"No." He groaned. A grin tugged at his lips. "But if I must . . ."

"Good." Alanis smiled. "You're off to a winter vacation in the country, then."

His eyes opened wide, and he stared at her sharply. "You'll be coming along?"

Alanis smiled with tenderness. "Of course I will. I only leave when you tell me to."

He shut his eyes. "Remember you said that, *Amore. Always remember you said that . . .*"

CHAPTER 23

"Where the devil did he stash the damn medallion?" Cesare ranted, marching up and down the most notorious boudoir in Rome—the one belonging to Leonora Orsini Farnese. Though she married Rodolfo Farnese, the idiot cousin of the Duke of Parma, by blood she was an Orsini and as fierce as her brothers' cuneated arms ranking them *de Militibus,* Defenders of Ancient Rome. The Orsini were forever busy with military undertakings and possessed tremendous political power in Italy. That made Leonora a valuable asset to Cesare, in addition to her private ones.

Emerald green eyes met his in the dressing table mirror.

"You don't need the medallion. Stefano is dead. La Feuillade is besieging Turin. Vendôme controls Lombardy. Go see Louis. He is the one controlling the north at the moment, and you have an agreement with him."

Cesare watched her brushing her fiery red mane and looking utterly desirable in her sheer penoir. He was not so slow that he didn't realize it was his new station in life putting him in the right light as far as Leonora was concerned. *She ached to be a Milanese Princess.*

Her scarlet-painted lips moved seductively. "When are we to be wed, *tesoro?*"

"Soon." He ambled to the window fronting Lungotevere, thinking that life at the Dado, the Palazzo Farnese, suited his sensibilities much better than the stark walls of the damned Castello Sforzesco. It sickened him to estimate the amount of gold needed to transform that brown wreck into something habitable—gold he had yet to put his hands on. Stefano had gold, but the bastard insisted on taking his gold with him. Staring at the calm, green Tiber, Cesare considered a few fat fish personally beholden to him. Pushing morbid thoughts aside, he attached his new title to his name and found he liked the sound of it—Prince Cesare Galeazzo Sforza. *Nice.*

Leonora's voice carried from across the bedroom. "What about Camilla?"

"Who?" Cesare turned around to watch her spraying herself with expensive perfume.

Leonora rolled her eyes. "Your wife. You really ought to do something about that graceless cow. She's been raising her fat chin in every palazzo in Rome and calling herself a princess."

"I'll worry about Camilla. You concentrate your pretty head on Rodolfo, that stupid husband of yours. How do you intend to silence the idiot? The old-fashioned way?" He snickered.

"I suppose you're referring to poison?" She sent him a dark smile in the mirror.

He came up behind her and delved his hand inside her

penoir, cupping a soft breast. "Or let your brothers place him *hors de combat.* Take him out of play, as the French say."

She swatted his hand. "Put a lid on it where my brothers are concerned. If you want them to help you take over Milan, don't attach it to assassinations. It is bad enough every palace in Rome is abuzz with gossip how you held Stefano in Ostia and tortured him to death." She got up and paced the room. "They say he married someone—an English duke's grand-daughter. Were my father alive, he'd skin Stefano for this! Our betrothal was final! I have the papers to prove it."

"Feed them to the fish."

"Duke Gianluccio wanted a bride of pure Roman blood for his son, but that coward!" She fumed. "Folded his tail and ran like a big baby. And I had to lie flat for Rodolfo the pig."

"You didn't lie flat for long, *caramella,*" Cesare reminded her with a nasty grin.

"They say she's a blue-eyed blonde," she spat acidly. "I wonder where he got that fetish."

Cesare was getting bored with the subject. "Forget Stefano. The Sforza and the Orsini *will* end up in bed together. Only this time, my sweet Orsini Rose, you'll be landing the right cousin."

"Before you add the red gules of the Orsini to your vipers and eagles, I suggest you pay a visit to your good friend, the King of France. Think of the appalling disgrace should an-other connubial contract between our families suffer the same fate as the first one . . ."

Curled in a wingchair, Alanis woke as morning chill swirled into the ducal bedchamber. She got up to shut the great mullioned window. Beyond it, heavy mist cloaked dark green forests and terra-cotta roofs of hillside villages. A week had passed since their arrival in Lucca, and she had yet to tire of the Tuscan landscape's beauty. She glanced at the four-poster bed and smiled.

"Good morning." She came to sit on the bed and put a

gentle hand on Eros's brow. Cool. Thank God. His recurring fever spells broke at last. "Shall I ring for breakfast?"

Blue-black fingers caught her wrist. "*Don't* . . . nurse me, Alanis. Please." He lowered her hand, whispering, "Lie beside me. Let me feel you. Hold you. *Close.*" He raised the covers and shifted aside, allowing her room where his body had warmed and dented the mattress. Alanis climbed in, and he wrapped the covers around her, draping a possessive arm over her midsection. He released a sigh in her hair. "You smell so good. Feel so good." He kissed her neck. A bolt of lightning shot through her. His head came up. "What's wrong? You don't like my kissing you?"

She met his startled blue eyes. "I do. I missed you terribly," she whispered, striving to keep the mushy timbre in hand. She snuggled against his shoulder, marveling at his proximity.

"I dreamed about this, the whole time I was in Ostia. The best thought in my head was the morning we spent together on the beach in Agadìr. I remembered the color of your eyes, the sound of your voice, the feel of your skin, the sweet taste of your mouth, the taste of you everywhere . . ." He squeezed her to him. "In my dreams, Morpheus brought you to me again. At times it was impossible to tell between a thought and a dream."

She looked into his eyes and melted inside. She saw darkness there, deep pain he carried with him from Ostia. "What did he do to you?" she asked softly.

"My cousin? He made me wish I were dead. But when he told me you were in Rome, looking for me, it brought me back. *You* brought me back. I hadn't realized how much I needed you." He ran his battered knuckles along her cheek. "How come you didn't return to England?"

"Did you want me to?"

"No."

"Well." She smiled. "One does not leave the wounded to die on the battlefield."

He grinned for the first time in days. "A very diplomatic

answer. One can see you are your grandfather's granddaughter. So why did you come for me, Alanis? The truth now."

Because I can't live without you. She couldn't find the courage to confess. "How could I forget about you and return home? You are . . . my friend." She smiled affectionately.

The spark left his eyes. "I see. So who protected you while I was imprisoned? Niccolò?"

So he had noticed. Perhaps Nico was too frequently at hand, inquiring after her well-being ten times a day, escorting her to the village on occasion. "He is just a friend, Eros."

"A friend like me?"

Her smile died. "How could you think that?" She reached inside her mauve gown's bodice and pulled out his medallion. "This belongs to you." She slipped the chain over his head.

"Thank you." Eros fisted the medallion but kept his eyes on her. On her mouth. He let go of the medallion and slid his hand up her bodice. His gaze found hers, searching, asking. The top pearl button popped open, exposing the cleft between her breasts. He leaned forward.

She laid a hand on his chest. "You need to regain your strength. You've hardly eaten—"

He stared at her glumly. "I'm not much to look at, am I? A pitiful *ragazzuccio,* eh?"

She bit her lip on a smile. "You look like a scrawny bear that was trapped in a cave for too long." His pirate tan was gone; thick, short hairs stood as thorns on his head; and he was too thin for his frame. She gently caressed his silky, jet beard. "Perhaps I should give you a shave and you won't look like a . . . *ragazzuccio* anymore."

He nodded in accordance, looking even glummer. "As long as you give me something . . ."

A week later Sallah called on his convalescing friend in the ducal apartment. Standing at the mirror, Eros was being helped into a superfine black coat by the majordomo, Bernardo.

"Well, I'll be damned," Sallah mumbled with appreciation. "Someone here certainly looks like a completely different person. Plumper too."

"Don't get any ideas." Eros cast him a smile and rolled his shoulders to get the feel of the tailored coat. He strolled to the dresser and retrieved his dagger. His fingers flexed around the bejeweled hilt and flipped it with the expertise of a juggler before sheathing it in the leather case riding his hip. "Where is Alanis? She wasn't in her bedchamber the last I checked."

"She went to the village with Nasrin. Said they'd be back for luncheon." Sallah frowned at the three bulky captains loitering about. "And to be perfectly honest, I understand why she was in need of fresh air. You've turned your bedchamber into a situation room the past week. Against whom are you planning to wage war? The Frenchmen up north or your cousin in Rome?"

Eros shot Giovanni a sharp glare. "Where's Niccolò?"

Giovanni shrugged. "He's back, but I can always send him on another errand."

"Send him to Venice." Eros turned to Sallah. "We need to talk." He steered him out the door, saying, "Before I answer your questions, I need to know what happened from the moment I was captured. Perhaps you'd be able to explain something Cesare told me in Ostia. And," his voice turned harsh, "I'd like to know why Alanis has grown a living male shadow."

"Ah, him. Nothing to worry about," Sallah reassured him as they took the stairs. "Niccolò was very kind and protective of her when you were held prisoner."

"I wasn't dead."

Sallah halted. "What is it that you expect of her precisely?"

Eros sighed and ran a hand through his thick, short hair. "When I think about what I want, it scares me to death."

"You have two options: Marry her or lose her. And bear in mind she won't marry a pirate and go live with him on a godforsaken beach. She has other responsibilities besides you."

Annoyance crossed Eros's brow. "I'm not her *responsibility*."

"She seems to think you are. She's the one who saved your life, if you haven't figured that out yet. I was ready to give up numerous times. Alanis wouldn't hear of it."

"What do you mean 'she's the one who saved me'? It was . . . that nun who—"

"Alanis took over from the start. She made the right decisions. She appealed to the pope." Eros's eyes burned fiercely. Sallah scowled. "Don't look so stunned." His friend had the face of a man who'd been served with the bill for the national debt. "She is . . . fond of you."

Eros's expression turned pained. "Sallah, I think you should tell me everything."

"You must question him about this army he's assembling." Nasrin frowned at a group of armed mercenaries ogling them as they walked past the local tavern. The strike of metal against metal rang from the blacksmith's. Poultry and venison garlanded with parsley hung outside the butcher's. Fruit and vegetables coated with dewdrops were sold beneath stone terraces decorated with red geraniums. Alanis loved the village with its tiny streets, charming piazzas, and scent of baked bread drifting from the baker's. She wished Eros took the time to stroll with her.

"There are thousands here," Nasrin persisted, "and I happen to know there are others billeted in the neighboring villages. Do you suppose he is preparing to march on Milan?"

"I don't know what he's about. He won't tell me," Alanis replied with a sigh.

"Most of the men pouring into the region are seamen off his ships, but he is hiring many more from every province in Italy. Let's be realistic. Cesare is one man, not a fortress. Eros must have grander schemes up his sleeve than a simple vendetta. You must discover what they are. After all," Nasrin added knowingly, "you will become the next Duchess of Milan." Alanis sat on a stone bench, silent. Nasrin sat beside her. "My dear girl, do not tell me you are shocked by this. The man is half-mad for you. And he is a prince. He won't be able to resist taking back the princedom he's lost, his heritage. When I think about the palaces you'll reside in, the glamour . . ." She sighed. "Ugh, you'll be royalty. Indeed, I feel as proud as a mother."

"I beg you, Nasrin, speak no more of this. He is not well yet and you're planning weddings and enthronements. Furthermore, there's a war in Milan involving the three major powers of the world—Spain, France, and the Alliance. How is Eros to overcome this hurdle?" And there was another force to take into account: Eros himself. She doubted he would rise from his sickbed ready to change his life. He wasn't an ordinary man. He was deep, complex and . . . unpredictable.

Nasrin eyed her suspiciously. "What troubles you? You've been restive for days."

"I don't think there will be a Lombard wedding, Nasrin. Eros will never consider taking a wife before he regains his stature in Milan, and I don't think he intends to do the one or the other. I don't know how I fit into his life, or how he fits into mine. I worry about my grandfather, but if I write to him, he'll send General Marlborough along with his troops to fetch me."

"You have to make a decision, my dear. Sallah has asked Eros to arrange for our departure, and you must decide if this is merely an adventure and you are coming home with us or if this is your life. If you truly love him, if he means more to you than the life you're accustomed to, you should let him know how you feel and give him a solid reason to fight for his home. As to your grandfather, he is a grown man. He's made his decisions. This is your life, Alanis. Not his."

Anxiety twisted her innards. "But if he doesn't love me, if I pressure him and lose him . . ."

Nasrin took her hand. "I have yet to meet the man immune to so much love. However, if you do lose him, then you will have lost nothing, for one cannot lose what one never had."

Tall shadows fell on the bench. Alanis looked up and saw three soldiers leering at them.

"Don't even think about it," a familiar male voice clipped

firmly. Alanis sighed with relief when she recognized the windblown, dark blond hair. Nico dismissed the pests, then bowed in greeting. "Signora. My lady. My apologies. These men will be sacked today. Eros wants to keep his affairs here quiet. We don't need drunken brawls over women."

"Niccolò." Alanis smiled. "We were about to return to the castle. Would you escort us?"

He beamed when she curled her hand around his offered arm and started walking.

"Where have you been? You haven't come to see me in three days," she admonished.

"Eros sent me to Genoa. More ships." He sighed. Alanis suspected ships were not the only reason Eros sent him away. Nico smiled sheepishly and produced an elegantly trimmed box. "I brought you a gift. I hope you won't find this too presumptuous."

Alanis pulled the golden string and opened the box. "Caramels! I love caramels."

"I know. I remember from Rome. These are a special Genoese delicacy."

"Thank you. I'm so glad you are returned. Come up to the house. We'll play whist."

"I . . . don't think Eros will approve," Nico said. "I'll escort you, but then I must be off."

They started up the road, Nasrin complaining about the floating drizzle, Alanis emptying the box of caramels. "So what is this army intended for?" Alanis inquired.

"Your guess is as good as mine. Ask Eros. He'd tell you before he'd tell me."

When they arrived at the castle, Nico took her gloved hand, his hazel eyes melting, and brushed his lips across it. He turned on his heel and left, whistling a sailor's ditty.

Nasrin stopped her before they went inside. "If you keep encouraging that fellow, things will get bloody. *El-Amar* may be an Italian prince, but he has the mentality of a Maghreb corsair. Jealousy won't bring him around, and someone will get hurt. Most likely your sailor friend."

* * *

At ten minutes to seven a firm knock rattled the door connecting the ducal bedchambers. Sitting at the vanity table, while her maid, Cora, arranged her hair, Alanis met her sparkling eyes in the mirror in front of her and called excitedly, "Come in."

Eros sauntered in, tall and dashing in smart eveningwear. He sought her eyes in the mirror. "*Buonasera.*" He smiled darkly. A snowy cravat foamed at his neck. He sported a new diamond stud in his ear in place of the one lost in Ostia. He was every bit the northern Italian prince, with his jet hair cropped haphazardly, his lordly pallor, and dark blue Lombard eyes. Alanis felt the heat of his gaze all the way down to her toes. To Cora he said, "*Finisci presto, ragazza.*"

"*Si, Monsignore. Subito.*" The maid bobbed and smiled reverently, as seemed to be the case with the entire staff since their long lost prince turned up on their doorstep two weeks ago.

Alanis followed his still too lean, though magnificent frame as he strolled to the luxurious damask curtains and swept them aside. Crimson-gilt sunrays poured in—the final moments of the setting sun. "I've something special to show you," he said. "If we don't hurry, we'll miss it."

Alanis thanked the departing maid and stood in a swish of silvery blue silk. They were alone. Her hands shook. They stared at each other, suspending the moment before . . .

In five strides Eros crossed the room. He cupped her small waist and pressed a searing kiss on the side of her neck. "How did I survive six weeks without seeing you?" he murmured.

Alanis was wondering the same thing about him. Even his musky scent teased her beyond reason. "Eros." She shut her eyes and thought she'd die if he didn't kiss her immediately.

He must have intended their first kiss to be slow, but the moment his mouth covered hers it spun out of control. Desire struck her, raw and aggressive, and she knew he felt the same rush. He devoured her, rubbing their tongues together, taking, needing. "*Santo Michele.*" He groaned. "How will we last through a three-hour dinner?" He crushed her mouth in another mind-melting kiss, emitting so much heat she was burning. She fisted his sleeves, too weak to trust her feet.

"Let's forget about dinner," he suggested hoarsely. "Stay here instead."

She locked her arms around his neck and kissed his mouth, his cheek, his neck, making him groan. "You wanted to show me something," she murmured, nipping his earlobe.

"*Diavolo.*" He looked pained. "Ugh, all right. Now." He took her hand and whisked her out the door and up the steps spiraling to the turret. Icy air welcomed them. He positioned her before him, wrapped his arms around her bare shoulders, and whispered, "Look ahead."

Alanis gasped. Evening was quietly descending over distant villages and stretches of vines, which appeared wild yet tended. Cloaked in purple mist, dense woodlands of oak and chestnut alternated with cypress trees. Terra-cotta roofs of clustered towns sparkled bronze under the dying sun. Ancient campaniles tucked away in steep hills sent metallic peals to announce the hour. And on the faraway horizon, the rounded Cupola of Florence touched the snaking Arno River.

"See the white peaks up north?" Eros's deep voice filled her ear. "They're the *Alpi Orobie,* the Milanese Alps. And the *alpeggio* beneath them, the emerald mountain pasture . . . *È Milano.*"

She looked at his profile. Tender longing liquefied his irises. "Your home," she whispered.

"My home." He squeezed her tightly, as they stared ahead until the last blazing sunray was no more. During these moments, she felt closer to him than she ever did to anybody else.

"Sallah told me everything," Eros said. "Sidi Moussa, the Roman prisons, the visit to Pope Clementino. How did you know I was in Rome? It was the one part Sallah couldn't explain."

"Sidi Moussa told Nasrin that you were taken to the eternal city that all the roads lead to. I remembered something from Latin lessons: 'All the roads lead to Rome.'"

"'*Tutte le strade portano a Roma.*'" He kissed her lips very tenderly. "Beautiful, intelligent Alanis, this is the second time you've saved my life. I thank thee from the bottom of my heart."

"You are welcome." She smiled. "Although I hardly deserve all the credit."

His eyes gleamed. "So do you put yourself out to such extent for all your friends?"

It was the moment of truth, the one she had been dreading. She turned around, slid her arms beneath his coat and around his waist, looked up into his eyes, took a very deep breath . . .

"I am in love with you," she confessed. "I love you, Eros. I loved you since I met you. I'd do anything for you. *Always.*" She felt so weak she was amazed she was still standing. "Do you love me?"

Eros was silent. Time ticked by. *Ages*.

"You . . . don't love me?" she asked, her voice as feeble as her knees.

He was silent.

She swallowed a sob. Where did one go from here? Hell wasn't sad enough. She stepped away from him, her limbs frozen, her teeth chattering, and walked to the spiraling flight of steps. She glimpsed at his shadowy back. Eros remained as frozen as the faraway Alps.

She found Sallah and Nasrin in the great dining room. "Where's Prince Charming?" Sallah inquired at the same time as his wife demanded anxiously, "What's happened?"

A tear slid along Alanis's cheek. "Nothing. He's on the tower. If you'll excuse me, I am not as hungry as I thought I was. I'll retire now. Good night."

Sallah and Nasrin exchanged apprehensive looks. "I'll go see what's keeping him," Sallah suggested and went upstairs. He ran into Eros on the gallery, where the Sforza dukes displayed their shining suits of armor and imposing portraits. "There you are!" he called with forced jollity.

Eros spared him not a glance as he threw a greatcoat over his shoulders and lunged for the stairs. Sallah hurried after him. "Eros, wait! What is going on here? Bloodshed again? Damn it, man, stand still for two seconds!"

But like a black storm, Eros's boots hit the foyer's marble floor and he strode to the front door. Wind howled as he tore the door open, swelling his black greatcoat and letting in the bustle of dry leaves and the scent of pending rain. Without a word he vanished into the night, slamming the world behind him.

A burst of wind stirred the fuggy air in the old Heartless Fortune Inn. Sitting amid sweaty faces engrossed in games of hazard—*cricca* and *tricchetrach* gave rise to a host of insults and quarrels, in which the players fought over a penny and were heard yelling as far off as San Gimignano— Giovanni raised his eyes from a demoralizing hand of cards, and scowled. Eros sauntered in, wearing a black greatcoat and a matching expression. Giovanni waved him over.

"You're the last person I expected to see here tonight." He sniggered as Eros took the seat next to him. "Who are you hiding from? Your beautiful blond angel or . . . yourself?"

"You remember there are things I do not discuss with anyone? Alanis is one of them." Eros signaled the innkeeper for a tankard of wine and dropped a bag of coin on the table. "Greco, count me in for the next round."

Giovanni leaned closer. "I'll let you in on a little secret, Eros. If I had a woman like yours, I wouldn't be here playing *cricca* with *you*." His gaze traveled to Eros's netherregions, and he frowned with concern. "Your captor, he didn't cause any . . . permanent damage, did he?"

"No. But *I* will if you don't *shut up*."

Giovanni shook his head. "I don't get you. There's a man"—he pointed his chin at a remote table—"who'd give his sword arm to be you tonight. I think the damage is in your head."

Eros's gaze shifted to the far corner of the inn, where hunched over a mug of rum sat Niccolò. Giovanni felt the sudden, black force of Eros's fury causing his hairs to stand on end. Nico must have felt it as well, because his eyes came up and he was staring straight at Eros.

"Don't do anything you'll regret," Giovanni advised quietly. "The poor man is miserable. I think he wants you to kill him."

"Well, I don't. So just keep him away from her, *and from me.*"

Nico stared at them for another moment, then dropped a few coins on the table and left the inn. Eros relaxed, and Giovanni gave silent thanks to a few patron saints. "You know he'd never do anything to hurt you," he pacified. "Trouble is he's not thinking clearly these days. And who can blame him? You're back from the dead, sleeping with the woman he's in love with. He's torn between his loyalty to you and his feelings for her, and he knows he doesn't stand a chance. Not only was she yours to begin with, now on top of everything else, you're a royal prince."

The innkeeper arrived with the wine, his face beaming. "*Monsignore.*" He sketched a bow. "The wine is on the house, in memory of His Highness's father, the Great Duke Gianluccio, whom I had the honor of serving in the *Lanze Spezzate* many, many years ago."

Shock struck Eros's features. Then bit by bit his countenance warmed. He got to his feet. A heartfelt smile expended on his face. "*Compaesano? Milanese?*"

"*Si, si!* My name is Battista." The innkeeper removed his apron and tore his shirt open, proudly exhibiting his belly and a purple leaf tattooed on his chest. "Thirty years of service."

"You served with the *Broken Lenses,* the Special Guard?"

The innkeeper heaved his chest. "*Sì, Monsignore.* At Vigevano, Novara, and Galliate, with honor and valor befitting the duke, God rest his soul, who inspired this in his soldiers."

"Then it would be a great honor to shake the hand of a veteran soldier of Milan." Eros offered his hand and released a soft chuckle when Battista grabbed it and shook it excitedly, his sweeping glance ensuring his neighbors were paying close attention.

"'Prince Stefano has a mind and heart for every great undertaking,'" Battista recited. "'He is the cleanest and noblest lord, the son of Mars, newly descended. An intelligent and charming youth, capable of speaking well and behaving with princely grace, a worthy future duke if Milan ever saw one.' Those were the words spoken by the Milanese chronicler upon His Highness's thirteenth birthday, and we've been celebrating His Highness's return for weeks now."

"Celebrating his return?" Eros blinked. His eyebrows drew together in a fierce scowl.

"Sixteen years we've waited for His Highness to return and hoist the Viper against our evil vanquishers," Battista continued wistfully. "Ever since the word spread that Prince Stefano is back and is building an army to liberate Milan, folk have been arriving here to enlist. For who better than a Sforza can lead the Milanese versus the French and the Spaniards— a prince who is a soldier, who'll be able to endure years of warfare, who'll know how to satisfy the people and secure himself against the nobles, who's spent years in exile and knows the taste of the cruelties, the prejudice, and the injustices that are the common man's lot? His Highness is our true and last hope for a savior, the extraordinary man Milan is calling for."

Tongue-tied, Eros merely stared at the man, and, Giovanni noted, was beginning to look extremely ill at ease. He himself felt a little homesick for his Sicily again, after decades.

"As our great Cicero wrote," Battista declared, "'The people may be ignorant, but they will readily follow a trustworthy man.' On behalf of the Milanese—I salute His Highness!" With a deep bow he excused himself and returned to his place behind the bar. Eros sat down stiffly.

Giovanni reshuffled the cards and handed Eros a pile. "Come on, Barbazan, give up some coins! Tightfisted Frenchman. Thinks his fortune is a woman that he cannot part with."

"Fortune *is* a woman," Barbazan replied, "and, my friends,

as any woman, she must be jogged and beaten, for she favors young men who are less inclined to caution in mastering her."

"I'm not introducing you to my sister," Greco muttered, examining his hand.

"Fortune is a courtesan," Eros threw in and drew a card off the deck. "Favorable yesterday, she'll turn her back on you tomorrow." He stared at the card for a long, tedious moment.

They were playing a deck of Visconti tarots, which was used commonly around these parts, thus Giovanni attributed Eros's slowness to his mood. But he jumped along with the others as, swearing, Eros stood up and dropped his cards on the table. A second later he was gone.

"What was that about?" Greco asked. "He stared at that card as if his entire future was revealed to him there. Do you suppose the portrait of one of his ancestors spoke to him from it?"

"Mind your own affairs!" Giovanni silenced their laughter. He collected Eros's pile and let the ominous card drop to the floor. He crossed it with his boot. Only when everyone's attention was focused on a new game did he lift his boot. Beneath it, face up, lay the card of *The Lovers*.

Alanis sat at her dressing table and one by one removed her hairpins. Blond hair tumbled on either side of her tear-stricken face. *Eros, I love you. Do you love me?* "Idiot," she sniped at her pitiful reflection. At least now she knew. He didn't love her. He wanted her as a mistress.

Someone knocked. She turned her head in time to see a note sliding in beneath the door. *Perhaps he did love her.* She darted to it and with shaky fingers quickly unfolded it. *Meet me at the lily pond.* She grabbed her cape and raced outside. Dry leaves and twigs twirled on the cold ground. She hurried down the trellis-covered flight of stone steps and ran to the secluded pond. Silvery beams shone between fast-approaching rain clouds. A dark figure stood with his back to her, observing the quaking ducks. She came to a halt, panting for air. "Eros."

He turned around, and her joy expired. "Lady Alanis." Nico smiled hesitantly. "Forgive me for dragging you out here at night, especially with a storm coming, but I had to see you."

"Really, Niccolò," she said crossly, her voice thick with disappointment. "You should not have sent that note. It was written in English. You tricked me."

"Michele wrote it for me. He knows a little English, and . . . I don't write so well, not even in Italian. I apologize."

"You could have at least signed it."

"Would you have come?"

"Probably not. Which is why you should not have sent it. If Eros finds us here, conducting a midnight rendezvous, he'll kill you. He has a thing about betrayal, and you are one of his men."

"Eros is at the village inn, drinking and gambling. He won't be back for hours. This may be our last opportunity to speak alone. Would you please hear me out?" Moonlight shifted across his features, making his eyes look large and anxious. She didn't have the heart to refuse him.

"All right. I'm listening. Why do you say this may be our last opportunity to speak alone?"

"Eros is sending me to Venice, but I'm considering staying there, if you'll come with me."

"To Venice?" she repeated, not quite grasping his intent.

"It's the most beautiful city in the world. I know this because I was born there. I grew up near the Rialto Bridge, amid Europe's busiest money market and bawdy houses."

She smiled, a little surprised. "You? A Venetian? A lion in the League of St. Mark?"

"A republican." He smiled proudly. "But my family was poor, so I went to sea at the age of twelve to make my fortune. I served on a merchant ship when Algerian corsairs attacked us."

"How did you escape?"

"I didn't. I was taken to Algiers and was put to work on the wall. Eros found me there, a slave. He was already established with the *Raises,* so when he learned I was Italian, he pulled rank with the Aga, the Captain of the Bagnio, and got me out. I've been with him ever since."

"So the republican became a warrior?"

Nico shrugged. "When one consorts with Milanese, war is business and a way of life."

She stilled. Eros had said the exact same thing to her. "You *knew* who he was?"

"We knew he was from Milan. He had the accent, the arrogance, a thing for vipers. Eros is fearless and dedicated to the pursuit of power. A typical Milanese. No big mystery."

"What do you know about the Sforza?" Alanis asked with interest.

"They were very powerful until the French came along, then the Spaniards. They had a popular boast at the time that the pope was their chaplain, the emperor their condottiere, Venice their chamberlain, and the King of France their courtier. Everyone feared them. Even Cosimo de' Medici paid them tribute to keep them out of Florence. Now, I—" He took her hand.

Alanis subtly pulled it free. "What happened? How did France conquer Milan?"

"The nobles quarreled with each other and provided support for any adventurer, internal or external, who favored their personal ambitions. There were class struggles, petty jealousies, vices, simony . . . Milan belonged to Mars, my lady. The entire world wanted to humiliate them."

Mars. The most physical, volatile figure among the gods— a fighter, a dancer, a lover, an immortal ruled by his heart and desires, driven by rage, loyalty, and vengeance. She didn't want to think about Eros, but the similarity was too strong. "I should be getting back," she said.

"Don't leave just yet," Nico pleaded. "Come to Venice with me. Let me take care of you. I have a small fortune saved. I'll start a merchant line. I'll dedicate my life to making you happy. If only—" He knelt on one knee. "Would you do me the honor and consent to be my wife?"

"Your wife?" Alanis staggered back, her jaw dropping. He was proposing marriage to her.

He pushed to his feet. "I love you, Lady Alanis. You are the noblest, sweetest, loveliest woman in the world, and I know your situation in life exceeds mine ten times, but I can make you happy. You deserve better than a man whose heart is locked, even if he is a royal prince."

She secured her cape against the biting wind. "I . . . I don't know what to say."

Nico took her shoulders, looking straight into her eyes. "Say yes."

She squirmed uneasily. "I, eh, am deeply honored, but I cannot accept your proposal. I—"

"Have eyes only for Eros," he finished grimly. "He'll break your heart, my lady. I've seen it many times before. While I . . ." He pulled her to him and touched his lips to hers.

A horse neighed. Alanis whirled around. A dark rider wrapped in a greatcoat loomed on the lane leading to the stables. Sitting in his saddle, he watched her in the bracing wind. Though his face was obscure, she knew who he was. His cold disgust iced her blood.

With bloodcurdling reserve, the rider stirred his mount and rode away. *You've lost him,* a frantic voice cried in her head, but another voice, a sadder one, said, *You never had him anyway.*

CHAPTER 24

Lost are we and are only so far punished
that without hope we live in desire.

—Dante: *Inferno*

The sky split open the moment Alanis ran up the front step. She hurried inside and shut the door on a gust of thrashing rain. She collapsed against the door's carved surface to catch her breath. Lightning flashed. An instant later the foyer's stained glass windows shuddered loudly. In the resulting darkness she saw a faint glow escaping the open library doors. A broad-shouldered silhouette filled the door frame. *Eros.* Her heart slammed against her rib cage.

"The back-stabbing harpy." His voice was deep and sarcastic. "Come in. Join me while I drink myself to a stupor. It is a state I strongly recommend."

Wariness crept up her spine. "You sound drunk already," she murmured.

"Not so drunk. When one is blind drunk he cares not that he has fallen into the same snare his father had and let a beautiful harpy enchain his soul. He is but the simple sum of his desires."

She stood paralyzed for a moment, then straightened away from the door and hung her cape. Her hair flew wild and tangled to her waist; her satin shoes were soaked in mud. She stepped out of them and considered waiting for the morning to have it out with him.

A heavy body leaned into her, and she could smell the expensive cognac on his breath. Eros flattened one hand on the wall and slid the other up her torso toward her left breast. Her breath caught when he squeezed her covetously, his thumb caressing the bare flesh swelling above the lace. "Your fickle heart speeds up when I caress it," he breathed roughly. "I wonder, what would my effect be on your lying lips?" He spun her around and took her mouth in a brutally possessive kiss. She pushed him away, but he caught her wrists in a vice-like grip and deepened his assault, pressing into her, forcing her tongue to fence with his. Desire licked her like a blaze, like a curse. She yielded to his kiss, hating herself but hating him more for dragging her down with him.

Almost in a daze, she felt him pick her up and carry her into the fire-lit library. A pleasant scent of burning pinewood perfumed the air. He meandered among heavy mahogany furniture upholstered in red velvet until he reached the couch fronting the hearth. He fell on top of her, his greedy hands and mouth attacking her without a preamble. He wasn't making love to her; he was punishing her. "No, Eros. Stop. *Stop!*" She shoved him aside and scrambled away from him.

Heaving, Eros rose from the couch and marched to the wine cabinet. He uncorked a semi-full decanter and tipped it over a glass. Cognac sloshed, bright and golden. Glass in hand, he turned to face her. The look in his eyes made her heart stop. *Hurt. Rage. Anguish.*

"You lied to me," he accused in a harsh whisper. "You lied this evening. You lied that night we spent together in Agadìr." Hot fury ignited his irises. "You kissed Niccolò, Alanis!"

"He kissed me!" she countered heatedly. "It wasn't even a kiss. It didn't mean anything. Nico knows how I feel. The only person in this chamber who feels nothing is you!"

"I ought to feel nothing. One would think I'd be immune to women of your sort. After all, I was given birth to and sentenced to death by one."

"Your mother didn't sentence you to death. Any man with half your brains would have fathomed it by now. If you hadn't been so keen on punishing her, you'd have seen the love in her eyes when she held your hand and called you 'her miracle.' It was *heartbreaking!* I didn't save your life, Eros. Your mother did. She took you out of that pit. She treated your wounds and told me where to hide you. She's your guardian angel, that poor, sad nun whom you despise, who teaches little waifs and strays in the city, who has dedicated the past sixteen years of her life to charity and penitence. Maddalena didn't abandon her son, Eros. *He abandoned her.*"

"I don't want to talk about this!" Eros growled.

"Fine. Don't talk. But you're the one who opened Pandora's box tonight, so you shall have to listen. A woman who puts her child to death is a harpy, but harpies don't turn to the Church. They don't fill their lonely hearts with orphans' love or risk their lives rescuing their sons. Whatever happened that tragic night, Maddalena is innocent. You know how easy it is for a man to overpower a woman. I'm convinced your uncle did something to her and locked her up in his residence to maintain his lie. I'm surprised you were so quick to believe him when you knew what a vile snake he was and how much your mother loved you. But you—her adoring son—you couldn't break that door to ascertain if she was his accomplice before you took your sister and disappeared? You left your mother alone. Didn't you ever for one moment think about her, what she must have suffered? Maddalena never stopped loving you, Eros, and if you had a pinch of compassion in you, you'd go back to Rome and beg her forgiveness."

"There is one fact your theory does not support. Carlo knew about the New League my father sponsored. How? Only my mother and I knew about it."

"You shall have to ask Maddalena. Return to the convent. She's earned your apology, or at the very least your gratitude."

He looked away and sipped his cognac. "I'm never returning to that convent."

"*Predictable.*" She gave a bitter laugh and shook her head. "Go ahead, keep your cynicism, your senseless hatred, and your warped memories. You find such solace in their company. Why bother searching for the truth when you can blame every mishap in your life on your poor mother? It is so much easier than looking in the mirror and seeing all the ugly truths."

"I know my ugly truths," he bit out. "It is time you own up to yours. You came to my bed that night for the most *obvious* reason of all. Sadly for me, I was so blinded by lust for you, so obsessed with having you, I let you convince me you wanted me as badly as I wanted you."

"The *obvious* reason?" she hissed unblinkingly, tears stinging her eyes. "And what might that be? That I'm a cold, manipulative harpy, out for your blood, your soul, and your princedom? I am a duke's granddaughter! Why should an old title lure me to a man's bed when that is precisely what I ran away from? If I wanted to hold court in a palace, I'd be in England now!"

"You came to me because you knew who I was."

"I came to you because I loved you!" she cried, unable to stem the tears.

"Don't lie to me!" he roared. "You don't love *me! This is what you love!*" He swung aside and with brute force hurled his cognac glass at the wall above the fireplace, smashing the fine crystal to dust and slivers against the Sforza coat of arms hanging there.

She stared at him in shock. "You're wrong," she whispered. "It's what *you* love, Stefano."

Eros looked as if she had run a stake through his heart. His eyes burned. His chest rose and fell laboriously. "Stefano Sforza doesn't exist anymore. That part of me is dead! I told you that months ago! There is only one man living inside of me, Alanis—*un dannato,* a damned one!"

This was not about him and her, she realized. It was about his past, about his being in Italy again after sixteen years and having to confront his old demons. And even more important—about his having to come to terms with who he really was. "You are not damned. Stefano Sforza is very much alive inside you, but you have buried him so deeply, he's . . . a little lost."

"A lost cause."

Heavy silence fell between them. He stood proud and handsome before her, and so terribly miserable, her heart bled for him. His worst scars weren't on his skin. They were in his soul.

She came to him and slipped her arms around his neck. "You are *not* a lost cause. You are wonderful, and you are mine. If you had died in that pit, my spirit would have died with you."

His head dropped on her shoulder. He embraced her so tightly she had trouble breathing. He didn't speak for a very long time. When he did, his voice was soft and apologetic. "One fears nothing when one has nothing to lose. I lost everything at sixteen, and I had nothing to lose ever since." He lifted his head. His eyes were dark and aching. "Until you came into my life, *Amore.*"

"Not true." She smiled tenderly, loving him even more. "You've always had you."

"And who is that, do you suppose?"

She fisted his medallion and tugged gently. "That's for you to find out."

He swallowed hard. "Everyone is expecting me to march on Milan, vanquish the invaders, and establish a new Sforza regime. I can't do it, Alanis. I'm not even sure I want to."

She considered the caged look in his eyes. "Why are you so averse to the idea?"

He blew out a haggard sigh. "Savoy is there. Vendôme is there . . . It's hell up north."

"'Better to reign in hell than to serve in heaven.'" She tried cheering him up a little but lost her smile when she saw his frown. "Perhaps you should consider joining Savoy. The Allies are at a stalemate with the French. An alliance with you will tip the scales in their favor, and you, as a single-ruling prince, will enjoy their future protection against recurring French attacks."

"I won't solve the problem by bringing the Austrians into Milan to oust the French and the Spaniards. That's what brought my ancestors' demise in the first place."

"The Allies are not interested in subjugating Milan. They only want the French out."

"The Milanese don't need another power-hungry prince coming to wage war on their land. Milan has been Europe's goriest battlefield for over a millennium."

"Didn't you just say you are the one they've chosen as a leader? Their rightful prince? The pope said the same thing to me. He asked why you were procrastinating in fulfilling your duty."

His hand furrowed his hair. "Don't pressure me, Alanis. I heard enough at the inn tonight."

"What are you so ashamed of?" she inquired softly. "What makes you so unworthy in your eyes to become the next Duke of Milan?"

"What do you think? Do you honestly believe the Milanese should welcome me back after I folded my yellow tail and jumped ship? They depended on me to take my father's place, and I let them down. I let my father down. I let myself down.

I left Milan to fend for herself, without leadership, without anyone to guide the army and protect her interests against France and Spain. I don't deserve their loyalty. *I* wouldn't welcome me back."

"Everyone knows you were very young when your father was murdered. If you had stayed, you would have been dead now and of no use to the Milanese. You had no choice."

"There's always a choice, and I took the craven way out." The self-loathing look in his eyes matched the derisive twist of his lips. "I'm thirty-two years old, Alanis. I own dozens of ships. I retain thousands of men. I have enough blunt to sponsor ten wars. So where have I been until now? What kept me from fulfilling my duty?"

"You were . . . otherwise engaged." She didn't want to dwell on his past thrills and sins. Not tonight. Not when they were alone in this fire-lit room with the rain battering the windows. Not when they were finally talking.

Eros smirked. "Yes. Otherwise engaged in frolicking with Louis and romp—"

Their gazes locked. He didn't have to say more.

"Why are you building this army?" she asked. "Revenge? You're going after Cesare?"

"I don't need an army to hunt down a coward. He's a social creature. I'll find him in Rome and kill him with my bare hands." The spark in his eyes chilled her bones. She had forgotten how dangerous he was when he had lain sick and wounded with the soulful eyes of a puppy. Obviously, he had recouped his old self and was deadlier than ever. "I had a lot of time to think in Ostia," he said. "I don't believe in coincidences. When we visited the Kasbah, Taofik warned me against an Italian nobleman. Then Hani arrived and tried to kill me. He was Taofik's pawn. Taofik sent him and Cesare to my house in Agadìr. Without his help they wouldn't have known where to look. So come spring I'm sailing to Algiers and razing it to the ground."

"So you'll punish Taofik for being the evil, corrupt individual you always knew he was."

"He was my mentor. He taught me valor *and* perfidy and . . . he was sometimes my friend."

"He was never your friend. He used you. You were young, angry, and vulnerable. When he discovered how gifted you were, he took advantage of all your qualities. Don't destroy yourself exacting revenge from him. He is not worth the trouble. He'll pave his own road to hell."

Swearing, he strode to the fireplace and grabbed a poker to stir the logs. "Taofik deserves what's coming to him. I can't erase what his greed and machinations have cost me. His enemies die in dark corners with a knife in the back. I won't spend the rest of my life looking over my shoulder. And the same goes for my cousin. Cesare has wanted me dead for years. He'll be back once he learns I'm alive. They should both burn in hell!" Sparks went flying up the flue.

She stared at his broad, rigid back. "Before you rush off to roast them, think about the rare opportunity you have here. Milan is but a few days' ride. You have a great army camped on the hills, and I've seen the way your mind works. You are a master strategist, ten times more capable than the generals conducting this war. You can accomplish anything you set your mind to. You only need to want it. Few ever get a second chance, Eros, and I know you want your home back. If you let this opportunity pass, where will you be when your enemies are dead and buried? You'll still feel as you do now—alone, adrift, and homesick. You'll have achieved nothing."

Eros raised his head and pinned her in his gaze. "You are leaving me."

Not wanting him to see her eyes watering again, she turned her back to him. "I don't know. I haven't made up my mind yet. I won't be sailing with you on your revenge expedition. It isn't the sort of life I want for myself. I hoped we would discuss things, but clearly your mind is set."

He came up behind her and wrapped his arms around her shoulders. "I had a dream when I lay in the convent," he whispered. "You promised certain things to me. You said you wouldn't leave unless I asked you to." He pressed his lips to a tear rolling off her cheek. "Don't you know me by now? Don't you know I'll never let you leave me? I need you. I want you. I think about you all the time. *All the time.* You don't get to up and leave whenever I irritate you."

"You want a mistress, Eros. Any pretty lightskirt can fill this post." Alanis shut her eyes against the flow of tears and wondered bleakly how the world could turn so mad as to make her feel the most protected in the arms of the man capable of causing her the worst pain.

"Not anymore." He turned her around and one by one kissed the tears clinging to her face. "You planted this ache inside of me that only you can make better." He took her hand, and staring blazingly into her eyes, kissed the inside of her palm. "Tell me what I need to do to keep you."

Love me, her heart cried out miserably. But one did not ask another person for his love.

"I know you worry about your grandfather. But if I became the Duke of Milan, there would be no scandal. Is that what you want me to do? Reclaim Milan?"

"I do want you to get your home back, but don't do it for me, Eros. Do it for you."

"For you, I'd do any silly thing." He smiled. "I won't sail to Algiers. We'll stay in Tuscany together and . . . talk more. That is, if you agree to stay here with me. I won't pressure you to—"

He was too tall to kiss without her shoes on, so she curled her hand around his smooth nape and pulled his head down. He inhaled sharply. "You want me?" His voice came out low, husky, and slightly insecure. "Because I want you. *Terribly.*"

"Will this answer your question?" She pressed her mouth to his, intoxicated by the velvety softness of his lips and aching for the spicy taste of his mouth. His response came as naturally as breathing. He slanted his mouth and kissed her as if their lives depended on it—on one kiss. The terrible longing she'd suppressed during the weeks of searching for him, of not knowing whether he lived or died, broke as a dam. She didn't want to suffer anymore. She wanted to lie with him and love him and rediscover that magical place they had found together on the sands of Agadìr.

"Don't move," Eros whispered, and marched to the doors. The latch clicked. He was at her side within seconds, bending and scooping her into his arms with no noticeable difficulty at all. He strode to the fireplace, to the long, dark red couch fronting it, and set her down on her feet. They kissed each other, unable to stop. She felt his fingers unclasping the hooks on her back as she fumbled with his cravat and peeled his coat off his shoulders. Eros released his hold on her to let the coat slide to the carpet, then unlaced her petticoats. They were in an awful rush to rid each other of their garments, and their hands kept bumping in the process. Finally when her last piece of clothing joined the heap at her feet, she unclasped the top button on his breeches.

He grimaced. "Let me do this or I'll make an ass of myself." He took over, but when he saw her standing before him, her nude body gilded by the fire, he took her blond head between his hands and whispered, "*Come puoi essere così bella? How can you be so beautiful?*"

Humbled by what she perceived in his eyes, she took his hand and guided him to the couch. She lay back and pulled him down on top of her. He reclined between her thighs, his breeches half open, his large body deliciously heavy on top of her. She ran her fingernails through the soft, jet thorns on his head. "Samson, Samson, your hair is so short. I loved your long, silky hair."

Deep laughter shook his chest. "Silly baggage. I'll grow it for you. Water it every day." He kissed her hungrily and wrapped her legs around him as he rocked against her. "I've craved this. I've craved you." He slid lower and licked her nipple until it stiffened into a pointed pink button. He sucked it into his mouth. She arched up, curling her hands to keep from clawing at his back, and wondered why the devil he still had his damn breeches on. His hand found the strong pulse between her thighs. He gently squeezed her hidden nub and drove her wild with slow, skillful fingers. She moaned and bucked, threatened to murder him when this was over, vaguely felt his lips moving lower, scorching her skin with kisses, and before she realized his intent, his mouth replaced his fingers. She cried out, blinded by an overwhelming rush of pleasure, and came off the couch in a perfect bow. He had to hold her thighs apart to prevent them from clamping.

Alanis bit hard on her hand as the pressure built rapidly inside of her. His mouth was hot, insatiable, relentless, and the shaking began. She climaxed so powerfully her release bordered on pain. Every cell in her body exploded with pleasure, and for a brief, sweet moment she floated between heaven and earth. When she opened her eyes, Eros was suspended above her, smiling.

She regarded him beneath long eyelashes. "Remove the rest of your clothing, villain."

Eros sat up and yanked off his boots and breeches. When he reappeared on top of her, his expression was taut with expectation, his eyes gleamed with desire. "Whatever you do to me, I'll die a happy man." He came inside of her in a sure, strong thrust and embedded himself so fully he groaned with pleasure. He didn't pause, though; his rhythm was hard and unbreakable, rolling their hips together in a furious dance. Their eyes sustained contact the entire time. A fine sheen of sweat broke on their bodies; their skin glistened in the firelight. Outside, wind howled, trees knelt under the assault of the rainstorm, but none of it permeated their passionate union.

"*Hold me . . . Love me . . .*" he murmured pleadingly, his eyes dark blue pools of yearning.

She did, all through the turbulent ride to ecstasy, while her body liquefied around him and her eyes became bright lagoons. Eros's release was rich and explosive. He cried her name and collapsed sweaty and limp in the sanctuary of her arms. They lay unmoving, damp limbs tangled, minds vacant of thought, the popping sounds of logs being consumed by fire filling the silence.

He reached for the burgundy velvet jacket on the back of the couch and flung it over their naked bodies. His sated, sleepy blue eyes shone with tenderness. "*Carissima*." He pressed his face to her cheek like a large, cuddly tiger and murmured, "Say you love me again."

Her eyelids fluttered lazily, but his plea went unanswered, for she was claimed by sleep.

Sallah and Nasrin looked stumped as hand in hand Eros and Alanis approached the lunch table on the terrace loggia the next day. The sun shone, and every leaf looked greener.

Eros assisted Alanis into a chair and stole her hand beneath the table to hold over his thigh. "I've seen to your departure arrangements," he announced. "You'll be sailing home from Genoa onboard one of my ships the day after tomorrow, but honestly, I wish you'd stay longer."

"My wife misses her daughters, and frankly I'd consider joining us if I were you. I hear there are hysterical grand-fathers pulling white hairs and scribbling arrest warrants in Yorkshire."

Four footmen stepped forth, brandishing porcelain plates artfully heaped with *Ossobuco alla Milanse*. Sallah got distracted and ended up recounting his unsuccessful attempt at playing *cricca* at the village inn that morning. Eros laughed the entire time and bated him pitilessly.

"The next time you go gaming in these parts, take me as a chaperone," he advised. "I can't believe you lost a hundred ducats to that bag of air, Rizo."

"There won't be a next time." Nasrin gave her husband a tight-lipped smile.

"How can one win anything playing with a host of bar-barians?" Sallah complained crossly. "I've never been as-saulted with such savagery of language and behavior in my entire lifetime!"

"Don't you have it backward?" Eros grinned and sipped his wine. "The barbarians were the Huns, the Celts, the Vikings, and well, practically every other tree-climbing, cave-dwelling clan in Europe. The civilized people were the Romans. That's us." He gestured at himself.

"Ha! Let me correct you on that, my dear Roman descendant. My ancestor, King Solomon, played chess with the Queen of Sheba while your ancestors, Romulus and Remus, still suckled on a she-wolf. Now who's the boor, eh?"

"Touché!" Eros gracefully inclined his head. "You are correct, of course."

"And see that you remember that!" Sallah harrumphed triumphantly. "Oh, incidentally, while undergoing this horrid experience, I happened to hear a very interesting rumor."

After rolling her eyes to the heavens, Nasrin urged tolerantly, "Enlighten us, dear."

"Well, it is not a widely spread rumor due to its sensitive nature, but my source was quite reliable. Apparently, a certain Venetian sailor proposed to a certain English lady last night."

"*Bastardo!*" Slamming his fist on the table, Eros shot up. "That does it! He's a dead man!"

Alanis jumped after him as he marched off to kill poor Niccolò. She caught his hand and forced him to meet her gaze. "I turned him down. Please make no more of it than it really is."

"He had no business proposing to you in the first place!" he ranted, looking flustered.

"I turned him down, Eros."

"You turned him down," he repeated, but his eyes still sought reassurance. Alanis's heart tightened. It was Nico's *willingness* to marry her that put the strain on him.

"What are you so rabid about?" Sallah called. "You should be pleased you are the one she does want to marry. Instead of murdering her suitors, why don't you propose to her yourself?"

Alanis crimsoned. Eros paled. And Nasrin kicked her husband's leg. "Shut up, Sallah, and eat your veal. You might burst of fat, but at least you won't choke on that foot in your mouth!"

* * *

Two days later a loaded coach waited in the yard outside the castle. As Eros walked Sallah out the front door, Alanis and Nasrin followed at an unhurried pace.

"Are you certain you want to stay with him?" Nasrin asked with a worried frown. "I know I encouraged you, but now I think you ought to sail home with us and give him the opportunity to realize he cannot live a single day without you. Believe me when I say that he'll follow at a jolly trot, wagging his very handsome tail, and beg for your hand in marriage."

Again that word: *Marriage.* Alanis's eyes were drawn to the tall dark head conversing with Sallah. The sun shone in his sapphire eyes. His smile was a blinding flash of white.

"He will melt if you keep staring at him as you do," Nasrin berated fondly. "But I confess, he does look happier than ever. There's a glow about him that is entirely your doing."

Alanis groaned inwardly. If Eros had a glow, she was afraid to inquire how ridiculously in love she looked, hopelessly in love with a pirate–prince who had trouble making up his mind which he preferred to be. "I'm drinking the herbs again," she whispered, expecting criticism.

"I'd be lying if I said I approved. If you do not trust him to do the right thing . . ."

"It isn't about trust. A baby shouldn't be the connecting force between us. I don't want to bind him to me with a child and become another duty in addition to the heavy ones thrust on him already. I worry about him, Nasrin. He hardly sleeps at night, thinking about Milan, about this war." Fear possessed her. It wasn't the first time she questioned the wisdom in sending Eros to fight for his home. A war was a war, and he was intrinsically a soldier. She felt a fierce need to protect him, to steal him back to the desert and hide him there, but she knew he needed to restore his life and fulfill his duty. Otherwise, he'd never find peace.

Nasrin put her slim arms around Alanis. "All will be well, dear. You'll see . . ."

Sallah was next in line for a hug. "You know you are a

daughter to me. Never forget that. And don't let this rogue vex you too much. Remember he's just a large, spoiled tot."

Alanis laughed and wiped her tears. She waved them good-bye as the coach bounced away.

Strong arms circled her waist from behind. "Alone at last." Eros buried his face in her neck. "And I have urgent matters to discuss with you in private, my lady."

Alanis leaned into his broad frame as he nuzzled her neck. "How urgent?"

"Burning." He took her hand and whisked her up the front steps.

"We're rabbits again." Eros's deep voice filled the shadows as they rested entwined in his huge brass tub, submerged in hot water, and stared at the flames leaping in the fireplace.

"Brrr . . ." Alanis grinned and rested her head on his slick, wet chest. Lying in his arms like this, their naked bodies glistening in the dusky glow of the fire, she should have felt happy. And she did, to some extent—as long as she didn't think about war and marriage. The two words hovered over her head like the Sword of Damocles. She shut her eyes and released a heavy sigh.

"What upsets you, my innocent water sprite?"

Alanis gave a soft, glum chuckle. "Not so innocent anymore."

"You are to me." He kissed her cheek. She looked up at him. The firelight gilded one side of his face while the other remained shadowed—two sides of the same man, one veiled, the other open and good. Her fingers traced his square jaw, finding the dark shadow of a day's growth of beard irresistible. She caressed his mouth, fascinated by its shape and texture. He was beautiful, like the god Mars, and just as contradictory. His blazing blue eyes; his strong, perfect features; the glossy blackness of his hair—they embodied the spirit burning inside of him.

"*Dai*, don't frown." He put a finger between her eyes and

smoothed away the tiny wrinkle. "Is this so terrible? We are together now. Isn't it what matters most—being lovers again?"

Lovers. A double-edged word, she thought. "Is that what we are—lovers?"

Eros was silent. He dipped a brass pitcher in the bucket heating on the iron grill. He poured the water over her hair and watched, entranced, as the clear flow coated her skin. He framed her head with his hands and slicked back golden wet strands off her brow. "Yes. We are lovers."

Looking into his eyes, she wanted so much to believe he loved her, but their color was the blue source of the flame and just as mystifying. At times, she believed she could feel rather than read the thoughts dwelling in the private regions of his mind. Yet she knew that a wistful part of Eros would always remain covert. She thought of Italian wine: One needed to consider the lie of the land to understand the wine's character, for it was not solely the grape but also the diverse soils of Italy—the volcanic ashes of Lake Bolsena, the lush Chianti region, the rocky terrain of Massa—that added their special flavor to the grape. Eros was no different: He was the creation of Lombardy and Algiers, Rome and Versailles. And as she explored his eyes she could almost sense those equally strong, equally compelling characteristics.

"I'm considering convoking the *Consiglio Segreto,* the Milanese Privy Council," he said. "It holds authority over all areas in Milan and is composed of the highest-ranking nobility. The *grandi* are a powerful lot and demarcated, and they retain standing armies of their own."

She straightened up with a splash and straddled his thighs. "Eros, are you saying you—?"

"This position is very distracting to me, Alanis, but yes, I am determined to give it my best shot." He smiled. "You do realize the odds are against us? Everyone wants Milan, and they're all there, with armies five times the size of mine and with limitless resources to pour into the field."

Her eyes lit up. "But you have the Milanese people on your side, and well, you're you."

He kissed her lips. "Only you think so highly of me."

"With good reason." She smiled. "Once you let your people know you're coming back, they'll flock to you."

"Even if I do obtain the support of the Milanese, I know my country. Intrigue. Corruption. Avarice. Italy is a tiger, beautiful and deadly." Holding her thighs, he slid deeper into the water's hot caress and rested his head on the curving rim of the tub. "Before my uncle's treason, the chain of command always led to the duke, but during the past sixteen years the *grandi* wielded complete power, with the Spaniards supervising at a distance. They are a team of sharks, but they possess one quality that may prove useful to me—their willingness to trade one master for another, believing thus to improve their lot. Perhaps they'll agree to join me. We'll see."

Curbing a smile, she recited, "'If you liberate Milan of this *hateful* domination, what gates will be closed to you? Whose envy will oppose you? What Italian will withhold allegiance? You will be received with love in all those provinces that have endured these foreign hordes for years. Let your illustrious house take up this task with boldness and hope, so that this nation may be ennobled under your banner and so that the words of Petrarch may come true.'"

His head came up. He looked astonished at first. Then a slow smile tilted his lips, and they recited the rest in unison, "'Against barbarian rage, virtue will take the field, then short the fight. True to their lineage, Italian hearts will prove their Roman might.'"

She shrieked when he lunged at her, draining half the tub. He held her nape, whispering to her lips, "Celtic witch, how dare you quote Machiavelli *to me?* I find it . . . incredibly arousing." His mouth was warm and seductive. He kissed her softly, slowly, deeply. "You make me feel so good about myself. I feel sane again when I'm with you. Tell me you love me, *Amore.*"

Alanis caressed his slick, muscular shoulders, wriggling her bottom in his lap. "I love your body. You are an excellent lover. I'm blinded by lust."

He gave her bottom a light slap, his eyes flashing wickedly.

"Monster. Cute little monster." He bent his head and licked a ring of fire around her erect nipple. He took it into his mouth and suckled hard. She whimpered in response. "Alanis," he groaned, dragging his mouth along her neck. "I need to be inside you."

"I want you too." She curled her fingers around his bone-hard flesh and squeezed gently. A grateful sigh escaped his lips as she lifted herself up and impaled herself on him. He wrapped her legs around him and took her in hard, rhythmic movements, his face expressing the effort it cost him to suspend his climax. The tension building inside of her was so strong, she feared she might culminate with a scream that would bring the entire castle down on them. It was a fierce battle. Her inner muscles clenched him as a fist, urging him on, and finally milked a powerful jet from him. He surrendered first with a shuddering groan and buried his face between her breasts.

Alanis stared at the cheerful flames and smiled with feminine satisfaction. The invincible Viper who rarely lost his self-control—and when he did, it was always in a controlled mode—wasn't so restrained anymore. It meant one thing: his heart was taking over his head . . .

"Promise me," he whispered, as she held him to her. "Promise you'll never, ever leave me."

A smile full of hope touched her lips. "I promise. I will never, ever leave you . . ."

CHAPTER 25

Lucas Hunter prided himself on being a hardy person. He survived Eton, Cambridge, the ironhanded Earl of Denton, and pirates, yet he was sweating. "Your Grace." His voice sounded winded and croaky. "I take full responsibility for this . . . acute state of affairs. Indeed, my conduct was . . . unpardonable. You have every right to demand satisfaction. I—"

"Put a lid on it, Silverlake!" the Duke of Dellamore bellowed. "Alis's life is at stake here, not the particulars of the time and place in which I'll put a bullet through your spineless arse! So I will leave the matter of your honor to your conscience and ask you again: *Who—has—Alis?*"

Lucas blinked, rooted to the spot by those icy blue eyes glowering at him beneath silvery eyebrows. Yet, by God, he owed Alis to set things right again. "My wife's brother has Alis, sir."

The duke leaned over his desk and seized Lucas by his cravat. "*A name*, Silverlake."

Swallowing the lump in his throat, Lucas shut his eyes and blurted, "Eros."

He was dumped in the chair, but nothing else happened. Perplexed, he opened his eyes and witnessed the saddest spectacle of his life: The Duke of Dellamore sat in his chair, his elbows on his desk, his hands supporting his head, and tears of terror trembling in his eyes. He was shaking.

"Your Grace!" Lucas grabbed a whiskey bottle and a glass and poured the duke a generous nip. "Let me get my wife, sir. She may be able to answer your questions better than I can."

The duke waved him off.

Minutes later, Lucas ushered his pregnant wife into the Dellamore library. The duke was not alone. His man, Hassock, was memorizing traveling orders while the secretary, Simms, was taking down a letter to Lord High Admiral. Dellamore was to set off for London straight away. Lucas heard the words: blockade, extradition, Maghreb. So the chase had begun. Eros would be hunted down like a rabid dog. Good. He hoped the bastard would be shot on sight.

His wife, however, lit up like a torch. "Your Grace!" She rushed to his side, pretty jet curls bouncing. "Before you set the entire Fleet upon my brother you must allow me to explain—"

The duke looked stunned, then murderous. "I see you did not waste time, pup."

"Your Grace," Jasmine placated. "Eros *did not* kidnap Lady Alanis. She left with him of her own free will. They were to travel the world together. She trusted him. They'd formed a—"

"Do you mean to tell me that my granddaughter *eloped* with that worthless blackguard?"

"They *did not* elope, and my brother *is not* worthless."

The duke dismissed his men and ordered the couple to sit down. "I suggest we discuss this at length. I should warn you, Viscountess, as a gentleman, that anything you say may be used against your brother when he is apprehended."

"I appreciate the warning," she said grimly, "but there are things that may put my brother in a better light." She glimpsed at Lucas. "Things I haven't even told my husband."

"I'm all ears, madam," the duke clipped. "Tell me about Eros."

"I gather you've heard of him, Your Grace?"

"Heard of him?" The duke snorted. "I sent fleets after him. Waged war against him. Your brother, my dear lady, is a bloody pirate. The worst of the lot!"

"A killer and a thief!" Lucas grumbled in accord.

"Shut up, Hunter," Jasmine muttered. To the duke she said, "Indeed, Your Grace, you've heard of him, but I should mention that Eros hasn't practiced piracy for nearly a decade. He is a respectable entrepreneur. He owns the royal mines in Agadir, among other prosperous ventures."

"So he has a head for business as well as for terrorizing the seas. Your brother's scheme of infamy had to be decidedly clever to tempt a girl as brainy as my Alis."

"There was no scheme of infamy, Your Grace. Merely a friendly transaction—Lady Alanis wished to see the world, and Eros, feeling indebted to her for saving his life, agreed to take her on a short tour of some intriguing spots on the globe. I'm convinced that Lady Alanis will return to

England shortly, with her reputation intact, if things are handled properly . . ."

"There's no reason for things not to be handled properly!" the duke thundered.

"Exactly. And Eros will be off to fight Lou—" She clamped a hand over her mouth.

"What's this?" The duke stirred. "The Viper fighting the French? Now that's an interesting bit o' news. My colleagues at the War Office will be delighted to hear this. But why hasn't Eros joined the Alliance if he is so openly challenging the King of France? Holding head on his own merit is a risky business. Could be worth his life."

"Eros has his own reasons, Your Grace. Personal scores to settle with Louis."

The duke's silvery eyebrows drew together in a scowl. "*Personal* scores?"

Looking pleased, Lucas muttered. "Excellent win–win situation. Either the King of France will do us the courtesy of ridding the high seas of this beast or Eros will aid us in bringing the downfall of the House of Bourbon. And then we'll eliminate him."

"I swear, Hunter," Jasmine seethed, "one more nasty word . . ."

"Madam, you must inform me of your brother's whereabouts at once!"

"I will not assist you in apprehending my brother, Your Grace. I give you my solemn vow that Lady Alanis will return in perfect form. He will not harm her."

"But what if he does not return her? Your brother is a man, and my granddaughter is a gem of the first waters. He cannot have her! Even if he dishonored—" The duke pushed to his feet. "There's a particular noose stored in the Royal Fleet with his name on it!"

Jasmine stood up. "Your Grace, please allow me to explain. Perhaps once I've clarified a certain matter you would feel less averse to . . . accepting him as a . . . grandson-in-law—?"

"You go too far, madam!" His thoughts were written on his

face: The fact that his oldest friend's heir married so low beneath him didn't mean he'd put up with similar arrangements.

Head high, Jasmine met the duke's glare at eye level. "Alanis is my friend. It is only out of concern and respect for her that I reveal this to you. You, sir, do not merit such honesty." She paused and steeled herself. "My brother was born in Milan on October fourth in the year of Our Lord 1674, the firstborn son of Gianluccio Sforza and Maddalena Anna Capodiferro of Rome. He was baptized in the Duomo as Stefano Andrea Sforza, Count of Pavia, Duke of Bari, and the future Royal Prince of Milan. I was born ten years later, as Gelsomina Chiara Sforza."

Lucas and the duke looked stumped.

"I remember fragments of our past. Eros wouldn't speak of it. He preferred to forget. About sixteen years ago my father was charged with national conspiracy against Spain and was put to death, but Eros and I escaped. In an unlucky twist of fate, we arrived in Algiers and were held as slaves. To rescue us from this adversity, Eros joined the Raises and became a corsair. A wise old woman in the Kasbah cared for me while he was at sea. We never returned to Milan since."

"The Prince of Milan . . ." the duke murmured. "Duke Gianluccio's son and heir. I imagine you have proof of this extraordinary tale."

"Imposters need proof." Jasmine's chin came up a notch. "Eros merely needs to show his face in Paris, Rome, or better yet—to your friend and ally, Prince Eugene of Savoy, who knew him as a youth. Find me one man in the courts on the Continent who disclaims my brother's legal birthright to Lombardy, Emilia, Liguria, and the southern Alps, and I will show you a liar. Stefano is the living successor of the Visconti–Sforza line, with a pedigree a thousand years old. He is royalty. Is this highborn enough for the granddaughter of the Duke of Dellamore?"

While Lucas struggled to overcome his shock, the duke clipped, "The situation has just gone from bad to worse, madam, because if your brother is who you claim he is, then

Alis is in much graver danger than I imagined. Now in addition to fretting about him keeping his hands off of her, I must worry about the rest of the world keeping hands off of him! The Duchy of Milan is the crux of this war. If word gets around that the Prince of Milan is alive and well and free to roam the seas as a fish, any number of parties will feel threatened. They'll want him dead."

Jasmine gave him a cool glance. "No one but you knows, Your Grace."

"That is where you are wrong, madam. Apparently, the King of France knows as well." He came to his feet and rang for his secretary. "I must set off to the War Office at once. Something tells me that His Majesty, the Sun King, is not resting idly on his golden *fleurs-de-lis.*"

"Ah! Cesare Sforza!" King Louis's foxy smile broadened as Cesare bowed his way into the royal office. "Come in, Cesare. Enter, so that I may growl at you!" He took a minute to doodle a majestic signature on several official letters, then dropped his gold *plume d'oie* and summoned his secretary to finish the mucky job of stamping the great seal over pools of hot wax. "'The pen is mightier than the sword!'" he declared, flourishing his bejeweled hand.

Eying the smug king, Cesare considered informing His Majesty that his proverb originated from the small island he so detested. Instead he said, "Politics is the art of the possible."

The king's humor evaporated. It was not every day that *un zèro,* an upstart such as Cesare Sforza, dared to outwit the Sun King. He subsided against the golden lilies embossing the blue silk upholstery of his bergère. "How very obliging of you to fetch yourself, Cesare. I am looking forward to detaching your incompetent head from your just-as-worthless body."

Cesare paled. "There must be a mistake, His Majesty. I kept my end of our bargain—Stefano . . . is dead."

"Stefano is very much alive!" the king shouted. "You owe me a ship, fifty-thousand gold *louis,* and your head on a platter!"

Cesare's ears throbbed. Surely there was a mistake. Stefano could not have survived Ostia. The last time Cesare visited him in the pit, he was all but a cadaver. "Indeed, I do not presume to have a finger on the pulse of so many intrigues as His Royal Radiance does, but in this instance I can safely guarantee that Stefano is sleeping with the fat fish in the Tiber."

"S'blood!" The king slammed his hand on the desk. "Stefano is fattening up in Tuscany!"

"Impossible!" Cesare cried. "He's dead!"

"Bicarat!" Louis yelled at his secretary. "Get over here, you good-for-nothing scribbler! Where's the communiqué I received from Milan two days ago? Bring it to me!" he commanded while Bicarat was already placing the missive before him. "Ah! There it is!" He skimmed the contents. "Here!" He offered it to Cesare. "Read it yourself. You do read, do you not? I imagine you recognize the florid signature at the bottom?"

Cesare's hands shook as he accepted the sinister missive. He was well acquainted with the mark of the Cancer imprinted on the stationery. It belonged to Count Tallius Cancri, the Eight-Footed Crab, as most called him, Milan's jurist and council chairman. *A council in Lucca, next month, the entire Privy Council summoned by no other than . . .* Cesare swore viciously. The part describing what excellent health his presumed-to-be-dead cousin was enjoying in Tuscany was not the worst part. *The bastard has returned from the dead to reclaim Milan!*

"Tallius Cancri is lying!" Cesare screeched, horror-struck. "Stefano is dead!"

Contempt written on his face, Louis said, "Tallius Cancri has no reason to lie."

"Yes, he does. I'm the heir! I'm the prince! He wants me dead so that he and his cronies will be able to keep what they stole from Stefano and maintain power!"

"You are not the heir, you are not a prince, but you are undeniably very nearly dead!"

Deaf to anything but his own misery, Cesare cursed. "It's

that English bitch! The blond whore he took for a wife! She rescued him!"

"What English wife?" Louis started. "Stefano married an Englishwoman?"

Cesare's mind spun on course again. "Stefano married the pretty blond granddaughter of the Duke of Dellamore, Anne's personal adviser and ambassador on special occasions."

Silence befell the royal office. "I don't believe it!" Louis leaped out of his throne. "Stefano would never do this to me—marry an Englishwoman after snubbing every French princess I offered him! He's only interested in chasing demireps!"

"Not anymore, His Majesty," Cesare drawled. "He's in bed with the Alliance."

Louis's eyes bulged. "*Working with the English dogs?* With that two-faced traitor, Savoy?"

Cesare was all blandness. "So it seems, His Majesty."

"The devil he is!" Louis paced the room, fuming. "I refuse to believe it! Stefano has been nothing but trouble ever since he turned sixteen, but he is no Judas."

"Well . . . His Majesty did order his death. Perhaps he took offense?"

"I was vexed with him!" the king grumbled. "He placed ten of my frigates *hors de combat* in less than a year, and those of my very best! That was too many, by God! One now and then I don't say much about, but ten in eleven months?"

Cesare sighed. "I can understand what induced His Majesty to order his death."

"His death! His death! If it pleased me to see him dead, I'd send someone more capable than you! Someone competent enough to finish the job!" Bitter disappointment etched the king's face. "I was fond of that *voyou!* As any king is fond of a rascal who beats him at his own gaming table, who openly flirts with his mistresses, who addresses him with little to no respect. Every time I offered him a dukedom in France, an admiralty in my navy, and what not, he laughed in my face and declared he had too much sense to enter the rat race of politics. He vowed he would never accept a sovereign over his head. Now I find out that he is no better than that backstabbing Savoyard. Self-ish, ungrateful, good-for-nothing jackals, the both of them! How well they suit the roles of Brutus and Mark Antony."

"I can still complete my mission, His Majesty," Cesare offered temptingly. "I can see to it that Stefano never emerges from the convocation."

"I was not aware you held the admiration of the Milanese Privy Council."

"I am well connected with certain parties, His Majesty—those who have much to lose if Stefano is proclaimed Duke."

"And you can vouch for their willingness to cooperate?"

"Merely by receiving this missive His Majesty may appreciate that at least one creature in the council objects to trading his current master with another. I could guarantee the council's full collaboration, if only . . . I were so fortunate as to be given command of His Majesty's great army in Milan. The Orsini Army, which serves under me now, has already left Rome to camp on the southern boarders of Emilia. They await my orders, sire."

"I always knew you were a skunk, Cesare, the kind who'd sell his country, his family, and his honor, but not the kind who'd turn brother against brother," Louis said scornfully. "To my deepest regret, and against my better judgment, these dire times call upon me to enlist a skunk such as you to introduce stability to my strongholds in northern Italy." He contem-plated Cesare's face, hankering for a premature smirk or an unwise retort that would save him from voicing his less than satisfactory decision. The miracle didn't happen. Thus, the king announced, "Eliminate the Prince of Milan, and I will make you Prince of Milan in his stead."

Cesare beamed. "I thank His Supreme Radiance. I shall not fail this time." He curtsied with a thousand flourishes, his cravat nearly scraping the royal office's marble floor.

Louis's lips twisted with disgust. "Make sure Stefano doesn't beat you to the laurels, Cesare. The council may grow to like him better than they do you and proclaim him duke. After all, it's only a formality. He already holds the privilege."

Cesare fashioned a broad, carefree smile. "As they say in Rome: 'He who enters a conclave as pope, leaves it a cardinal.' Where I come from, the same rule applies to dukes."

"But just as a precaution, let us invite this English bride of his to Versailles to attend my ball of spring. You have four weeks. I trust you are capable of arranging something . . . elegant?"

Cesare nearly kissed the decaying bag. "Excellent idea, His Majesty! I'll send the invitation immediately by special envoy." And in his head he thought: Roberto. He left with a deep bow.

"'The labor of the God-fearing is by others done.'" Louis smirked. It was always gratifying to have the last laugh, or clever proverb, as the case demanded. However, there was work aplenty for the righteous as well. "Bicarat! Take down a letter. Now, how should we begin?" He eyed the forty-carat emerald perched on his little finger. "Aha! I have it: To the Estimable Duke of Dellamore, it would be our royal pleasure, etc., etc. . . . to host his lordship at the traditional Masquerade Ball of Springtime, which will take place in Versailles on the first of April . . ."

CHAPTER 26

Roberto knew his occupation well: First, one began to contaminate the area a week before executing his mission. One studied routes and routines and blended in, becoming so familiar he was invisible. One planned and bided his time until the right opportunity presented itself.

And it did. On the morning of the convocation, the *Consiglio Segreto* arrived with a large entourage of guards, servants, coach drivers, and Count Gonzaga's pack of rowdy dogs. Roberto entered the kitchens with the lot of them while their betters were invited to freshen up in private chambers. His plan was simple: He would wait until everyone was in his cups, then take the servants' stairs to the duchess's chambers. He would leave the same way he came in—unnoticed.

Alanis found Eros in his bedchamber, sprawled in an armchair and idly flipping his dagger.

"Hoping to impress your nobles with your Algerian tricks today?" She swished in, freshly bathed and gowned in Laguna green silk, which set off the color of her eyes and fair complexion.

Slender, tall, and graceful, she enticed his eyes as a forbidden fruit. He grinned. "Throw daggers, you mean?" He set the blade aside and came over to gather her in his arms. "No, *Amore*. There's an old Italian trick I'm hoping to impress them with. It's called 'the game of trust.'"

"Sounds frightfully alarming," she murmured before their mouths locked in a kiss. She slid her hands beneath the lapels of his superfine coat, reveling in the familiar feel of warm muscle swathed with fine cotton, and kissed a sensitive spot below his jaw. "Promise you'll be careful."

"I'm always careful."

Her gaze clouded with concern. "Not always. Remember the counts are not to be trusted."

He smiled slyly and winked. "Don't worry. I'm not to be trusted either."

She laughed, but knew better. After watching him meticulously drilling his army during the past weeks, she understood why his men worshiped the ground he walked on. He was strict but also considerate, honorable, and reliable. He was the sort of man who'd strip to his cambric shirt despite the everlasting drizzle and instruct the less-seasoned soldiers in dueling and other forms of close combat. He was the sort of man who'd risk his own life before anyone else's.

"There is nothing fortuitous about this meeting. Every

nuance is planned down to the last detail. But you must promise me you'll stay in your room until I come to you. *Capisce?*"

A hurtful look etched her eyes. "Am I an errant child that I'm to be sent to my room?"

He caught her arm as she moved away from him. "Please don't make me out to be an ogre. I'm not hiding you. I'm protecting you. These counts have a long-standing debt with me. They'll use anything to destroy me, and you—" He tightened his arms around her and whispered against her hair, "You are my weakness, Alanis. Please say you'll remain out of sight."

"You will come to me as soon as they leave?" she inquired crossly, making him smile.

"With whom will I share my triumphs and failures if not with my . . . best friend?"

She liked that. "I will hole up in my room like a good girl and wait for you to come to me."

"Wait naked." As his mouth touched hers, firm knuckles rapped on the door. Swearing, Eros released her and called out, "*Entra!*"

Bernardo rushed in, carrying a dispatch on a silver tray. Eros broke the seal and skimmed the missive. The air grew thick with the tension he radiated. "*Mannaggia.*" He crushed the note in his fist and tossed it into the fire. "The Orsini are camped on the southern border of Milan."

Alanis exchanged apprehensive glances with Bernardo. The faithful servant had been Duke Gianluccio's man and confidant, and now he served his son. "Who are the Orsini?" she asked.

Lines of frustration etched Eros's brow. "They're a powerful Roman family, five brothers and a sister. Ten dukedoms won't satisfy this brood. Damn Cesare! I had it all planned. Savoy is in Vienna. Vendôme is cantoning in Mantua. But now Cesare will ignite the whole blasted area."

Delicately Alanis suggested, "Perhaps you should reconsider joining the Alliance?"

He pinned her with a glare. "I will *never* accept a sovereign over my head. *Never.*"

"*Monsignore.*" Bernardo coughed. "Pazzo Varesino is here. He came with the council."

"Varesino is a Genoese baron. He is not a council member." Understanding dawned in Eros's eyes. His hands curled into fists. "They brought their assassin with them. Find Giovanni. Tell him to stay close." He grabbed Alanis and gave her a quick parting kiss. "Lock your door."

"Eros, *wait.*" She clutched his arms. "If you are doing this because I pestered you—don't. I'm sorry I pushed you. You don't need to be or do *anything* you don't want yourself. Cancel the meeting. Return to the desert. I will always love you. *Always.* I'll stay with you no matter what."

"I *am* doing this because of you, *Bimba,* but not because you pestered me. You made me realize one cannot escape himself forever, live without roots, without a sense of identity. Some things are worth fighting for. I'm a better man thanks to you. For the first time in almost two decades I know the meaning of pride and purpose. My name doesn't feel foreign on my lips. I'm whole. And I am not afraid to admit that I miss Milan like crazy. I want to visit my father's grave that I haven't seen. I want to do my duty by my people. And . . . *I want to go home.* With you."

Her eyes shone with love. "In that case—*in bocca al lupo!* Good luck, my love."

Eros pulled her up against him, whispering, "My heart stops when I look at you, Alanis. When you lie in my arms at night, I cannot believe that you are mine." He planted a possessive kiss on her lips, then released her and walked away, his boot heels pounding the marble floor.

Stock-still, Alanis watched his tall back through huge, crystalline tears. This time she was certain her heart would burst.

"You know what you have to do," Eros uttered softly in Bernardo's ear as he marched past him to greet his guests.

"My lords, welcome." He tipped his head upon meeting them at the foot of the stairs in the stately hall. "It's good to see old, familiar faces after so many years."

The counts exchanged shocked glances. They were staring at a replica of their late duke—the man who had instilled fear and obedience in their shaky hearts—Prince Gianluccio Sforza. Stifling their bitter reluctance, the prominent counts stiffly sank to one knee, grunts gulped, pride curbed, and bowed their heads before the Prince of Milan in acknowledgment of his supremacy.

When the formal greeting was over, Count Vitaliano exclaimed, "Stefano! What a surprise! How well you look! And to think that we've all mourned your death for sixteen years." He gave a look of unconvincing disbelief. "Incredible! You're alive and well, and all grown up."

"All grown up." Eros smiled coolly. His eyes narrowed on an elderly man who faced him. "Count Tallius, our honorable chairman and Eight-Footed Crab. How are those lawful claws?"

"As those of an old, rusty crab." The count chuckled. Informally he threw his arm around Eros's broad shoulders. "It is good to see you, my boy. You are the spitting image of your father, God rest his soul." A hum of accord swept the hall with everyone reverently nodding heads.

"Your reception is heartwarming," Eros thanked them politely. "I'm convinced that even a tough Lombard Gun such as my father would've shed a tear now, though very discreetly." His comment won a round of laughter. "Let us proceed into the *Sala Ducale* and toast his memory."

A stout Bernardo carrying an empty silver tray barricaded the double doors.

"What's this?" Count Tommaso da Vimercate cried, appalled.

"Only to unburden the load of your dagger, old friend," Eros explained while indicating the jewel-incrusted hilt on the count's belt. "This is a friendly reunion, is it not?"

"Preposterous!" Count Bossi cried. "Our daggers are an

ornament, a part of our costume. You cannot expect us to strip down to our hoses!"

Eros parted the silvery-edged lapels of his black coat and presented his front to his guests. His medallion rested over a purple satin waistcoat and a blinding white cravat of ruffled lace, but no dagger was strapped to his hip. "Gentlemen," he smiled candidly, "I expect no more of you than I do of myself. So, please, let us make our conference a happy event and not a bloody one."

The counts objected loudly. Count Tallius intervened smilingly. "Why sour a sweet reunion with unnecessary suspicion? We all recall the sad lesson of Senigallia when Cesare Borgia lured his mutinous captains to a peace conference and had them seized and slaughtered by his personal guard while their escort was left at the door. Would you have us fretting and eaten by doubt?" He chuckled. "Faith is a frame of mind, Your Highness. You either trust or you don't."

Eros regarded the shrewd adjudicator. "You have the right of it, my scholarly friend. Do forgive my overzealous suspiciousness. I've been walking among jackals and wolves for so long I have forgotten the meaning of blood kin." He nodded to Bernardo, and the doors were opened.

As the ranting group poured in, Tallius fondly slapped Eros's shoulder, chuckling. "There's a recent rumor floating about that you, our own prince, to whom we swore fealty as he wailed throughout his christening in the Duomo thirty-two years ago, have become a ruthless sea wolf!"

Eros smiled at the floor. "What a nasty rumor. How recent did you say it was?"

A legion of liveried footmen filed in imperially to seat the counts, each carrying a bottle of wine. Crystal goblets were filled garnet red to the rim, and the meeting was officially launched in good spirits. Count Gianfranco Visconti, a blood relative, received the honor of offering the first toast. Occupying the prestigious spot at the other end of the richly decked table across from his prince, he rose to his feet. "Dearly assembled, we are convoked today not by any prince, as this land thrives with princes, but by the one upon whose birth the whole of Italy acclaimed: the newly descended son of Mars!" Everyone saluted Eros. "We rushed through hostile territory controlled by the voracious Florence, traveling furtively in merchants' disguise, with but a few companions, to stand before him now. Honorable friends, today we don't only kneel before our prince, we're embracing a long lost brother, soon to be our father, into our loving bosom. Prince Stefano Andrea Sforza, the future Great Duke of Milan, in memory of your excellent, cherished father, Duke Gianluccio Sforza, a great man and a true leader—*Salute!*"

A moment of indecision ensued. No one dared sip the wine. Hiding a grin, Eros summoned Bernardo. "Please exchange my glass with that of an esteemed councilor of your choice."

Bernardo scowled at the strange request—touching a nobleman's glass before he drank of it. Nevertheless, he took his master's glass and circled the table until he halted behind Varesino's chair. With a haughty flourish he switched the glasses, then brought Varesino's glass to his lord.

Eros raised his wineglass. "Gentlemen, now that we have ascertained that poison is not on the menu, I invite you to drink a toast in honor of my father." His gaze clashed with Tallius's.

The count's cold gaze revealed that he was acridly aware he had been tricked, for he had been fool enough to initiate the game of trust. "*Salute.*" He put the glass to his lips while urging the others to follow his example of good faith. Crystal clinked and a spirited "*Salute!*" followed.

As they drank, Eros held Tallius's gaze over the rim of his glass. An ominous look passed between them: By the end of the war there would be only one victor, and he would take it all.

The golden lady confined herself to her chambers all day. Servants came and went with her meals, but none other than Stefano was allowed inside her private rooms, the man being insanely jealous of even the staunchest of his captains, especially of the Venetian who couldn't keep his eyes off her.

Roberto snickered with satisfaction as he rushed up the convoluted back stairs of the castle. Soon Cesare would be duke, and he would be there at his side to reap the glory. Hence he would carry out his mission to the letter and ensure his master received his prize unscathed. A hired cart awaited him outside the walls; its driver turned blind, deaf, and dumb for a few coins. He quietly unbolted the side door and crept in. She lay on her bed, asleep, her long tresses fanned out on the pillow. Producing a patch of cloth and a bottle of chloroform he brought with him from Paris, he drew up to her serene form. His heart raced at the sight of her so lovely up close. She was a little on the tall side. He hoped that the sack he planned to carry her in was large enough.

"Come, my beauty," he murmured as he pressed the anesthetic saturated cloth to her pink mouth. "You are invited to a grand ball in Versailles . . ."

The hour was getting close to midnight. Eros was becoming restless. Bernardo noticed his master's eye kept veering to a spot in the ceiling above which a certain bedchamber was located. A scheme of attack against the dormant French and Spanish strongholds scattered across Milan was laid out in detail. All that remained was for the counts to vote. Yet they dallied over old arguments and old wine. One would think they were doing so by design.

"I still maintain that leading the army as commander-in-chief is a gross mistake that we shall all live to regret except you, Stefano, because you will be dead," argued Count Corrado of Bergamo. "I respect your passion to command the shocking arm of our joint forces, God knows we Bergamese commend valor above all else, but who will take the reins if you fail?"

"I will not fail," Eros asserted succinctly.

"Be reasonable, Your Highness," Count Castiglione droned, his red cheeks attesting to the number of wine refills he'd put away. "If you are taken or killed on the battlefield, there'll be no one to direct the campaign. You are our strategist. You can't march as an ordinary soldier."

"Vendôme does, and so do Savoy and Marlborough," Eros pointed out tersely.

"With the van of the cavalry, yes, but not at the head of the shock arm. That's suicide!"

"So I'm suicidal," Eros muttered. Unnoticeably he summoned Bernardo. "Go up to her," he whispered, "see if she needs anything—some company—and tell her I'll be up soon."

"Francesco Sforza made his way to power by skill in arms," Count Carlino reminded them. "He had little to sell but the strength of his men and the ambition burning in his blood, and the people went wild with delight, rushing him and his horse into the Duomo to acclaim him duke."

"Ancient history," Tallius grumbled. "I admire your fortitude, Stefano. However, there are doctrines on how to conduct warfare, and placing a country's sovereign at the point of its spear is simply not done nowadays. It goes against every rule in the book."

"Worry about your end of the deal," Eros suggested. "You have much to see to."

On the other side of the long table Count Gonzaga was making his case in favor of a treaty with France in place of a surprise attack. "We speak as if Louis, damn his soul, would allow us to throw him out and continue to stay out. Hasn't he all the tricks of a demon at his command? So long as Philip retains the Spanish Crown, France is not one but two powers."

The debate heated, with opinions bombarding Eros on all sides—half the table calling the other "barbarian lovers" while the other half riposting in kind. Count Rossi stood up and yelled, "The French infantry is formidable and is considered the most effective in the world!"

"The French infantry cannot sustain recurring cavalry attacks," Eros replied calmly. "They conduct their campaigns according to the old fashion, by maneuvering instead of fighting, and by besieging forts. We'll take them doubly by surprise because we'll use mobile artillery, the kind used to tear up sails but which is also effective at clipping many of the enemy forces in one shot. Our campaign will show the world that entrenched lines, fortresses heavily garrisoned, and other defensive vices crumble under offensive energy and skill on the battlefield."

The counts looked intrigued. Mustering his patience, Eros launched his final lecture. "The Old World is entrenched in tradition. The French are guided either by the narrow rules of the art as they understand them or by the instructions of Louvois, who, I admit, is a great war minister but does not understand war. His one maxim is, take the enemy's strong places and the enemy will fall. And although he has seen the most splendid victories won by men who disregarded the rule and moved on the enemy, he spends too much time and money spying on what the enemy is doing and robbing its means of subsistence when he should keep the initiative. It's done with immense outlay and lacks that divine spark to which the genius of war is due. And that is but one example. The Spaniards are more direct, but their instructions are not to indulge in battle unless victory is secure. Sultan Kara Mustapha is fearless and smarter. Though he lacks the men and the means to lead on large-scale attacks, he improvises. He plots and schemes to overcome Western prosperity. Just consider tiny Algiers and what a thorn it has been in your flesh for centuries."

"And the guns?" Count Marco Rossi interjected. "What about the Spanish Gun?"

"Their cannons will be ineffective," Eros promised. "My men are experts at stealth, and my chief gunner has a special fondness for tampering with Spanish steel."

"Won't it be wiser to wait for the conclusion of the war to see what's what?" asked Count Pietro Fogliani, the ambassador at the Papal Court. "If the Allies win—"

"Then we shall have new Hapsburg masters," Eros stressed, "only our new lords will speak German instead of Spanish. How long are we prepared to be vassals to the kings of Europe?"

"The Alliance is not interested in ruling Lombardy," Pazzo Varesino exclaimed.

"Perhaps," Eros concurred, "but they won't liberate it,

either. They'll bleed the land dry, for they do not own gold mines in Panama, and their coffers will be drained by the end of the war."

Varesino's lips twisted disdainfully. "Our Roman ancestors began as a republic, and history has proven that councils make far better choices than princes do. What could possibly persuade us to bestow authority upon a man of disreputable and corrupt habits? What talents qualify *you* to save Milan—the mental capacity to maintain your calm under fire? You are versed in pillage, robbery, extortion, and, as I recall, spearing knights at tournaments. You were bloodthirsty at thirteen. No wonder you became a cold-blooded pirate. You had the makings of one."

A hush gripped the table, yet the faces around him looked curious, not surprised. Were they waiting to see if the Viper would demonstrate that which had earned him his chilling reputation? Eros wondered. Deciding to toy with them a little, he sipped his wine. "You've done well for a parvenu whose lethal ability with the assassin's dagger has won him not only a position at Court but also a tidy pension for dotage. I've been following your success attentively, Pazzo. What you were unable to achieve through honest means during my father's reign, you stole after his death. You took the Torelli House for your mistress, the Martesana for your bastard son. Private assets of mine. Did it not seem peculiar to you that my father's man switched your cup and not someone else's?" He smiled. "You see, mine was the only cup that was poisoned."

Varesino's face turned crimson. His hand flew to his collar and yanked loose his cravat.

"A small quantity of cantrella takes hours to permeate one's blood system but is enough to kill a bull," Eros drawled with satisfaction, "as you well know. *Assassino.*"

Varesino choked. His arm moved. Light flashed off a thin blade. Eros bolted to his feet. He leaned toward Rossi, drew the startled count's dagger from his scabbard, and threw it at Pazzo. The blade impaled the baron's knife hand at the wrist a split second before he aimed to throw his own stiletto. An enraged scream of pain tore from Pazzo's lips. He doubled

over, clasping his skewered hand. His bloody fingers opened
stiffly and let the stiletto drop to the table.

"You tricked me . . ." He squealed, as his weight tugged on
the tablecloth, causing porcelain and crystal to smash onto the
floor. He collapsed on the floor, rapping a stream of invectives.

Astounded eyes shifted between the empty, gory place at
the table and between the cool man standing at its head, his
aloof, crescent-marked face etched with disgust.

"Your assassin won't die of poison, but your intent has been
noted and, I should say, was sadly predictable," Eros said. "I'm
aware you knew I was alive, and I'm well informed of your exploits these past sixteen years. You stole my lands, my houses,
my every possession in my princedom, and divided them
among yourselves. You came here determined to eliminate me,
assured that if your attempt failed, you'd alert France and thus
set me up neatly. Knowing that, I *endeavored* to change your
minds, nonetheless, because we're brothers. Without me,
Milan will remain occupied and your power as a council a
joke. With me, you'll lose some of your domestic power, but
we'll be regaining our country. With or without you, *I am
coming back.* Now it's your turn to start courting." He left the
table, declaring the convocation adjourned.

The double doors burst open. Giovanni and Bernardo
rushed in, nearly colliding into him.

"She's gone!" Giovanni stated as Bernardo presented the
acrid smelling rag.

"*Bastards!*" Eros roared. He drew Giovanni's pair of pistols
from his belt and spun around. His eyes glinting, he marched
up to Count Bossi, aimed at his head, and pulled the trigger.

The deadly blast jumped the counts out of their seats. Gory
pulp jetted out of the count's cracked skull, spraying his close
neighbors as well as the white tablecloth.

"You executed Bossi!" Tallius cried, wildness in his bulging eyes. "You're mad!"

"Worse. I'm utterly sane." Face as hard as stone, Eros
started in their direction, his stalking pace causing them to
skitter away like a flock of chicks before a mighty predator.

"Bossi was a sick pervert," he bit out icily. "He won't be missed by anyone, especially not by the little boys he imprisoned and molested in *my* Villeta Maiella, which he appropriated *two months* after I'd left Milan. You, however, my dear counts, I will relish executing, one by one, until one of you steps forth and tells me where the devil you took her!" he bellowed, eyes flashing murderously blue.

"We had nothing to do with that!" Gonzaga squeaked from behind a tall chair.

"Varesino yes, but not that!" Visconti verified from his hiding spot behind the drapes.

"Be rational, Stefano!" Corrado pleaded from a remote corner, cowering beside a Roman marble bust. "What would we benefit from lying?"

"Speak up, cowards!" Eros barked, looking less tolerant by the second. His strides echoed menacingly off the polished marble floor. "This is your last chance!"

"It's your cousin's doing!" Rossi yelled. "Cesare also plotted your assassination!"

"*Where?*" Eros's gaze collided with Tallius's over a chair. He raised the second pistol.

"Wait!" Tallius stood up, his hands in the air. "Louis is holding his Spring Masquerade in Versailles ten days from today. If you don't catch up with Cesare's man, you'll find her there."

CHAPTER 27

Versailles was as glamorous as Alanis had remembered it. White wax *flambeaux* glowed in every window. Fireworks slashed the sky, showering colorful sparks over the artistic grounds. A long line of carriages pulled up to the magnificent palace, fetching countless guests in dazzling costumes. *Le*

Bal Masqué Printanier was King Louis's favorite gala, and no expense was spared.

The vile man who had thieved her from Tuscany and with whom she had spent ten trying days on muddy roads poked her ribs, urging her to quicken her step down the servants' corridor. She elbowed him back, fed up with being pushed and prodded. He was Cesare's man, so it was no great surprise when he opened a gilded door and Cesare's impressive shape came into view.

"Finally!" Cesare growled at Roberto and ushered Alanis inside his luxurious apartment. It amazed her yet again how chillingly he resembled Eros. No wonder he carried a large chip on his shoulder. Ostensibly, they were equals, yet his cousin was born to all the privilege while Cesare had nothing. "We have less than an hour to smarten you up for your audience with Louis," he told her. "The king is anxious to meet the Englishwoman who's captured our Lothario's heart."

"Eros will come for me." She glowered defiantly and hoped in her heart that he would.

Cesare smiled. "I am counting on it. However, all is not lost for you. After Stefano dies, you may still become the Duchess of Milan. You simply need to repeat that performance—"

Alanis slapped him. "Not in a million years," she hissed, deriving visceral satisfaction from seeing the ugly red mark her hand left on his cheek. He would exhibit it to all of Paris tonight.

Cesare pulled her up roughly against him. "I'm beginning to wonder what Stefano found in you that was so titillating, but perhaps if I sampled the goods . . ." He tried to force his mouth on hers, but an enraged feminine screech broke his concentration.

"*Cretino!*" A redheaded beauty stormed into the room, emerald eyes glinting, ruby skirts bustling. Alanis shoved him off, and the instant he turned aside another fast palm met his cheek. "You're dead, *stupido!* My brothers will cut you up into a thousand pieces!"

"Don't be silly, Leonora." He touched his smarting cheek. "She'll serve Stefano to us on a platter. Now let her have the costume you're wearing. *Red Passion,* isn't it? Precisely the part she'll be playing tonight. Wear the green one I like so much. You do wish to look your best for your old betrothed, do you not?" He sent her a spiteful leer.

With a testy sniff Leonora lifted her chin and grabbed Alanis's elbow. "Come with me."

The leading showcase of Europe, Versailles celebrated the birth of spring and the greatness of its monarch with all the extravagance of a ball thrown on Mount Olympus. The entire crème de la crème of aristocratic France came to rub shoulders with the Continent's highest-ranking figures and openly mingle with famous courtesans, acrobats, poets, and artists who supplemented the ribald atmosphere with great pomp and splendor. Squeezed inside Leonora's indecently low-cut, ruby silk gown, Alanis was grateful for the matching plumed mask concealing her face.

As the couple from hell stirred her amid the hedonistic carousers engrossed in drinking and flirting, she realized one could easily lose his companions in a throng such as this. She had to stay sharp, bide her time, and wait for an opening to disappear.

"Don't cultivate false hopes, *caramella,*" Cesare warned softly and tightened his grip on her arm. "Stefano's competence may be legendary in situations in which the guns start blazing, but his pirate skills won't save him from what I have put together for his benefit tonight."

Alanis gnashed her teeth as sharp pain shot up her arm, but she kept her mouth shut. Better to assume docility than willfulness and wait for his guard to slip, she decided.

They began searching the ballroom for Eros. Their hunt should have been easy, considering their quarry's height and build, but in the lively swarm of monsters, faeries, sultans, queens, and beasts, it proved impossible. They explored the balconies, the passages, the grand buffet, and the gaming rooms, where Cesare's focus blurred upon spotting the red-felt tables active with games of hazard. Hooked, feverish greed burned through the eye slits of his black satin mask. If only the temptation took over, Alanis prayed. Unluckily, Leonora intervened and hauled them away.

At ten o'clock the scene dimmed and the king's new curio, a Chinese gong, announced the appearance of the Sun King. Flanked by rows of footmen in figurative liveries of spring, each carrying a burning *flambeau,* King Louis, masquerading as Apollo, all golden and glittering with diamond studs as a sole star in the heavens, led the *Dauphin,* Their Royal Highnesses, the Grand Prior, and the first ten of his ministers toward his throne. A mad dash of creatures ensued, the prospect of being noticed by the king urging the courtiers to range themselves along his path. In royal events being viewed with a distracted eye was preferable to not being seen at all.

Taking advantage of the mayhem, Alanis stomped her heel on Cesare's toe, severed his grip, and lost herself in the tide of courtiers. Running, she scanned the crowds on all sides for a tall dark head, acutely aware that in addition to her fair coloring, her body blazed in the bright red gown. She had no wish to stumble upon her pursuer, or upon any other villain. The Lord knew the *haut monde* had its own fair share of degenerates. Only Eros, if he were here at all . . .

The lights were revived, and the king took his throne with full state regalia, signaling for the *Spring Ballet* to commence. No longer performing, he invited Their Royal Highnesses to engage in the first *entrée.* Alanis checked the strange masked faces folding in on her. Never before had she felt so crowded upon, so exposed. She pressed on, head turning in every direction to ensure Cesare wasn't on her heels. She saw a dark head towering above the rest, keenly searching the crowd. Tears of relief filled her eyes. Pushing forward, she took satisfaction in ruining Leonora's tasteless gown and glued her eyes to the beloved raven head. She saw a flash of blue through the slits in his black mask. *Eros*. Her pulse sped up. She came within an arm of him when a glimmer of emerald silk at his side caught her eye. Leonora spotted her as well and alerted Cesare. He bounded forward, moving with startling swiftness. Alanis staggered back, almost tripping in her haste to evade him. He was big and strong and ruthlessly determined to catch her—the precious lure his future rode on. Masked strangers cast her passing glances, but no one interfered, either sozzled senseless or too jaded to help a lady in distress. Forcing her way in the sea of gaudy faces absorbed in revelry, she fled fast. Her throat went dry; her pulse pounded in her ears. She was running, but there was nowhere to run, nobody to run to.

The second *entrée* began. The prominent Ten were invited to dance the minuet with their wives. Space cleared on the parquet floor, and suddenly she was grabbed from behind and carried out of the way. She kicked and screamed, but her captor clamped a gloved hand over her mouth and hastened toward the rear of the crush. She was doomed now, and worse—*so was Eros*. The steely hands whirled her around, and she met glittering blue gemstones shaded by a black satin mask. They were not cold, the eyes, but gleaming, gulping the sight of her in the seductive gown.

This was *not* Cesare, Alanis realized. The masked man curled a hand around the back of her neck and drew her closer. "Say my name," his deep voice requested, thrumming her heart.

"Eros." She gripped his neck and embraced him tightly, dizzy with joy. She never wanted to let go. "You came for me," she murmured, a little breathless, "into the lion's den."

Eros pulled off his mask, baring his crescent scar and a face carved of feelings. "We go together," he whispered. He kissed her lips, as a desert nomad drank at an oasis.

"We must get out of here, my love. Cesare is here. He's planned something horrible for you. And I have reason to believe that the King of France is behind——" A movement caught her eye beyond his shoulder. "Eros, *look out!*" she cried, as a lustrous thin blade pressed to his neck.

"We meet again, cousin," Cesare spoke over Eros's shoulder, pointing the deadly tip of his stiletto to Eros's gullet. "They say dead men have nothing to fear save the wrath of God, but you look very much alive, Stefano. I don't think the same rule applies to living mortals."

Alanis's gaze darted between Cesare's masked face and Eros's eyes. He was cuing her to clear off. Obeying his tacit command, she edged rearward and saw him reaching inside his cape.

All blandness, Eros inquired, "How do you intend to explain to Louis slitting my throat on his ballroom floor during his favorite gala? The old man has a penchant for me. You should see how he flirts and bickers with me over two *pistoles* when we play baccarat at his gaming table."

"Your glory days are over," Cesare hissed. "Who do you suppose set up this brilliant snare? I'd love to take credit, but . . ."

A forceful elbow met his stomach, and he went flying back. Algerian dagger in hand, Eros whipped around to face him. He flashed Cesare a blinding smile. "You were saying?"

"You're dead!" Cesare ripped his mask off and withdrew his rapier. "*En guard!*"

People began to take notice and formed a ring around them, urging Eros to engage. Alanis held her breath, watching his fingers squeezing the dagger's hilt. A pulse hammered in his jaw. Throwing his dagger seemed to have become an itch he had to restrain himself from scratching.

"This isn't the Circus Maximus, Cesare," Eros rasped. "Don't make a spectacle of us for all of Paris to regale about. We are not this king's courtiers. We are Milanese, progeny of the Houses of Sforza and Visconti, greater houses than the Bourbon."

"Make your peace with your maker!" Cesare snarled. "For

I intend to finish what I started in Ostia right now." He leaped forward, wielding his sword. Eros stumbled back. He switched his dagger to his left hand and pulled out his rapier. They circled each other as gladiators in a ring.

"You brought the Orsini into Milan. For that alone I ought to kill you!" Eros lunged at his cousin and slashed, nicking Cesare's arm.

Undaunted by the graze, Cesare smiled. "I knew you'd appreciate my ingenuity. Did I spoil your scheme of attack?" To the delight of the crowd he struck again. Eros deflected the blow and impaled his rapier into the lustrous loop created by their scuffing blades. Their rapiers locked at breast point, bringing the duelers eye to eye. "You should've remained in the sewers of Algiers, Stefano. You left Milan at sixteen, too green to achieve the degree of guile Italy demands of her princes. With or without me, you wouldn't last a day as duke in Milan. You'd find your death on the sacristy floor of Santo Stefano, assassinated by your own courtiers."

"You give me too much credit when you say my virtue remained intact. I wish to God you were right." Clenching his jaw, Eros bashed his forehead into Cesare's face, cracking the bridge of his nose. The crowd winced. Blood splattered the parquet floor.

"Savage!" Cesare growled. He produced a lace handkerchief and pressed it to his bleeding nose. "You're as coarse as the monkeys you've served in the Kasbah!"

Eros looked amused. "You whine like a woman, Cesare. It's only blood."

"*Ventrebleu,* Stefano!" The sudden bellow gripped everyone's attention. Hastening to clear a path for His Royal Radiance, the tight circle of spectators split into two flocks of buzzing bees. Walking briskly and looking displeased, King Louis advanced without a mask. He halted in front of Eros, scowling ferociously. "You are here, in my palace! Have you not thought it proper to present yourself when you know it would please me to see you?"

"Good evening, Majesty. A splendid ball. Superlative, as always." Eros lowered his rapier and gallantly tipped his head. *But he did not bow,* Alanis noticed with a smile.

"So," the king prompted, "have you no excuses to offer me? No apologies?"

A self-assured grin curled Eros's lips. "I was on my way to pay my respects when a family matter demanded my attention. They are taxing affairs, His Majesty's balls. One never knows who one might run into and be forced to exchange pleasantries with." He pointed his rapier at his bitterly neglected, nose-bleeding cousin standing not too far off. "Here's one example."

"Aha! You too are here!" Louis cried. "I'll deal with you shortly. So!" He glared at Eros. "The prodigal returns! And a ubiquitous one at that! Where have you been? What have you been up to? I hear different tales about your exploits every minute. One day you are here, the other there. One never knows what to believe!" A genuine smile crinkled his powdered face. "I was beginning to worry you had a wicked twin running around, conducting affairs in your name."

"An alarming thought, Majesty." Eros shuddered daintily. "Another like me?"

"Indeed, an alarming thought." Louis pursed his lips. To Alanis, their dialogue seemed a bit surreal. Not to mention the blades in hand and the pending duel, they conversed as old cronies who haven't gone on a carousing rampage in a while. "Well," the king finally addressed a very disgruntled Cesare, "you mean to finish one another off tonight, in my ballroom no less?"

"His Magnificence." Still pressing the handkerchief to his nose, Cesare grandly brandished his sword in a formal bow. "I deeply apologize for—"

"Don't give me that contrite, repentant face of yours, Sforza. I place no confidence in your hypocrisy." Cesare tried to speak, but Louis held up a silencing hand. "I'm not

interested in your excuses either. I know them all by heart.
Especially the one in which you blame your cousin."

Flushing vividly red, Cesare clammed up.

"My favorite cousin and I were about to remove ourselves
to the gardens," Eros informed the king. "We wouldn't dream
of spoiling His Majesty's favorite gala. Duels are so vulgar."

"Spoil? Why do you say spoil? Let's be vulgar tonight!"
The king grandly flourished his bejeweled hand. "My ballroom is at your disposal, *Messieurs*. Carry on if you must."

Eros's amusement perished. It was clear to Alanis that he
was loath to air his family's dirty laundry for the benefit of
every gossip on the Continent. Yet the matter was out of his
hands. Louis had given his consent. With mock severity Eros
brought the gilded hilt of his rapier to his nose. "Hail, Caesar!
Morituri te salutamus—we who are about to die salute you!"

"Ha!" Louis snorted. "That depends on you!" He leaned
closer to Eros. "Come see me later in private, Stefano. I
intend to scold you." In a whirl of golden silk he spun around
and strutted to the gilded dais, and while doing so exclaimed,
"May the best man win!"

The orchestra ceased playing. Eyes alight in anticipation of
imminent bloodshed, everyone waited for the duel to proceed.
The people who conquered the world now had only two interests: bread and circuses, Alanis thought morbidly, imagining
the crowd in togas instead of rich satin.

A cheer went up, and Eros moved swiftly to block Cesare's
swinging sword. His aggression redoubled by the king's indelicate slight, Cesare thrust hard and moved faster, yet parried as a man who had the greatest respect for his epidermis.
Disciples of the best Italian fencing masters, they sparred
dazzlingly, the lethal elegance of their strikes exhibiting rare
skill and intelligence. Their rapiers crossed time and again,
scraping shrilly, glimmering in the iridescent light of the
chandeliers, almost imaginary. They fought as furious tigers,
turning ceaseless times around each other while inflicting
lightning fast strikes. In the thick of the fray they shed their

coats and were forging a path through the spellbound crowd, their white shirts soaking up sweat and blood.

Alanis saw women fainting with graceful care and heard bets being placed and men encouraging the duelers to slash at each other. It was impossible to tell whom they were rooting for with cries such as, "My gold's on you, Sforza!" or "Give him the cold steel!"

Eros lost his footing and sprawled on the floor. The crowd booed. A man behind her yelled, "Here go my hundred *louis!*" Yet Eros sprang to his feet and reengaged. Alanis turned her head and hissed, "Hold your tongue, *Alfred!* Let's see you holding your own out there." By chance, her gaze locked with Leonora's. The redheaded barracuda stood right behind her, chatting with a female friend. Alanis suspected Leonora had deliberately chosen this spot.

"This is exciting, *chérie!*" Leonora's French friend clapped her hands. "If Cesare wins, you'll become the Duchess of Milan and I'll be your bridesmaid in the Duomo."

"How wearisome you are, Antoinette." Leonora slid Alanis a cool smile. "It doesn't matter who wins tonight. The pirate Cesare is fighting is Stefano Sforza, the *real* Prince of Milan. And although they say he married a mousy thing from The Little Island to secure the good faith of the Alliance, according to Lombard Law his troth is worthless. Duke Gianluccio's greatest wish was that his son marry pure Roman blood, as he had. And I am an Orsini. Stefano will never marry a Celt. He'll follow his father's testament to the letter and forget all about the English chit."

"Oh!" Antoinette bubbled with excitement. "Eros, the mysterious blackguard who had all the courtesans of Versailles go through his bed as yesterday's linen, is your Milanese prince!"

"Precisely." Leonora smirked. "After all, we are still engaged."

Engaged. Like manacles the word crushed Alanis's heart. No wonder Eros was prickly on the subject of marriage. He was already engaged to a Roman princess his father had handpicked for him. Worried and miserable, she watched Eros backing Cesare against the wall.

"We can finish this off on our own time away from this circus," Eros said to his cousin.

Wheezing and sweaty, Cesare snarled, "Has your blood become thin or are the iron chains of Ostia to be praised for breaking your backbone?"

"Oh, I wish to kill you," Eros rasped icily, "be at rest as to that, but to kill you quietly, in a snug, remote place, where you won't be able to boast of your death to anybody."

"We fight to the death now!" Cesare growled.

A determined gleam lit Eros's eyes. "We fight to the death." With renewed vim he lunged at Cesare, feinting right and left, as his cousin staggered rearward to the center of the ballroom. He changed his guard constantly and wielded his rapier with ruthless brutality. There was neither pity nor tolerance left in him. With deliberate savagery he went for Cesare's weak spots, slashing his cousin's shirt to shreds while inflicting nicks on every bare piece of skin. The masked crowd tripped back to clear space for the duelers but kept squeezing for ringside positions. Cesare's fencing turned desperate. He parried, ducked, and bent his knees, turning the swings with his gloved hand while keeping his head well back, but a calculated *demi-vaulte* sliced his arm to the bone. Blood ran. The crowd went berserk, cheering in a chorus that undulated as surf in a storm. Covered with sweat, his chest heaving, Eros sprang forward and ran his thin blade through Cesare's liver. Cesare collapsed on the floor, his body leaking a pool of blood.

"Stefano . . ." Fear rounded his eyes. His gaze darted to where his sword lay a good few feet away. "My blade . . ." he murmured, impotently reaching out for it.

Eros looked as sapped as his cousin. He sheathed his rapier. "Draw your knife," he ordered.

Cesare hesitated, not quite trusting his cousin's generosity.

"Draw your knife, bastard!" Eros growled. "I'll grant you

your last wish, only you'll die by the knife, as befitting a traitor."

Cesare flashed his dagger. "You're dead too, Stefano. Only you don't realize it yet." With a brutal kick he felled Eros to the floor. He rolled onto him and stabbed.

Alanis's shriek was swallowed up by the gasp of the crowd. Even the king shot to his feet.

Flat on his back, Eros gripped his cousin's wrist and fought to repel the advancing knife. Cesare was fatally wounded, yet he demonstrated tremendous force as he pushed the trembling dagger downward inch by inch toward Eros's chest. Alanis's eyes were glued to the knife, mere inches away from Eros's taut face. Then, when all seemed lost, Eros lunged up and threw Cesare off of him. With a guttural cry he crashed into Cesare, pinning him to the ground, and buried his dagger in Cesare's chest. The gem-encrusted hilt protruded from his cousin's chest as a headstone.

Cesare's eyes widened; his lips spattered blood. "*Stefano . . .*" He clutched Eros's torn shirt, agonizing pain transforming his features from cruel to desolate. "What did you win from Louis?"

Kneeling beside him, Eros's eyes filled with regret. "Milan would have been free today if we had joined forces, cousin. You've been a worthy foe and could have been a worthier ally, but greed and jealousy poisoned your soul." His smile seemed sad to Alanis when he said, "I only won ten *pistoles*. Did you think that old miser would endanger a *sou* more?"

"Miserable scrooge." Cesare smiled weakly. His eyes grew dark with fear. His bloody fist tightened on Eros's shirt and pulled. "Listen to me. The sinister hand of the Eight-Footed Crab is what you must fear." His head dropped, ocean-blue irises frosting over with oblivion.

Profound sorrow creased Eros's brow as he smoothed his hand over Cesare's gaping eyes. "Forgive me, cousin," he whispered, swallowing a tight lump. "I forgive you . . ."

Alanis leaped forward, but a strong hand seized her arm. Her head lashed around. A silvery-haired gentleman disguised as a Greek philosopher faced her. Her jaw dropped. "*Grandfather?*"

The duke's icy blue eyes glinted. "Hello, Alis. I'm so glad you remember me."

She bit her lip. What rotten luck! She forced a smile of greeting. "Grandfather, please," she beseeched. "I must have a moment with Eros. I'll explain everything later."

"Indeed, you will, Alis, on our way home. We're leaving!" He started toward the entrance.

Alanis squirmed to be free. "No! I can't disappear without a word. I need to go to him . . ."

The duke halted. "Take a look at your *hero*." He gestured at the rush of females flocking to Eros. Farcically, while Cesare's body was being hauled away, Eros had to fight off champagne glasses, salmon tartlets, and lace handkerchiefs offered to wipe his brow. The ladies surrounding him didn't look offended by the crude display of sweat-slick muscles smeared with gore.

"Well, Alis," her grandfather demanded sternly, "are you ready to depart before the King of France decides to put me on the rack for interrogation?"

She hardly heard him. Glumly, she saw Leonora approaching Eros. He smiled, looking surprised. Alanis swore. She considered leaving: Let him come after her, all the way to England, wagging his tail. In the corner of her eye she saw rows of halberdiers closing in on him.

Her grandfather urged her into motion. "We're English on French soil. We must be off."

"No. Wait!" she cried, her head pounding. "I cannot leave him. They aim to trap him."

"Forget him, Alis! He'll have to sort it out with his good friend, Louis."

Dragged off against her will, Alanis's mind reeled with anxieties.

"*Alanis!*" The deep roar immobilized her. She disengaged from the duke's grip and turned to see Eros marching determinedly toward her. The guard was almost upon him, yet he seemed oblivious to the danger. His sharp gaze went to the elderly duke at her side, then sought hers. *Don't leave,* his potent plea pinned her to the spot. She hung pleading eyes on her grandfather.

"*Please.* Leave without me, grandfather. England needs you, and I . . . I love Eros."

"Damnation, Alis! Now none of us will be leaving." The noose converged on the three of them while the other guests were respectfully vacated to the gardens.

"Arrest him!" Escorted by two of his highest-ranking courtiers and a squadron of palace guards, the King of France strutted toward them. The halberdiers rushed to surround Eros in a tight loop while two guards seized his arms, containing his dynamic resistance.

"Well, well, well!" the king bellowed at Eros. "So the skunk did not lie! You are in bed with the Alliance! Aha! The estimable Dellamore! Rise, *Monsieur le Duc,* and introduce me to your charming granddaughter, who has bedeviled my Stefano's heart so that he has forgotten what he's about and who his friends are." He strode to Alanis and to her utter disgust put a finger beneath her chin, lifting her face to the light. Static as an ice queen in ruby silk, her aquamarine eyes slanted wrathfully at the king. "Ravishing," he murmured. "Now I understand everything."

"Leave her alone, Louis!" Eros vaulted forward and was brutally restrained by the guards. His muscles bunched as he fought to be free; his eyes blazed. It took four men to contain him.

"I'm shocked, *Monsieur.*" Louis glared at the duke. "How could you let this exquisite flower fall into the hands of a notorious rake, a philanderer, and a blackguard?" He slid Eros a spiteful leer. "Perhaps after tonight, with her new status as widow, we'll put our heads together, play matchmakers, and find her someone more suitable. The Marquis Du

Beq would be an excellent choice." The king introduced one of his courtiers. "One can see he's already in love."

Du Beq took a bow. Alanis felt his eyes gliding over her cleavage like unwanted hands. Her eyes found Eros. He worried about her, seeming more disturbed by the king's fondling than by his dire situation. She jerked her chin free, not caring that she was snubbing a royal finger.

"Oh, she's a fiery one!" Louis chuckled. "Do I rile you, my beautiful wildcat? Have you fallen so madly in love with our Stefano as so many before you?"

The duke's silvery mustache bristled. "His Majesty, my granddaughter is not attached to Prince Stefano Sforza in any way. She will be returning home with me."

"Nobody will be returning home so fast!" Louis's foul mood resurfaced. "You, my dear duke, will be escorted to your chambers with your lovely granddaughter. And you"— he pointed an emerald-burdened finger at Eros—"have a special cell with your duplicitous name emblazoned on it—in the Bastille!"

"You can't put a finger on me, Louis, and you damn well know it!" Eros rasped fearlessly, shocking everyone, including Alanis, with his blunt address. "I'm a royal prince. Only the Holy See and the emperor have the power to sentence me to death. If you kill me, the Church will mulct you so heavily, you'll go bankrupt within a month. The pope does not take too kindly to foreign monarchs who dare execute royal Italian blood. I can well imagine the Cardinal of Rouen's face when he hears his chances of becoming pope went down the drain along with my chopped head. What a field day you'll have with your Catholics."

"Shut up!" Louis barked. "You've crossed the line once too often and I put a blind eye to it, but no more! *Mortbleu,* this is as far as it goes! You shouldn't have sides with that backstabbing Savoyard! Did he offer you Milan? Did he promise you the kingship of Italy? How dare you presume you could make a mockery of the King of France. Did you think your treachery would go unpunished? I'd have made you a god in France! An Admiral-in-Chief! The toast of Paris!"

"The toast of Paris?" Eros snorted. "I know a sea captain who'd love that."

The king's temper went through the ceiling. "Let's see if you still maintain your wit after a few cooling days in the Bastille!" And at the halberdiers he yelled, "Take him away!"

CHAPTER 28

"His execution will take place at La Place de la Concorde a week from today," the Duke of Dellamore announced two days later upon entering the apartment he shared with Alanis.

Alanis sat down, spots swimming before her eyes. She hadn't slept in days. "Please help me get him out of France," she begged. "Use your contacts, perhaps Madame de Montespan—"

"Damnation, Alis! You'll get no sympathy from me. You let that bastard compromise you thoroughly and stayed on as his mistress for months! Your mother must be turning in her grave."

"My mother would want me to find happiness!" she retorted, angry with the duke and with herself. Why the devil had she confessed everything to her grandfather? "Eros makes me happy. He respects me. He confides in me. He came here to rescue me *despite* the danger to himself!"

"I don't understand this—your absolute loyalty to him! What did he do to merit such blind devotion? Did he declare himself? Has he asked you to marry him?"

She glanced at her lap. "I explained about Lombard Law," she murmured uncomfortably.

The duke paced the room. "For the love of God, Alis, how could you take off with a man of his repute? He took you to

Algiers, for heaven's sake! Are you so dim-witted to have placed your life in that cur's hands?"

She rolled her eyes. After two days of incessant scolding she hadn't a drop of strength left to hear any more. "He is *not* a cur. He's the man I love and a royal prince!"

"A soon-to-be dead prince. And good riddance, I say! That man used and abused you!"

"He never abused me! I fell in love with him, and I went to him of my own free will."

"Free will! Of course he made you care for him! Did you think he was the peach-faced pup Silverlake was? Stefano Sforza is a shrewd predator. What do you think made him a terror of the seas? He's no fondling, Alis. He's precisely what he was cultivated to be—a Milanese Viper, sly and ruthless in every interesting way. I make no allowances for him. Nor do I absolve you of stupidity. You fell for his charms when he had no intention of doing the right thing by you. He's as slick as that glossy black head of his. A pox on his head, I say! I hope he rots in the Bastille!"

Alanis kept silent. She needed her grandfather's help, and she was failing miserably.

"A damnable prince," the duke muttered, "and it didn't stop him from treating you very ill, Alis, very ill indeed. He should've known better than to drag an innocent to the worst haunts in the world! He should've exercised prudence and taken your escorts along instead of placing you at the mercy of his cutthroat crew. And he should have bloody well kept his hands to himself! A disgrace! Coming from anyone else I'd get it, but from a man of *his* background? That scoundrel hasn't one redeeming quality in his entire outsized body. He's corrupt through and through."

"So the only thing standing to his credit is his title?" she asked frostily.

"A title is a title, especially one as important as his. If he'd approached me in a gentlemanly manner, I might have come around. Might have introduced him to Marlborough. Perhaps even furthered his cause. But not now! Never now! Stefano

Sforza chose the cowardly way. He took you to his bed without the slightest regard for your reputation. He manipulated your feelings and took advantage of your naïveté. Can you not see that as the truth?"

Stoically she said, "I had no wish to cause scandal or distress. You've been an excellent grandfather, and I cannot justify my actions. Except that . . . unlike Lucas, Eros wanted me for me, not because he felt obligated or because I had the makings of a suitable, well-bred wife."

An affectionate smile softened the duke's scowl. "Why shouldn't he fancy you? You are precisely the sort to tempt a man as jaded as he. He can have all the painted trollops downstairs, but none of them will reestablish his sense of worth. You are his trophy, his rightful due in life, everything that was deprived of him and can compensate for lost years."

Remembering Leonora, Alanis said dolefully, "When he becomes the Duke of Milan the world will forget his notoriety. He'll have his pick of the Continent's prime stock of princesses."

"You heard the king. He is finished. Even if he survives this adversity, Stefano Sforza will never have Milan. Whatever reputation he once sported as a force to be reckoned with is ruined. His allies will desert him, his army will fall apart because he will no longer be able to deliver the triumphs he has promised, and his captains will scramble for the service of some luckier master. The Milanese people will remember him with hate and disgust. He'll be viewed as a cringing, whimpering, blustering, dithering creature; be avoided as possible; and be looked upon with cold contempt. Is this the sort of man you want for a spouse, Alis? A failure? A wreck?"

Tears welled in her eyes. "You have no idea how wrongly you misjudge his character. He is loyal, strong, and clever, and I love him with all my heart. Please speak to the king. You know his politics. If you wished to, you could prevent this execution."

Alarm crossed the duke's brow. "Alis, dearest, are you in a . . . family way?"

Alanis put her hand over her flat abdomen. Today she wished she could say *aye*.

"You must be anxious to return home, *Monsieur le Duc*," Louis remarked with a sly smile. "However, I have a lovesick prince in my dungeon pining for your granddaughter. And as I am famous for my benevolence, I cannot refuse a condemned man his last request."

Dellamore eyed the man behind the royal escritoire. "His last request, Majesty? Which is?"

"That I allow Lady Alanis to visit him in the Bastille. He's been harassing me for two days, sending his guards." Louis's eyes narrowed foxily, interested to hear the duke's reply. "Well?"

The duke gritted his teeth. "Alis will respect His Majesty's command, naturally, yet I must insist that the insignificant connection between her and your prisoner does not merit this visit."

Louis leaned closer. "I hear otherwise, *Monsieur*. My sources tell me they are married."

"They are not married."

" . . . and that Stefano is with the Alliance."

"As Queen Anne's representative, I may guarantee conclusively that he is not."

Doubt crept around the king's eyes. "You do not mind if I hang him?"

"By all means, hang him."

Snorting, Louis subsided in his throne. "I see. You are in no hurry to return home."

The duke realized he had no choice but to play along. He bent forward, softly saying, "May I have his Majesty's discreet ear? This is a very delicate matter indeed . . ."

"It is?" Looking as eager as a cat before a bowl of cream, Louis leaned toward the duke.

"Well, they are not married, but there might have been an indiscretion. You see . . ."

A Frenchman before anything else, Louis's face beamed in anticipation. "Yes? *Yes?*"

"Prince Stefano held my granddaughter captive for months, Your Majesty. *Unchaperoned,*" the duke added with a meaningful wiggling of his slivery eyebrows.

Louis shifted closer. "*And—?*" he encouraged.

"That's it."

Looking sourly disappointed at being denied the torrid details of the affair, Louis clipped, "My sources at the Papacy claim that the marriage certificate she presented to the pope verified they'd been married in Jamaica several months ago. Now, what say you about that, *Monsieur?*"

Maintaining his impersonation of an old gossip, the duke explained, "He tricked her. He promised marriages, princedoms . . . His Majesty must know how impressionable young girls are. Alis took the bait, and lo and behold! It appears he's already engaged, and what's more? His wedding vows are valid only if they are taken in the Duomo in Milan. Lombard Law."

"That's right!" Louis stirred. "Lombard Law! I remember now."

"So His Majesty understands why Alis has no cause to visit with this despicable rogue."

"That he is, but she will visit him nonetheless, under guard, of course." When the duke opened his mouth to object, Louis looked at him righteously. "My benevolence, *Monsieur!*"

"Ah, yes . . ." The duke stifled a curse. "His Majesty's benevolence . . ."

The king signaled for the opening of the doors. "So the matter is settled. Lady Alanis will pay Stefano a visit and then you may return to your little island." The audience was over.

When evening came, Capitan La Villette arrived to escort Alanis to the Bastille. She bade him wait in the foyer and sought her grandfather in his chamber.

"So, you're off to the Parisian Pit," the duke said. "Do you need me to come along?"

"I'll manage." She refused his halfhearted offer. "I've become quite the pit scout since I met Eros. For a prince, he has a peculiar tendency to inhabit the most unpleasant spaces."

"Hmm. I trust you're not entertaining thoughts of smuggling him out in your pocket?"

Alanis smiled brilliantly. "As you pointed out this morning, he is too outsized for that. But never fear. We'll put our heads together and come up with a clever scheme." Indeed, the mere of thought of putting heads and mouths and bodies together charged her with excitement and hope.

The duke removed his eyeglass. "Louis believes your pirate has switched sides to our camp. How do you intend to convince him that his personal favorite is still loyal?"

"Eros never pledged allegiance to anyone. He'll have no king over his pox-cursed head."

"And yet," the duke reflected aloud, "there is nothing more dangerous than having a sense of normality without the reality to back it up. There is a way to convince the king that his favorite pet isn't collaborating with us. You want to save him, Alis? Leave him. Renounce him."

Her smile collapsed. She, too, had come to this abject conclusion, but to convince the king, she would have to convince Eros first. The most awful feeling assailed her; as if she had taken poison, sickly frost pervaded her system. A large, warm tear rolled down her cheek.

"I won't lie to you, Alis. The idea of you forsaking Sforza is very appealing to me, but I'm not heartless. I realize *your* feelings, as least, are sincere. This is the best advice I can offer you."

She returned to the foyer. Capitan La Villette looked impatient. "Mademoiselle is ready?"

Another city, another pit. She straightened her spine. "Mademoiselle is ready."

Cupid read the name and title of this book:
  "Wars," said he, "wars are in store for me, I perceive."
  —Ovid: *Remedia Amoris, The Remedies For Love*

Murderers and thieves, libertines and prostitutes, forgers and debtors populated the most sinister prison in Europe— the Bastille. They existed in filthy, dank cells, enchained in irons, at the mercy of sick, hardened jailors. The air reeked of human stench: death, disease, and misery, taking form in the ghostly eyes peeping through barred slits. Alanis followed La Villette down endless torchlit tunnels, descended hundreds of steps, and shuddered at the insalubrious spaces.

"Ten minutes, Mademoiselle," the captain said when they arrived at the bottom of the pit.

A grunting hunchback who seemed an indigenous beast of this ghastly haunt unlocked the cell. The door opened with a metal clang and squeaked on its medieval hinges. Alanis stepped in. At first she perceived nothing, only blackness. The door slammed shut, and a pair of strong hands gripped her. Her heart jolted violently. "Alanis." Warm lips touched hers, soft and familiar. The desire to respond to his kisses was overwhelming, yet she held back, knowing that if she showed any sign of warmth, Eros would never believe her. She would be digging him a grave.

"The king sent me here," she uttered impassively. "He claims you've been asking for me."

"Day and night." His face was sooty, yet his eyes gleamed in the feeble torchlight leaking in through the eyehole; his smile was the sun. "God, you are beautiful." His hands caught her fair head and he planted another kiss on her lips. "I missed you, *ninfa*. Did you miss me?"

As filthy as he was, she came alive under his touch. She ached to run her fingers through his thick, oily hair and devour his mouth. Instead she asked, "How have you been holding out?"

Suspicion flickered in his eyes. "Fine. And you? I hope my cousin's brutes didn't—"

"You arrived in time. Thank you. It seems my little lie to the pope got you in a lot of trouble. Louis believes you joined forces with the Alliance. With Marlborough and Savoy."

He grinned. "Imagine that."

"He scheduled a rendezvous for you with the executioner of Paris next week."

Eros hesitated. "I've decided to give in to Louis's ultimatum. I'll take the admiralty."

"*What?* You'll accept him as a sovereign? Become a French marionette and serve him as a captain in his navy?" she asked, horrified. *The Milanese will remember him with loathing and disgust.* "If you do this," she whispered, "you'll never win your country back. Why, Eros?"

"For you. Will you live with me in France?" His voice thickened. "As my wife?"

Her heart kicked with brute force, and if Eros's arms hadn't curved around her waist, she would have squatted on the grimy, straw-spread floor like a dumbstruck idiot. "Your wife?"

He pressed his cheek to hers. "I can't wait to give Louis my consent, get out of this foul hole, and make love to you in a clean bed. You and I, Alanis, man and wife."

At that moment, Alanis knew beyond doubt that she would walk through fire before she allowed him to sacrifice his princedom. Watching him go through life castigating himself for abandoning his *paesani* and siding with their enemy would be a torment far greater than giving him up altogether. It would destroy them both bit by bit. She *had* to let him go. For his sake. She tilted her head back. "I'm sorry. I cannot accept your proposal. I won't live in France."

His mouth curved in a grin. "I understand your aversion, *Inglese.* Believe me, I don't much relish living here, either. It won't be forever, though. We'll abscond the first chance we get."

"What about Lombard weddings? I know all about your Milanese laws."

"You do? Well, it doesn't matter now." He shrugged negligently. "Lombard Law applies to royal Milanese princes, not to nameless, homeless French sailors."

The pain he concealed shredded her heart. Her resolve hardened. "You won't be a prince?"

He embraced her closer, his smile full of trust and warmth. "You see, this nymph I want to marry won't mind. I happen to know that she loves me." He sought reassurance in her eyes and when she subtly averted her gaze he stiffened with alarm. "You . . . have doubts?"

"Well . . . I rather hoped . . ." Now was the time to launch another broadside. "Louis assured my grandfather that if I visited you, he'd allow us to return to England. We leave tomorrow."

His arms dropped to his sides. "I don't believe you. You're lying. Why?"

She met his gaze. "Because you were right from the start. I did come to you that night as a result of what you told me. I want to be a princess, and if not in Milan, then somewhere else."

Terror crossed his brow. "*You love me.*"

Commanding her tears, she sustained his stunned glare. "I never did."

Eros seemed briefly in doubt of his sanity, or at the very least—*his hearing.* "I must be a real idiot," he whispered. "I . . . I'm not catching on . . ."

His misery turned her stomach. "Yes you are. You simply refuse to accept it."

"*Accept what?*" he growled despondently. "That the woman who hauled me out of the pit of hell, who pieced my soul together, who slept in my arms night after night for weeks, is a creature I don't even recognize? Why are you so heartless?"

Heartless was an accurate definition, for what she had left inside her chest was debris.

He cupped her face and stared into her eyes. "Alanis, haven't you considered the possibility that we might be expecting a baby? *Our baby?*"

Alanis blinked. "*Now* it bothers you?"

"It never bothered me." He held her gaze, conveying more than she cared to see.

She shut her eyes briefly to collect herself, then peeled his hands off her, drawling acidly, "There is no baby." Let him despise her. Let him curse her name to all eternity. At least he would live to do so, in Milan. Stepping back, she landed the final blow. "I took care of the business."

Her words struck him with the force of a sledgehammer. "You came to me a virgin, Alanis! How would you know about things like *that?*"

She throbbed under his fury. "A virgin. Not an idiot."

He seized her arms and shook her brutally. "What have you done to your body? *Tell me!*"

She was a rag doll in his hands. The contempt in his eyes made her cringe. "Special herbs," she confessed expressionlessly, "brewed and imbibed every morning."

He shut his eyes, believing at last. He let go of her and stepped away.

In her mind she was crumbling at his feet and weeping. "Good-bye, Eros."

He looked at her—a blue-eyed black leopard, his jet forelock falling over his tiger eyes. He removed the heavy gold chain from his neck and took her hand. Commanding her glassy gaze, he put the medallion in her palm. He gathered the chain-links onto it and closed her fist. "Keep it. You've earned it. It's what either of us will ever have of Milan."

You will never see him again, the small voice inside her head wept inconsolably. Her spine rigid, she walked to the door and asked to be let out. Her last glimpse of Eros was through the barred eyehole in the cell door. He stared at her, and in his beautiful eyes glittered unshed tears.

Tall waves crashed against the cliffs of Dover. Standing at the railing in the nippy morning air, Alanis viewed England's coast and felt as bleak as the gray crags. In her heart she knew that she had done the right thing. Eros would live. He would escape France and establish himself as the next Duke of Milan. He deserved happiness. She knew that she had lost him forever.

The chill in her bones was familiar: misery, nausea, loneliness. She recognized all of these symptoms. A sound that was partly a sob but also a bitter laugh escaped her lips. What a paragon of kindness she was, and what a bloody hypocrite. She burned with jealousy and pain, already despising the woman who would spend the rest of her life with him, for she doubted not a second that Eros would not embrace chastity. He would find solace, he would find pleasure, and ultimately— he would find love.

And she would pine for him ad infinitum, as Dover's cliffs pined for sun.

It started with soft wails. Then the pain increased, becoming unbearable. Burying her face in her folded arms, she succumbed to heart-torn sobs. *Ah God! Eros. I love you . . . I love you . . .*

The day of the execution arrived. Suspending the order, Louis had entrenched himself in the Trianon since sunrise and refused to admit any of his ministers or courtiers. Dusk enveloped the royal cache when the king finally sent for his *valet de chambre,* his faithful Jacquoui.

"Ventrebleu, mon Jacquoui!" Louis cried. "I have the power to send the traitorous *voyou* to his ancestors with a snap of my finger, and yet my finger refuses to be snapped!"

Watching his king plowing a track in the red carpet, Jacquoui offered humbly, "Perhaps the royal finger is fond of the culprit and therefore it refuses to part with him."

"Mortbleu, my wise Jacquoui! The royal finger is terribly vexed with the culprit. It wishes to be snapped yet shows great reluctance with the slightest launch of a snap. It is as impudent as the blackguard it has chosen to advocate."

"Has the royal finger shown any of these worrying signs in the past, Monsignor?" Jacquoui asked with the airs of a man discussing a most weighty business and not the tantrums of a finger.

"Yes. It has," the king grumbled. "The troublesome

business commenced at the beginning of the week when the English duke left with his granddaughter."

"Ah, the tall, fair lady with the cat eyes." Jacquoui was unable to hide his smile. "Is she the one responsible for damaging the royal finger and causing these rebellious fits, Monsignor?"

"Indeed, she is, *mon Jacquoui.* She has the blood of a superb English charger. She sent the poor *voyou* to the devil and charged back to The Little Island. Heartless, absolutely heartless!"

Jacquoui looked pensive. "Well, it appears the *voyou* wasn't entirely culpable of the crimes alleged to him. Perhaps he deserves another hearing. I'm of a mind it will do wonders for the royal finger, Monsignor."

"You think so?" A royal eyebrow cocked inquiringly.

"Positively, Monsignor. Once the royal finger listens to the *voyou*'s story after he's spent an entire week in the Bastille contemplating his sinful conduct, it will behave obediently."

"*Superb!* Now, run along and fetch that captain, what's his name?"

"La Villette."

"Find La Villette and tell him to bring Stefano to me at once."

"But isn't His Majesty ready for his afternoon nap now? A royal head does need its sleep."

"Sleep! Do you think I ever sleep with the ministers always at hand, who never leave me a moment's repose, who talk to me about Spain, who talk to me about Austria, who talk to me about England? I sleep no longer, *Monsieur.* I sometimes dream, that's all. Now go! Release my Stefano from prison."

Accompanied by four guardsmen, Capitan La Villette escorted Prince Stefano Sforza to the Trianon. The prisoner seemed uncharacteristically passive, yet noticing his strong deportment, La Villette deduced it was melancholy rather than general debility causing his strange behavior. A week in the Bastille could not ruin such a man's health, but it could break his spirit. La Villette had seen tough men fall apart within days when a death sentence hung over their heads.

The king started when the prisoner entered the miniature palace. "*Jacquoui!* Do something about this . . . this . . ." He gestured agitatedly at Eros's deplorable state of cleanliness. "Bring him a new shirt, soap and water to wash his face, and raspberries with cream and champagne for me."

Minutes later, Eros washed his face in the king's presence and exchanged his frayed shirt for a crisp one. Yet he declined the refreshments and remained aloof and unresponsive. Louis banished his attendants and circled his prisoner as an inquisitor. "Stefano, how did you come to know the blond wildcat? I'm curious." When no response came, he halted and glowered at the tall Italian. "She left, you know. Went back to The Little Island with her grandfather." His remark caused a slight twitch in his prisoner's face. "Ah, you are still alive. For a moment I feared you were already dead. So tell me. How did she come to be with you? When she was presented to me three years ago she was promised to an English viscount and seemed pleased with him."

Eros stabbed the king with a black glare. "I took her from her stupid fiancé."

"You took her? Just like that?" Louis's eyes shone with admiration. "What? No protests? Was she so enamored of your handsome face she agreed to abandon the viscount? Hmm?"

"She protested."

"*And—?*" the king encouraged eagerly.

Eros merely glowered at him. The king snorted with displeasure. He hated being kept in the dark about such juicy affairs. "I reconsidered your sentence, but there is one stipulation: You will remain in Versailles. There is much to be discussed between us. You avoided my court for three years, Stefano. That was very rude of you. You have a lot to make up to me."

Ignoring etiquette, Eros slumped in a chair and fixed Louis with an exasperated look. "You want to keep me here to discuss the Duke of Dellamore's granddaughter?"

Louis sat on the opposite sofa. "This isn't like you,

Stefano. Usually the women make fools of themselves over you. How did you allow yourself to come to such ruin?"

Eros smirked blackly. "Everybody has the right to make a fool of himself once."

"Ugh, you are intolerable today." The king lifted the bowl of raspberries and plopped it in his lap. He selected a berry and dipped it in the cream. "How did I ever put up with you?"

"A mystery."

"I expected *you* to know better. You used to be an authority on women. There were times when you ran my palace as if it were your private harem." He suckled the berry into his mouth.

Eros slid him a slow contemptuous look. "What is your point, Louis?"

The king gobbled another berry. "Everyone knows a woman will sell a man for ten *louis*. How come the blond wildcat agreed to marry you if she disliked you so much?"

That got Eros's full attention. Uncertainty clouded his eyes as he contemplated the king for a long moment. "She didn't agree to marry me. She wanted to become the Duchess of Milan."

Louis sighed. "Ah, young man, young man. Take care—I repeat to you—take care. It is woman who has ruined us, still ruins us, and will ruin us as long as the world stands. Listen to an old Frenchman when he speaks of love. Take my advice and forget about her." When Eros's eyes flashed angrily, Louis dropped a berry in the cream. "*Ventre saint gris!* You unhappy devil! You are still in love with her, after all she's done. The lady deceived you, rejected you, spat in your face, and left you for dead. Tomorrow she will do the same to another. If you tell me that your heart still bleeds for her, I'll be forced to put you out of your misery."

"Go ahead. You'll be doing me a favor."

That did it. Louis licked his fingers and pointed at the door. "Go! Clean up, eat something, and get some sleep. Find yourself a woman, or get drunk, whatever poison carries success with you. Then, when you are improved, we'll discuss the position of admiralty I made open for you in my navy. Perhaps if I take you under my wing, you'll forget this idiocy."

Eros leaned forward and rested his elbows on his knees. "Did you release me because a woman broke my heart?" he inquired suspiciously.

"Can you blame me?" Louis cried. "Look at you! A week in a cell and you are nothing."

"You are not worried I'll leave this place and join your enemy, Savoy, just to get even?"

"*Ah, pardieu!*" Louis smiled charmingly. "Let us speak no more of this misunderstanding. It'll be as it has always been between us, Stef. While my son entertains himself with his brainless cats and my ministers fret about Savoy's next move, we'll play a little faro, discuss politics, and contrive brilliant war strategies to crush our enemies."

"England and Savoy." Eros smiled perceptively.

"Precisely. And when by the end of this year the whole of Italy will be ours to run, your heartless blonde will dye her hair a different color!" The king laughed.

"*You* will give me Italy?" Eros looked doubtful.

Louis grinned with satisfaction. "Who else can give it to you? Not Joseph, and certainly not your council. Not even the English dogs are in your corner, as we have learned. Reputation is a delicate commodity. Once it is lost, it cannot be mended."

"If the whole of Europe labels me a failure, why would you want me to rule Italy for you?"

"Because you are the perfect candidate. You are reputed to be a ruthless man. You have the savvy to secure fear and thus unswerving obedience. They will think twice before undermining your authority. Fear of one's ruler brings a country into peaceful unity and induces loyalty. Now, I am not telling you to rule with a vindictive hand. Absolutely not. You have the liberty to act more mercifully than another who has yet to establish the evil tendency of his nature. But bear in mind that a wise ruler must rely on what he and not others can control. If you know this, you know everything."

His shrewd eyes glinted as he said, "I'll make you King of Italy, Stefano. You'll have Milan, Naples, and Sicily, Savoy and Sardinia . . . Marry a Roman princess and you'll secure Rome! You have the right blood flowing in your veins. You also possess the arrogance, the brains, and the ambition to become a very dangerous power. You, my proud young Milanese, were born and raised to be exactly what I intend to make of you: a sovereign!"

"You want a puppet, Louis. And I'm no good with strings."

"A puppet! A puppet! I have enough puppets to put on another of Monsieur Moliere's silly plays! What I *need* is a strong, capable son to accede to the throne when I'm no longer available to maintain the *Gloire!* Alas, you are more Sforza than Bourbon, as I am more Bourbon than Sforza. So Italy it must be for you, while I hope my grandson, Philip, manages to hang on to Spain, and while the *Dauphin* and his cats will eventually take over my Versailles . . ."

He was to accommodate the prisoner in the palace but keep a tight watch on him. Capitan La Villette prided himself on being a patriot, yet the amethyst bracelet burdening his pocket had a necklace sister. It was left for him with a certain Madame. Were his prisoner to escape, he'd be reuniting families. Heavy mist descended on the park as he followed the four guards leading the prisoner to the palace. La Villette's mind was so deeply preoccupied that he failed to notice the suspicious movements up ahead until he was upon them. The prisoner knocked down the rear guards and snatched one of their halberds. He buried the halberd in one of the remaining guards' chests, then slammed his fist into the second man's face. He brought down his elbow on his nape.

La Villette saw a squadron of guards patrolling farther down the lane. In a moment they'd become aware of the situation and his necklace would be lost to him forever. La

Villette drew his sword. The king may treat this man as a prince, but everyone knew that vicious crescent scar.

"Desist and surrender your arms!" he ordered him in a harsh whisper.

The prisoner looked at him, then glimpsed beyond his shoulder at the approaching patrol.

Fear crawled up La Villette's spine as a procession of ants. He lowered his sword. "Don't kill me," he implored huskily. "I'll help you secure a horse without being noticed."

In Italian-accented French, the Viper ordered, "Show me!"

CHAPTER 29

Thick smoke and vigorous brainpower condensed the air at the Imperial War Council in the Schönbrunn Palace in Vienna.

"The French are everywhere, entrenched in strongholds. I see no way to take over Milan," General Marlborough complained to the elderly duke at his side. "'If I had been aught but a fool, I should never have endured what I do endure for this place amid the swords of the Lombards.'"

"Quoting dead popes, are we?" His old friend chuckled.

"Damned Milanese let the French right into their midst. And to think you almost gained their top dog as a grandson-in-law . . . Oh. Beg pardon, Dellamore. That was done in poor taste."

The Duke of Dellamore scowled deeply. "I would not have minded much if it were not for my poor Alis, John. She's heartbroken over him. Trouble is, the blackguard is still alive."

"Did you find out anything about him? Is he still in France?" Marlborough asked.

"Wish it were so, John. Unfortunately, the bastard's vanished without a trace."

"That should put your mind at rest. He'll leg down to Algiers and never bother her again."

"Not bloody likely." The duke sighed.

"Oh?" Marlborough's brows knitted. "You believe he has a soft spot for her?"

"That, or something much worse." The duke looked up. "Have you ever met him?"

"Met whom?" Savoy interrupted the private conversation. "Hopefully not a Milanese."

Dellamore pinned Savoy with a no-nonsense glare. "Stefano Andrea Sforza."

Savoy's brows lifted. "Stefano Sforza . . . Yes, I knew him well. Many years ago, in Milan."

"I seem to be the only one who hasn't met the Viper," Marlborough grumbled. "How very unflattering. I take it you did not much care for the young prince?" he prodded.

"Quite the opposite, actually," Savoy replied. "I liked him very much. In his youth, Stefano showed great potential. He excelled at everything, at military studies and all-embracing topics alike. There was no undertaking so great that did not seem a minor thing to him. He feared no effort or danger. But today . . . well, today he is a man to treat with caution."

Dellamore nodded. "He's the sort one cannot quite put a finger on. Almost every man who ends up in Algiers has his soul sucked out of him the first year, and only a handful ever manage to escape. Stefano Sforza became a *Rais*."

"Precisely," Savoy said, sphinxlike.

"Damn. Now I am intrigued." Marlborough's keen gaze shifted between his companions. "So what is the verdict—is Stefano Sforza one of the good or the bad ones?"

Dellamore and Savoy exchanged glances. "Good question," Savoy finally said.

Minutes later, His Imperial Majesty, Ruler of Austria, Hungary, and Bohemia, the Emperor Joseph, joined the council. "Gentlemen"—he summoned everyone's attention—"brace yourselves for another Milanese surprise. It appears this night is about to become much more interesting."

While the chamber buzzed with speculation, Dellamore's nerve endings prickled. The great doors reopened. Silence gripped the chamber as every pair of eyes fixed on the tall man striding to the head of the long table opposite the emperor. Dressed in black uniform embroidered with silver and purple vipers snaking up the cuffs, his natural hair slicked back to his nape, he radiated supreme self-confidence. Chairs moved as the councilors turned to inspect the newcomer. Some recognized the youth in the man's face and appeared just as astounded as those who'd never met him. Dellamore's gaze briefly locked with those intense eyes, and he realized his skin was on fire.

"Esteemed members of the Imperial Council." The emperor's voice swept the table. "I present to you Prince Stefano Andrea Sforza, the Count of Pavia, the Duke of Bari, the Royal Prince of Milan. *Buonasera, Sua Altezza*. Which winds bring you to Vienna?"

"Winds of change, Your Majesty." Cold and inscrutable, Eros's gesture of respect was a crisp nod, as a captain salutes his condottiere. "I've come to join the Alliance. I acknowledge the supremacy of His Majesty, the emperor, and yield to the authority of his commanders-in-chief."

The councilors eyed him, as a pack of veteran wolves assessing a bold young male.

The emperor smiled broadly. "Generals, should we enlist Prince Stefano to our ranks?"

Savoy narrowed his eyes. Marlborough lit up with curiosity. He fired the first question. "Your Highness, what is your experience in commanding full-scale inland campaigns?"

"None."

A disappointed hum arose among the councilors. The Dutch Attaché asked, "What is your understanding with the Privy Council in Milan? May we expect their support?"

"My understanding with the Milanese Council is null and void. They are hostile."

The exclamations around the table grew louder and more articulate.

"What is your personal ambition in joining forces with the Alliance?" the emperor asked.

"My ambition is not personal. My reason for joining is to liberate the Milanese people."

"Surely you expect to emerge with some power in Milan by the end of this war?"

"I nurture no such aspirations."

The Portuguese ambassador looked doubtful. "You lay no claims to Lombardy, Emilia, Liguria, and the southern Alps?"

"It is up to the Milanese to elect the leader of their choice."

"Milan is not a republic!" cried the Austrian secretary of state. "It is up to the Holy Roman Empire to make this decision, and you ought to be very grateful, Your Highness, for without the Empire's traditional supervision of such matters, your opportunist cousin would have nominated *himself* duke many years ago!"

"Come now, Count Bartholomeo," the emperor drawled, "Prince Stefano is aware that his demand is unorthodox. The Empire will establish the leadership of Milan when the time is right."

"No. It will not," Eros stated, shocking everyone. "My family obtained imperial investiture hundreds of years ago, and as the legitimate Sforza successor, I inherited this claim. I now bequeath it to the people of Milan. It is their natural right to choose their leadership. This is my one proviso in pledging allegiance to The Cause."

"You arrogant Lombard!" cried the Archduke Karl, the younger brother of Emperor Joseph and the Austrian claimant to the Spanish throne. "How dare you stipulate to us!"

"My proud young prince," the emperor said. "I advise you to balance *bravura* with caution, and practice *prudentia* before *fortitudo.* What have you to offer that you dictate provisos to us?"

"Myself."

Marlborough's soft whistle pierced the resulting uproar. He

leaned aside and whispered to Dellamore, "He must have
been born in Bergamo, for he has a pair of big, shiny, brassy
ones. Your Highness," he called, "I'm somewhat puzzled. You
come alone, audacious, with a not-too-distant a past of destruction trailing behind you, materializing straight out of the
realm of our enemy, and striding as bold as brass into the
lion's den. What *do* you hope to achieve?"

Eros met the Duke of Dellamore's sharp assessing gaze.
"Redemption."

The assembly exploded with laughter. "We're not in the soul-
saving business, Stefano," Savoy exclaimed. "Try the pope in
Rome." His comment elicited another round of laughter.

Eros stabbed Savoy with a personal glare. "Perhaps you do
not deal in salvation, Eugene, but you've certainly grown rich
on the taxes you've rung out of the occupied nations you took
from Louis. But of course, you are liberators of the World,
fighting the darkness of Tyranny."

Savoy's expression hardened. "Your sarcasm discredits
you, Stefano."

Eros smiled darkly. "If I sound sarcastic, Eugene, it's because I've long since ceased to believe in human altruism.
Louis may be a voracious bully, but you serve your own interests just as he does." He readdressed the council with a
firm voice. "Emperor, Councilors, Milan is ripe for the
taking. Louis is overconfident, and the people of Milan are
burning for independence. To oust France, you must draw
on the basic need of every man to be free. Enlist the Milanese! Convince them to raise the standard of revolt and end
this Franco-Spanish occupation!"

His speech aroused both positive and negative exclamations.

"Italians take this xenophobic feeling too far," the Danish
emissary protested.

Eros tightened his jaw. "One day soon the divided states of
Italy *will* unite under one banner, and all the foreign powers
in the world combined together won't be able to stop it. If you
understand this and kindle the patriotic flame, you'll win the
war."

"How do you propose we do that?" the emperor asked. "Vendôme's forces are planted in fortresses all over Milan, which is highly populated. La Feuillade is entrenched in Turin, and the Duke of Savoy is standing on the brink of ruin. Every attempt to reach him was checkmated by the French. The King of France keeps moving his chess pieces, and we are losing the game."

"Empower the Milanese instead of subjecting them to bloodbaths."

"You've some nerve lecturing us on humanity," the Portuguese retorted, "when, in fact, you've been practicing piracy quite flagrantly up until late."

"I haven't practiced piracy for over eight years, except against Louis."

"A fine web he's spinning around us!" the Dane echoed the collective disgruntlement.

"Today the duty of serving Milan's interests lies with its Privy Council," the emperor said.

Eros smirked. "Tallius Cancri serves himself. Confide in him, and you may be certain that whatever strategy you design will reach Louis's ears before you blow the trumpets of war."

Marlborough's voice had a trace of optimism when he demanded, "Have you a strategy in mind or have you come here to ascertain ours stands up to your satisfaction, Your Highness?"

"I command an army of professional soldiers. Most of them serve on my ships, but I have also recruited expatriated Milanese whom the Spaniards banished after my father's death. They are all Italians and superlative warriors, brave men who'd readily give their lives to free Milan."

"Fortune-seeking privateers and a militia of farmers?" the Dane mocked.

"Prince Stefano, are you offering to lead this . . . ad hoc army against Marshal de France, le Duc de Vendôme?" Marlborough inquired with a bemused expression.

"Put your mind at rest," Eros replied sternly. "My men are ferocious soldiers. They are service hardened and have all seen war. And if in the past war meant profit and excitement, I assure you that today these men have an interest that goes far beyond the career of arms. They want their country back, free of foreign powers. They want a home."

"Exactly how many men are we discussing?" Savoy inquired pointedly.

"Twenty thousand."

The assembly ceased arguing. Everyone stared at the tall, dark prince looming at the end of the table. Amazed, Savoy asked, "Are you saying you command *fourteen battalions?* That's two-thirds of my army cantoning in Verona." He sent Marlborough a meaningful glance.

"Trained as cuirassiers, divided into five mounted brigades," Eros specified.

"Where the devil are you hiding them?" Marlborough demanded. "In your pocket?"

"In Tuscany."

Strident exclamations of disbelief arose. Marlborough looked dazzled. "Twenty thousand cuirassiers resting supine five minutes away from Milan? Savoy, did you hear that?"

The emperor started. "Quite a statement, you leading an army flying the Viper into Milan!"

"I will fly the Sforza colors alongside those of the Alliance," Eros conceded.

"The decision to include Prince Stefano with the Alliance must be put forth to a full vote!" the Dutch attaché insisted heatedly. "It necessitates an official agreement of The Hague!"

"Prince Stefano is an enemy of his own council!" the Dane asserted. "He is King Louis's personal favorite and a pirate! I strongly object and move to dismiss the motion forthwith!"

Savoy silenced the furor. "We commend your sense of duty, Stefano, but your joining us is not a feasible prospect at the present state. I assure you nonetheless that Milan will be liberated."

"In other words: Go to the devil, you French spy!" Eros

growled. "Do you honestly believe I sold my soul to the French tyrant, Eugene?"

"I'm well acquainted with Louis's phenomenal powers of persuasion. No doubt he offered you the stars and the moon for this. He keeps the sun to himself," Savoy added sardonically.

Eros clamped down on his rage. "You've known me since childhood. You knew my father. The King of France tagged me another protégé-come-traitor and threw me in the Bastille because I refused to become a French marionette. Because he thinks I take after you, *Savoiardo*. The only reason I'm standing here before you tonight is because a clever bird convinced me your aims were noble. To my deepest regret, I see now that she was mistaken."

"Have you any assurance to discredit you as a French agent?" the emperor demanded.

Eros drew himself up. "*None.*" His disillusioned gaze swept the table. He recognized most of the faces—old friends of his father's, old enemies. They all longed to see him squirm.

The Duke of Dellamore didn't fail to perceive the emotion burning in the prince's eyes. He didn't aim for gain. He truly ached to partake in his country's liberation. Alis was right about her pirate after all. The duke rose to his feet. "You have *my* word, Councilors, as Special Emissary of Her Majesty, the Queen of England. Prince Stefano Sforza is not collaborating with the French."

All eyes settled on the duke. One particular pair of eyes looked stunned.

"England has been monitoring Prince Stefano's undertakings for a while now," Dellamore continued. "We know that he's been faring secret maritime warfare against France. He rejected Louis's offer of an admiralty in his navy, including French peerage befitting his consequence, and was sentenced to death. Luckily, after serving time in the Bastille, he managed to escape. We should commend his resistance and laud his valor. I confidently vouch for his integrity."

The councilors gaped with awe.

"Well then," the emperor said, "it appears the matter is settled. Do join us, Your Highness. We can benefit from your expertise. Gentlemen, let us proceed. The night is not getting younger, and frankly, neither am I. We need to decide which of our goals will take precedence: Milan or its western neighbor— Turin."

Accepting a chair with a nod to the footman, Eros inquired, "Why choose?"

Savoy came over and debriefed him on the situation, concluding with, "Vendôme employs seventy-seven thousand men on the bank of the Adige River near Salo at the north. La Feuillade holds Turin with forty-two thousand men and two hundred thirty-seven guns and mortars."

"Our forces are not nearly as strong, only thirty-two thousand," Marlborough chimed in.

"Fifty-two thousand," Eros corrected and received an appreciative nod from Savoy.

Marlborough continued, "The Duke of Savoy has taken refuge with eight thousand men in the Cottian Alps at Luserna and is loudly calling to Eugene for aid. Except that if Eugene leaves the Milan region, Vendôme will cut him off along the route to Piedmont. His superior numbers will impede Eugene from reaching Turin, and we'll lose the position we already hold in Milan."

Eros examined the map. "Not necessarily. Let's say we set off from Verona jointly, taking every fort up to Piacenza, where we'll split forces. I'll press north to the city of Milan while Savoy breaks off westward toward Piedmont. Vendôme will lose precious time trying to decide which force to follow, and if he chooses to go after you, Eugene, then by the time he catches up with you, you will have reached the Stradella Pass where a small army can resist a larger one."

"Of course!" Savoy cried. "The Stradella Pass is the key to northwestern Italy! From there it's Voghera, Tortona . . ." His finger slid on the map. "Up to Villastellona, where I'll arrange for the Duke of Savoy to meet me. Between us, we'll crush La Feuillade in Turin." He gave Eros an apologetic glance. "A sound plan, Stefano. Has all the right ingredients: optimal utilization of the topography, an element of suspense, a surprise for the enemy—"

"And teamwork?" A glint of hope lit Eros's eyes.

"Our team took a hard beating from Vendôme recently," Savoy confessed. "Are you certain you wish to come onboard?"

Eros smiled. "Without a doubt."

"Excellent. Welcome, *paesano!*" Savoy grabbed Eros's hand in a firm shake.

Heartened by the moment, Marlborough remarked, "That will leave Milan to you. You are aware of the enormous risk you're taking, Your Highness? If Vendôme crowds after you—"

"Bearing in mind that Louis is hot after your head . . ." Savoy added with a smile.

Eros laughed. "Precisely why I cannot play Charlemagne and toddle off to Algiers. Louis will be terribly disappointed. Now about Vendôme, though he is a hyperindolent character, he has consummate ability. If he comes after me, I'll be ready for him. I know all his vices."

"Still," Marlborough persisted, "you're to expect strong opposition, even if Vendôme rushes after Savoy. You'll have his crony, Mendavi, to deal with and a number of strong garrisons. Are you certain your troops can carry off vigorous fighting? You could be slaughtered by the French and the Spanish armies at any point along the route to the capital."

"That is a risk I shall have to take," Eros stated resolutely.

"The whole idea is for you to reach the capital, not to perish on the way," Savoy stressed.

"I'll get there," Eros vowed, his eyes gleaming with determination.

"Your proposed strategy is intelligent and daring," the emperor complimented Eros. "I see great logic in it. Your ancestors were formidable warriors. Will you live up to their image?"

"I won't fail my people, Your Majesty. However, there is

one last thing that remains to be settled right now: the Empire's guarantee that it *will not* interfere in Milan when this war is over. The Milanese will elect the leader of their choice, even if it turns out to be a council."

Everyone objected. "Silence!" the emperor commanded, though the heightened color in his cheeks attested to his own frustration. "You are very shrewd, Prince Stefano. You have seduced us with your wits and charm and made yourself indispensable. I agree."

Eros nodded. "Very good, Your Majesty. And I in turn pledge to the council that no matter what happens on the way to the capital, I *will* arrive in Milan, if it's the last thing I do."

"See that you do," the Duke of Dellamore muttered, catching Eros's full attention. "And for heaven's sake, man, endeavor to preserve yourself in one piece . . ."

CHAPTER 30

Hopping mad and screaming murder, the King of France assembled his marshals, ministers, and advisors in Versailles to discuss the tide of war moving inexorably against the French forces in northern Italy. "The cavalry has done defectively, quite defectively!" he roared. "We're losing garrisons and towns, being outmaneuvered at every turn! Splitting forces at the Stradella Pass is an old trick. None of you could anticipate this ploy? What sort of a circus am I running here?"

Louis's war staff plunged into offering endless apologies, excuses, and explanations, but the king cut them all short. "Imbeciles! Idle-brained idiots! You're dismissed! All of you! I'm taking over now! I want Stefano dead, his army wiped out, and I want it done *yesterday!* If he reaches the city of

Milan, this war is *over* and your heads will *roll!* Do I make myself clear?"

"Their ruse upset all calculations within our command," Field Marshal Marsin mumbled. "Vendôme had to rush after Savoy to Turin. If we leave Marshal La Feillade unprotected—"

"La Feillade commands ninety battalions," de Orleans muscled in, "one hundred thirty-eight squadrons, sixty thousand men. How much more does one need to hold on to one city?"

"Surely His Majesty cannot deem an ex-pirate and his amateur militia of daredevils capable of conquering an entire region fortified with twenty-three strong places?" Marsin insisted.

"*Amateur?*" Louis bellowed. "Indeed I wonder who is the amateur here!" He glared at de Orleans. "Can you do better than the incompetent Vendôme?" When the duke nodded firmly, Louis muttered, "And take Marsin with you as second. Clearly one French brain is not enough!"

After receiving counts of losses and establishing an operation room in Cremona's palace, where he was invited to stay, Eros found his captains emptying a carafe of wine on the loggia.

"Nico, take ten squadrons and hunt down the runaways. I want no nocturnal surprises."

Greco scrutinized his captain's filthy linen shirt, his dusty breeches, scuffed boots, and the thick leather belt heavy on the hips with his personal arsenal. "Shouldn't you prettify yourself for tonight's feast?" he asked humorously. "*We* are coarse peasants, but the townsfolk are expecting a prince, not a common soldier dressed in bloody uniform."

Eros poured himself a full jug of wine. "After two months of fighting, I assure you I'm my usual insulting self. Besides, the banquet fêtes the men, not me."

Music and song approached the piazza. Carrying flower

bouquets, the locals approached the loggia, demanding, "Which one?" And all at once the captains pointed at Eros. "Him!"

The entire force in the piazza cracked with laughter as their commander was carried aloft by crying men, plump grandmothers, and small boys whose eyes shone with hero worship.

The banquet commenced as evening fell. Wine poured, warm speeches were given, and a chorus sang madrigal. Yet only once Eros relaxed with a glass of cognac did he notice the most arresting sight of all: High above their heads, vipers and eagles flapped proudly in the wind.

The celebration continued well into the night. When Eros finally got to his feet, more cheers arose. It took forever to cross the piazza toward Palazzo Fodri and the soft bed awaiting him there. He stopped to check with the captain of the guard, to whom he issued orders for their early departure the next day, and cut through the park. There, sprawled on daybeds, his captains were entertaining the local beauties in a private party complete with candles, wine, and gentle music.

As Eros approached, Giovanni came over, dragging two giggling females. "This is Sofia." He presented the brunette, who curtsied and batted her eyelashes. "And this one is Maria."

The first stirred nothing in him, but this one caught his eye. "*Buonasera*," Eros said softly.

"Blondes, always blondes!" Giovanni chuckled, and dragged Sofia away.

Smiling, Maria took Eros's hand and led him to a remote daybed. He accepted a glass of wine and let her engage him in easy conversation, but when she leaned her soft breasts into him and kissed him full on the mouth, he stiffened. He pulled back and shut his eyes, swallowing.

"Is something the matter?" she asked uneasily.

"No." He raked a hand through his hair. He stood up, mumbled an apology, and walked off.

A heavy hand on his shoulder halted him. "What's wrong

with you?" Giovanni demanded. "You've been running yourself to the ground for weeks, always leading the first attack, planning, directing, pushing onward through the heaviest fighting. Why not let go and enjoy for a change?"

"Let me be, Giova. I'm tired."

"Tired for a woman? *You?* It's that damnable bitch who left you in France to die!"

Eros grabbed his collar and slammed him hard against a shadowed wall. He said nothing.

Giovanni grimaced. "Forget her, Eros. She's gone. What purpose does it serve to carry on as a lovesick Orlando? I see the risks you take on the battlefield. You're begging to die. Isn't what you're bringing to these people more important than a pair of smooth white thighs?"

Eros's eyes glinted. "One more word and you'll wish you were back on the battlefield. Now, return to your party and don't forget we're folding at first light." He released Giovanni and stalked away, hearing behind him a stream of curses and an exasperated, "Do as you please!"

"Listen to this," Alanis called the attention of the young mother cradling a plump angel on the couch beside her. "'We are often told about the untutored soldier whose courage and keen military instinct make him superior to the bookworm who is full of military saws and warlike instances,'" she read from an article in the *Gazette*. "'Yet with his industry and intelligence, Prince Stefano is the finest example of both qualities: Though his past is a mystery, it is said he has Xenophon and Polybius by heart and was educated to war; with his unique stamina he demonstrates to us repeatedly that the greatest captains are men to whom providence gave the two qualities.' Then they go on and on, comparing his tactics to those of Caesar and Gustavus and extolling his fighting for being the hottest even after remaining five days on the battlefield."

Jasmine smiled warmly. "You miss him."

Alanis paled. "I miss him." *Terribly.* She missed looking at him, touching him. She missed everything about him. She slept with funny red slippers beneath her pillow and a gold medallion between her breasts. Neither item was a substitute for the man . . .

"I knew you two would fall madly in love. All the signs were there. Eros was practically scraping for excuses to whisk you off with him. And he never took any woman anywhere."

Alanis failed to contain her own sad smile. "You think so?"

"Positively. He wanted you for himself right from the start."

"As I wanted him," Alanis confessed. "There is no other like Eros. He is perfect."

Jasmine grimaced. "My brother is far from perfect. He is quick-tempered, domineering, capricious, arrogant, *unmanageable* . . ."

"He is wonderful, isn't he?" Alanis's tearful eyes shone with longing and sadness.

"I'm glad he found you. You had the patience and staying power to reach his softer side. I used to fear I'd never find a man worthy enough to stand in his shadow, but later I realized what a handful he was. I needed someone of a more . . . agreeable disposition."

Alanis still held that Eros to Lucas was fire to porridge, but she understood Jasmine's preference. Not everyone enjoyed playing with fire *all the time*. She, however, wilted without him, as a flower deprived of sunlight. And she worried about him day and night . . .

"When the war is over and there is a new duke in Milan," Jasmine declared, "I'll take my two men to attend the enthronement. You should come too. Perhaps you'll convince Eros to join me on a visit to our mother. Now that I know she's alive, I can't wait to see her."

Alanis would have loved to witness the reunion, alas . . . "I'm not a member of your family. And to be perfectly blunt, I don't want to see him again, and I know he wouldn't want to see me."

"You owe him an explanation."

Alanis imagined herself coming to congratulate him and Eros presenting her with his back.

"You are afraid," Jasmine concluded solemnly, "that he would spurn you."

Alanis shut her eyes and let out a weary sigh. "I'll give you his medallion when you leave for Milan. But please, let us speak no more of him."

He was tired of fighting, so tired of fighting. He'd taken dozens of fortified towns, but all this hard work wasn't enough. He in control of the capital was in control of the duchy, and no one knew that better than Eros. Moving amid rows of cannon, foot, and defense pikes, his eyes drew north to the line the French and the Spaniards called "*Ne Plus Ultra.*" Nothing Further Is Possible. Miles of contravallation and circumvallation stretched around the city. Steel wrought by masters, cannon by the thousands. A firewall. Beyond it, prospering over a stream-run plateau heavy with morning dew, rose the city of his forefathers, of his childhood, of his heart, the city he forsook in a time of strife, against all the blood vows he had taken as a dutiful, optimistic youth: *Milano.*

La Feuillade almost destroyed Turin during his siege. Could he bombard his home, Eros asked himself for the millionth time. A city two thousand years old, the seat of Roman emperors, which Leonardo Da Vinci reconstructed as the Ideal City linked by streams and canals to the Po. He breathed in the cool air blowing from the Alps and surveyed his city's soaring domes. Among them, ivory pinnacles and gables glistened under the sun—the Duomo. His chest tightened at the sight. Hemmed inside the Spanish Wall, his city thrived and he lived to see her again—*his home.* Only there was no one there to welcome him with open arms: no father, no mother, just hopeful strangers expecting him to save them. He couldn't barrage Milan. She had to remain intact for future generations, maybe even *his* future generations . . .

He slumped on a rotten tree trunk, chopped of roots and leaves, which served the men as a convenient bench, and commiserated with the wood. Evidently he too was doomed to go through life chopped of past and future. A lost cause. "'Wars,'" he said, "'wars are in store for me . . .'"

Five officers approached. Though they hardly slept, his men looked as fit as ever and ready for action. "What are our orders?" Niccolò asked. "When do we attack?"

"We don't." Eros propped elbows on knees and buried his fingers in his hair.

The men exchanged puzzled looks. Giovanni stepped closer. "Do you want us to wait for General Savoy's reinforcements when he returns from Turin?"

"No. We'll be surrounded by the time he gets back. If he returns."

"We can launch a minor assault," Daniello offered. "Sniff their guns up close."

"It will be driven back. They are stronger than us."

"But their strength is wasted in the extent of their lines," Nico pointed out. "And the men in the entrenchments probably lost much of their spirit, knowing they are in a superior force."

"Let's send a careful reconnaissance to discover their weaker places," Giovanni proposed. "We can then break through at that point and cut the enemy in two."

Eros's head came up. "And risk getting blown to smithereens as we mount the field? I don't think so." His cuirassiers would be burned alive under the guns.

Barbazan scowled. "So what do you want us to do, Eros?"

"I don't know." He had less than twenty thousand men in line, all horse and situated just beyond the artillery range. And though it was in the highest degree unwise of the French to hold a strictly defensive line, they believed the enemy was too weak to attack without exposing himself to a dangerous sortie and that therefore he would not try. They were right.

"May I make a suggestion?" Greco said. "I think the only solution would be to take their artillery out of action. We can wait for nightfall and creep into the lines."

Eros glimpsed beyond his shoulder. "Pity! I left my golden wings in Agadìr."

"It's very risky," Giovanni conceded, "but not impossible."

"No, it's suicide," Eros stated tersely. "No one will return from this mission."

"It's all or nothing!" Nico tried cheering them up and received a glare in return. "We have to do something," he mumbled, joining Eros on the tree trunk. "We can't swim there."

Eros froze in his place. He stared at Nico. He stared at the tube-shaped trunk they sat upon. He glimpsed at the immured city—immured with a *Spanish* wall—and linked by streams and canals with every body of water in the area so that it would never dry up.

"He has a plan!" Giovanni exclaimed, punching a fist into a palm.

"Not yet." Eros got to his feet. "I need to sleep on it."

"Go! Sleep!" Giovanni called after his retreating back. "I'll put ten guards around your tent to ensure you sleep like a babe."

Alanis woke up with a start. She had expected to sleep like a log after spending the entire day visiting the Dellamore tenants with her estate manager and inspecting the new repairs done to their houses, but a terrible premonition crept into her dream. *Eros was in grave danger.*

She lit a night candle and held his medallion to her heart. "Why did I insist on sending you to war?" She remembered Maddalena saying that Eros's greatest ambition was to become a great duke like his father—the Duke of Milan. "Think positive thoughts," she ordered herself. "Let him feel how much you love him, even if he's forgotten all about you." She curled onto her side and envisioned his face. "*Please, please be careful . . .*" She shut her eyes tightly and prayed.

* * *

Blazing torches and chains of sentries formed a tight loop around silent rows of tents. The ring of fire securing the Liberation Army emitted hope for miles away, straight into the hearts besieged in the great city. Someone out there had come to set them free—someone of their own.

The tranquility of the night banished the god of war, Mars, and attracted the god of dreams, Morpheus, to weave delusive magic in his head: She came to him that night, all blonde and eyes and beautiful—stole into his bed and into his sleep-drugged mind, her lips begging love, her body a mystery of haunting ivory curves. Her sweet sighs drifted over him like warm zephyrs—a Siren's lethal call to doom, to surrender his heart, his will, his soul . . .

Eros. I love you. I will never ever leave you . . .

As a simple sailor reaching for the smoky islands of gold scattered beyond the equator, he almost touched the golden silk spread on his pillow, almost caressed her soft, nude body, almost drowned in her clear lagoon eyes, and she vanished. Another image appeared—a nun. She turned around, and he saw her face—Alanis's face—and she laughed. She viciously laughed at him.

Eros awoke. If his spirit were a wolf, it would howl with pain. Shaken, perspiring, he sat up and buried his hands in the damp roots of his hair. Desperation—depression. Kindred words. He was coming apart, and there was nothing, absolutely not a damned thing, he could do to stop it.

Darkness engulfed him. A powerful urge to get the cognac bottle out of his trunk and pour it down his throat seized him, but tomorrow was another day, and there were over a million lives and dreams relying on him. He didn't even have the dratted luxury to put an end to this . . . *agony.*

He got up to wet his parched throat with water. It was then that he saw the three shadows skulking outside his tent, outlined by moonlight, their fists fastened around thin dirks.

Assassins. Honed by years of violence, his reflexes kicked into full capacity. He slipped his dagger out of its casing and stuffed the pillow under the sheet to make the bed appear as if he still slept in it. Barefoot and half-naked, he kept to the carpeted floor and lay in wait for his assailants.

The flap-door swayed. Moonbeams poured over the still bed. One man remained at the entrance while the other two tiptoed toward the misguiding lump. Eros let them approach it, and just as they went for the pillow with daggers, he grabbed the watcher from behind and slit his throat in one clean motion. Warm blood sprayed his fingers. The man fell to the carpet. The other two realized they were trying to murder his pillow, for the tent filled with floating down. They whipped around. Eros threw his knife at the first to advance, burying it between his gaping eyes. The second lunged at Eros and they tumbled down, rolling one atop the other. Eros wrenched the assassin's dirk from his fingers and pressed its sharp tip to the man's neck, whispering, "Tell me who sent you and you're walking out tonight. Lie, and you'll never spend the blunt. Now talk!"

The alarm sounded. The camp surged to life with shouts and activity. Giovanni flapped the tent's lid open and walked in. He lit an oil lamp and surveyed the crowded floor. "I see you had guests. Acrobats." He cast Eros a broad smile. "Nice work."

"Thanks." Pushing up with one arm curved around the assailant's neck and the dagger pointed, Eros sighed. "Unfortunately, they're not the guests I've been dreaming of."

Giovanni scowled. "I don't understand how they managed to make your guards disappear. There's not a trace of a struggle outside, or the guards."

"I dismissed them." Eros gave his captive's neck another squeeze. The man squeaked but gave nothing. "You know I can't sleep with people around me."

"Better get used to it, Your Highness. Might even consider employing a valet. You know, someone to help you into those fancy coats and shave your princely face . . ."

Making a face, Eros wanted to comment on allowing anyone to put a knife to his neck and remembered an occasion when he had allowed someone else . . . He focused on his prey. The idiot upheld his silence. "Giova, see what's this weight in his pocket. Smells like gold."

A quick search by the one-eyed giant's indelicate fingers produced a leather pouch full of coins. He whistled as he lightly tossed it in his palm. "Heavy. You should be flattered. His dead mates must be carrying similar pouches each. Someone wants you dead, Eros."

"Fancy that." Eros brought his elbow down on the man's collar, rendering him senseless. He swept his forelock off his brow and reached for the water trencher. After draining it, he beckoned Giovanni to toss him the bag of coin. "Hmm. French francs. Means nothing. Anyone can pay in francs, and there's that confusing double or triple meaning—the man who paid wants me to think he is French, wants me to think he wanted me to think he's French, and so on . . ."

"I'll leave this to you." Giovanni discharged a bellow that immediately summoned sentries.

Eros rubbed a coin. "We can rule out Philip as an imaginative killer. He's brainless. So it's either Louis, or . . . 'The sinister hand of the Eight-Footed Crab is what you must fear.'" A second warning tinkled in his head. Enigmatically, he said, "'Beware when the moon is in Cancer.'"

"What does *that* mean?" Giovanni looked all at sea.

Alanis would understand, Eros mused sadly. She'd remember Sanah's warning. He glared at the man coming to on the floor and bounced the gold pouch in his palm. "Hey, *Stupido,* how would you like to earn this back *and* those of your dead friends?"

The funeral cortege started off at dusk the next day. A trail of torches snaked up to the blockaded city, monks dressed in black robes carrying the remains of the assassinated Prince of Milan, begging entrance at Porta Romana. Their sole wish was to lay to rest the last of the Sforza princes with his ancestors in the cold, grand stone of Milan's cathedral.

The captain of the guard consulted with his superiors. All day the rumor that Prince Stefano was murdered in his army bed spread like the Black Death throughout the city. Now the rumor was established: Stefano Andrea Sforza was dead. The sentries on the wall watched the enemy camp being taken apart peg by peg. The absence of two hundred of the enemy's forces went completely undetected. It was too dark and even less worthy of note to investigate the floating tree trunks coursing up the southern canals into the city. At the circumvallation lines, where grids of iron filtered trash from water, the trunks remained inert in the waterways, slapping at the bars.

"Take a deep breath," Eros told the man teaming with him beneath the sawed in half, hollowed-out tree trunk. "We have a long dive ahead of us."

All Nico saw was a flash of white against dark burnished skin, glittering eyes, and the wink of a diamond. "It's all or nothing," he said before they plunged deep into the black.

The water was ice cold, fed by melting glaciers in the Alps. Only the bursting force of his limbs kicking and cutting through the fluid darkness infused heat into Eros's bloodstream. God help him if the irrigation system's sketches he had drawn from memory were faulty; two hundred of his men would drown. He refused to think about it and rowed harder. They swam for yards, dark shapes honed in seas, navigating with hands along the mossy canal walls. When at last they surfaced for air, they were almost blue in the face. His lungs burning, Eros gave silent thanks and hauled himself out of the inner pool. They were inside the Spanish Wall.

Other teams surfaced. Some were to enter the city, incapacitate the sentries, and open the gates. The rest were to infiltrate the passages in the wall, sweep them clean of metal and men, and join forces outside where the formidable battery of cannons lay. By this time, Eros calculated, his army will have supposedly broken camp and withdrawn from the battlefield.

They split into pairs again and entered the wall's dark, convoluted corridors. Barefoot and dripping, Nico and Eros moved as phantoms. They spotted a pair of sentinels, crept up, clamped a hand over each guard's mouth, and silenced them forever. They continued systematically and met their teammates on the battlements, where they disabled the guns. By the time Eros grabbed a secure rope and slid off the curtain wall, stripes of gold striated the eastern sky. He crouched to pull his boots on, which he carried tied to his back, and marched to the cannon line.

"Mission accomplished!" Greco greeted him. "They're all loaded and ready to go, lovely steel monsters. And, as you instructed, they're pointing at the other direction. At their own wall!"

Eros scanned the long contravallation line pointing the wrong way. "Good work, Greco. Now let's raise the dead." He waited for all the teams to arrive and take position behind the guns. He raised his hand. "Fire!" he shouted, and the Spanish Wall came crashing down.

The city came alive to the sound of thousands of guns roaring all at once, to crashing walls, and to dust rising as high as the dawn sky. Panic and mayhem ruled the streets. Officers yelled at the top of their lungs. Bedraggled soldiers poured out of barracks. Everyone stampeded south toward the source of the devastation, and halted. Slack-jawed, they stared at the southern border where instead of the fortified wall of their city lay a dust-clouded pile of debris. Very little was damaged inside the wall, but the effect of the sight was horrifying. Then the earth shook.

Like a swarm of locust, an army of cuirassiers emerged from the south. Mounted on armed warhorses, their bodies protected with blackened steel, their flanks stretching to the east and the west, they arrived by the thousands in a roar of ironclad hooves, trampling every patch of green and brandishing the crowned banner of the Sforza and a red cross over white—Milan's insignia.

The French commanders improvised battle positions, anxious mothers hustled children into homes, and even the sturdiest man would have fled if not for the imposing figure climbing onto the crashed blocks. Unfazed by the threat of salvoes from the French infantry squatting at the fore, Eros swept the hundreds of thousands of faces with a hawklike glance and raised his arms.

"Milanese!" he called, his deep voice carrying to the farthest alley. "The time has come to fight off the barbarian sword, to take up arms, and to kick the foreign hordes out of Italy!"

The Milanese roared with ecstasy.

"Noble Latin blood!" Eros addressed his people. "How long must we suffer these burdens? How long do we allow the copious shedding of *our blood?* Do not make an idol an empty name! By God! The hearts that proud, fierce Mars makes hard and closed will open and soar and break free!" He drew his sword and pointed it at the ivory Duomo gilded by the rising sun.

Always prepared, the Milanese drew their pistols and blades and emulated his salute.

Eros's blood rushed thick and hot. "'*Italia mia!* Against barbarian rage, virtue will take the field, then short the fight! True to their lineage, Italian hearts will prove their Roman might!'"

The crowd went berserk, shouting the words with him, cheering and waving their fists. The cuirassiers attacked. The French musketeers fired. The Milanese swooped in. The battle began.

Giovanni hopped to Eros's side, his weapons drawn. "Remember to stay in one piece!"

"If you are the last to survive," Eros shouted over the tumult of battle, "go home to Sicily and marry the farm girl who's been keeping a candle in her window for you!"

"Aye, aye, Captain!" Giovanni grinned and dove into combat.

Eros followed. He blocked a storming French soldier, then another, paying no heed to the blasting grenades spitting earth and metal in his face. The enemy's battalions played a torrential fire, but the Italians' spirit was strong and the fight was tenacious to the last degree.

Eros saw the grenade flying his way a moment too late. Something slammed into him. His head hit the ground, but he felt no burning sensation of an open wound.

"Eros . . ." The weight holding him down moaned, coughing blood. Eros recognized the voice instantly, and the bloodied dark blond head. Nico lay in a pool of gore, his flesh torn—torn by the grenade he had taken for *him*. Why in blazes had he done such a crazy thing?

"Niccolò." Eros slid aside and put a hand beneath Nico's head. He pressed another on the open gut wound, feeling the intestines pushing out. Shells kept shrieking past his head, but he scarcely noticed them. "You did well, my friend, up until the moment you decided my life was more precious than yours."

"It is." Nico smiled faintly. "For Milan, and for the whole of Italy. Pity I won't live to see our country reunited again."

"You will, if you save your strength." Yet Eros knew it was hopeless. He hated seeing the signs. "You will go home to Venice, as you've always wanted, start that merchant line . . . "

"Nah. Too stuffy." Nico laughed and choked on blood. Moaning with pain, he looked up at Eros. "I never imagined I'd have a prince for a friend and that he'd hold my hand when I died. You gave me twelve years of freedom, Eros. I wouldn't have lasted a year as a slave in Algiers."

"You owe me nothing," Eros insisted. It wrenched his soul, realizing what had induced Nico to dive between him and the grenade. "You never did."

Nico's breathing thinned. "Do something for me," he murmured.

Eros swallowed hard. "Anything."

Violent spasms raked Nico's body, and his eyes rounded with sudden urgency. "Tell her—"

Eros steeled himself. "Yes?"

A soft smile touched Nico's lips. "Tell her you love her." Then he was gone.

Eros gently rested Nico's head on the ground and smoothed his eyelids shut. His vision was hazy. A comforting hand squeezed his shoulder. He raised his head. Giovanni and Daniello stood beside him. Now he understood how come he wasn't shot down yet. They protected him.

"I want him buried in Venice," Eros said, swallowing the lump in his throat. "Daniello, will you see to it that he gets a proper Christian burial? That his family is well taken care of?"

"I will," Daniello promised hoarsely, tears paving thin trails down his blackened cheeks.

Eros shook himself and pushed to his feet. "Now let's take this city."

The fighting spread throughout the city, establishing chaos and demolition. The ground was unsuitable for the operation of cavalry, and the clash became a brutal bloodbath. Every yard was gained with an enormous effort, the enemy persevering. Deep in the mêlée, Eros slashed right and left, hacking away at whatever crossed his path. Everything blurred from then on. An inner chill overtook him, hardening his heart, numbing his thoughts. The sensation was not a foreign one: the separation of mind from body when the scenes became very bad, when his conscience refused to accept the horrors he himself inflicted, when his arm nearly gave, when blood and sweat washed his face, when cries of pain penetrated his reason yet he ignored them, and when sickened of death, he begged God to have mercy on his soul and knew he deserved none.

The cool obscure interior made him think of the kingdom he had scarcely escaped that day. Memorial candles flickered in remote corners, elevating the souls of the dead higher in heaven. Fifty-two giant piers decorated with saints and prophets were erected to create an ambiance of greatness. His great ancestor, Duke Gian Galeazzo Visconti, constructed the Gothic edifice as a symbol of power, but for Eros the Duomo symbolized something else entirely.

His eyes red with fatigue, his boots clomping heavily on the marble tiles, he descended into the dim underground crypt. Peace and a deep feeling of bereavement mingled in his heart. He returned, but not to the full, wealthy life he had enjoyed here before—but to a cold lifeless tomb.

Feeling his way in the blackness, he found the first slab of stone, a changeless casket of cold immortality—the tomb of the first Sforza duke, Francesco. Only a few people knew that his son, Galeazzo Maria, the fifth duke of Milan, shared this casket instead of receiving one bearing his name, so that in aftertimes one could not show it, saying, "Here is placed the duke Galeazzo, who was murdered by his own courtiers." *Eros's father was murdered by his own brother.*

He stumbled onto blocks of marble embossed with grand names, moving sightlessly, until finally he distinguished another tomb, one that hadn't been there before. He splayed his fingers over the smooth stone, carefully feeling for an imprint. When his fingers read the sharp Latin etching, he sank to his knees and rested his cheek on the cold, hard marble. Throat constricting, he whispered, "I've returned, Papa. I'm home."

Dellamore's October was warm gold and auburn. Passing a quiet evening in the library, Alanis contemplated the flames dancing in the fireplace while her grandfather leafed through the *Gazette.* Six months had passed since they returned from France, and she was thinking of Malaga wine, salty sea breeze, and fiery red blossoms. She shut her eyes and released a sigh of the heart.

"He has Milan, you know," the duke stated, his icy blue eyes watching her with concern.

She didn't want to talk about him. She didn't want to hear his name spoken. Although she was past the crazy yearning, the gutting pain, and the clenching of the heart, thoughts of Eros were reserved strictly to the privacy of her bed at night, where scalding tears lulled her to sleep.

"The French reinforcements came too late," the duke continued, "and now he is sweeping the country of the remaining French forts. Milan is a duchy again, though not yet formally."

Alanis frowned. "Why not? Didn't the Milanese proclaim him duke right after the battle?"

"They did, but he postponed the coronation ceremony."

She touched the heavy medallion concealed inside her bodice. If Eros needed it, he would come. *Soon*. Fear and anticipation quickened her pulse. She should give it to his sister, but would she? She so ached to burn again . . . even if it destroyed her completely, forever.

"A delegation of counts is begging audience, *Monsignore*."

Eros raised his head from a stack of papers and rubbed his tired eyes. He frowned at the secretary looming beyond his massive escritoire. "A delegation of counts? What counts?"

"The Privy Council, *Monsignore*. They wish to congratulate His Highness on his victory and welcome him home."

So the double-dealing, bootlicking bastards are here to make amends. Eros smiled slyly. "Show them in, Passero, but make sure you tell them I'm in a foul mood."

"Very good, *Monsignore*." Passero hid his smile and bowed his way out.

Eros knew the scheming counts were the ones who had sent the assassins to his tent, yet he would let them live. Why? Because he needed them. Because they shared the sacred duty of healing and rebuilding a nation together. As to healing his private scars . . .

He poured himself a glass of cognac and stared out the window. The Castello's reddish-brown walls planted a fierce sense of belonging in him, something he hadn't felt for nearly two decades. He sipped his cognac standing up, waiting for the counts to enter. This way, when the weasels bowed their scheming heads, they would be well and truly humbled. For the first time in his life, for one brief, petty moment, Stefano Andrea

Sforza was about to derive immense satisfaction from the power his prestige and royal blood afforded him. *And gloat.*

CHAPTER 31

" . . . in penitence that is poured out in tears."
—Dante: *Purgatorio*

The old Roman road ambushed her thin soles at every tread as Maddalena made her way back to San Paolo, but the children in the orphanage expected her daily visits, and she couldn't let a small matter such as a cart's broken axle keep her away from them. Children were the light of life, and she had lost hers. Yet she was granted the miracle of seeing her son again, of stroking the black silk of his head, and being there when he needed her. No mother could ask for more.

Maddalena embraced the memory. She'd always known Stefano Andrea would grow up to be a wonderful man; he had all the attributes of his father but also, she smiled, one or two small qualities from her. She tried to imagine Gelsomina as a grown woman. She was surely stunning. Maddalena's heart warmed at the knowledge that her daughter found true love. She had also known true love once, and it had been both heaven and hell. Time had healed the scars of the past, and she could now think of Gianluccio with tenderness, and even derive comfort from it. The memory of the man who had smashed her heart with his countless infidelities and whom she had destroyed in one unbridled burst of jealousy would stay with her forever. One day she would meet him and beg his forgiveness, but until then, she had a holy duty to perform on earth—to care for parentless children and fill their lonely hearts with maternal love.

"Sister Maddalena!" Sister Maria rushed toward the convent gate. "Come quick. Hurry!"

Maria was a young woman of eighteen years. She had recently joined the convent after her parents passed away, leaving her penniless and alone. She hadn't adapted yet to the serenity of convent life. "Hello, Maria." Maddalena smiled. "What has you in high spirits today?"

"The most amazing thing! A visitor, for you! A nobleman. Sister Picolomina put him in the small prayer room. He's been waiting for over an hour."

"Hush, Sister," Maddalena scoffed gently, as they entered the cool chapel. "The man may have a sick child or is plagued with another misfortune. Your glee will offend him."

"This man has no sick child!" Maria bubbled with excitement. "He's a young, handsome nobleman with fine clothes."

"The hand of misfortune does not distinguish between the poor and the rich. Nor does it spare the young and the pleasing to the eye. In God's eyes we are all equals, regardless of our clothes." Maddalena neared the altar, knelt with a prayer, then rose and signed the cross.

"He only asked to see you," Maria said. "And when Mother Superior inquired as to the nature of his business he would not say, except that it was personal and that he would wait. He was very polite. He has been sitting by the window this entire time, waiting."

"Maria," Maddalena frowned at the girl, "have you been spying on him?"

Maria's cheeks warmed. "I did not disturb him. I remained outside the window."

"You are not to moon at men that way. Remember, you are married to the Son of God."

"I've not sinned, Sister. Honestly. It is just that he . . . looked so sad. I wondered what could have possibly brought sorrow to his beautiful eyes. He seems such an amiable, kind gentleman. He gave Mother Superior a heavy sack of gold coins for charity."

"We shall soon find out what ill luck brought him to us,

won't we?" Maddalena quickened her pace. It wasn't the first time a nobleman requested her aid. Sometimes it was the case of a sick wife or child, other times the sad case of an un-wanted child. Yet curiously, she sensed that whatever brought this nobleman to San Paolo, it was of a different nature.

Aware of Maria eagerly hanging over her shoulder, Mad-dalena turned the metal knob in her raw palm and glimpsed through the crack between the door and the frame. She saw an arm clad in dark velvet. The man, as Maria had described, sat on a stool fronting the garden window, absorbed in his thoughts. His elbow was propped on the windowsill, a black suede glove held negligently in his hand. She swung the door open and walked inside. "*Buongiorno, Signore*. I am Sister Maddalena. Did you request to see me?"

The moment the man's back came into full view, her heart jolted. Hair as black and glossy as a raven's was slicked to his nape in a thick cut. His elegant, skirted black coat was exquis-itely trimmed with silver and shaped to fit the expense of his broad back. Maddalena stifled a sob.

The tall, dark-haired man came to his feet and slowly turned around to meet her. "Good afternoon, Mother," Eros said quietly.

Maddalena heard Maria's gasp of surprise. The door closed softly behind her, and light feet scurried away. She stared at her son, outlined by a halo of October sunlight. His eyes glit-tered, his throat visibly constricted. He was tanned and strong and healthy. There wasn't a sign of the bony fledgling she had brought from the dead last winter. And he was a duke, as his father had been. "Eros," she whispered, the moisture in her eyes betraying the serenity she struggled to maintain. Her throat felt clogged and dry. Was he here for a specific reason? *Or was he simply here?* She smiled a mother's smile, full of love and pride and tenderness. "Eros, my beautiful angel. You are here," she murmured diffidently, not sure how he would react.

Eros's Adam's apple moved with difficulty. He took a step toward her. "I'm here."

There was so much to explain and to apologize for, but that

would have to come later. After seventeen years of separation, her son was here, no longer a boy but a man, and she longed to squeeze him to her bosom and never let go. Unable to repress her tears, Maddalena opened her arms and to her utter amazement and joy, Eros stepped forward, letting her embrace him to her aching heart. Her hand shook as she stroked his head. "Forgive me, my child . . . Forgive me . . ."

He straightened and tenderly peeled the wimple and veil off of her head. Silvery-blond hair was swept into a tight chignon. Her teary, sea-blue eyes shone. A warm glow spread in his eyes.

"*Mama.*" With a smile full of memories, he threw his arms around her neck and hugged her fiercely, like a little boy. She wept and offered more apologies, but he hushed her. "No, Mama. Forgive me, forgive me . . ."

Maddalena choked on tears. She stared beyond his shoulder at the modest figurine on the wall; He seemed to smile at her with timeless compassion. Her lips moved soundlessly, *Thank you, Merciful Father. Thank you . . .*

"A toast." The Duke of Dellamore raised his wineglass. "To our valiant general and war hero—the Duke of Marlborough!"

The grand ballroom rang with applause. Crystal clinked and great quantities of wine were tossed back in salute. Standing between her two favorite dukes, the Queen of England, Anne Stuart, smiled with delight, her eyes twinkling. "What I wish to know is what they are saluting in Versailles at this very moment. How unsporting of Louis not to have invited us!"

Everyone laughed. "Indeed, Your Majesty," Marlborough said. "How mean-spirited of the King of France to begrudge us our successes. Haven't Sforza and Savoy let his troops exit Italy without occurrences? He should be grateful they allowed him to give up the rest of his garrisons in peace, for he could no longer hold himself in Italy."

"Hear! Hear!" exclaimed Godolphin, Lord Treasurer, with

the hoisting of his glass. "Both Milan and Turin now make a sharper sally on the French rear!"

Another round of laughter and applause swept the large circle of dignitaries assembled in Hampton Court in celebration of the victories. Stuffed among them, Alanis forced her lips to smile and joined the salutes. She hadn't been too keen on making an appearance tonight, but the thought of spending another evening at home, moping, when every soul was out there making merry was even more depressing than having to put up with sloshed strangers.

Anne said, "Thanks to our new ally, the Prince of Milan, Italy is decontaminated of French, and not only that, but the war is now fought on the very borders of France. Let us hope we shall be as successful in Holland and Germany and win this war!" Everyone saluted, and the queen gave the signal for the orchestra to commence playing.

As the ballroom floor was transformed into a colorful sea of silks and jewelry, a man came to stand beside Alanis. "Lucas." She greeted him smilingly. "Where's your lovely wife?"

"Right there." He pointed at the matrons bombarding Jasmine with attention. "Now that her identity as Prince Stefano Sforza's sister is known, she's all the rage." He looked at Alanis. "I'm sorry, Alis, for what happened in Jamaica. Please accept my apologies. I behaved horridly."

Alanis patted his arm. "I, too, owe you an apology, Lucas. I should have settled matters in a civilized manner instead of taking off as I did. Can you bear to forgive me?"

"Please," he put his hand over hers, "let us speak no more of this. We should be friends—*a brother and a sister*—as we've always been."

Alanis nodded in wholehearted agreement. "I should like that very much."

The Duke of Dellamore and Lucas's father, the Earl of Denton, joined them.

"I say, Dellamore," Denton said, "rumor has it General

Savoy is to make an appearance tonight. And he's said to be bringing—" A stern glare from Dellamore shushed him up.

Alanis shot her grandfather an accusing glower. Heat and frost in a peculiar mélange spread through her body: Her icy hands cupped flaming cheeks. *Eros. Here. Tonight.* She couldn't speak, couldn't think, couldn't breathe . . .

Jasmine approached briskly, smiling, her bright eyes loudly conveying the message. Alanis cringed. She couldn't bear this. She had to get out. Had to flee . . . She commanded her wooden legs to begin operating when an adamant fist closed on her wrist.

"You'll brave this to the end, Alis," her grandfather whispered crisply. "Your pirate is an esteemed figure now. I won't have you running for cover whenever he sets foot on English soil or whenever you cross paths somewhere in the world. I didn't raise you to be a coward."

Fluttering and skittish as a trapped bird, Alanis hung desolate eyes on his stern face. How could she encounter Eros now? See the odium in his eyes? She would die . . .

The Master of Ceremony signaled the orchestra to commence playing the traditional formal notes to announce the arrival of a grand party. Alanis stared at the ballroom doors. And indeed, it didn't take long for her to distinguish a painfully familiar dark head . . .

Accompanied by a large party of superbly dressed gentlemen and their female escorts, Eros ambled inside, staggeringly handsome in black, white, and a hint of purple. He was grinning at something the man at his side was saying. Eugene of Savoy looked ridiculously pint-sized beside the tall Milanese—an attribute that always managed to astound and amuse those who expected a great general to look the part. Alanis's eyes remained solely on Eros. Tanned, poised, radiating strength and vitality, he melted her to a state of pottage. His thick jet hair spilled to his shoulders. His frame was bulked up to his natural proportions. He was her pirate from the Caribbean, only this pirate was a prince, the much admired, highly praised Prince of Milan.

Everyone gathered around him, bubbling compliments and salutations. Alanis heard a cry of delight and saw Jasmine flying into her brother's arms. He picked her up, hugging her tightly, and kissed her cheeks. Tears swam in Alanis's eyes. Eros had yet to learn he was an uncle.

She was shaking. So when her grandfather took her arm and towed her toward the queen's circle, where everyone who was anyone stood by to gain an introduction, she stumbled like a duck. Dellamore, Marlborough, and Savoy clapped backs. The Milanese counts shook hands with the English nobility. Eros addressed the queen, charming her with a drawled "*Buonasera, Sua Maestà,*" a kiss on the hand, and a dimpled smile. Alanis did her best to become invisible, but just as she stole a glimpse at his arresting profile his head turned in her direction.

Hard sapphires lanced right through her. She felt his heat with such blazing intensity, she was gasping for air. His gaze coolly veered to her grandfather. He nodded politely and joined in the conversation with Savoy. A sob died in her throat. She stood as a statue, draped in mother-of-pearl silks, golden locks cascading over her bare shoulders, frosted by the cut direct.

"Vendôme was a worthy opponent," Eros said. "His recall to the Netherlands delivered the deathblow to the French. And de Orleans, despite his assurances to Louis, was unable to defend two places at the same time. He should have come after me, but instead he rushed to Turin."

Marlborough grunted in accord. "After Vendôme's recall, the French operated badly. They opened the road to Piedmont for Prince Eugene to break through, did not dispute the defile at Stradella, and remained in the Turin lines to be beaten."

"And by the time they sought to retire on Milan," Savoy said, "they had nowhere to return to. Stefano had secured the region, proceeding with an impertinent Italian élan. A true Caesar."

"Even Julius Caesar had to thank mere fortune now and then," Eros admitted humbly.

"You are too modest, Stefano. Your special skills allowed

you to do what none of us could. Milan was impregnable. Yet you did the possible, the impossible, and then the unthinkable. Your sub-aqua operation to infiltrate the enemy was exceptionally bold and brilliant."

Eros wouldn't look at her, not even fleetingly, but Alanis saw what the others didn't—Savoy's praise made his color rise. She smiled, delighted to see him shine and acknowledged by his peers—by princes and queens—as he well deserved. She had done the right thing in France.

"Prince Stefano," Queen Anne spoke. "We are all dying to hear the tittle-tattle the tongues are wagging on the Continent. Do tell us *everything,* and don't be stingy about it."

Bestowing the queen with another of his dazzling pirate smiles, he drawled, "I imagine Her Majesty wishes to hear what Louis's tongue is presently wagging."

"Of course." The queen exchanged naughty looks with a few high and mighty matrons.

"*Allora,* I confidently report that the King of France is having a hard time swallowing the frog, figuratively speaking, of course." Eros winked at the queen, who blushed and tittered. "He fired three of his ministers, retired two generals, and is no longer on speaking terms with Philip."

"Not speaking with Philip?" The queen laughed. "Delightful! Why, it was in support of Philip that he has started this war in the first place!"

Alanis heard an English tongue wagging behind her. "Isn't he the handsomest devil! Such a young prince, and a bachelor at that! What a pity my Carol has already given her consent to Lord Bradshaw. *That's* the shape our ladies dote on."

"Indeed we do, Lillian," agreed a younger voice, one Alanis identified as belonging to a rich, attractive widow on a perpetual hunt for male consolation. "'Thou shalt value prurience over prudery,' that's what I always say. Let's beg an introduction."

The mingling continued. Alanis gripped her grandfather's arm and hissed beside his ear, "One more instant of this and I will surely scream. With or without your permission I'm leav—"

Abruptly, the duke shifted his attention. The air stirred beside her. "Your Grace." The deep voice nearly caused her to faint. She looked aside, words lost. Eros smiled graciously at the duke. "I haven't yet thanked you for lending your gentlemanly word to my credence in Schönbrunn. I am in your debt." He inclined his dark head elegantly, then settled his gaze on Alanis.

Longing and misery tore at her heart, and when her grandfather said, "Please allow me to present my granddaughter, Lady Alanis." she felt a sudden urge to rip a tile off the floor and dive beneath it. Yet she remained cool, and following etiquette, put her fingers in Eros's hand.

"Your Highness." She curtseyed, lowering her eyelashes to conceal the shock effect of his lips on her hand. They were playing the most dratted game, yet all she could do was play along.

"*Piacere,*" his deep voice murmured. "What an unexpected pleasure."

Her eyes flew to his. He had greeted her with the exact words upon their first encounter in his cabin. The world stilled, as he sustained her anguished, damning gaze, betraying none of his thoughts—not odium, not disdain, not anger, not a hint of emotion. He let go of her hand.

Dinner was announced, and everyone ambled in the direction of the dining room. Alanis glanced beyond Eros's shoulder. Her grandfather was abandoning her to her fate!

"It appears I am to escort her ladyship to the royal dinner table," Eros observed blandly, offering a negligent arm. He wouldn't even look at her when he offered. She studied his granite profile, mentally shrinking with angst. *My heart stops when I look at you.* Nothing. She took his arm and they followed the tail of silks, behaving as perfect strangers. She was physically aware of every breath he took, of every muscle bunching on his arm, and sensed her last spark of hope dimming out. His indifference was such that he didn't even gloat at his ultimate triumph.

The colorful procession disappeared around a corner. All of a sudden, Alanis was yanked aside and channeled through a side door into a drawing room lit by a soft blaze. Heart pounding, she watched Eros shutting the door behind him, *and latching it.*

So much for indifference, she thought nervously, as he turned around and nailed her with a glare as effective as an iron ram. The hard glitter in his eyes made her want to run for cover. He started toward her, his pace deliberate, his gaze unwavering. *Revenge*—the word reverberated in her head. Swallowing panic, she edged back and clumsily bumped into a table. A lamp teetered. She turned in time to set it upright again. When she raised her head, Eros was standing in front of her, his handsome, masklike face looming inches above hers. "Alanis," he said.

Her name on his lips sent a tremor through her heart. "Why are you here, in England?"

"I came to collect something that belongs to me."

Without tearing her gaze from his, she stuffed her hand inside her reticule. She usually wore his medallion over her heart, but not in this gown; the deep décolletage barely left room for flesh and bone. Her stiff fingers closed around the gold chain. "You are the Duke of Milan. You did it," she said softly, wondering why in damnation she was still hoping . . . "Was coming home as . . . you had hoped it would be?" she braved on, hoping to ignite a spark of intimacy in him, *something* of what they had had between them.

Eros said nothing. His expression confirmed that he remembered every word spoken in the Bastille. How stupid of her to hope he would share his moment with her. She'd abandoned him. She had made him believe the magical thing between them was false. And now he was the Duke of Milan, admired by every ruler in the universe, including the emperor and the pope—what she had claimed was her requisite for a husband. She offered him the medallion. "This is the reason you postponed the enthronement ceremony, isn't it? You need to display it."

"No."

Alanis didn't know what to think anymore, except that if

he continued staring at her so intently, her frail composure, whatever was holding her together, would break.

Eros moved closer, his eyes unforgiving, unrelenting, his tan a soft bronze in the dim light. His fingers closed around her pulsing wrist. He shifted her hand aside, encouraging her fingers to open and let the medallion drop to the ebony table. He caught her other wrist and tugged. She stumbled forward. He tugged again, slowly sliding his hands up her bare arms. They stood toe to toe, the air between them charged with electricity, and she wondered if he could feel the fast rush of her pulse. The look in his eyes grew fiercer, and they were no longer inscrutable; they were *miserable*. "Alanis." He bent his head and pressed his warm cheek against hers. His lips opened in her ear and he whispered, "I love you."

She grabbed his waist to keep from folding to her heels. "W . . . what?"

His arms locked around her. She felt his soft lips on her neck. Huskily, almost brokenly, he confessed, "I can't live without you. I don't . . . *want* to live without you."

With unspeakable relief, she buried her face in his shoulder, hugging his waist, dampening his coat with tears. "I love you too." Could this truly be happening? Could fate be so generous?

They stood embraced, oblivious to anything except their pounding hearts. He was her soul mate and he had come for her. She raised her head from his shoulder. "I lied in the Bastille."

His raw gaze touched hers. "I know. You were . . . almost convincing. When Louis saw how flattened I was, it got my wits working again, and I appreciated what you had done. It was Louis you wanted to convince, not me." He caressed her cheek, his thumbs collecting crystalline beads she wasn't aware she was still shedding. "You wanted me to take my home back, *Amore*."

"I did. Leaving you in that cell was the hardest moment of my life. But I wanted you to be happy and whole. Thank God it worked."

"At times, I thought perhaps you had meant it, but I would have come anyway." He pulled her closer and kissed her with so much love and yearning, sunshine filled her heart. "I love you, Alanis, more than is sanely possible," he confessed, not allowing more than a whisper between slow kisses, and dazedly she realized not every tear washing her face belonged solely to her.

"Eros." She embraced him so strongly, she feared he might break, but this was Eros, she reminded herself; he wasn't so easily broken, not by the worst pits, not by the worst lies. "Do you suppose Louis realizes he's the one who made you side with his enemies?" she asked.

"Perhaps. And perhaps one day he'll even deign to forgive me." He smirked.

She regarded him perceptively. "You'll miss his friendship, won't you?"

"The diversion. My new definition of friendship is a tad different than his."

"And Taofik?" she asked, worried again. "He may want to rid himself of your shadow and decide to come after you to regain his peace of mind."

"I don't think he would. Though he's anything but gutless, he'll hesitate to venture so deep into our world. My best revenge would be to ignore him. Taofik is a man who lives on the dark side, who sees everything in the form of violence and perfidy. Which is why he'll never enjoy a full night's rest, worrying I might be lurking somewhere in the shadows. Nevertheless," Eros sighed, "if he does come after me, I'll . . . handle him."

Alanis smiled. "You are changed."

"Softer, eh?"

"Your thirst for blood is gone."

Exhaling, he touched his forehead to hers. "I'm sick of death. Sick of mutilated bodies lying in rivers of gore. Sick of burying my friends . . ." He lifted his head. "Niccolò is gone."

"No. Not Niccolò." Tears of anguish flooded her eyes. "He had so many dreams and plans, so much to look forward to. I shall miss him dearly."

"So shall I. He saved my life. He stopped a grenade meant for me. A hero. His last thoughts were of you, Alanis. He said, 'Tell her you love her.'" Eros's eyes reflected great sadness.

"We may visit him together and light a candle for his noble soul. He is buried in Venice."

She nodded, her throat clogged. Loving her, Nico saved the man she loved. No man was ever braver or nobler. A hero indeed. "You must give me a full account of the war. I was terrified something might happen to you . . . that I had sent you to die."

"You cannot begin to imagine how I've missed having you by my side, to consult with and confide in, share everything together. To hold at night . . ." Groaning, Eros claimed her mouth in a hungrier kiss—a lover's kiss. She clung to him, sending a thousand thanks to God.

"I didn't think you'd come for me," she admitted softly. "I thought I'd lost you forever."

"I prayed to God I wouldn't find you married to someone else. I couldn't throw the French out fast enough to come to you. If I had lost you, there wouldn't have been a place sad enough for me to hide. Not even Agadìr. Milan would have had to find another duke."

"You postponed the enthronement ceremony because of me?"

"My people need a sane duke, *Amore*. Not a lovesick wreck."

"And they shall have one. I love you just as insanely, Eros. I was afraid my grandfather would commit me to Bridewell if I didn't show promising signs of improvement soon."

Eros laughed. "Your grandfather is a great gun. He vouched for me at the War Council in Vienna. Did he tell you about that?"

Her aquamarine eyes rounded in disbelief. "The old fox told me nothing."

"Well, he trapped you with me tonight. Do you suppose he'd like us to be together?"

"Hmm." She frowned thoughtfully. "Sanah did mention something about my grandfather finding me a pompous prince—an odious creature, forever engrossed in politics . . ."

He playfully yanked a blond lock. "And as I recall, Sanah also mentioned that the next time we paid her a visit, you'd be pregnant. Therefore, I suggest that one of us give up her use of anticonception vices and that we begin working on filling out the Castello *immediately* . . ."

His words and following kisses stirred a delicious flutter in her stomach. "Agreed."

Eros relaxed his grip, straightened his back, and taking a fortifying breath, said, "Will you marry me, my beautiful, fair nymph? Come live with me in Milano?"

Her heart leaped, but before she screamed *yes,* Alanis asked smartly, "What about your barracuda of a fiancée, and her brothers—the Orsini?"

That surprised him. He half grimaced, half smiled. "How do you know about Leonora?"

"I know everything." She poked his chest. "You ought to remember that."

"I will." He chuckled. "As for Leonora, the Orsini are ancient history. With Cesare dead and my joining the Alliance, they folded their cuneated arms and plodded back to Rome."

"So no Roman princess for you, only a savage Celt from The Little Island."

"A golden sea sprite in lieu of a—what did you call her— a barracuda? I'll take that any day. And just that you'd know, there's a lot of Celt in me as well. Milan's origins lie in a remote Celtic past. In Roman mythology, Mercury's wife was a Celtic goddess named Rosmerta."

"Was she beautiful?" Alanis asked hopefully.

"Not particularly. Not like Venus." His smile softened. "Not like you, *Amore.*"

"You know," she said, "this sort of offer is generally made with a ring."

"Ah, baggage." Eros sighed. He stuffed his hand into his pocket and produced a ring—an exquisite viper embedded with tiny diamonds, black ambers, and a pair of amethysts for eyes, snaking around a huge sparkly diamond. "You know to whom this ring belonged."

"*Your mother.*" She gasped. "You went to see her. Oh, Eros. Tell me everything."

"You were right about everything. She did go to Carlo that night, after she'd caught my father with one of his mistresses. He was forever unfaithful. I was aware of his peccadilloes, in a passive way, and accepted them as a way of life, never giving thought to what it did to my mother. She loved him, and for years he paraded his conquests as status symbols, humiliating her, neglecting her. God knows why she put up with him for so long. Her family lived in Rome. She never quite fit in among the Milanese. My father's transgressions and the resulting gossip made her feel even more isolated and lonely. When you talked about her in Tuscany, memories flooded me. I realized I did need to know the truth. When I saw her, she was—" He gave a boyish smile, shrugging. "*Mia mama*. It didn't matter anymore. I missed her. I needed to hear her say that she missed us and that she did care. That she loved us always. Still."

"And when you visited her, she told you what had really happened that night?"

"With great reluctance. She was ashamed to tell me—the one who'd abandoned, despised, and accused her wrongly— that Carlo tried to seduce her to obtain information about the League, and that when she fought him, he threatened to kill my sister. I should have killed the bastard slowly for what he did. God help me, but I was an idiot, a righteous little *cazzo* no better than my father." His blue eyes glistened with remorse. "My mother wasn't a harpy. She was a victim. Carlo beat her and . . . abused her and locked her in his chamber, *and she was ashamed . . .*"

Alanis held him to her, desperate to take away his pain. He was shaking.

"I created my own hell," he said. "I don't want us to end up as my parents did, our children losing everything, as Gelsomina and I have. Nothing is worth the pain. *Nothing*. Especially not an easy tumbling. I want a real home, Alanis, a loving, happy family." He stared at her resolutely. "I swear to you on *everything* I hold sacred that I will always be faithful to you. Will you swear the same to me?"

"I swear it, with all of my heart."

Eros took her hand, slipped the ring on her finger, and kissed her knuckles. "This ring binds you to me as well as to the people of Milan, but you should know, *tesoro,* in Milan, we don't call our emblem 'Viper.'" He smiled wryly. "It's called *il biscione.* You'll see it crawling on walls and pillars. Even on coaches. I think this ring will match your amethysts very nicely, no?"

She studied her new ring, too dazed to absorb it all. "I don't have my amethysts anymore. I gave them to the captain in charge of you in the Bastille. He agreed to—"

"Help me escape. He did." He looked at her in astonishment. He raised her hand and kissed it. "My God, Alanis, I can't believe you did all that for me. I swear I'll get them back. I—"

"I don't care about the jewels, Eros. I only care about you." Just looking at him, seeing the love in his eyes was compensation far greater than she ever wanted. She embraced him achingly. From now on she would never have to let go. "I love you."

"I love you," he said gruffly. "Without you, my life is meaningless."

She tilted her head back, her eyes shining with humor. "So you want an answer?"

"I need witnesses." He grabbed her hand, collected his medallion, and headed for the door.

She flew after him, laughing, her gown sashaying along the polished tiles. "Eros, wait! You don't know what my answer is yet!"

He threw her a smile over his shoulder. "That's why I need an audience, *Amore,* to ensure you give me the right one. I dare you to refuse me in the presence of the Queen of England . . ."

When they entered the dining room, every head came up questioningly. Eros steered Alanis to the last vacant seats and tapped a fork against a glass, coughing pointedly. "Your Majesty." He nodded at the queen. He sought the Duke of Dellamore's gaze. "Your Grace." He waited for an approving nod. When he had it, he smiled at everyone else. "Lovely ladies. Honorable lords." He sank on one knee, holding Alanis's hand. She very nearly expired of embarrassment.

Chairs scraped the floor as the party settled down comfortably to hear the spongy words.

Alanis shot Eros a beseeching look. He ignored it, conveying that this is how it should be and that she had no say in the matter. He stared into her eyes, his smile meant only for her. "I beg you, angelic lady, be mine."

The large party held its breath. His mother's ring already adorned her finger, so the only thing remaining was to say "Yes." She collapsed around his neck, kissing him full on the mouth to the shocked gasps of everyone present. The guests recovered rapidly. Cheers went up. Glasses clinked. Everyone saluted the pair of lovers while speculating whether the affair had blossomed right under their noses in the moments these two had been left alone. It was icing on the cake that the Prince of Milan came to London to celebrate his victory and snagged him a bride to boot.

Taking advantage of the brief mayhem, Eros whispered to Alanis, "Come to my apartment in the palace after the ball tonight. I'll send Rocca for you."

Also unnoticed, Alanis pressed her soft lips to his ear, mercilessly caressing its whorls with the tip of her tongue. "Wait naked."

Eros groaned.

Eros stood before the fireside, wearing the black silk dressing gown he'd lent her the night they returned from Algiers and contemplated the painting hanging above it. The firelight gilded his profile and the smooth triangle of burnished skin exposed on his chest.

As Alanis entered his Tudor-styled bedchamber, his head turned and their gazes touched.

"*Carissima,*" he said, and she flew across the room, flinging herself into his open arms.

Eros crushed her to him, murmuring against her hair,

"You are my heart. I'm never letting you go." He kissed her with so much love, it hurt the heart. His embrace spoke of agonizing longing, of lonely nights spent in the field. "I'm dying to make love to you, *Amore,* but before that—I have a gift for you, a wedding gift." He turned her in his arms and pointed at the painting hanging over the fireplace. "Prince Camillo Borghese of Rome has kindly agreed to lease it to me for a period of twenty-five years. It's one of his villa's masterpieces, painted by Tiziano—*La Venere che benda Amore. Venus blindfolding Cupid.*" He rested his chin on her shoulder. "You asked me once why my mother called me Eros. This is the reason."

Alanis looked up. A golden-winged, bare-bottomed Cupid stood between Venus's thighs, letting her blindfold him, even as clear danger approached from every direction. The absolute trust of the boy in his mother touched the deepest corner in her heart, evoking the sweetest memory of a mother's caress. She was spellbound by the beauty and strength of the painting.

"My mother *loved* this painting," he said, "and it haunted me for years. Just thinking about it maddened me. Though I had ripped the blindfold from my eyes, I still envied the boy, because he had someone he felt so completely safe with— a sanctuary." He pressed his lips to her cheek. "Thank you, Alanis, for becoming my Venus and for loving me as you do. Your blindfolding me with love was my miracle—and my salvation."

"I love my gift," she whispered. She turned around and slid her hands inside his silk robe. "You are the love of my life, Eros. Always know that." She kissed his lips, his neck, his chest, every warm rippling muscle, needing to make sure he had returned from the war safe and sound.

His robe spilled to the floor. Eros took her hand and pressed it to his heart. It was pounding hard and fast. "Can you feel it? When you touch me . . . I shake."

"I feel it." She sensed the vibrations coursing through her as though they were one.

His fingers unlaced her gown, then her corset and petticoats. Somehow, they made it to the bed, tripping over undergarments and stockings in their haste to come together. His mouth closed on hers, rough and arousing, and she found herself flat on her back with Eros between her thighs. His scent, his body, everything about him was so familiar, it seemed they had never been apart.

"You and I, *Amore,* we are forever . . ." he whispered, and the burning began. They united in a storm, promising a future of love and joy, and when the call of rapture became too potent to draw out, Eros held her to him, two words pouring from his lips, "*Ti amo. Ti amo. I love you . . .*"

EPILOGUE

This is the land that gave you birth, this your fairest home; here you should seek the high office to match your noble birth.
   Here are citizens for your eloquence to sway, here rich hope of offspring, here awaits you perfect love from your bride to be.

—Propertius: *Elegies*

The city of Milan was abuzz with wedding preparations. The ducal wedding was originally planned for June, but the Duke of Milan, whom the Milanese declared "*È malato d'amore. He is mad with love,*" kept advancing the date until it was settled on the beginning of spring. Sadly, the date coincided with the King of France's favorite gala—the famous Masquerade Ball—and most of his guests excused themselves politely and rushed to attend the Lombard Wedding instead.

The pope sent his special blessing; the emperor sent his brother; everyone else came in the flesh: royals, nobles, ambassadors, and friends. The faithful citizens of Milan, who were invited to participate in this joyous affair, flowed to the city from every district, keen on making merry.

Upon hearing the news of the upcoming nuptials and not receiving an invitation, Leonora Farnese said to her husband, Rodolfo, "People will marry anyone, these days."

Sallah and Nasrin brought a special gift—an exquisite pair of candlesticks, which Nasrin insisted were a Jewish mother's privilege to present her daughter with on her wedding day—and their six unmarried girls, who all vowed that they, too, would marry princes some day.

Gold poured to cover the cost, the scope of which equaled the extravagance unseen in Italy since the time of the Borgias. Yet according to rumors, half the sum was a wedding gift from the Sultan of Morocco.

The Duke of Milan had so much on his mind desiring to please his bride that he couldn't keep track of his intentions. He established a committee to oversee these essential matters, some of which were duties such as picking fresh flowers for the new duchess's boudoir and collecting feathers for her feather bed. Her one request, however, that he adamantly denied was the spot where they should spend their honeymoon. He chose a private villa on a non-death-defying cove along the Amalfi Coast and promised to take her to Constantinople at a future date.

Many of the wedding preparations concerned wardrobe materials, as fashion was a serious business in Milan, and some of the fabrics for the bride's wedding gown and trousseau had to be sought as far afield as Brussels, Florence, and Rome. The duke had Milan's jewelers working frenziedly to supply the items he intended to give to his bride; the list running to thirty closely printed pages. He also arranged for participation by more than fifty musicians, supplementing his own corps with others from the cities of Genoa and Ferrara.

As the new Abbess of Milan, and assisted by her daughter, Maddalena organized all the orphans in the city to put on a grand public spectacle on the wedding day. She also appointed herself Alanis's secret consultant on matters best kept between bride and mother-in-law. In their spare time, she tutored Alanis in Italian and other important Milanese subjects.

Amazingly, a true friendship blossomed between the Duke of Milan and his brother-in-law. It even survived the prince's annoyance upon discovering that the viscount had imbibed a full bottle of port before his own wedding, which had caused him to faint.

The continuous arrival of guests caused a logistical nightmare. Housing had to be provided, and the situation in Milan was difficult because so many prominent persons were attending the wedding. It was whispered that the prince himself, in his magnanimity, offered his quarters to Prince Eugene of Savoy and moved in with his bride . . .

By the time the wedding day finally arrived, the prince and his bride were in a state, terrified that something might go wrong. Only the strict warnings from the Duke of Dellamore and the Archbishop of Milan kept them from raising their hackles and eloping to Sicily.

The third largest cathedral in the world was packed to the rim that day. The bride's veil, made of fine Brussels lace, covered the cathedral aisle from the front steps to the altar. The esteemed archbishop blessed the union, and soon after, the bridal couple emerged on *Piazza Duomo* to greet the expectant Milanese. A sea of flowers and beaming faces crammed the square and every street and alley connected to it. The orchestra launched a cheerful *Te Deum,* a flock of pigeons exploded into flight, and rains of flower buds and candies came from every direction.

A formal royal banquet was to be held at the Castello Sforzesco, but instead of climbing into the ducal carriage, the Duke of Milan gripped his bride's hand and, shocking every official, lord, and lady, marched straight into the heart of the throng. They merged with the ecstatic well-wishers, shook hands, clapped backs, nodded greetings . . . And when they were surrounded with no hope of an easy retreat, Eros swept Alanis into his arms, eyes glowing, dimples showing, and kissed her thoroughly to the raging delight of the crowd.